"Lush, eerie, and compulsively readable, this story got under my skin and stayed there."

—ALEXIS HENDERSON, author of *The Year of the Witching* and *House of Hunger*

"Despite its dark story of oppression and cruelty, Moreno-Garcia . . . instills the novel with action sequences showcasing violent conflicts between humans and hybrids. And she injects the novel's gory battles with cinematic energy equal to that seen in the Universal Studios monster movies and other genre classics. What Moreno-Garcia really does, though, is explore who the real monsters are in the world. Those are definitely not the hybrids, despite 'the fur and fang and fury' that Moreno-Garcia unleashes as justice claws its way through the book's final pages."

—*The Washington Post*

"This is historical science fiction at its best: a dreamy reimagining of a classic story with vivid descriptions of lush jungles and feminist themes. Some light romance threads through the heavier ethical questions concerning humanity. Readers of Isabel Cañas's *The Hacienda* will be drawn in by the setting and themes; fans of other classic remixes, such as Megan Shepherd's *The Madman's Daughter*, will also enjoy."

—*Library Journal* (starred review)

"Told from Carlota and Montgomery's points of view and clearly inspired by H. G. Wells, this wholly new novel paints a vivid picture that is as alluring as it is unsettling, filled with action, romance, and monsters. However, it is Moreno-Garcia's ability to mesh the unease of the scientifically created beasts with the real-life terrors of a life on the margins and the horror of colonialism that elevates this story. Readers will fall into this tale immediately, enchanted."

—*Booklist* (starred review)

"The imagination of Silvia Moreno-Garcia is a thing of wonder, restless and romantic, fearless in the face of genre, embracing the polarities of storytelling—the sleek and the bizarre, wild passions and deep hatreds—with cool equanimity. . . . [*The Daughter of Doctor Moreau*] immerses readers in the rich world of nineteenth-century Mexico, exploring colonialism and resistance in a compulsively readable story of a woman's coming-of-age. . . . The visceral horror of what Carlota has endured, combined with Moreno-Garcia's pacing and drama, makes for a mesmerizing horror novel."

—*The New York Times Book Review*

"With her well-crafted gothic style, Moreno-Garcia draws readers into the lush setting and asks them to think carefully about the morality of experimentation, the damage wrought by colonization, and the unpredictable fancies of the heart. From the European racism toward the Maya people, to the horrific work of Dr. Moreau, and the ways in which women are vulnerable to misogyny and violence, the author infuses her romantic vision with deadly serious themes and topics. The result is an entertaining and thoughtful tale—a page-turner that is both creepy and fanciful, and always smart."

—*Bookreporter*

"Over the 300-ish pages that comprise *The Daughter of Doctor Moreau*, Silvia Moreno-Garcia breaks your heart just to help you put it back together again. [In this] emotional novel dense with both mystery and the unsettling sense that something is slightly off, Garcia instantly captivates you through vivid imagery and characters that tug at your heartstrings from the book's first few scenes. . . .

"By no means a light novel, *The Daughter of Doctor Moreau* commands your attention at every turn and asks heavy questions about some of the beliefs we hold most dear. With sentimental character arcs and a haunting feel that will have you mulling over the novel for days, Moreno-Garcia delivers one of the most evocative books of the summer, if not the year." —*Paste*

"Moreno-Garcia's previous work has spanned genres—horror in *Mexican Gothic*, noir in *Velvet Was the Night*—and in this volume, she deftly combines fantasy, adventure, and even romance; the result is hard to classify but definitely a lot of fun. This isn't the first book to riff on H. G. Wells's *The Island of Doctor Moreau*, but it's definitely one of the better ones. A fun literary remix."

—*Kirkus Reviews*

"If there are two things I love in this world, it's contemporary reimaginings of Victorian era horror and sci-fi, and joyful genre mashups in literature. Thank the Lord, then, for Silvia Moreno-Garcia . . . who brings her chameleonic powers to bear on H. G. Wells's 1896 'exercise in youthful blasphemy.'"

—Lit Hub

"Moreno-Garcia weaves a story about how life is often hard and full of unwanted surprises, and how finding your own inner strength to face these challenges is as important as accepting help from those who love you, just as you are. It's a story you can get lost in, and it's a tale whose bittersweetness will pull on your heart just enough for it to ache but will also leave you with hope that the characters are moving on to something better, no matter how hard getting there may be."

—Tor.com

The Daughter of Doctor Moreau

THE
DAUGHTER
OF
DOCTOR MOREAU

A Novel

SILVIA MORENO-GARCIA

NEW YORK

2023 Del Rey Trade Paperback Edition

Published in the United States by Del Rey, an imprint of
Random House, a division of Penguin Random House LLC,
New York.

DEL REY and colophon are registered trademarks of
Penguin Random House LLC.

Originally published in hardcover in the United States by
Del Rey, an imprint of Random House, a division of
Penguin Random House LLC, in 2022.

This book contains an excerpt from the forthcoming book *Silver Nitrate* by Silvia Moreno-Garcia. This excerpt has been set for this edition only and may not reflect the final content of the forthcoming edition.

ISBN 978-0-593-35535-0
Ebook ISBN 978-0-593-35534-3

Printed in the United States of America on acid-free paper

randomhousebooks.com

2   4   6   8   9   7   5   3

Book design by Fritz Metsch

To my husband,
my joy and inspiration

The Maya vocabulary . . . employs the word "peten" promiscu-
ously for both island and peninsula. The cartographers nearest to
the epoch of the conquest are therefore fairly excused for having
represented Yucatán as an island torn off from the Mexican main.

—*The Magazine of American History with Notes and Queries*, 1879

PART

ONE

(1871)

CHAPTER I

Carlota

THEY'D BE ARRIVING that day, the two gentlemen, their boat gliding through the forest of mangroves. The jungle teemed with noises, birds crying out in sonorous discontent as if they could foretell the approach of intruders. In their huts, behind the main house, the hybrids were restless. Even the old donkey, eating its corn, seemed peevish.

Carlota had spent a long time contemplating the ceiling of her room the previous night, and in the morning her belly ached like it always did when she was nervous. Ramona had to brew her a cup of bitter orange tea. Carlota didn't like when her nerves got the best of her, but Dr. Moreau seldom had visitors. Their isolation, her father said, did her good. When she was little she'd been ill, and it was important that she rest and remain calm. Besides, the hybrids made proper company impossible. When someone stopped at Yaxaktun it was either Francisco Ritter, her father's lawyer and correspondent, or Hernando Lizalde.

Mr. Lizalde always came alone. Carlota was never introduced to him. Twice she'd seen him walking from afar, outside the house, with her father. He left quickly; he didn't stay the night in one of the guest rooms. And he didn't visit often, anyway. His presence was mostly felt in letters, which arrived every few months.

Now Mr. Lizalde, who was a distant presence, a name spoken but never manifested, was visiting and not only visiting but he'd be bringing with him a new mayordomo. For nearly a year since Melquíades had departed, the reins of Yaxaktun had been solely in the hands of the doctor, an inadequate situation since he spent most of his time busy in the lab or deep in contemplation. Her father, however, didn't seem inclined to find a steward.

"The doctor, he's too picky," Ramona said, brushing the tangles and knots out of Carlota's hair. "Mr. Lizalde, he sends him letters, and he says here's one gentleman, here's another, but your father always replies no, this one won't do, neither will the other. As if many people would come here."

"Why wouldn't people want to come to Yaxaktun?" Carlota asked.

"It's far from the capital. And you know what they say. All of them, they complain it's too close to rebel territory. They think it's the end of the world."

"It's not that far," Carlota said, though she understood the peninsula only by the maps in books where distances were flattened and turned into black-and-white lines.

"It's mighty far. Makes most people think twice when they're used to cobblestones and newspapers each morning."

"Why did you come to work here, then?"

"My family, they picked me a husband but he was bad. Lazy, did nothing all day, then he beat me at night. I didn't complain, not for a long time. Then one morning he hit me hard. Too hard. Or maybe as hard as every other time, but I wouldn't take it any longer. So I grabbed my things and I went away. I came to Yaxaktun because nobody can find you here," Ramona said with a shrug. "But it's not the same for others. Others want to be found."

Ramona was not quite old; the lines fanning her eyes were shallow, and her hair was speckled with a few strands of gray. But she spoke in a measured tone, and she spoke of many things, and Carlota considered her very wise.

"You think the new mayordomo won't like it here? You think he'll want to be found?"

"Who can tell? But Mr. Lizalde's bringing him. It's Mr. Lizalde who's ordered it and he's right. Your father, he does things all day but he never does the things that need done, either." Ramona put the brush down. "Stop fretting, child, you'll wrinkle the dress."

The dress in question was decorated with a profusion of frills and pleats, and an enormous bow at the back instead of the neat muslin pinafore she normally wore around the house. Lupe and Cachito were giggling at the doorway, looking at Carlota, as she was primped like a horse before an exhibition.

"You look nice," Ramona said.

"It itches," Carlota complained. She thought she looked like a large cake.

"Don't pull at it. And you two, go wash your faces and those hands," Ramona said, punctuating her words with one of her deadly stares.

Lupe and Cachito moved aside to let Ramona by as she exited the room, grumbling about all the things she had to do that morning. Carlota sulked. Father said the dress was the latest fashion, but she was used to lighter frocks. It might have looked pretty in Mérida or Mexico City or some other place, but in Yaxaktun it was terribly fussy.

Lupe and Cachito giggled again as they walked into the room and took a closer look at her buttons, touching the taffeta and silk until Carlota elbowed them away, and then they giggled again.

"Stop it, both of you," she said.

"Don't be mad, Loti, it's just you look funny, like one of your dollies," Cachito said. "But maybe the new mayordomo will bring candy and you'll like that."

"I doubt he'll bring candy," Carlota said.

"Melquíades brought us candy," Lupe said, and she sat on the old rocking horse, which was too small for any of them now, and rocked back and forth.

"Brought *you* candy," Cachito complained. "He never brought me none."

"That's because you bite," Lupe said. "I've never bitten a hand."

And she hadn't, that was true. When Carlota's father had first brought Lupe into the house, Melquíades had made a fuss about it, said the doctor couldn't possibly leave Carlota alone with Lupe. What if she should scratch the child? But the doctor said not to worry, Lupe was good. Besides, Carlota had wanted a playmate so badly that even if Lupe had bitten and scratched, she wouldn't have said a word.

But Melquíades never took to Cachito. Maybe because he was more rambunctious than Lupe. Maybe because he was male, and Melquíades could lull himself into a sense of safety with a girl. Maybe because Cachito had once bitten Melquíades's fingers. It was nothing deep, no more than a scratch, but Melquíades detested the boy, and he never let Cachito into the house.

Then again, Melquíades hadn't liked any of them much. Ramona had worked for Dr. Moreau since Carlota was about five years old, and Melquíades had been at Yaxaktun before that. But Carlota could not recall him ever smiling at the children or treating them as anything other than a nuisance. When he brought candy back, it was because Ramona asked that he procure a treat for the little ones, not because Melquíades would have thought to do it of his own volition. When they were noisy, he might grumble and tell them to eat a sweet and go away, to be quiet and let him be. There was no affection for the children in his heart.

Ramona loved them and Melquíades tolerated them.

Now Melquíades was gone, and Cachito slipped in and out of the house, darting through the kitchen and the living room with its velvet sofas, even stabbing at the keys of the piano, ringing discordant notes from the instrument when the doctor was not looking. No, the children didn't miss Melquíades. He'd been fastidious and a bit conceited on account of the fact that he'd been a doctor in Mexico City, which he thought a great achievement.

"I don't see why we need a new mayordomo," Lupe said.

"Father can't manage it all on his own, and Mr. Lizalde wants it all in perfect order," she said, repeating what she'd been told.

"What does the mister care how he manages it or not? He doesn't live here."

Carlota peered into the mirror and fiddled with the pearl necklace, which, like the dress, had been newly imposed on her that morning to assure she looked prim and proper.

Cachito was right: Carlota did resemble one of her dollies, pretty porcelain things set on a shelf with their pink lips and round eyes. But Carlota was not a doll, she was a girl, almost a lady, and it was a bit ridiculous that she must resemble a porcelain, painted creation.

Ever the dutiful child, though, she turned from the mirror and looked at Lupe with a serious face.

"Mr. Lizalde is our patron."

"I think he's nosy," Lupe said. "I think he wants that man to spy on us and tell him everything we do. Besides, what does an English-man know about managing anything here? There are no jungles in England, all the books in the library show snow and cold and people going around in carriages."

That was true enough. When Carlota peered into books—sometimes with Cachito and Lupe looking with interest over her shoulder—magic lands of make-believe spread before her eyes. England, Spain, Italy, London, Berlin, and Marseille. They seemed like made-up names to her, jarring in comparison with the names of the towns in the Yucatán. Paris especially surprised her. She tried to say the name slowly, the way her father did. *Paree*, he said. But it wasn't merely the way he said it, it was the knowledge behind it. He had lived in Paris, he had walked its streets, and therefore when he said Paris he was invoking a real place, a living metropolis, whereas Carlota knew only Yaxaktun, and though she might conjugate her verbs correctly—*Je vais à Paris*—the city was never real for her.

Paris was the city of her father, but it wasn't her city.

She did not know the city of her mother. An oval painting hung in Father's room. It showed a beautiful blond woman wearing an off-shoulder ball gown and sparkling jewels around her neck. This, however, was not her mother. This was the doctor's first wife. He'd lost her and a baby girl; a fever took them. And then, afterward, in his grief, the doctor had acquired a lover. Carlota was the doctor's natural daughter.

Ramona had been at Yaxaktun for many years, but even she could not tell Carlota her mother's name or what she looked like.

"There was a woman, dark and pretty," she told Carlota. "She came by one time and the doctor was expecting her; he received her and they talked in the little parlor. But she came round only that one time."

Her father was reluctant to paint a more detailed picture. He said, simply, that they had never wed and Carlota had been left with him when her mother went away. Carlota suspected this meant her mother had married another man and had a new family. Carlota might have brothers and sisters, but she could not meet them.

"Listen to your father, who gave you life, and do not despise your mother when she is old," her father said, reading the Bible with great care. But he was both mother and father to her.

As for her father's family, the Moreaus, she knew none of them, either. Her father had a brother but he lived across the sea, in distant France. It was the two of them, and that was enough for her. Why would she need anyone but her father? Why would she want Paris or her mother's town, wherever it might be?

The one place that was real was Yaxaktun.

"If he brings candy, I won't care if he's nosy," Cachito said.

"The doctor will show him the laboratory," Lupe said. "He's kept himself there all week, so he must have something to show them."

"A patient?"

"Or equipment or something. I bet it's more interesting than candy. Carlota is going into the laboratory. She'll tell us what it is."

"Are you really?" Cachito asked.

He had been pushing an old wooden train across the floor, but now he turned to Carlota. Lupe had stopped rocking her horse. They both waited for an answer.

"I'm not sure," Carlota said.

Mr. Lizalde owned Yaxaktun; he paid for Dr. Moreau's research. Carlota supposed that if he wanted to see her father's lab, he would. And they might show it to the mayordomo, too.

"I am. I heard the doctor talking to Ramona about it. Why do you think they got you in that dress?" Lupe asked.

"He's said I might receive our guests and walk with them, but nothing is certain."

"I bet you get to see. You have to tell us if you do."

Ramona, walking down the hallway, paused to look into the room. "What are you still doing here? Go wash your faces!" she yelled.

Cachito and Lupe knew when their merriment was at an end, and they both scampered away. Ramona looked at Carlota and pointed a finger at her. "Now don't move from this spot."

"I won't."

Carlota sat down on the bed and looked at her dollies, at their curly hair and long eyelashes, and she tried to smile like the dolls smiled; their tiny mouths with a cupid's bow looked perfectly pleasant.

She grasped the ribbon in her hair, twisting it around a finger. All she knew of the world was Yaxaktun. She'd never seen anything beyond it. All the people she knew were the people there. When Mr. Lizalde chanced to appear in their home, he was, in her mind, as fantastical as those etchings of London and Madrid and Paris.

Mr. Lizalde existed and yet he didn't exist. On the two occasions on which she'd glimpsed him he had been but a figure in the distance, walking outside the main house, talking to her father. But during this visit she would be up close to him, and not just to him, but to the would-be mayordomo. Here was an entirely new element that would soon be introduced into her world. It was like when Father spoke of foreign bodies.

To soothe herself she took a book from the shelf and sat in her reading chair. Dr. Moreau, wishing to cultivate a scientific disposition in his daughter, had gifted Carlota with numerous books about plants and animals and the wonders of biology so that, in addition to the fairy tales of Perrault, Carlota could be exposed to more didactic texts. Dr. Moreau would not tolerate a child who knew only "Cendrillon" or "Barbe Bleue."

Carlota, always agreeable, read everything her father put in front of her. She had enjoyed *The Fairy Tales of Science: A Book for Youth*, but *The Water Babies* scared her. There was one moment in which poor Tom, who had been miniaturized, met some salmon. Even though the book assured her salmon "are all true gentlemen"—and even though they were more polite than the vicious old otter Tom had previously run into—Carlota suspected they would eat Tom at the slightest provocation. The whole book was full of such dangerous encounters. Devour or be devoured. It was an infinite chain of hunger.

Carlota had taught Lupe to read, but Cachito stumbled over his letters, jumbling them in his head, and she had to read out loud to him. But she had not read *The Water Babies* to Cachito.

And when her father said Mr. Lizalde would be visiting, along with a gentleman, she could not help but think of the terrible salmon in the book. And yet, rather than turn away from the image, she stared at the illustrations, at the otter and the salmon and the horrid monsters that inhabited its pages. Though they were all getting too big for children's tales, the book still fascinated her.

Ramona returned after a while, and Carlota put the book away. She followed the woman into the sitting room. Carlota's father was not much for fashion, so the furnishings of the house had never concerned him, and they consisted mostly of the old, heavy furniture that the previous owner of the ranch had brought, supplemented by a few choice artifacts the doctor imported through the years. Chief among these was a French clock. It struck a bell upon the hour, and its sounds never failed to delight Carlota. It amazed her that such precise machinery could be produced. She pictured the gears turning inside its delicate, painted shell.

As she stepped forward into the room she wondered if they could hear her heart beating, like the song of the clock.

Her father turned toward her and smiled. "Here is my housekeeper with my daughter. Carlota, come here," he said. She hurried to her father's side, and he placed a hand on her shoulder as he spoke. "Gentlemen, may I present my daughter, Carlota. This is Mr. Lizalde and this here is Mr. Laughton."

"How do you do?" she said, automatically, like the well-trained parrot that slept in its cage in the corner. "I trust your trip has been pleasant."

Mr. Lizalde's whiskers had a bit of gray in them, but he was still younger than her father, whose eyes were bracketed with deep wrinkles. He was dressed well, in a gold brocade waistcoat and a fine jacket, and dabbed at his forehead with a handkerchief as he smiled at her.

Mr. Laughton, on the other hand, did not smile at all. His jacket was of brown and cream wool tweed, with no embellishments, and he wore no vest. She was struck by how young and dour-looking he seemed. She'd thought they'd get someone like Melquíades, a man balding at the temples. This fellow had all his hair, even if it was a bit shaggy and untidy. And how light his eyes were. Gray, watery eyes.

"We're doing well, thank you," Mr. Lizalde said, and then he looked at her father. "Quite the little princess you have there. I think she might be of an age with my youngest child."

"You have many children, Mr. Lizalde?" she asked.

"I have a son and five daughters. My boy is fifteen."

"I am fourteen, sir."

"You're tall, for a girl. You might be as tall as my boy."

"And bright. She's been schooled in all the proper languages," her father said. "Carlota, I was trying to assist Mr. Laughton here in a matter of translation. Could you tell him what *natura non facit saltus* means?"

The "proper" languages she'd learned indeed, though the smattering of Mayan she spoke she had not obtained through her father. She'd learned from Ramona, as had the hybrids. She was, officially, their housekeeper. Unofficially she was a teller of tales, an expert in every plant that grew near their house, and more.

"It means nature does not make leaps," Carlota replied, fixing her eyes on the young man.

"Right. And can you explain the concept?"

"Change is incremental. Nature proceeds little by little," she declaimed. Her father asked questions such as these frequently, and the answers were easy, like practicing her scales. It soothed her fragile nerves.

"Do you agree with that?"

"Nature, perhaps. But not man," she said.

Her father patted her shoulder. She could feel him smiling without having to look at him.

"Carlota will guide us to my laboratory. I'll show you my research and prove the point," her father said.

In its corner the parrot opened an eye and watched them. She nodded and bid the gentlemen follow her.

CHAPTER 2

Montgomery

IT WAS NOT a river, for there were no rivers atop the thin soil of northern Yucatán. Instead, they followed a lagoon, which stretched into the jungle, like fingers gouging the land and slipping inland. Not a river and yet very much like one; the mangrove trees shaded the water and wove their roots together, sometimes so close they threatened to choke the life out of unwary visitors. The water seemed dark green in the shade, then grew more turbid, stained a murky brown by lush leaves and dead vegetation.

He thought he was used to the heath of the south and the press of the jungle, and yet this place was different than what he'd seen before, near Belize City.

Fanny would have hated it here.

The boatmen moved their poles swiftly, like the gondoliers in Venice, steering away from rocks and trees. Hernando Lizalde sat next to Montgomery, looking flushed and uncomfortable despite the fact that the boat had been fancifully equipped with an awning to protect them from the sun. Lizalde lived in Mérida and did not venture far from home even though he owned several haciendas throughout the peninsula. This trip was strange to him, too, and Montgomery gathered he did not like visiting Dr. Moreau often.

Montgomery didn't exactly know where they were headed. Lizalde had been reluctant to share any coordinates. He had been reluctant in many respects, but the money he'd been offered served to keep

Montgomery interested in this venture. He'd worked for low men, for crumbs. Lizalde was yet another bothersome job.

Besides, there was the issue of his debt.

"We must not be far from Yalikin," Montgomery said, trying to build a map in his head. He thought there were Cubans there, extracting palo de tinte and fleeing the war back on their island.

"We're at the edge of Indian country. Damn those godless bastards. They grip the shores," Lizalde said and spat into the water, as if to underline his opinion.

In Bacalar and Belize City he'd seen plenty of free Maya people, macehuales, they called themselves. The British traded with them regularly. The white Mexicans in the western lands, children of Spaniards who'd kept to their kind, had no love for them, and it was no surprise to see Lizalde was ill-disposed to those free folk. It was not that the British liked the Maya for their own sake, nor that they always remained on friendly terms, but Montgomery's countrymen thought the Maya rebels might help them carve out a piece of Mexico for the Crown. After all, disputed territory could become a protectorate with a bit of negotiation.

"We'll get rid of that heathen scourge, hack those mangy cowards into pieces one day," Lizalde promised.

Montgomery smiled, thinking of how the dzules like Lizalde had fled to the coast, boarded a boat, and escaped to the safety of Isla Holbox or else stumbled all the way to Mérida in haste during previous skirmishes against the Maya rebels.

"The macehuales think God speaks to them in the form of a talking cross. It's not exactly heathen," he replied, simply because he wanted to see Lizalde's flushed face grow even redder. He didn't like the hacendado, even if the man was paying him. He didn't like anyone. All men were to him worse than dogs, and he reviled humanity.

"It's heresy all the same. I suppose you don't properly worship the lord, Mr. Laughton? Few of your kind do."

He wondered if he meant men in his line of work or Englishmen and shrugged. Piety was not necessary to do his employer's bidding, and he'd lost any faith he'd ever had long before he ever touched the shore of the Americas.

They took many turns through the mangroves until the water grew shallow and they spotted two lonely wooden poles. There was a simple skiff tied to one of them. This must be what amounted to the landing. A road of bright reddish-yellow dirt ran from there. In the rainy season it would no doubt turn into a muddy trap. But for now it was dry, and there was a clear path through the dense scrub and brush.

One man walked ahead of them, and behind them there were two others, carrying Montgomery's belongings. If he decided to stay he'd have a few toiletries; the rest might be sent later, though there wasn't much else to bring. He tended to travel light at all times. The possessions he couldn't do without were his rifle, which he slung over his left shoulder, the pistol at his hip, and the compass in his pocket. This last item had been a wedding gift from his uncle. It had seen him through British Honduras, through swamps, creeks, rickety bridges, and sharply pointed ridges. Through dampness and swarms of mosquitoes. Through lands rich with limestone and teeming with mahogany, past ceiba trees with buttresses as sturdy as the towers of a castle, their branches festooned with orchids.

Now it brought him here, to Mexico.

They walked until they reached two ceiba trees shading a tall Moorish arch. In the distance there was a white house. The whole of Moreau's property was surrounded by a huge, tall wall and anchored by those arches. The house and other buildings—he spotted the stables to the left—lay in the middle of this long, walled rectangle where plants grew wild and unkempt.

It wasn't a proper, grand hacienda by a long shot—he thought it too small for that; the property might pass as a ranch—but it was still a sight. Lizalde had told him the previous owners had thought to run a sugar mill. If they had, their efforts had been poor; he couldn't spot the telltale chimney stacks. Maybe there was a trapiche in the back, but he couldn't see that far. There was a shorter, dividing wall at the rear. It had been painted white, like the house. The workers' housing must be behind that dividing wall, along with other structures.

The Mexican way of building houses, inherited from the Spaniards, involved walls behind walls and more walls. Nothing was easily exposed to the curious eyes of passersby. He bet there was a delightful interior patio behind the house's strong façade, a cloistered haven of hammocks and greenery amid a row of arcades. The house's portón itself was tall, nine feet in height, made of wood so dark it almost looked black, contrasting with the whiteness of the house. There was a postigo that could be opened to allow people on foot passage so that the double doors didn't have to swing open.

Montgomery was proven wrong when a woman opened the postigo to receive them, and they walked across the interior courtyard. There were no lush gardens, nor lazy hammocks. He was presented with the sight of a dry fountain shaded by a fiddlewood tree and empty planters. Unpruned bougainvilleas hugged the stone walls. Graceful archways led into the house proper, and windows with iron grilles looked onto the courtyard. Despite the cloistered quality of Mexican dwellings, the inside and the outside also seemed to mix freely, and above the archways there were carved images of leaves and flowers, evoking the presence of nature. It was a paradox that he enjoyed, this meeting of stone and plant, darkness and air.

The woman told the men carrying Montgomery's things to wait in the courtyard and then asked the gentlemen to follow her.

The sitting room Lizalde and Montgomery were led into had tall French doors and was furnished with two red settees that had seen better days, three chairs, and a table. Not the finest abode, not the pride of the wealthiest hacendado, definitely more of a haphazardly maintained country manor, but they had a piano. A massive, handwrought iron chandelier was dramatically suspended from wooden beams, drawing the eye, further indicating a certain amount of wealth.

Preposterously, a delicate clock had been placed atop a mantle. It was painted with a courting scene, showing a man in French livery of a previous century kissing the hand of a woman. Cherubs served as further ornamentation, and the top of it was painted a pale blue. It did not match anything else in the room. It was as if the owner of the house had ransacked another property and then hastily tossed the clock into this chamber.

A man sat on one of the chairs. When they walked in, he stood up and smiled. Dr. Moreau was taller than Montgomery, and Montgomery regularly towered over others, a good six feet and two inches in height. The doctor was also powerfully built, with a fine forehead and a resolute mouth. Though his hair was growing white he had an eagerness, a vitality, that did not give at all the impression of a man approaching his golden years. In his youth, Dr. Moreau could have been a pugilist, had he wanted to.

"Did you have a good trip? And would you like a glass of anise liqueur?" Dr. Moreau asked once Lizalde had introduced them. "I find it cools one down."

Montgomery was used to meaner stuff, to aguardiente. The thimble of liqueur was not his drink of choice. But he would never turn a spirit away. It was his curse. So he downed it with a swift twist of the wrist and set the glass back on a circular ceramic tray.

"I'm pleased to meet you, Mr. Laughton. I'm told you are from Manchester? An important city, very large these days."

"I haven't been in Manchester in a long time, sir. But yes," Montgomery said.

"I was also given to understand you have some interest and experience in engineering and are also equipped with a grasp of the biological sciences. If I may say so, you seem a tad young."

"I am twenty-nine as I stand before you today, which perhaps you may think young, though I might protest at such a claim. As for my experience, I left home at fifteen with the intent of learning a trade and took a ship to La Habana, where my uncle maintained various types of machinery. I became a maquinista, as they call it there."

He left out the reason why he'd abandoned England: his father's insidious beatings. The old man had also possessed an affinity for liquor. Sometimes Montgomery thought it was a vile affliction, transmitted through the blood. Or a curse, even though he didn't believe in curses. But if that was the case, then his family had also transmitted to him their easy way with machinery. His father had understood cotton machinery, belts and pulleys and boilers. His uncle, he knew, too, the way of machines, and young Montgomery had been more fascinated by the motion of a lever than any toy or game.

"How long were you in Cuba?"

"Nine years in the Caribbean, in total. Cuba, Dominica, several other places."

"Did you fare well there?"

"Well enough."

"Why did you leave?"

"I've moved around frequently. British Honduras suited me for a few years. Now I'm here."

He wasn't the only one who'd made such a trek. There were a motley group of Europeans and Americans crowding this part of the world. He'd seen ex-Confederates who'd fled south after the Civil War in the United States come to an end. The bulk of those Confederados were now in Brazil, attempting to establish new settlements, but others had gathered in British Honduras. There were Germans left over from Maximilian's failed imperial efforts and British merchants plying their goods. There were Black Caribs from Saint Vincent and other islands who spoke excellent French, mulatto laborers who extracted chicle and others who chopped mahogany, the Maya who held tight to settlements by the coast, and the dzules like Lizalde. The upper crust Mexicans, the Lizaldes of the peninsula, would often claim a pure, white ascendancy and some of them were indeed fairer than Montgomery, blue- and green-eyed and mightily proud of this fact.

Montgomery had chosen British Honduras and then Mexico not because of their natural riches, though there were opportunities to be had, and not because this vibrant collage of people attracted him, but simply because he did not wish to return to the cold and the fires that crackled at night in tiny rooms that reminded him of his mother's death and afterward of Elizabeth's demise, too. Fanny couldn't understand it. To her England meant civilization, and his aversion for colder climates struck her as unnatural.

"Tell him about the animals," Lizalde said, lazily waving his hand in Montgomery's direction, like a man commanding a dog to do a trick. "Montgomery is a hunter."

"Are you, Mr. Montgomery? You enjoy the sport?" Moreau asked, sitting down on the chair he'd been occupying before they walked in. He twisted his mouth into a faint smile.

Montgomery sat, too, on one of the settees—all the furniture was in need of a good reupholstering—one elbow on the armrest, his rifle set aside but within easy reach. Lizalde remained standing by the mantelpiece, examining the delicate clock set there.

"I do not do it for sport, but I've made a living at it for the past few years. I procure specimens for institutions and naturalists. I then embalm the specimens and prepare them and ship them back to Europe."

"Then you are familiar with biological matters and certain lab items, taxidermy requiring it."

"Yes, although I wouldn't pretend to be formally schooled in this matter."

"Yet you don't enjoy it? Many men hunt for the mere thrill of see-ing a beautiful animal mounted and stuffed."

"If you mean to ask if I'd rather have ten dead birds than ten live ones, then no, I don't enjoy the dead specimens. I am not looking for feathers to pluck and would rather let them lie upon the breast of a scarlet tanager than see them on a lady's fine hat. But biological sci-ences being what they are, you need those ten birds and not just one."

"How is that so?"

Montgomery leaned forward, restless. His clothes were rumpled and a trickle of sweat was running down his neck. He wanted nothing more than to roll his sleeves up to his elbows and splash cold water on his face, yet here he was being interviewed for the job without the courtesy of sparing him five minutes to tidy himself.

"When you are trying to take a look at the world you must make a thorough look of it. If I were to capture one specimen and send it back to London, people might take it as the one and only model of the organism, which would be incorrect since, at the very least, male and female birds often differ to a striking degree.

"So I must send male and female specimens, smaller and bigger ones, scrawny and plump, and attempt to provide a varied sample of their morphology so that the zoologists will arrive at an understanding of the species in question. That is, if I've done my job well and provided accurate specimens and the notes that must go with them. I am looking for the essence of the bird."

"What a splendid encapsulation of it all," Moreau said, nodding. "The essence of the bird! This is precisely what I attempt to find here with my work."

"If you permit me to say so, I don't know what your work entails. I've been given little indication of what I might find at Yaxaktun."

Montgomery did ask around a bit, but the details had been damnably scant. Dr. Moreau was a Frenchman who'd come to the country sometime around the time of the War of Reform. Or perhaps it had been shortly after the Mexican-American War. Mexico was constantly buffeted by conquering forces and internal strife. Moreau was but another European man who'd arrived with a bit of capital and great ambition. But Moreau, despite being a physician, opened no practice and did not remain in a large city for long, as might have been expected of any fellow wishing to establish himself in Mexican society. Instead, he was in the jungle running a sanatorium or clinic of some sort. Where, exactly, was a question mark.

"Yaxaktun is a special place," the doctor said. "We have no great staff, no mayorales, caporales, vaqueros, or luneros, as you might have at a proper hacienda. You'll have to do a little of everything.

"Should you take up the post of mayordomo, you'll be occupied with a number of chores. The old noria is useless. We have a couple of wells, of course, but it would be good to have real gardens and irrigation. The house and ancillary buildings and the grounds, and handling the upkeep of those, should keep you busy enough. But there's also the matter of my research."

"Mr. Lizalde said you are helping him improve his crops."

In passing Hernando Lizalde had mentioned "hybrids," but only once. Montgomery wondered if Moreau was one of those botanists who liked to graft plants together, who would compel a lemon tree to birth oranges.

"Yes, there's some of that," Moreau said, nodding. "The land can be stubborn here. Thin, poor soils. We sit atop a block of limestone, Mr. Laughton. Sugarcane and henequen may grow, and yet it's no easy feat to farm here. But there's more to my pursuits, and before I may come to the specifics of my work I must remind you, as no doubt Mr. Lizalde has made clear to you, that your labor here would mean a vow of silence."

"I signed papers to that effect," Montgomery said. He'd, in fact, practically signed his whole life away. He'd gone into debt for Fanny, bought her as many dresses and bonnets as he could manage. This debt had been sold and sold again, landing on Lizalde's lap.

"The boy has been thoroughly vetted," Lizalde said. "He's capable and discreet."

"That may be, but it takes a certain temperament to remain at Yaxaktun. We are isolated, the work is hard. A young man such as yourself, Mr. Laughton, might be better suited to a large city. Certainly your wife might prefer that. She wouldn't be joining you, would she?"

"We are separated."

"I know that. But you wouldn't think of getting in touch with her again, would you? You've done so in the past."

Montgomery tried to maintain an impassive face, but still he dug his fingers into the sofa's arm. It wasn't a surprise that Lizalde had included such information in whatever dossier he'd sent to Dr. Moreau, but still it stung to reply.

"Fanny and I have ceased any correspondence."

"And you have no other family?"

"My last living relative was my uncle, and he passed away years ago. I have cousins back in England, whom I've never met."

He'd also had a sister, once. Elizabeth, two years older than him. They'd gamboled together until he went away to make his fortune. He promised he'd send back for her but Elizabeth had been married off a year after his departure. She wrote often, mostly to tell him about the misery of her marriage and her hopes that they might be reunited.

They'd lost their mother when they were young, and he recalled the long nights in her room, while the fire burned. Henceforth, they had each other. Their father could not be trusted. He drank, and he beat his children. Elizabeth and Montgomery, it was the two of them. Even after she'd married, she thought he was her salvation, and Montgomery agreed to send money for her passage.

But by the time Montgomery had established himself in a solid position he was twenty-one and his sense of brotherly duty had been greatly diminished. There were other matters on his mind, most notably Fanny Owen, the daughter of a small British merchant who made a home for himself in Kingston.

Rather than spend his precious savings on sending for his sister, he'd used that money to buy a house and wed Fanny.

A year later his sister committed suicide.

He'd traded Elizabeth for Fanny and killed his sister in the bargain.

Montgomery cleared his throat. "I have no relative to write to about your scientific work, Dr. Moreau, if that is what you fear," he said after a moment. "Though I still have no idea what the work may be."

"*Natura non facit saltus*," the doctor replied. "That is my work."

"My Latin is lacking, doctor. I can jot down species names, not recite pretty phrases."

The clock struck a note, marking the hour, and the doctor turned his head toward the doorway. A woman and a girl walked into the room. The girl's eyes were amber-colored and large and her hair was black. She wore one of those bright dresses that were in vogue. It was a ferocious shade of pink, unnatural, bristling with ornamentation and almost glittering with a certain brutal beauty. The dress of a little empress who'd come to hold court. Like the clock, the outfit was misplaced in this room, but Montgomery was beginning to think that was precisely the effect Dr. Moreau wanted.

"Here is my housekeeper with my daughter. Carlota, come here," the doctor said, and the girl walked to his side. "Gentlemen, may I present my daughter, Carlota. This is Mr. Lizalde and this here is Mr. Laughton."

The doctor's daughter was of an age when she could still cling to her girlhood. Soon, though, he imagined they'd make her trade her youthful dresses for the maturity of the corset and the weight of long skirts. That's what they'd done to Elizabeth, wrapped her tight in colorful velvet and muslin and choked her to death.

Elizabeth hadn't killed herself. She'd been murdered. Women were butterflies to be pinned against a board. Poor child, she couldn't know her fate yet.

"Could you tell him what *natura non facit saltus* means?" the doctor asked, apparently attempting to jest. Montgomery wasn't in the mood for jesting.

"It means nature does not make leaps," the girl said.

His tongue still tasted strongly of the anise he'd sipped, and he wondered what should happen if he didn't obtain this job. He could drink himself a storm back in Progreso, he supposed. Drink and then blindly make his way to another port. South, possibly to Argentina. But he had debts to pay before even entertaining that thought. Debts Lizalde held.

CHAPTER 3

Carlota

SANCTUS, SANCTUS, SANCTUS. Three times holy. Her father's laboratory was a sacred space, more so even than the chapel where they prayed. Ramona said there was something holy in every rock, in every animal, in every leaf, and also in things. In stone and clay and even the pistol her father never used and kept by his bed. This is why you had to offer sakab, honey, and a few drops of blood to the alux, so that the crops might grow. Otherwise the corn would wilt. For the alux that lives inside the house there were also offerings to be made, or it would move the furniture and break the pots. The world, Ramona told them, must maintain a delicate balance, like the embroidering of a handkerchief. If you are not careful, the threads of life will tangle and knot together.

Melquíades claimed the mere thought such a thing might be possible was sacrilege: holiness could not reside in a flower or a drop of rain. Offerings to spirits were the devil's work.

Nevertheless, the laboratory was sacred, and therefore Carlota was not admitted in there without her father. When she was, he mostly kept her to the antechamber and assigned her readings or tasks he supervised. Cachito and Lupe were not permitted inside. Not even Ramona could enter this precinct. Only Melquíades, when he had worked for them, had been allowed to freely turn the key and make his way inside.

That day, though, her father handed her the key, and Carlota turned it, opening the door to the men. Then she began walking around the room, throwing the shutters open. Light streamed in through three tall windows, unveiling the doctor's secret world.

A long table dominated the antechamber, and upon it were set several microscopes. When her father did allow her in, he'd show her arrangements of diatoms that he'd ordered from distant places. Under the lenses, minute algae became kaleidoscopes of color. Then her father would change the slide and offer a peek at a bit of bone, a feather, a section of a sponge. For a child, it was more whimsy than scientific fact.

The wonders of microscopy were not the only ones to be found here. Taxidermied animals were stored in cabinets and jars, feathers and fur neatly preserved. The naked skeleton of a large cat was arranged on a table. The walls of the antechamber were festooned with illustrations of an equally fantastic nature. Drawings depicting the flexing of muscles, the naked skeleton, veins and arteries that looked like rivers, tracing their course across the human body. There were a number of books and papers set upon tall bookshelves and also piled on the floor. This was not, by far, the sum of her father's books. He also kept a well-stocked library, but he worked mostly in the antechamber because it was somewhat isolated from the rest of the house.

"Have you heard of Darwin's discussion on pangenesis, Mr. Laughton?" her father asked as the gentlemen walked around, looking at the drawings on the walls, like guests who have been admitted into a museum exhibit.

"Pangenesis is somewhat linked to heredity," Laughton said. "The specifics evade me. You must instruct me once again."

Carlota wasn't sure if the young man spoke honestly or if he was merely bored or wished to brush her father off. There was a wryness to his face, the barest hint of mockery.

"Mr. Darwin suggests that each animal or plant is made up of particles called gemmules. And these in turn provide the elementary constitution for an organism's progeny. Of course, these gemmules cannot be seen by our eyes, but they're there. The problem is Mr. Darwin has found an answer, but not the proper one."

"How so?"

"Darwin's vision is too shallow. What I seek is to explore the essence of all matter of creatures and then leap beyond that. Which I have. I've managed to surpass him, to look at life and isolate the most basic unit of it and from it build something anew, like a brick-layer might build a house.

"Picture the axolotl of the lakes of Mexico City. It is but a small creature, much like the salamander, but should you slice off a limb, it will regrow it. Now imagine if you had the capacity to regrow a limb like the axolotl. Imagine all the possible medical applications, all the treatments that could take place if man had the strength of an ox or a cat's keen eyes in the dark."

"I'd say that is impossible," Laughton replied.

"Not if you were able to somehow look at the gemmules of two organisms and mix them."

"You mean you'd take a characteristic of a salamander and blend it somehow with that of a man? That sounds even more impossible, Dr. Moreau. If I were to inject the blood of a salamander into your veins you'd die, even the most obtuse naturalist will tell you that."

"Not the blood, but the essence which hides in the blood," her father said. "I've done this. My daughter is proof of it."

Laughton now turned to look at Mr. Lizalde as if silently asking if they were meant to take this seriously, and then he looked at her, frowning.

"I was once married, a long time ago. My wife and daughter died. It was disease that carried them away, and there was nothing I could do despite my medical training. But the tragedy did spur my interest in certain biological studies. Years later Carlota was born of a second union. But just like the first time, my life seemed poised for sorrow. My daughter had a rare condition of the blood."

Her father moved toward the glass cabinet and threw it open as he spoke. Inside he kept numerous bottles and receptacles. She knew them all. Out came the wooden box with its velvet lining and the brass syringe, as well as the porcelain container with the cotton, the bottle of rubbing alcohol.

"To save Carlota I pushed my studies forward as much as I could until I found a solution, a way to combine certain unique elements found in the jaguar with the essential gemmules of my child. With this medication I keep my daughter alive. Time for your injection, Carlota."

Her father motioned for her to step forward. "What do you intend to do with that?" Laughton asked, sounding concerned.

"He does not lie. I am ill, sir," she replied, calmly glancing at the man. Then she went to her father and held up her arm.

The pinprick of the needle was hardly noticeable. A red flower bloomed on her skin, and then she gently pressed the piece of cotton her father handed her against her arm.

"Now a tiny tablet that aids in my daughter's digestion; nervous girl that she can be, sometimes she gets stomachaches and the injections make this worse," her father said, uncorking a bottle and handing a tablet to Carlota, who placed it in her mouth. "There and done. An injection once a week, that's all there is to it."

On seeing that no harm had befallen her, Laughton's frown relaxed once again into doubtful scorn, and he even let out a low laugh.

"You are amused, sir?" she asked. "Do I make you laugh?"

"I'm not laughing at you, young miss, it is only that this proves nothing," he said, and he looked at her father and shook his head. "Dr. Moreau, it is an interesting tale, but I do not believe you have given the strength of a jaguar to a girl with an injection."

"I have found a way to keep her healthy and whole by relying on the strength of animals, which is not exactly the same. But this does bring me to the main point of my investigations and the sort of research I am conducting for Mr. Lizalde."

"Perhaps you mean to gift men gills so they can breathe under the sea?"

"The opposite: I mean to fashion animals into something different, to carve them into new shapes. To make the pig walk upright or the dog speak a variety of words."

"Well. Only that!"

"It is possible to transplant tissue from one part of an animal to another, to alter its method of growth or to modify its limbs. Why couldn't we change it in its most intimate structure? Come now, follow me."

Her father motioned for her to open the door that led into the laboratory, and they walked in. Little was visible at first in the darkness. The windows were again tall but the lower half had been bricked, and she went around opening shutters, this time with the aid of a long stick with a hook at one end. The sunlight came in great streaks, neatly illuminating the many shelves, bottles, tools, funnels, tubes for stirring, scales, and beakers that constituted her father's arsenal. There were vessels for heat and porcelain plates for evaporation. There were cabinets with labeled drawers and all manner of apparatus that he'd had custom made with copper, steel, and glass. A table in the center of the room was littered with papers, jars, and even a few stuffed animal specimens. The lab also housed a furnace and an oven. A row of hooks had been placed above them, and from there hung small shovels, tongs, and pincers.

One could easily discern how chaos was taking hold of the lab. Melquíades had helped keep it all tidier. It wasn't that her father was sloppy, but his moods fluctuated. At times he would enter into periods of frenzied activity, then languish in a listless state. When lethargy and melancholy attacked him, he spent his waking hours sprawled in the great chair in the library, gazing out the window, or in bed, staring at the oval portrait of his wife.

At such times, Carlota, despite loving her father beyond all words, felt her heart twist with bitterness because the way he gazed at the portrait and that other way his eyes seemed to skim over her told her clearly in his heart his dead wife and child reigned supreme.

She was a poor substitute.

But her father's lingering melancholia had given way that month, perhaps in anticipation of this visit or for some other reason. He was, at any rate, almost giddy as they stood in the laboratory and he spread his arms out, pointing out several pieces of equipment and then motioning for them to go toward a red velvet curtain that had been set at the other end of the room.

"Come here, Mr. Laughton. Allow me to show you the fruits of my labor," her father said, and he pulled the curtain aside with the flair of a showman.

Behind it there was a large box with the sides made of glass and set upon wheels so that it might be rolled around. Laughton knelt down to better look at the box. Laughton then quickly turned to Mr. Lizalde and whispered something she could not hear, and Mr. Lizalde whispered something back, but by their faces it was clear the young man was shocked.

For Carlota, the sight was unusual, too. She had never had a chance to gaze at the hybrids at this stage; her father kept them from her until they were more mature. The creature inside the box had the body and size of a large hog. But its limbs were all wrong, and instead of hooves it was developing fingers, thin protuberances of flesh. Its head also looked misshapen, squashed. It had no ears, and its eyes were closed. It was asleep, suspended in a murky substance that could not be water but instead resembled a film or mucus, and the same mucus covered its mouth.

She wanted to press her face against the glass or tap it with a finger, but she did not dare. She suspected that Laughton wanted to do the same, and he couldn't move, either. They both stared at the creature behind the glass, at the way its back was arched, and the backbone that seemed to stick out, razorlike, all the nubs tracing a long line against the taut skin. The eyes . . . she wondered what was the color of the hybrid's eyes. It had no hair, not even a bit of fuzz even though Cachito and Lupe had fuzz over their faces. Soft as down yet plentiful, it also covered their arms and legs.

"What is that?" Laughton finally asked.

"A hybrid. They are all developed in the womb of pigs. Once they reach a certain point of maturation, they are transplanted into this chamber. The solution is a mixture of a type of algae and a fungus which together excrete certain chemicals that spur the growth," her father said. "The hybrid is also provided with a nutritive solution to ensure bones and muscles do not atrophy. There is more to it than that, of course, but you are looking at a creature that will have, in a few weeks, the ability to walk upright and manipulate tools."

"Then this is . . . you've mixed a pig with a man?"

"I've gestated an organism inside a pig, yes. And some of its gemmules are from another animal, and some others are from humans. It is not a single thing."

"It's . . . it's definitively alive?"

"Yes. Sleeping for now."

"And it'll live? You'll eventually take it out of there and it'll breathe and *live*?"

It barely seemed alive now, but it *was* breathing. You could tell because it twitched a bit. But it looked for all intents and purposes like a deformed animal that someone had pickled.

"Sometimes they don't," Carlota said, remembering the hybrids the previous year and the year before that. They'd all died in the womb, and her father had complained about the quality of the animals he could get, that he couldn't work if all he had were pigs and dogs.

But Melquíades was no hunter to drag in big cats or monkeys. Melquíades was already rather upset that her father wanted jaguars every six months and this necessitated going to a city and talking to people Melquíades didn't want to talk to. Hunters normally traded in pelts and demanded an exorbitant price to drag a jaguar to Yaxaktun. And Melquíades had that pain in his gut and didn't like going on tiresome errands.

Her father nodded. "No, they don't always live. It's part of what I'm trying to perfect. The process is not yet entirely without its problems."

"It'll live," Laughton whispered.

Her father clapped his hands and smiled. The sound was loud; it seemed to bounce off the ceiling.

"Come, gentlemen, let's meet a more developed hybrid," her father said, and he ushered them out of the room. "Lock up, Carlota."

So she did, closing the door behind the gentlemen, first the laboratory, then the antechamber.

Her father guided them to the kitchen, which was patterned with azulejos, each tile showing a drawing of a flower or a geometric shape, evoking the days of the Mudéjar. Glazed pots hung next to the doorway. The trasteros were stacked with baskets and clay dishes—the porcelain was stored in the dining room, along with the glasses and serving bowls. Cooking pots were heaped upside down, waiting to be filled with beans and rice. There were two cast iron comales to cook the tortillas and two metates to grind the corn, as well as a wall rack containing a multitude of wooden spoons, ladles, chocolate whisks, knives, and all manner of tools.

In the center of the kitchen there was a big, rough, old table with benches on each side. Ramona, Cachito, and Lupe were sitting there. When they walked in, the three of them stood up.

"You'll be wanting food, doctor?" Ramona asked.

"No, Ramona. It's fine for now. I wanted to introduce Mr. Laughton to our two young friends. These are Livia and Cesare," her father said, using the formal names of the young hybrids.

Her father had a good Latin name for each of his creations, but Ramona had nicknamed each and every one of them or they called one another another thing. Cachito was small, hence his moniker. Lupe simply looked like a Lupe to Ramona. No, Ramona did not use the names the doctor liked. Even the doctor's daughter had a nickname. Carlota was Loti and sometimes she was even Carlota Hija del Elote Cara de Tejocote, when Cachito and Lupe giggled and thought themselves funny with their rhymes and puns.

Naturally, her father didn't approve of them using nicknames—it was lowly, he complained—but there wasn't much he could do about it and even he had grown accustomed to their monikers. Ramona told them stories, taught them words, and they lived by the doctor's rules but also Ramona's habits. That, Ramona said, was as it should be, for the world is a constant compromise, a greeting of the other and of yourself.

"Hello, Mr. Laughton," Cachito and Lupe said in unison.

"Give him your hand."

Laughton extended his hand and shook the hands of both of the children, nodding. He looked dazzled. His wry grin had vanished.

"Witness here, the ears," her father said, pulling Cachito forward. He had pointed ears, covered with a fine brown fur, which her father now gently poked at. "But with Lupe, they're somewhat smaller and the fingers are better developed. See here, too, the jaw. It protrudes, but it's not as bad as with the boy's."

As he spoke her father cupped Lupe's face, tilting her head up. "They're still young and their features haven't settled. But you can see how well formed they are. Can you say something else to Mr. Laughton?"

"We're pleased to meet you," Cachito said.

"Did you bring candy?" Lupe asked.

"I . . . yes. I'm pleased to meet you," Laughton said. "I'm afraid I didn't bring candy."

Laughton pressed a hand against his mouth and simply stared at Cachito and Lupe for a moment before turning his face away and looking at her father.

"Sir, I need to sit down and I need a glass of water."

"Yes, not a problem. Ramona, brew a pot of tea and bring it to the sitting room. We'll chat there. Carlota, please take the key to the laboratory back to my room, will you?" her father asked, his palm settling on her shoulder and patting it twice. "Later we will have supper."

"Yes, father. It was a pleasure seeing you, gentlemen," she said, remembering her courtesies. She was good when it came to minding such details, her voice soft, her head lowered to indicate her agreement.

Chapter 4

Montgomery

THE DOCTOR OPENED a box and offered them cigars. Montgomery shook his head. He watched Moreau light his cigar with dexterous fingers, watched him sit on the couch and smile as Ramona walked in with the tea.

He reached for a dainty cup, felt the porcelain beneath his fingers. Yet he still wondered whether he had hallucinated. Perhaps the drink had finally rotted his brain. Sometimes he dreamed of Elizabeth—he could swear she was whispering in his ear. But he had never seen things.

No, what he'd witnessed had been real, and now they were sitting in this room, calmly drinking tea. As if nothing were amiss. As if they had not gazed at a miracle or a curse made flesh.

The hybrid called Livia was taller than her male counterpart, slender, and had a shorter snout and rounded ears, resembling in coloration and features the jaguarundi. The boy, Cesare, had the black spots and streaks of an ocelot. His fur was a tawny color, his face rounder. Though looking at them one could immediately link them to wild cats, they also possessed human form, and he was left thinking of an Egyptologist who had once shown him drawings of gods with animal heads. Or else the carvings in ancient Maya temples where one could spy the face of an ancient god conjoined with a beast from the jungle. Montgomery could not begin to imagine how Moreau had managed to fashion such creatures. In fact, he could hardly form a sentence.

"Feeling any better, Mr. Laughton?"

"I'm not exactly sure what I'm feeling," he said, letting out a nervous laugh. "Doctor, what you've shown me is . . . there are hardly words to describe it."

"It's a leap, is what it is," Moreau said.

"Yes, I suppose so. But what is the purpose? I can understand attempting to heal your daughter's illness, but how could the creation of the hybrids benefit you?"

"It doesn't benefit him. It benefits me," Lizalde said. He sat in a high-backed mahogany armchair which didn't look the least bit comfortable, but upon which he had perched in a kingly manner, an unlit cigar in his right hand. "The hybrids might address our worker issues."

"Worker issues?"

"The Indians of the region have always worked the fields. They have been traditionally laborious and orderly, when the right pressure is applied. But then came trash like Jacinto Pat to stoke violence. Sugar is valuable. And henequen might be, too, but if and only if we have enough hands to work the land, which can't be done when half the damn peninsula is in revolt and the other half cannot be trusted. I view every Indian with distrust these days, Mr. Laughton. They have a conspirator's streak in them.

"Now, it's true that in the old days we could import black workers from the Caribbean, but now that is no longer possible. It was, in any case, always too expensive. In Mérida I've heard gentlemen say we ought to bring men from China or Korea. I can't tell you what the expense might be to do *that*," Lizalde said, pausing to light the cigar he'd been toying with.

"Besides, even if we were able to bring these Chinese folk, it might be for naught. I have a friend who tried importing a crew of Italians. They died of yellow fever. Not everyone can acclimate to our land," Lizalde said, his thin lips twisting with displeasure. "Local workers, workers reared in the peninsula. That is the trick."

"You hope the hybrids will cultivate sugar instead of employing the macehuales?"

"You've seen Moreau's work. Hybrids walking upright on two legs, with hands to handle tools. It can be done, if the good doctor can fix a few minor issues."

"What minor issues?"

"As my daughter noted, some hybrids die. The maturation is a challenge," the doctor said. "Accelerating their growth is necessary, but sometimes the process can cause defects. All hybrids have shorter life spans, which makes perfect sense. Think of a cat. At twelve years of age, it is already an old cat. That is not so for a human."

"How old are the hybrids we saw?"

"They were born some seven years ago but would now be comparable to a twelve- or thirteen-year-old child in terms of their faculties and physical development. They have proven to be my greatest success. Their maturation has slowed down, and if it proceeds at this rate they should be able to live, oh, thirty or thirty-five years without any issues. More than that and they might develop severe bone problems."

"Thirty years still does not strike me as a particularly long life span."

"It's longer than a year," Lizalde said.

"Is that how long they used to live?"

"In the beginning it wasn't long, no. When I extended the life span there were setbacks. Skin issues, muscle and nerve twitches," the doctor said.

"And yet these two might develop bone problems, too."

"At thirty, perhaps. Which is a good deal better than at eight. But that is not the only complication. Just as Carlota must receive injections to maintain her good health, in turn the hybrids must receive medication to ensure they remain stable. They'd sicken without it. As you can imagine, this makes it implausible for us to send our current set of workers over to Mr. Lizalde's haciendas, but that is the ultimate goal."

"How many hybrids do you have now?"

"Over two dozen. You can see them later, if you'd like. I do wonder if it's true, what Mr. Lizalde said about you."

"What did he say?"

"We have conducted an exhaustive search, trying to find a man of the right caliber to work as the mayordomo at Yaxaktun. I require someone who can procure animal specimens for me. There are supplies that must be brought over, there is business in Mérida you might have to attend to. There are a thousand things you need to do. But the most important thing you must do is look after the hybrids. You've worked at a logging camp and in other arduous conditions, dealing with a variety of people. I think that is useful experience. However, the reason why you stand before me today is because Mr. Lizalde assured me you are not afraid of wild animals."

Montgomery's porcelain cup was decorated with yellow flowers, edged with gold. He ran his thumb around the rim and smirked. "Mr. Lizalde lied. I am afraid of wild animals. Only a fool wouldn't be."

"Yet, the jaguar," Moreau said. "Mr. Lizalde wrote me about the jaguar."

"The jaguar," Montgomery said.

That story. The story that had given him whatever renown he had. Mad Montgomery Laughton. El Inglés Loco. He realized he'd have to tell it, for Moreau was looking at him with interest.

"I was in a small town, south of Belize City. Jaguars are opportunistic killers and they tend to stay clear of humans. I don't know why this one came close to the town, but the people there had seen it twice before. But it had done nothing on those occasions, and they'd chased it off. There were a few women doing their washing by the river. One of the women had taken her daughter with her that day. She was a little girl, about four years of age. The girl was milling around, not too far from her mother, when a jaguar pounced on her from the bushes. It clamped its jaws on her head and dragged her away.

"I went after it. I didn't have my pistol with me, so I had to use what I did have, which was a knife. I managed to kill the jaguar."

He didn't mention that the reason he didn't have his pistol was that he'd been drinking the previous night and he'd been washing his shirt by the river, since he'd soiled it with vomit. He didn't mention the hideous quantities of blood staining his fingers. Nor his tears, nor the fact he tried to retch after it was all over and could not. His stomach had already been emptied. But maybe Moreau could discern the totality of the story. There was something knowing in his eyes.

"And you were not hurt?"

"I have scars on my arm from it." He paused, his fingertips tingling, as if his nerves were remembering the struggle. Sometimes his arm ached, echoes of the battle embedded in his flesh. "The child died. It was useless in the end," he concluded.

"Nevertheless, it was brave."

Montgomery grunted and drank his tea. It was not brave to come upon a jaguar as it was chewing on a child and stab it while it was distracted. The people of the village had known better. The mad Englishman.

After it happened he had written to Fanny. He didn't know what he expected. Perhaps for her to say that, yes, it had been a heroic act. Perhaps to pity him and return to his side, to nurse him back to health. But she had not cared, and she'd sent him a single, brief, cold letter.

"The work at Yaxaktun requires you to be surrounded by animals at all times. It's a difficult skill set," Lizalde said.

"No lion tamers around?" Montgomery quipped.

"I don't know if I like you yet, Mr. Laughton," Moreau said calmly, the half-consumed cigar dangling from his fingers. "I'm not sure you're the correct man for the job."

"Frankly, I'm not sure I'd take the job."

"There's no need to make decisions now, is there?" Lizalde replied. "We all ought to have a nap before supper. Tomorrow morning we can discuss business."

Montgomery agreed, mostly because he wanted to take a sip from the pewter flask nestled in his jacket's pocket, and he did exactly that as soon as he reached the room he'd been assigned. He removed his jacket and his shirt and took a sip, then another.

The room was large, and the furniture was old and heavy and made of precious mahogany. The bed was wrapped with mosquito curtains, which pleased him after having spent many nights in ratty hammocks. A massive chest lay at the foot of the bed. The chest's lock plate was decorated with delicate birds. There was also a type of traveling desk he'd seen before in these parts, a vargueño. Its panel of marquetry was overlaid with silver, showcasing an abstract pattern that pointed to a certain Moorish influence inherited from the Spaniards, like the azulejos. A friar's chair, with its distinctive brass nails, had been set by the window.

There was also a large mirror. He had not been staying in nice enough places that they'd ever own such a thing, and Montgomery saw himself as he hadn't in a long time. His body was wiry, unhealthily thin. Fanny had found him somewhat handsome, or at least sufficiently pleasing, once upon a time. He doubted she'd think so now. But perhaps that had been a lie. Money was what she found most beautiful. Money he didn't have. He'd known Fanny liked the finer things in life, but he had not begrudged her extravagances during their courtship, and he'd thought her happy when they wed.

But when Montgomery's uncle died, Fanny had been livid that he'd received no inheritance.

"He has children, back in England," he'd explained.

"But he didn't love them. And you said he thought of you as his son."

"What does it matter?" he'd asked.

It had mattered quite a bit. Fanny wanted a decent life, she said. Although Montgomery didn't think their living was indecent, he, too, began to observe the deficiencies in their household, and he admitted that Fanny was too charming to be living a drab, dry existence. She must sparkle as the jewel that she was. She must be happy. He examined the ugly curtains and the cheap rug and felt it was all a reflection of him. He knew himself inferior and foolish, and worried about the frown on his wife's face and the way other men looked at her.

Montgomery purchased a new, large house, imported fabrics from London and Paris, sought rare perfumes, bought golden bracelets and a pair of diamond earrings for Fanny, as though he were a wealthy man. He borrowed vast quantities of money, then borrowed more to pay that back. But wasn't it worth it to see Fanny happy? Wasn't it worth it to feel her arms around his neck, to see the flash of that perfect smile?

Eventually Montgomery packed their bags. He told Fanny there would be more opportunities for them in British Honduras. But she didn't like it there. She'd never liked the Caribbean, and this, she said, was worse. Their arguments multiplied. She cried often. She was distraught: this was not the kind of life he had promised her. She accused him of lying to her about the extent of his means.

Montgomery didn't know how to talk to Fanny. He grew quiet, retreated, focused on work.

He went to a logging camp for a two-month assignment. By the time he returned, his wife had left. Their money woes had intensified, and Fanny, made aware of their precarious financial situation, had decamped.

He couldn't blame her. He was not rich enough, not enough of a gentleman, too taciturn, too haunted even before he regularly reached for the bottle and wrapped himself in self-pity. Too moody, too damn much. She couldn't understand him. He'd loved her because she was different from him, but in the end that was what broke them.

He ran his fingers down the scars on his arm and looked at himself in the mirror, smirking. If he stayed at Yaxaktun perhaps he'd have a chance to improve his diet and put on weight. His work in British Honduras hunting animal specimens was haphazard. It paid better than his work as a maquinista, but he undertook it when the money ran out and to keep his debtors off his back. He saved nothing. The little profit he had, he drank and played away, and once in a while he hired a prostitute to share his bed. Blond and blue-eyed, if it could be had. Like Fanny Owen.

Yet he wasn't certain he wanted the safety of this roof over his head, of Lizalde's money. The comforts he could have here were considerable. The inviting bed, the nice furniture, they made a change from being bitten by fleas and having to check his hair for lice. But the price tag . . .

He stretched out on the bed but did not nap. A knock came later, and Ramona walked in with a porcelain pitcher and a washbasin for him. He thanked her and tidied himself for dinner.

They ate a light meal, and Montgomery made liberal use of the wine. They didn't speak of business, and Montgomery mostly listened to the others rather than conversing.

After dinner they went to the sitting room once more, and Moreau's daughter played the piano for them. She wasn't terribly good at it. He supposed Moreau did what he could when it came to his daughter's education, but without a governess, miracles could not be expected. Fanny had played beautifully. She possessed all the fine qualities a well-bred young woman should have.

Ramona eventually collected the child, and the men decided to smoke a cigar.

Montgomery excused himself, bid them good night, and went back to his room. Again he considered the situation, this place.

Animal hybrids, experiments. It was like a fever dream, and yet would it be worse than what he'd already experienced? He'd weathered the harshness of the logging camps and the peculiar cold of the jungle, when the sun couldn't filter through the trees and you were chilled to the bone in the never-ending rain. The wind cracked the sky in this corner of the world, making the houses moan. Many people toiled in misery, serving the hacendados. The Maya rebels had not risen against the landowners solely out of spite, as much as the white Mexicans liked to tell the tale like that. But then, so what? Everywhere Montgomery had been he'd spied the same misery under a different guise. In England it was in the factories, in Latin America it was in the fields. There was always someone with a little more money, a little more power, and he owned you. The hacendados extended credit to the Indians, and the Indians were indebted forever. But if it wasn't the hacendado, then it was the priest who came collecting, and the result was the same: weed cutting, sugarcane cutting, you had to work for them. Work like a dog, live like a dog, and die like one, too.

He'd heard fellow Englishmen say that the Maya were stupid for incurring such debts. But Montgomery, indebted as he was himself, understood that it was easy to lose control of one's life, that the reins could be yanked away with a smooth brutality. If he'd been a braver man, Montgomery might have put a bullet to his own head. But as he'd explained to Moreau, he wasn't brave. He was a perfect coward. He lay on the bed, placed his pistol under his pillow, and closed his eyes. The bedsheets were soft under his palms. He tried writing a letter to Fanny in his head, like he did sometimes at night.

I have come to stay at a small rancho which is the property of a wealthy hacendado. You'll wonder what is the difference between a hacienda and a rancho. It's merely a matter of scale. But the lodgings here are good and the place is clean. It is not always so in these distant parts of the world, wrecked by conflict. I've stayed in places where the floor was all dirt and my bed was a filthy hammock and chickens ran beneath me as I slept in a pitch-black darkness because there were no candles to be had. I know what you'll say: that I ought to head back to England. But I feel as if I've lost England or I never really knew it. I am a creature aborted, torn from the womb and homeless.

He'd never jot these words down or mail the letter. But it soothed him to imagine himself writing and Fanny opening the letter, her elegant hands holding up the letter to the light, and her voice as she read it out loud. But he didn't like picturing her face, he didn't like remembering those blue eyes and the mass of golden curls, nor her languid body, pale as alabaster, stretched out next to him.

No, when he pictured her, he had to further the illusion. He had to bury his face in a woman's hair, close his eyes, and breathe in slowly. Whisper her name while he held another and tried to bring a phantom back to life.

The words slipped away, his mind spent.

He dreamed of the jungle and flowers and a great jaguar sitting atop his chest, pressing him down as heavy as a stone. When he woke it was to the sound of a scream.

He sat up and reached for his pistol.

CHAPTER 5

Carlota

RAMONA HAD GONE to deliver the tea and then to check that all the visitors' luggage was in their rooms. Lizalde's servants had been allotted a room, told to wait there, and the children had been instructed to be good and quiet and stay out of sight. They'd decamped to Carlota's room to play since they could not run free.

Cachito spun the zoetrope and made horses gallop. Lupe lined the toy soldiers up. There were soldiers on foot and cavalry soldiers with their sabers wielded high, and even a toy cannon. The soldiers' coats were painted blue with white lapels, the cuffs red, and the trousers white, mimicking the uniform of Napoleon's Grande Armée. They each wore a black shako with a diamond-shaped plate on the front. Her father was a great admirer of Napoleon and had thought to name his daughter Josefina, but had changed his mind at the last minute.

He called her Carlota because it meant "freedom," and he thought it would suit her. Yet in the end she still shared a name with an empress: Carlota, who reigned in Mexico for a few scant years and who had visited Yucatán when Carlota Moreau was eight years of age. Yet, of those imperial times she recalled little of note and could not have said if the presence of the French army had altered the nation much having been cloistered away her entire life.

What she did know was that Carlota had gone mad after they'd executed her husband at the Cerro de las Campanas, and she thought it was an odd thing to have the same name as a madwoman locked away in Brussels. It struck her as unlucky. But her father assured her Carlota of Belgium was a great lady and he didn't believe in luck.

"That Englishman has no color in his eyes," Cachito said. "Ramona told me so."

"Everyone has color in their eyes," Carlota replied. She had taken off the fancy dress and was wearing a simpler frock and lay on her belly on the floor, watching the soldiers. She was getting too old for toys. But her father did not demand they cease their games, and she feared that when she was a grown woman he'd send her away, which sometimes made her want to cling ever so strongly to girlhood.

"Not that one, he doesn't. He's got eyes like a cloud. That's not real color."

"Did you go into the laboratory with them?" Lupe asked.

"I did. I saw everything inside. Father has a hybrid in there. But it's not full-grown. It's in a tank and it looks like something that should be in the womb, but not really, either. It's odd, its skin looks all wrong."

"In the womb?" Cachito said and scratched his ear. "It'd be tiny then."

"No, it's not like the homunculus people used to write about."

"The what?"

"A drawing I saw in Father's books. People thought you could make tiny people and grow them in a bottle."

"How do you spell it?"

Carlota sounded it out. Her father had taught her to read, and she in turn had shared her storybooks with Lupe and Cachito. Lupe was dazzled by the illustrations, but Cachito was interested in the words and loudly sounded out each new word he learned, then used it in conversation.

"Can you hold the hybrid in your hand?" Cachito asked.

"No, it's not like that. That's what alchemists thought."

"Your father is an alchemist. I've heard him say so."

"No, he knows chemistry."

"How's that different?" Cachito asked, making the zoetrope spin.

"Stop asking silly questions," Lupe said and she set the soldier she was holding down. "You should show it to us so we can see what you mean."

"How could I?"

"You have the key."

"I'm supposed to return it to his room."

"With guests around he won't go work in the laboratory tonight, which means he won't need the key. I bet we could take a peek when they've gone to bed and he wouldn't know."

"He'd be cross with us if he found out," Carlota said. "And all for what? So that you may be amused?"

"He showed the gentlemen the laboratory for their amusement," Lupe replied.

"That's different."

"How's it different? We should go tonight."

"I'm telling you, he'd be angry."

"If you don't give us the keys we'll swipe them and take a look without you and then you'll be terribly upset we left you out of it, like when we ate all the candies Melquíades kept hidden under his bed."

"That's not the same!"

"It's the same. You complain later when we leave you out."

Carlota bit her lip. She didn't like it when Lupe was stubborn like this. Cachito asked questions because he wanted to know, but Lupe dug into the same subject because she wished to have the last word. But no, Carlota didn't like to be left out. She didn't want them treating her like she was an invalid, which her father still did sometimes, fussing about her, taking her temperature, commanding that she stay in bed. She was better now. So much stronger.

"Fine," she said. "But we'll do it after they've gone to sleep and we must be quiet."

Lupe smiled for the rest of the evening, that smile that meant she was pleased with herself, and Carlota thought she'd done wrong in agreeing, but there wasn't more to say. If she backed down, Lupe would tease her, and Cachito would, too. He did as Lupe said. She hoped her father would check that the key was in its place, but he did not. Perhaps he was too busy talking to Mr. Lizalde.

Late at night Cachito and Lupe came knocking, and Carlota grabbed the oil lamp by the bed. She pressed a finger against her lips and they nodded. Barefoot, they rushed through the hallways until they reached the door to the antechamber. Carlota took out the key but did not place it in the lock.

"What is it?" Lupe whispered.

"My father could be inside."

"There's no light. Don't make excuses. You're a big coward."

"Am not," Carlota muttered furiously, turning the key, unwilling to endure a week of teasing from those two. Anyway, she wanted to see the hybrid again. Yet it wasn't right to sneak around against her father's instructions. Maybe in the morning she could visit the chapel and pray a rosary.

Carlota opened the door, and they walked in. In darkness, the antechamber, filled with its many books and animal specimens, did not seem like a vault replete with treasure as it had earlier to her. It was unpleasant. She clutched the oil lamp tight.

"Come on," Lupe whispered. "We are not turning back now."

Carlota opened the second door, the hallowed door to the lab. This time, rather than hesitating, she breezily moved in. The lamp's flame made the shadows dance, and she turned around, triumphantly looking at Lupe and Cachito, who were still standing by the door.

"Well?" she whispered. "You wanted to see."

They hesitated. Perhaps they had expected her to change her mind and run back to her room like a coward. Slowly they walked into the laboratory. They raised their faces and looked at all the glass on the shelves and the worktables. Finally, they tiptoed to where she stood.

"Where is it?" Lupe asked.

"Hold this," she told Cachito and handed him the lamp.

She pulled the red curtain aside. She lacked her father's flair but still managed to astonish them as she pointed to the box. They all stood close together.

"It doesn't look like a baby," Cachito said.

"It's not one," Carlota said.

"What is it?"

There was no answer. The creature floated in the dark, pale and still and full of secrets. Lupe leaned forward, breaking formation, pressed herself close to the glass and tapped her finger against it.

"Hey there," she said.

"Don't," Carlota warned her.

"Why not?" Lupe replied, she kept tapping against the glass.

Carlota had wanted to touch the glass when she'd first seen the hybrid but hadn't dared. Lupe raised her chin and slammed her palm against the glass, and then she giggled. Cachito giggled, too, touched the glass, and Carlota shook her head. She tapped her finger against the glass, not wanting to be the one who didn't dare. It felt warm against her skin.

Her nail traced a circle on the glass.

An eye opened. It was shrouded by a white membrane.

Lupe and Cachito gasped and stepped away. Carlota stared at the unblinking eye. She opened her mouth to tell the others they ought to go.

The hybrid slammed its head against the glass, making Carlota spring back and clutch her hands.

"We should leave," Cachito whispered.

The hybrid slammed its head against the glass again, and the membrane slid away, revealing an eye that was golden and huge. It was the all-seeing eye of an ancient god, a Leviathan, terrible and hungry. Its mouth opened, revealing razor-thin teeth, like the maw of an eel. It screamed, but the water muffled the noise, and in silence it unleashed its agony. The hybrid's body rippled, swinging back and forth against its prison. It was scratching itself, drawing lines of red across its throat.

"It's dying," Lupe said. "We need to get it out of there, it's dying."

"We need to fetch my father," Carlota whispered.

"It can't breathe. It's drowning."

"Give me the lamp," she told Cachito. But the boy held on tight to it, like it was a talisman. "Cachito, let go of it!"

Instead of obeying her, Cachito scrambled away, bumping his back against a table. She turned her head to tell Lupe that she needed to wake up her father. But Lupe was not next to them anymore. She had grabbed one of the iron shovels above the oven and was heading toward the box.

"Lupe!" she yelled.

"We have to get it out of there!" Lupe yelled back, and she swung hard.

A crack ran down the glass. She swung again, and a third time. Carlota rushed toward her and shoved the girl aside. Lupe fell on the floor, and the shovel fell out of her grasp, clanging and landing under a table.

Carlota looked at the glass box with its deep cracks, and for one brief, brief second she thought they might be able to fix this. Then the hybrid threw itself against the glass with uncontrollable violence, and the glass shattered, sending shards flying through the lab. Water spilled out over the floor. It smelled bad, like meat that had spoiled. Carlota pressed a hand against her mouth to keep herself from gagging.

The hybrid twitched and stood on all fours. Its limbs were slick and looked fragile; its skin was almost translucent, like something that had been plucked from abyssal depths. It let out a sound that was between a mewl and a growl. Then it turned its head in Lupe's direction and rushed forward. It didn't walk. It seemed almost to slide but at such a frenetic speed Carlota was barely able to yell a warning. Lupe scrambled to her feet but was not quick enough and the thing lunged at her, digging its teeth into her leg.

Lupe screamed, and Carlota threw herself against the creature, tried to pull it away from the girl. But it was slippery, like a fish, and even though she tugged at it and pounded her fists against its body, the creature would not let go.

She remembered the shovel and reached under the table. Her fingers were slick, and the shovel almost slipped from her hands as she hit the creature in the head. She had to hit it twice more before it let Lupe go, and even then it was not dead. It growled and flopped around the floor.

She dropped the shovel and tried to pull Lupe to her feet. The girl was crying, and she clung to Carlota.

"We have to leave," she said.

"It hurts!" Lupe bawled.

Carlota looked around. Cachito had jumped on a table and was covering his eyes. She tried to drag Lupe out of the laboratory, but they hadn't taken more than a few steps when the hybrid stood up again and rushed toward them. They shuffled back, then stumbled and fell.

Lupe screamed again, and Carlota joined in the scream as the pale thing leaped toward them, its back rippling and arching, its fangs bared.

A shot rang loud in the semidarkness, and there was an equally loud, wet thud.

Breathe in. Slow breath in, then let it out. That's what Carlota's father said when she grew nervous, when one of her old attacks threatened to wreck her body. But Carlota was gulping for air, unable to control her breathing, and Lupe whimpered.

Carlota turned her head. She saw the hybrid shivering on the ground, blood spilling from its belly. It growled and snapped its jaws in the air.

A pair of boots crunched over broken glass.

The Englishman got close to the hybrid and discharged his gun again, the barrel pointed at the head of the creature. The hybrid let out one last shiver and lay still as its blood mixed with the water coating the floor. Carlota had bitten her lip, and there was the taste of blood in her mouth and all around her the thick, coppery scent of death. She clutched Lupe, and Lupe pressed her face against her shoulder, crying.

"Carlota!" Her father had burst into the room and knelt next to her, touched her face. "Carlota, are you hurt?"

He helped her sit up. Carlota shook her head and took a shallow breath. "No. It . . . it bit Lupe."

"Boy, bring that light!"

Cachito jumped off the table and held the lamp up. Her father asked Lupe to show her the leg, and Lupe obeyed. Her father muttered something and then stood up. His eyes fell upon the dead creature and then up at the Englishman.

"What is the meaning of this carnage?"

"It was my fault, papa," Carlota said, clutching his hand. "We wanted to see the hybrid."

"Your fault!"

Carlota did not want to say anything, but she nodded a weak yes. Her father stepped aside, his eyes hard. She wondered if he was going to hit her. He'd never punished her physically, but she might have preferred it to the coldness that spread across his face.

"Mr. Laughton, I must tend to Lupe's wounds. Would you assist me?"

"Yes, sir."

"Papa, what should I do?"

"You get out of my sight," he said. The words were close to a growl, and she felt the tears brimming in her eyes, but the Englishman was there and he was looking at her with such pity, and her father looked at her with such rage that she dare not cry.

Carlota rubbed her hands together and quietly exited the laboratory.

She heard them talking the next morning, in the sitting room. Her father and Laughton. If Mr. Lizalde or anyone else had been aware of the commotion the previous night, she did not know. She prayed it was not the case.

"It shan't be like that, it was a singular accident," her father said. Carlota pressed herself close to the door, out of sight but listening carefully.

"But the risk remains."

"As you yourself pointed out, there is always a risk when it comes to wild animals. I'm thankful for what you did last night. I think you are the right man for the job."

There was a pause. The tinkling of glass.

"Did Lizalde tell you in his detailed notes about me that I drink?" the young man asked.

"Is that a serious problem for you?"

"Wouldn't it be a serious problem for *you*?"

"What you do in your spare time does not concern me, as long as you can function in the daytime."

The young man laughed. There was no mirth to it, and the sound resembled the barking of a dog. "I always do my job."

"Then we'll get along. Do you want the position?"

"Yes," the man declared without hesitation.

She wondered how he could say that after what had happened, how he could sound dignified and composed after standing in the middle of the laboratory in a pool of blood with a corpse by his feet.

She poked her head through the doorway to look at them. Her father did not see her, but Laughton was at an angle so that his eyes immediately fixed on her. Like Cachito had said, they had no color. Gray and watery and void of sentiment.

She recalled what Ramona had said, that Yaxaktun was the end of the world. And she thought that yes, this man was here because he believed that was the case, that he had reached the end of the world and he was simply waiting for the annihilation of all things.

PART
TWO

(1877)

Chapter 6

Montgomery

HE WOKE UP to a piercing headache and the sun bright on his face and cursed himself for being lazy. The doctor did not chide him for his drinking, because Montgomery fulfilled his duties. In fact, Montgomery suspected the doctor was pleased that he drank. How he could have ever imagined the man might object, he didn't know. It was a way to control him, similar to how he controlled the hybrids, with his sermons and his mystique.

The drink kept Montgomery in check. He'd tried to abstain more than a few times in the six years he'd been at Yaxaktun, but then he'd head into town to run an errand and there he'd be, sitting in a cheap den, inhaling the scent of rank tobacco and downing glass after glass. Or else he'd find one of the many bottles of aguardiente stashed around the house and uncork that.

But it was Friday, and Moreau would want to administer the injections. He splashed water on his face and dressed, eyeing the clock with a frown, and headed to the kitchen.

Ramona and Lupe were making tortillas, palming the dough into shape. The rhythmic clapping of their hands was a familiar melody.

"Good morning, Mr. Laughton," Ramona said. "You want a cup of coffee?"

"Good morning. Yes, thank you. Is the doctor in his laboratory?"

"No. The gout is bothering him. Loti said he was tossing and turning last night. She gave him something for it early this morning. He's napping and she's out for a walk."

Ramona stood up and set water to boil while Lupe continued with her work. The coffee was efficiently, quickly prepared, and he downed it with equal haste.

"I'm going to hazard a guess that Carlota has gone to the cenote," he said, rubbing his temple and setting the clay cup down. The previous night he'd been thinking of his sister. It was the anniversary of her death, and this made him sink into a foul mood; not even writing his letters to Fanny could soothe him.

"Same as always," Lupe said, her tone as caustic as quicklime.

"Can you fetch her?"

"She won't come with me if I go. She takes forever when I ask," Lupe said. "You want her, you better yell at her."

Montgomery sighed and marched out of the house. He did not understand what the trouble brewing between Lupe and Carlota was, but lately they had made it a habit to constantly bicker. He had been close to his sister, there had been no fights between them, so such tiffs struck him as odd. But Carlota and Lupe were not sisters. Perhaps it was as simple as that.

There he was thinking of Elizabeth again, and he walked faster, hoping to reach the cenote quickly and quickly walk back. It was idleness that plagued his brain; once he was busy with the chores of the day his melancholy ought to subside.

The cenote where Carlota liked to swim was called Báalam because near the path that led to it there stood a solitary, white stone carved in the shape of a jaguar-man. The cenote was small, or at least the part visible from above ground constituted a modest circle of blue-green water dappled by sunlight that was easily accessible by climbing down a few rocks. It was a delight to sink into this pool of water when the sun was high in the sky.

Carlota wasn't swimming in there that day. She lay stretched out on the ground in her linen tea gown with an arm draped over her eyes and a fan—the indispensable trinket of any well-bred Mexican lady—resting by her side. In any large city a wealthy woman would have never ventured out of her house dressed like this. She would have needed layers of silk and a fashionable bustle, a fancy hat, and gloves, but the doctor's daughter could do as she pleased because it was Yaxaktun.

He didn't doubt one day soon her father would cart her off to Mérida in one of her finer outfits to find her a proper husband. She was now twenty and therefore of an age for courting. At eighteen, his sister had been married.

He didn't yell, as Lupe had suggested. No need for that. "Carlota, get up. It's time to head back."

When his shadow fell over her, she lazily lifted her arm and blinked, fixing her remarkable honey-colored eyes on him. Her lips twisted into a sly pout.

"I've hardly been here a minute," she said. She had a lush voice, like velvet and pearls and the flutter of her fan, and her hair was the blackest of black. It tumbled free down her shoulders that day.

Yes, her father would have no trouble finding her a husband. Beauty like this was sure to draw the eye.

"Dr. Moreau will be needing you soon."

"You have dark shadows under your eyes, Montgomery. When you drink, it shows. You're better looking when you don't," Carlota said. She was blunt, yet charming. For all the fluttering of her fan, she didn't know the way of soirees and salons, nor the language of flowers.

"It's a good thing I'm not vain, then," he said, his voice cool.

"I don't want to depart. Lupe was cruel to me this morning and I don't wish to return to the house until she's happy again, and she won't be that until later in the afternoon."

"I don't care if she pounces on you and scratches your face. It's Friday. You'll have your injection and then you'll help your father give the hybrids their medication," he said, his voice still cooler than the blue-green waters of the cenote next to which they stood.

"No," she said, pouting again, but when he stretched out his hand, she took it and stood up.

They began the walk back, following the narrow trail. They passed the white carving of the jaguar, and Carlota stopped to look at it. He drummed his fingers against his thigh.

"Tell me again about England and how cold it is. Tell me what snow feels like on your skin."

"Why would you want to hear about snow?"

"I want to know everything there is. Like my father."

Your father is a madman imagining such a thing is possible, he thought. But so was Montgomery for staying in this place for so long. Six years, gone in a blink. He always told himself he'd save his money and take off the next year, but the compound interest on his debt was ridiculous. Lizalde sent him a little money once in a while, as if to show he was magnanimous. Montgomery drank whatever salary he had drawn when in town, gambled the rest.

"You can't know everything," he said as they began walking again.

"You can if you talk to enough people and you read enough books," she replied, sounding sure of herself.

"No, you can't. Certain things you must experience in person."

"You're annoying today! And you sound like Lupe! Were you gossiping together?"

"No. Why are the two of you fighting?"

She sighed, those beautiful eyes glancing up at him, the thick lashes as sharp as daggers. "She wants to leave. She says she wants to see what's outside Yaxaktun. She wants to see Progreso and Mérida and other places. It's ridiculous."

"Why?"

"She couldn't, how would she have her medication? And why would anyone want to leave Yaxaktun?"

"Not everyone can see the world solely through books like you do. Others seek more excitement."

"You think me dull?"

"I didn't say that."

"Yaxaktun is perfect. It is better than any other place in the world."

"You don't know enough about the world to pontificate about it," he said, unable to suppress a laugh.

"Really? What do you find so enticing about the city? That you can lose all your wages on a game of tute or baccarat?" she asked, her voice hot as a coal.

He knew her fury was not directed at him, that she was angry at Lupe, and it was because he was walking next to her that he now faced the brunt of that anger, which must be turned somewhere. He nevertheless stopped in his tracks and stared at the girl. He didn't insulate anyone from the knowledge of his vices, but he didn't want them tossed in his face like stones.

Moreau liked to think his daughter, like the gentle bees of the peninsula that stored their honey in round sacks of black wax, lacked a stinger. But Montgomery knew her words were not always sweet, and at times she stung him all the same.

"One insult a day is quite enough for me, Miss Moreau," he said. "Two is more than I will bear on an empty stomach."

She looked immediately contrite; she often was when she was involved in some small mischief. Regret came easy to her. "I'm sorry," she said, her fingers falling gently against his arm, grasping his sleeve. "Forgive me, Monty."

The endearment was so unexpected, so rare, that rather than be cross he merely nodded his acknowledgment, and they walked in silence. She seemed rather miserable, but he didn't add a thing. He did, however, look at her.

It was impossible not to look at her. In the city, the women who commanded the highest prices at the best brothels were the whitest ones. Girls of milk and honey. But it was obvious that Carlota's mother had been no whey-faced lady. Carlota's skin was healthily bronzed, the hair tumbling in a thick wave to her waist was jet-black; the honey was in her eyes. And yet she would have made the finest courtesan in the city, and Montgomery might have spent his wages not on tute or baccarat, as she'd chided him, but on a different sort of pleasure.

She had only to stretch herself upon a divan to become an oda-lisque, and when she moved it was with such utter grace, with such delicious poise . . .

Not that he ought to be thinking about Dr. Moreau's daughter in those terms, which is why he kept his mouth resolutely shut on the walk back, wishing they had not started that damn conversation and she hadn't touched his arm.

When they reached the house, she went inside and he dawdled by the entrance, resting on one of the built-in masonry benches. He hadn't been long there when a group of men on horseback appeared in the distance. Without haste he stood up, then walked inside and fetched his rifle. Carlota and Lupe saw him and raised their faces, looking curious.

"What is it?" Carlota asked.

"Stay inside," he replied, and he walked out, past the decorative iron gate, back through the strong wooden doors and to the bench. They were not expecting visitors and he was wary.

It was a party of six. Two young men dismounted. They did not wear the white cotton shirts and trousers of a laborer but were instead attired in the way of city folk. Their dark clothes were inappropri-ate for the heat of the jungle; their stiff-collared shirts and fancy, embroidered waistcoats seemed outright ridiculous. Rather than sporting something similar to Montgomery's Toquilla straw hat, which protected him from the sun, they had donned dark felt hats with upturned brims.

Montgomery wondered if they weren't cooking themselves alive underneath their grandiose outfits. When Montgomery went out of the house and ventured into the jungle, especially in the rainy season, he might don a long leather coat and a pair of worn chamois gloves. But he didn't wrap his fingers in soft kid leather, nor did he resemble a dandy out for a stroll.

"Is this Yaxaktun?" one of the young men asked, taking off his hat and handing it to one of his companions. His hair was a light brown and his eyes were green. He had a perfectly trimmed mustache to match his immaculate clothes and new leather boots.

"That's right," Montgomery said. His rifle was resting casually on his lap.

"We're on the trail of an Indian raiding party. Have you seen anyone go by?"

"Where are you coming from?"

"From Vista Hermosa."

"What are you doing this far?"

"You know it?" the young man asked, now tugging at his gloves, which he also handed to his companion. He ran a hand through his hair.

"I know it," Montgomery said, nodding. "It's pretty far for a casual horse ride."

"It's no casual ride. I told you, we're on the trail of an Indian raiding party."

Not dressed like that you're not, he thought, and then he frowned, remembering something he'd heard a while back. That Lizalde's son was coming for a visit. Could this be him? The family owned so many haciendas that it was hard for Montgomery to remember if the doctor had said he'd be at Vista Hermosa or not. But it would make perfect sense. It was the nearest hacienda to their ranch. Montgomery normally obtained supplies from other places; therefore he wouldn't have known if the young mister was lodging there even if he'd been visiting for a whole month already.

"We've had no trouble here," Montgomery said, eyeing the two ostentatious rings on the young man's right hand.

"Well, we've noticed the signs over at Vista Hermosa, and they were headed this way. We thought we'd see if we could catch up with them. They're like rabid dogs. You wouldn't want them wandering around, would you?"

"They're long gone if they were ever around."

"How about you lend us a few men? They could help us track them down. I bet they're going east, over to Tórtola."

"This is a sanatorium. I've got no men to spare, only patients. As for following your invisible Indians, if you cut a trail through the jungle what you'll be doing is opening the way for them, and after you find nothing, we might have a *real* problem if *real* Indians follow that trail back. A trail is an invitation. You don't cut trails east. We keep to ourselves here and we keep out of trouble."

He wasn't lying. The Maya rebels did raid. They took food, live-stock, prisoners. But Yaxaktun was out of the way, and luck had been on their side. If they had a quarrel with the people at Vista Hermosa he wanted nothing to do with it.

The young man snatched his hat back and fanned himself with it. "What is your name, sir?" he asked. He sounded irritated. It was no polite inquiry.

"Montgomery Laughton," he said, doffing his hat with a flourish. "I am the mayordomo at Yaxaktun."

"Perfect. I'm Eduardo Lizalde. My father pays your wages. Why don't you get me a few men and we'll be along."

"I work for Dr. Moreau and this is a sanatorium."

"Then fetch me Dr. Moreau so I can get him to give you your orders."

"He'd be napping right now. Can't bother him. Not for this."

The young man's companion laughed. He had the same brown hair as his young friend, but his eyes were dark. "Didn't you hear him, sir? This is Eduardo *Lizalde*."

"And I've told you. An idiot would cut a trail and try to ride with his horse to Tórtola or wherever you think you're going."

"Are you calling us idiots?" Eduardo asked.

"Climb back on your horses, gentlemen."

"How dare you, you swine! You don't order us around!"

Montgomery stood up and pointed his rifle at the young man with the casual air of someone lighting a cigar. "I'm *suggesting* you climb on your horses," he said.

"I cannot believe this! Isidro, can you believe this?!"

"You better believe I'll put a bullet through your stomach if you don't leave now," Montgomery said. He ought to have been more measured, but he was in a foul mood and couldn't be bothered to sweeten his words. Moreau might chide him for this later, but for now Montgomery stared the men down and watched them mutter and glare at him.

A voice came from behind Montgomery, pleasant and clear. "Gentlemen, if you'll forgive me, I've taken the liberty of having my father woken up. Dr. Moreau will be with us in a few minutes."

Carlota had stepped out of the house and was standing next to him. She fixed her eyes on the men, and they bowed their heads. Montgomery also inclined his head, acknowledging her presence.

"Will you come with me to the sitting room? I'm afraid your companions will have to wait here, with your horses, but I can see if we can bring some drink out to them," Carlota said, her hands fluttering gracefully, indicating the inside of the house.

"That would be appreciated," Eduardo said, and then he smiled. "I'm sorry, you are the doctor's daughter?"

"I am Carlota Moreau," she said and extended her hand to them.

The men pressed a kiss upon it and exchanged a look of astonishment before following the girl. Carlota, in her airy tea gown, looked like a woman in her dishabille, so he couldn't fault them for gawking. Then again, even if she had been bundled into a tight corset and buttoned up to her neck, she would have evoked notions of assignations and lovers. It was she, not the dress.

Still, he would have shot two bullets into their stomachs for that impudent look that passed between them. Even though that would have done them no good. "Lead the way, Miss Moreau," he said instead.

Then he waited a minute and walked into the house, the rifle resting on his shoulder.

CHAPTER 7

Carlota

THE FIRST THING Carlota liked to do in the mornings was feed the birds in the courtyard. She listened to their eager chirping, then went around the house and crossed the dividing wall that led to the old workers' quarters, where the hybrids made their homes. There Ramona and Carlota kept an herb and vegetable garden. They grew onions, pungent epazote, chiles, sweet smelling mint, all arranged in patches or clay pots. If you boiled mint, yerba buena, and bark from the pixoy tree, Ramona said you could induce a woman's labor. The yellow, bitter juice of the xikin cured cacochymia, the calabash tree helped settle the stomach, ix k'antunbub countered poisons.

These were the things she knew, along with the Latinate names for many species, gleaned from her father's books, and the long names of chemicals carefully written on her father's flasks. She'd been tutored well, if haphazardly, but she could find no fault in her upbringing.

When she was younger, she had feared her father might send her off to a finishing school, as the gentlefolk of Mérida did with their children, but her father had been entirely indifferent to such structured learning. Schools leave you without ambition, he said.

She'd grown, therefore, in the solitude of Yaxaktun, tended to by her father and Ramona, playing with Cachito and Lupe, and jumping into the welcoming cenote on the days when the heat wrapped itself taut around their limbs.

That day she'd risen late. Sometimes she had chores to complete in the lab, either helping her father or practicing taxidermy, which was Montgomery's art. He knew many tricks that astounded her. For example, mounting a feline specimen required great skill, especially when it came to the mouth. One had to fill the inside of the lips with clay until they were fixed in the desired position and one had to be careful that the skin didn't shrink when drying. The inside of the mouth was stuffed with papier-mâché; clay would have been too difficult to remove.

Her father fostered such botanical and zoological interests, though he also demanded that she apply herself to the piano. It was wildly out of tune, but Carlota obeyed and always did as her father said, reading the books he put in front of her and saying her prayers at night. Domestic activities occupied her evenings, when she embroidered or darned her father's socks. Her life was pleasant. Whenever something was amiss, when her perfect world tilted a little, she retreated to the perfect solitude of the cenote.

After feeding the birds that morning, she went into the kitchen. Ramona was busy by the stove, while Lupe was drying dishes with a rag.

"My father's leg is paining him. I'm thinking we might brew him that jasmine tea he likes instead of the usual chamomile."

"If we had any. We're all out," Ramona said.

"Truly?"

"Mr. Laughton should head to the city soon. You can add it to his shopping list."

"Bad idea, that. He's back on the bottle," Lupe said, taking her dishes and placing them in the trastero. "If he gets anywhere near Mérida, he'll gamble his wages away."

Carlota hated when Montgomery was in such a state, though she supposed it was about time. Montgomery cycled in and out of sobriety. Her father didn't seem to mind, saying Montgomery's productivity didn't diminish during his drinking bouts, but Carlota disliked the way he looked, with his hair in his eyes and smelling sour.

She'd asked her father to put an end to it, to order that Montgomery keep a dry house but her father had laughed her off. Men need their crutches, he said, and those that are unfit for human kindred need them most, leaning on their vices.

But then, she'd said, the hybrids were not men, and he let them drink, too. And he'd said she was right, they weren't, but still they needed that crutch. It was a form of compassion, her father assured Carlota.

"Poor Montgomery," she muttered.

"It's not your fault he's a fool. But I should go to the city. I'd do a fine job instead of him, and I wouldn't come back sniffling about all the money I've misplaced in games of chance," Lupe said cheekily.

"As if you could."

"Why not? It's not that hard to put in a few orders and count coins."

"You know why. Don't be silly. What if someone saw you? And you've never been in the city before, so you wouldn't know anything."

"You're not the only one who can read a paper and know what's what," Lupe replied and she showed Carlota her fangs, her mouth twisting into an acrid smile. "Maybe I'll go one day, with or without telling you."

"Don't start with that again. You'll give me a headache."

"No, we wouldn't want to give the little miss a headache."

"You're impossible," Carlota muttered, and she whirled out of the room, not wishing to prolong their verbal sparring. Lupe was dreadful these days. Now she'd have to contend with Montgomery being stinking drunk and Lupe being a nuisance, a combination that was more annoying than a mosquito buzzing in an ear late at night.

She fled toward the cenote, intent on staying there for the rest of the day. The path she followed was being slowly swallowed by the jungle. Soon Montgomery and his crew would have to clear it again, while also tending to that other path that led to the lagoon and the third path that connected to the main road, which snaked west from them, the road that led to the rest of the world.

The path to the cenote was like the lines of a rhyme, recited by heart, known in the marrow of one's body. She could walk the path with her eyes closed and still find her way to the cenote. In fact, she knew the jungle more by sound than sight. It wasn't that she didn't appreciate the beauty one could see, but sound struck her as the most powerful of the senses. Ramona had explained the jungle was full of spirits and Carlota listened carefully for them, tried to feel them in stone and earth. When she lay on the ground she paid homage to the symphony of the jungle: the growls of the monkeys, the squawks of lime-green parrots, the whistle of the quail, the quiet murmur of the water, and the even quieter whisper of the blind fish of the cenote's depths. She imagined herself as that fish, that quail, that monkey. She imagined herself as the vines and creepers climbing upon the trees, as the ceiba with its branches extending high with a quivering butterfly brushing against its flowers. And sometimes she imagined herself stretched out, under the rays of the sun, in the shape of a jaguar, the taste of meat thick on her tongue.

She loved the rhythm of the Yucatán, the ferocious rainy season and the calm of the dry months. She basked in the humid heat that still made her father mutter under his breath and hide inside his room, trying to cool down. She chased the rays of sun and ran her hands down the bark of the trees.

Sometimes she felt she could lie by the cenote for years and years, patient and quiet, while other times she whirled around, a feeling she didn't understand making her tap her fingers and stare at the clouds.

That day, as she reached the cenote, she wondered about the texture of snow. It was hot, so it was an odd thought to be having, but it was precisely the heat that inspired her. Ramona said you could cool your body down by thinking about cold things, such as the splash of water against your face. Carlota didn't believe it worked, but still she amused herself thinking of water and now of snow. If one looked at a snowflake under a microscope it became a series of silvery triangles and hexagons and stars. That is what the textbooks said.

When she lay down on the ground and draped an arm across her eyes, she tried to conjure the taste of ice. The textbooks didn't talk about the taste of rain or ice, nor the scent of red earth.

She could have lived forever by the water hole, lying peaceful like that. But Montgomery came, stern and serious, and she followed him, hand brushing against the old carving of the jaguar, hand brushing on his sleeve, down the trail, her steps light, barely making the leaves crunch, and his heavy leather boots loud against twigs and minuscule plants.

She liked Montgomery in the same way she liked the ring-tailed coati, the bez-muuch whose croak resembled the baying of the calf rather than the croaking of other frogs, or the cry of the owl, which Ramona thought unlucky. She liked Montgomery because he was part of her world and she loved everything in it. He was like that well-trodden path.

But he could be difficult, and sometimes she wanted to dig her nails into his hand, leave half-moons behind. Lupe could be difficult, too. Not Cachito—he was always friendly. And not her father. She was never cross at her father. She respected him too much, and if they had a disagreement, Carlota was quick to blame herself and never the doctor.

She was to be docile and sweet. That is how Dr. Moreau wished his daughter to act. She attempted to comply. Nevertheless, that morning she had spoken spiteful words, feeling as if Montgomery was baiting her. "Really? What do you find so enticing about the city? That you can lose all your wages on a game of tute or baccarat?" she asked.

"One insult a day is quite enough for me, Miss Moreau," he said. "Two is more than I will bear on an empty stomach."

Despite their occasional verbal sparring, Carlota did not seek to hurt Montgomery's feelings, and she felt contrite as they walked together. When they arrived at Yaxaktun, he stayed by the portón while she went into the courtyard. Lupe was standing by the bird-cages, and Carlota sighed, remembering she hadn't been good to Lupe that day, either.

"You forgot to feed the parrot before you took off," Lupe said.

"I can do it now."

"No need. I fed it."

"Are you still angry at me?"

Lupe looked at Carlota, lips pursed. "I thought *you* were angry at *me*."

"Maybe for a minute or two."

They walked back into the house slowly, Carlota whispering an "I'm sorry" and Lupe mumbling the same. Then Montgomery brushed past them, and Carlota watched in surprise as he opened a glass case and pulled out one of the rifles. But the surprise was not alarm. It was when Montgomery raised his voice sharply that her body tensed.

"Stay inside," he said, rifle in hand, and she wondered what he was up to. She followed him quietly, and stood in the shadows, not far from the doorway, and heard him speak.

There were visitors outside. Montgomery talked with that steady tone that concealed his aggravation like a knife in its sheath, while the men spoke back in indignant voices, their words growing louder. She remembered that Montgomery was drinking again, and this troubled her. Drink could deform a man and cloud his brain. What if Montgomery made a mistake?

"Get my father," she whispered to Lupe, who was standing next to her, also listening intently.

She could picture Montgomery's finger brushing the trigger of his rifle, and she felt compelled to act. Carlota stepped forward, her agitation never reaching her mouth. The words came out politely.

"Gentlemen, if you'll forgive me, I've taken the liberty of having my father woken up. Dr. Moreau will be with us in a few minutes," she said.

There were six men, four still on their horses and two who had dismounted and were quarreling with Montgomery. This pair was dressed properly, like gentlemen out of fashion plates. One of them grasped his hat tight between his hands, looking embarrassed the moment he spotted her. She saw the resemblance with Mr. Lizalde, but the young man's eyes were green and his features were finer than his father's.

And just like that, it was as if she'd thrown a bucket of water onto a fire. The green-eyed gentleman stumbled forward, kissed her hand, then the other one followed suit. She guided them inside, to the sitting room, which had seldom seen visitors. The mangy old parrot, in its cage, let out a loud cry as if greeting them.

"I must apologize for this unorthodox introduction. My name is Eduardo Lizalde, and this is my cousin, Isidro," said the handsome young man as she sat down, her hands carefully joined together, resting on her lap.

He had said nothing as they walked through the courtyard, though she had felt his sidewise glances.

"I am pleased to meet you. Though perhaps you do not owe *me* an apology. Mr. Laughton was merely safeguarding our home," she said. Her voice was firm, but there was no malice in it. She did not resent the visit.

"Why, of course, I apologize," the young man replied amicably, turning to Montgomery and pressing a hand against his chest. "It's been a bothersome day, and I'm afraid the heat got to me."

Montgomery did not speak, merely placing his rifle down and crossing his arms.

Carlota nodded, accepting the apology even if Montgomery had not replied.

Both men were good-looking and sleek in their dark suits. They stood up straight and didn't slouch like Montgomery, who was leaning a shoulder against the wall. She knew few men. Aside from the members of her household there were the men from books, from pirate novels. Men from the pen of Justo Sierra O'Reilly, Eligio Ancona, and Sir Walter Scott. Her static world was being invaded by a different sort of man.

Eduardo Lizalde looked at her with his lively green eyes, and she lowered her gaze, her eyes firm on her fingers.

"Gentlemen, good day," her father said as he walked in.

She felt Eduardo's gaze lifting, heard him turning to her father as he spoke, apologizing again, introducing himself, while she stared at her hands. When Eduardo Lizalde had kissed her hand, he'd been clumsy. His lips had latched on to her wrist for a brief moment. She touched that spot.

"Well, sir, Isidro and I have been away from the peninsula and recently returned. My father, thinking we might as well become acquainted with our properties, asked if we might want to tour the haciendas in this region and take stock of them, seeing as he's had little chance to visit. There is much business to attend to in Mérida. That is how we've wound up staying at Vista Hermosa."

"And how exactly did you end up in Yaxaktun?" Montgomery asked. She looked at him. He was still leaning against the wall, arms crossed, his brow furrowed.

The parrot was making a racket, apparently invigorated by the presence of the strangers. It yelled a nasty phrase that he'd learned from Montgomery and Carlota stood up, pressed her fingers against the bars of the cage, attempting to soothe the bird. Hush, she told it. Hush now, pretty bird.

"As I mentioned to you, Mr. Laughton, there was word that an Indian raiding party had been spotted near my hacienda and they seemed to be headed in this general direction, which is why I requested laborers to support us."

"We don't run a hacienda, but a sanatorium. There are no laborers. Perhaps your father did not inform you of that."

"My father did say you conducted research here. Tuberculosis, I think?" Eduardo said, his voice amiable while Montgomery sounded gruff. "But there must be attendants for the sick."

"Mr. Laughton and I manage Yaxaktun, with the assistance of my daughter," her father said, as he sat down. He motioned to Carlota. She sat down again and he patted her hand. "We have a cook and two young servants who tend to the animals we keep."

This was the lie her father and Montgomery dangled in front of all strangers. No one was to know about the true inhabitants of Yaxaktun. She supposed they must consider the young men strangers, even if they were related to their patron.

"So few people? Are you not afraid? The Indians keep close to this area."

A breeze swayed the white curtains inward and Montgomery shifted his stance. The parrot yelled once more, a shrill scream, no words this time.

"We'd be of little interest to them," Montgomery replied. "They might take the main road, but they'd leave us be. Which is why I don't recommend trying to hack your way to Tórtola. You'd get nowhere or get within the reach of people you do not want to meet."

"The Indians are bellicose, but surely no match for brave men and guns," Isidro said.

"I can see you've spent scant time in Yucatán. Perhaps you were reared in Mérida and then went, where? Mexico City?" Montgomery asked.

"Of course."

"Then you haven't seen much of this part of the peninsula. The Maya rebels have the east for good reason. They know the land, they have the courage, and they are moved by their faith in their leaders. I wouldn't go stirring an anthill and I wouldn't disturb them."

"Yucatán will be cloven in two, should such attitudes be followed by the Mexican government. What we need is President Díaz to send soldiers to put all these seditious Indians back in their place."

"I doubt that'll ever happen."

"It's not surprising an Englishman should think such a thing," Eduardo said. "After all, you British folk trade with them. Mr. Laughton, the reason why we came to Yaxaktun is not only because of the threat of an Indian party, but because we've been told Indians have found this farm an amicable place. That they've been trading here, obtaining supplies and assistance."

"Now that is a lie, and I wonder who told you that."

"Vista Hermosa may not be around the corner, but the people there hear stories all the same. They say Juan Cumux walks around these parts as though he were lord and master."

Cumux was one of those names that always made Carlota pause.

He was a general, and though not nearly as powerful or well known as other rebels such as Bernabé Cen and Crescencio Poot, he commanded enough men that people took notice and prayed he wouldn't stray into their lands. He'd been around for many years, since before Montgomery arrived at Yaxaktun, and Melquíades had muttered curses when he spoke of him while Ramona didn't say a thing. Best you don't invite bad luck by naming it, that's what Ramona told them.

"We wouldn't welcome such a man into our home. Surely you've been misled."

"People speak tall tales, sometimes, I'll admit that," Eduardo said with a frown. "But I must be careful when it comes to my lands and I don't really know you or the inhabitants of Yaxaktun."

"Not that we'd have much interest in knowing you, sir, with the way you push your point, making veiled aspersions," Montgomery said.

"If I'd even heard Cumux was nearby, I think I might have died of fright," Carlota said, which was not quite true, but she didn't want Montgomery and Eduardo to begin pecking at each other again, like the roosters Montgomery bet on when he went into the city.

She looked at the young man with a timid flutter of eyelashes, hoping to distract him.

"My lady, that would be tragic," Eduardo said, a smile quickly appearing on his face, chasing away his frown and he turned to her father. "Pardon me once more. As far as I'm concerned there is no need to disturb you any more than we already have. We should head back."

"I'm glad the matter is cleared," her father said, standing up and extending his hand, which Eduardo shook.

"I lament we had to meet like this. I wish I would have sent a letter introducing myself when I arrived. Now, you'll all think we are terribly rude."

"No, of course not. But you must come back another time. Perhaps stay for a few days. Living in the city, you must be used to going on visits, and this isolation might be jarring."

"We have been rather confined, that is true," Isidro said. He wasn't as good-looking as his cousin, but he did have a pleasant smile, which he now turned toward her. "We've greatly missed the sound of music. Do you play the piano, Miss Moreau?"

He gestured toward the upright piano and she nodded. "A little. My father has taught me."

"She sings, too," her father said.

"Then we must return," Eduardo said. "It would be lovely to hear a lady singing."

There was more shaking of hands, and Carlota rose from her seat. The parrot in its cage had finally grown bored and ceased laughing and making noises. "May I guide you back to the entrance?" she asked. When she moved, Montgomery followed, a fourth party, her shadow, walking three paces behind her and the gentlemen.

Isidro walked to her left and Eduardo to her right, and she moved with leisurely steps to better look at them. They didn't belong in Yaxaktun, in her world, and therefore the novelty was exciting, and there was also something about the way Eduardo's eyes swept over her that made her press her palm tight against her middle for a second, feeling the soft fabric of her dress beneath her fingers. When she was a child she'd been afraid of gentlemen, afraid they might gobble people whole. But she'd lost her fear of Montgomery quickly, and she'd never thought he'd peck at her.

Eduardo, though, she thought he looked like a hungry man, and when they reached the entrance he took her hand and kissed it again, and she blushed.

"I'm sorry we disturbed you. It really was audacious of us. But I'm glad we met, and had I known Dr. Moreau's daughter was as pretty as she is, I'd have come sooner. If I hadn't been hotheaded, perhaps this might have been a more pleasant introduction," Eduardo said, releasing her hand. "You won't think poorly of us, will you?"

"No, sir. It was a misunderstanding."

"You are kind; it eases my embarrassment," he said, his voice low, his smile sweet and only for her, then he raised his head and looked toward Montgomery. "Mr. Laughton, I apologize to you once more. Have a good day."

The men mounted their horses again, and soon they were riding away. She watched them disappear in the distance.

"I wonder if we'll ever see them again," she said.

"You best be sure we will, although I would hope their horses would trip and break their backs."

She turned around in surprise. "Montgomery! What a thing to say!"

"They're sniveling, rude men. What do you expect me to do? Sing about them in verse?"

"They apologized to you, and I heard you loud and clear when you were barking at them like a mad dog."

"A mad dog. My, my, well, they've certainly made a good impression for you to defend them like that. Which one do you like best? The green-eyed lad with the pretty hair? Or the one with the brown eyes and the lovely set of teeth?"

She didn't say a thing, aware she was wading near quicksand, but still Montgomery smiled slyly, leaning down against the doorway to look at her. "The green-eyed one, then. Have I guessed right?"

She elbowed him as she walked back inside, but still she said nothing.

"Take it from one dog who knows other dogs: that one has teeth."

"You are impossible! Stop it!" she yelled at last.

His boisterous laugh was a slap to the face, and she crossed the courtyard quickly, her cheeks aflame. Once inside, she sat on a leather chair by an open window, looking outside at the plants in their clay pots and the bubbling fountain until her face wasn't burning and she could breathe calmly. Five, six, seven. Count to ten and wait. Strong emotions were no good, her father said. Keep calm. Her childhood affliction did not manifest anymore, but in the past she'd had dizzy spells and her heart had beat wildly out of tune. Her first years had been misery and the sickbed.

Lupe came from behind Carlota. She knew her by her steps,

which were measured and different from the slower, heavier steps of Ramona and the quick shuffle of Cachito's feet.

"Are they gone now?" Lupe asked.

"Yes, they've gone. No need to trouble yourself over them."

"What did you talk about with them when you were in the sitting room?"

"They said there was an Indian raiding party and also that someone at Yaxaktun was providing supplies to Juan Cumux. They almost accused Montgomery of helping him."

"It wouldn't surprise me if Montgomery was selling supplies to Cumux."

"Why would you say that?" Carlota asked, turning to look at Lupe, and Lupe shrugged.

"English people sell them bullets and gunpowder, everyone knows it. And Montgomery is English and he always needs money so he can drink. He has a sickness of the soul, that's what Ramona says, always looking for aguardiente to drown himself in it."

That much was true, and not just aguardiente. Brandy or whiskey or anything would do. Lately he'd been firm and resolute and abandoned his imbibing. But then, that morning she'd looked into his eyes and noted the telltale signs: it was true, he'd turned to the bottle once again. He was to blame, but also her father, who allowed it, who let Montgomery and the hybrids partake in their liquor.

Her father would do nothing, and Montgomery floated in and out of inebriation, a season healthy and whole, another tumbling into the abyss. But would Montgomery really endanger them? He hurt himself, but he didn't harm others.

"Maybe he's trying to keep us safe by being nice to the cruzob," Lupe said, as if guessing her thoughts. "Their god speaks to them through a cross, you know? He really speaks, not like the Christ in the chapel or the donkey's skull."

There was a building in the back, near the huts, where someone had once affixed a donkey skull on a wall. Ramona said it had been there before her father arrived at Yaxaktun, and in those days the workers who'd done something wrong went there and the donkey whispered the number of lashes they should get for their misdeeds. Lupe and Carlota had feared it when they were children.

"A cross can't talk," Carlota said. "It's ventriloquism."

"Ramona says it can."

"You think you know everything, but you don't."

"You don't, either."

She pushed her chair back and stood up. "I should see if my father needs me."

"Don't tell him what I said about Montgomery. If he thinks Montgomery is disloyal he'll dismiss him, and then we'd have a new mayordomo pushing his nose into our business. At least Montgomery lets us be and he doesn't stomp and yell like that man today."

"Which man?"

"That Mr. Eduardo."

"Were you listening to everything? Why did you ask what we talked about if you were spying on us?" she asked, incensed.

Lupe knew better. She should have stayed far from the visitors, lest they spot her. When she covered her head and face with a rebozo, Lupe could be confused with a human. She didn't have the strange gait of the other hybrids. But barefaced as she was, it was easy to spot the reddish-brown fur on her face and peer into her small, brown eyes, which were set together closely. Her features recalled those of the jaguarundi, and anyone would have been startled by the sight of her face. The other hybrids were no less surprising.

"I listened to some," Lupe admitted with a shrug.

"He didn't yell."

"You're deaf, Loti."

Carlota marched out of the room and away. It seemed to her everyone was cruel and mad that day, and for no reason. She wished she were still resting by the cenote, maybe even swimming in its depths, the water cool against her skin.

CHAPTER 8

Montgomery

MONTGOMERY WALKED QUICKLY, venturing behind the dividing
stone wall, to the area where the huts of the hybrids were arranged
together. These were all made in the traditional manner of the region,
with a roof of palma de guano that could withstand the rains and
which was replaced every few years. Aside from those dwellings, there
were a few other buildings in the back. One of these was a wooden
structure that housed the machinery that had once been used to press
sugarcane. Most important, there was the noria and the donkeys
going around and around, making the water flow. They alternated the
beasts so that they wouldn't exhaust themselves. A donkey must not
work more than three hours in the morning and three in the evening.

The watering system at the hacienda had been one of his first
projects at Yaxaktun, and he was rather proud of the improvements
he'd made and the work of the hybrids, who cleaned the fields, kept
the irrigation canals clean, tended the roads, so that weeds would not
overtake their efforts.

Rather than produce sugarcane, they stuck to the rearing of pigs
and chickens, and the cultivation of a modest assortment of veg-
etables. In March, they planted tigernuts; in May it was the time for
chayotes and tomatoes; come June it would be the season for beans
and corn. Each month of the calendar was marked with tasks, from
the cutting of the wood to the careful collection of honey. The land
set their rhythm, like a metronome. Such efforts would have been
laughable to any hacendado, who would regard these agricultural

activities as suitable for poor peasants when there was more money to be had with other ventures, but Montgomery liked their operation and the sense of self-sufficiency it brought him. He enjoyed feeding the animals and caring for the couple of horses that they kept. Besides, they needed to work. Lizalde paid for bandages, medical supplies, and Moreau's trinkets in the lab, but his money alone would have never kept all twenty-nine hybrids fed, especially the bigger ones like Aj Kaab and Áayin.

He paused for a moment, pondering both the conversation with the young men and Carlota's reaction to them. Montgomery had teased her about the boys because she had been cruel to him before. But now he thought better about it and decided he shouldn't have bothered her. Should he apologize? Yet it was such a small thing, and he felt embarrassed to imagine himself sinking to his knees, pressing his hat against his chest, and begging the lady's forgiveness. If she should refuse the apology, it would sting. What he should do, Montgomery decided, was to think less about Carlota Moreau and more about something, anything else.

It was damnably hard, though. Carlota got under one's skin, like a splinter.

"Good day, Montgomery," Cachito said, springing beside him. Although full-grown, Cachito hardly reached Montgomery's chest. He was skinny and quick and his fur was tawny, darker around the ears, with the spots and streaks of an ocelot. He possessed a youthful voice that was often merry. He was friendlier than Lupe and more tractable than Carlota, who despite her sweetness could turn sour in an instant. The girl was spoiled, a miniature empress.

"Good day to you, too," Montgomery said, thankful for the interruption. "We're running late, but we best pull the table outside."

"We've been waiting," Cachito said eagerly.

Fridays it was time for all the hybrids to receive their injection and a tablet, which helped keep their stomachs in check, since the injection could make them queasy. Without this regimen they'd die. But it was something else that also inspired Cachito's enthusiasm.

Along with whatever treatment Moreau provided the hybrids, he also administered a substance that sent them into a dreamy stupor. He'd seen men who consumed opium and observed the same dull expression on their faces, and he didn't doubt this was the same. It lulled them, like the alcohol the doctor let the hybrids have each week.

Montgomery couldn't even fault the doctor for this. Through the years he'd seen the way the bodies of the hybrids twisted, he'd seen the pains they endured. Moreau's experiments produced creatures that were not whole, that were sickly, that often died young. Their lungs didn't work right or their hearts beat erratically. They could have no progeny, as the doctor had seen to that, but if they had been able to produce offspring Montgomery doubted any would have been able to come to term.

He'd never wanted any children. Fanny hadn't liked that about him. She dreamed of a big family. Montgomery feared his children would take after him, that they'd be drunks and braggarts. Or even worse, that they would bear a resemblance to Elizabeth. What a horrid discovery it would have been to see his sister's face again, haunting him during his waking hours.

The doctor had not created any new hybrids in the last three years. For that, Montgomery was grateful, recalling some of the creatures he'd had to bury. Fragile things that were wrapped in cloth and rested in their makeshift cemetery. Ramona lit candles for them, and Carlota said prayers. Montgomery said nothing at all.

"How long until the doctor comes?" Cachito asked.

"Dr. Moreau will be here soon, no doubt," Montgomery muttered.

"Maybe you can ask him to give us a bottle of rum afterward?"

"It's Friday, not Saturday, and far too early for drink," he said, feeling like a complete hypocrite because he'd sometimes drunk himself well and good around the early hours of the morning.

"It's not for merrymaking. Aj Kaab's tooth has been hurting."

Aj Kaab had teeth in two rows, teeth that never ceased to grow, and if they were not pulled they might pierce through his skull. He was the oldest hybrid, thick-voiced and gray, born before Lupe and

Cachito and therefore afflicted with more deformities. Then there came Peek', who looked like he was all bones these days, his skin gone mangy. Áayin was an aged creation, too, his caiman's skin always peeling in large patches. Most of the hybrids wore clothing. In the case of the more humanlike ones, such as Cachito and Lupe, regular clothes would do. But others had shapes that defied a common tailor or else buttons and laces proved a challenge to their malformed hands. In Áayin's case, he had a long tail and he found most fabrics itched. Carlota boiled chaal che', rubbing the soothing liquid against his back.

"The doctor better see about that tooth. I'll let him know," Montgomery said, stopping to look at the black pigs in their corral, half-buried in the mud, taking their nap. Pork was one of those dishes you could count on in Yucatán, but the doctor used the pigs for his experiments and thus Moreau and his daughter were more likely to dine on turkey or fish. The hybrids had a mostly vegetable diet with the occasional chicken. When Montgomery hunted, something else might go into the pot.

He didn't hunt that often, and when he did Ramona took care to make an offering for the aluxes, so that the hunt would fare well. Ramona had grown up in a town where they followed the tradition of primicias, not in the city where people might forget the old ways. So he followed the tradition, to please her, and even asked the stones for their favor. Ramona was strict about these things, and the others enforced the proceedings as rigorously as Moreau enforced his sermons.

Lupe was the one of the lot who was not pious.

Cachito leaned forward on the fence. "I heard there was one of the Lizaldes here today."

"Now was that Lupe or Carlota telling you things?"

"Are we in debt with them, Montgomery? Is it like the nohoch cuenta?" Cachito replied rather than provide him with a name.

The hacienda owners controlled their workers through two forms of debt. The little debt was when they bought products at the tienda de raya. But the large debt was incurred when they married or a burial was held; the money borrowed covered all the church and municipal fees. Slavery was forbidden by law. In practice, a quick note by a mayordomo in a ledger, indicating a sum that was owed, ensured the workers never left. There was no tienda de raya at Yaxaktun, there was no ledger where he noted fees, and thus it was a strange comment.

"What could make you say that?"

"Carlota reads the doctor's letters out loud for him when he's tired."

"You and Lupe spend your waking hours listening behind doorways," Montgomery said. "How could you be in debt with Lizalde when you've never met him?"

"Well . . . *you* are in debt with him."

"Because I'm an idiot. You on the other hand are smart."

"The doctor is in debt, too. That's what I've understood behind doorways."

"Let's get that table," Montgomery said, because he couldn't be discussing Moreau's financial dealings with Cachito.

They brought the table out from its storage and set it before one of the huts. It wasn't long until the doctor and his daughter appeared, she carrying his bag and supplies, while he leaned on his cane.

Carlota laid the instruments that would be needed on the table. She was careful to keep her eyes on the task at hand and did not glance at Montgomery, by which he knew she was still upset.

The hybrids lined up and received their medication, the youngest ones first. La Pinta and Estrella and El Mustio were at the front of the line, skinny, flat-faced, doglike creatures, slight of size and hardly that remarkable when you compared them to some of the other specimens, for there were a dizzying variety of shapes and animals represented.

Moreau, afflicted with a strange creative streak, had made furry hybrids with hunched shoulders and short forearms, but also apelike things whose knuckles could brush the ground when they walked, their spines curved. He'd created a squat hybrid that had the round, startled eyes and the long tongue of the kinkajou, another painted with the telltale dots and stripes of the paca, and yet a third with the small ears and distinctive bony, transverse bands of the armadillo. There were those with malformed ears and protuberant jaws and bristly hair that almost hid tiny eyes. It was a confusing medley of fang, fur, scales, showcasing the plasticity of bones.

Yet, despite the twisting and turning of their flesh, it was possible to spy the original animal that had originated them: Cachito and Lupe clearly resembled wild cats, while in other faces one could identify the fox and the playful coati. Parda had a wolf's snout and moved in great leaping strides, Weech was small and limber, while others shuffled or limped by, catching their breath with effort.

In the beginning Montgomery had been surprised by their countenances, even alarmed by their odd gaits. He thought of them as creatures from myth, beings that might have belonged in a medieval manuscript, the product of a feverish scribe's imagination. Or else they were the monsters that inhabited the edges of maps. Here be dragons!

Montgomery now regarded the hybrids simply as the people of Yaxaktun.

And so they came in order, and he chided El Rojo for attempting to move ahead of the line, as El Rojo always did, and patted Peek's shoulder and chatted with Cachito.

It was like every other week, only it wasn't. Montgomery took out a cigarette and lit it, watching as the doctor worked, thinking of the young men who'd stopped by, and the more he thought of those nosy idiots, the more irritated he felt.

Afterward, when all the hybrids were dismissed and had returned to their huts, Montgomery helped Carlota gather the doctor's things and took everything back inside. The girl did not linger in the laboratory, excusing herself.

Montgomery knew he was about to be reprimanded, and perhaps the girl knew it, too. Or else Carlota's stubborn anger compelled her out of the room, since she normally liked the laboratory, and they had, more than once, spent a good hour there, cleaning and sorting Moreau's tools and supplies. At times, he'd show her how one could cut an animal's skin and mount a specimen. "Are you picking fights with the neighbors because you are bored, Laughton, or is there another reason for the performance you gave today?"

"I was trying to get rid of them quickly. I might have managed it, if your daughter had not intervened."

"Then it is Carlota's fault?" the doctor asked, a trace of impatience in his voice.

"No, sir. It's just I didn't need her assistance, but I realize I've mucked it up. Maybe you should send a letter to the Lizalde boys telling them not to visit. We could make up something to keep them away."

The doctor examined a bottle with a yellow liquid, holding it up to the light. "Why would I do that?"

"They don't understand the work you perform."

"They don't. They think I run a sanatorium for the poor," the doctor said, as he carefully placed the bottle back on a shelf.

"Best you pen the letter, sir. I can take it tomorrow. If they visit they might discover the truth. And to be frank, sir, they strike me as the type of men who might show undue interest in your daughter."

"I hope so," Moreau said with a firm determination that caught Montgomery off guard.

"Sir?" Montgomery asked in confusion.

"Lizalde has grown impatient and tired of me. For years now I've promised him results and have little to show."

"But the hybrids are real," Montgomery protested.

"Yes, yes, they're real, and we also both know how frail they can be," the doctor said, grimacing. "There is still something in everything I do that defeats me. I fall constantly short of the things I dream. Limbs are crooked, deformities spring up, errors mar my work. Once have I come close to perfection, and well . . . it's not a success I've been able to replicate."

He was no doubt speaking of Lupe and Cachito, who were strong and agile and quick-witted. The rest of Moreau's creatures were prone to inspire pity. The oldest ones were more mangled, but the young ones had their infirmities, too.

"I spot more gaps each day, imperfections that ought to never have been," Moreau continued. "Even if I was given three decades I don't think I'd be able to unknot this puzzle. But I don't have three decades; I don't even have a year. Lizalde is fed up. To him Yaxaktun is fallow land which could be put to better use and my project has lost its luster. I've written to him, but he's become intractable. Our funds are dwindling and he is unlikely to provide us with more money or supplies."

Then Cachito was correct. The doctor was in the midst of an economic emergency, and Montgomery had been kept blind to this fact. He disliked secrets and sleights of hand, but before he could complain, the doctor spoke again.

"This is why the arrival of the young Lizaldes seems like divine providence. Montgomery, they might be our salvation."

"I don't understand."

"Carlota. Isn't she young and beautiful? If one of them were to court her, we might be able to survive this dry spell. They won't toss us out, and if she were to marry, everything is assured."

Ah, so that was the plan! Rather than have to drag Carlota to Mérida in search of a husband, it seemed the doctor had determined a husband had presented himself before her. It made sense. His sister had married at eighteen. He, himself, had been twenty-one on the day of his wedding. Montgomery had married for love. Carlota would be wed to a fortune. Perhaps she wouldn't mind. Fanny had a love for fine things, and when a husband could purchase pearls, many flaws could be forgiven, as was obvious by her second union to a wealthier man. "Have you discussed this with your daughter?"

"No. It's not for her to decide," Moreau said, his eyes adamant and calm.

That was true for the law favored Moureau's course of action. Even when a woman had attained the age of majority and turned twenty-one, she was not allowed to live outside her father's home without his express permission, or to do much of anything on her own. Therefore, should Carlota find her father's plans disagreeable, she still would not be able to extricate herself from him. And yet he thought it cold to not even inform the girl that she might be paraded in front of two gentlemen like a fine horse and quickly sold.

"If they come to visit you must be polite to them. Don't worry about my daughter, I'll see that she behaves herself. No more squabbling with those boys, you understand?"

"I understand, sir," he said, without any inflection in his voice.

That night as Montgomery sat in his room and poured himself a glass of aguardiente, he thought again about Fanny. He hadn't in a while. In the first months of her departure he drank to forget her, but time had done its work, and he didn't dwell on her as he'd once done. His imaginary letters to her had dwindled. What use was it to write solely in his head? Yet that evening he found himself composing a missive.

We are all commodities at Yaxaktun. Commodities to be sold and traded and bartered. Our prices vary, of course. Carlota Moreau is worth gold and rubies. Though, with a man like Eduardo Lizalde, I wonder if he'll know it. Do not give what is holy to the dogs; nor cast your pearls before swine, lest they trample them under their feet, and turn and tear you in pieces.

He drank his aguardiente and closed his eyes. He'd spent too much time in this place. He ought to leave. He'd been able to lull himself into a state of half-contentment, but the arrival of the Lizaldes was a sign. If he remained here, he'd grow mad like Moreau, who spent his days in obsessive pursuit of a secret that could never be had.

CHAPTER 9

Carlota

SHE FED THE parrot and whispered a ditty to it. When she was done tending to the birds, she took her father's medical bag and headed toward the old workers' huts. Dr. Moreau was supposed to look at Aj Kaab's teeth the previous day, but again he was remiss in his duties and again Carlota decided to provide assistance. Aj ts'aak yaaj, the healer, that was what the hybrids sometimes called her father in Maya, copying Ramona's words. But it was Carlota who most often worried about tending to their teeth and bones and limbs. She did not mind such tasks. In fact, she delighted in them. She liked keeping busy; she liked helping others.

Aj Kaab still looked sleepy when she called for him that Saturday morning. It was indeed early, before mass or breakfast, but it was best to get such matters out of the way. Aj Kaab yawned and stretched his arms while Cachito dragged a chair and a table outside his hut. Carlota set the medical bag down and went to fill a pitcher with water, so she could wash her hands and rinse Aj Kaab's mouth.

"Bet he screams and makes a fuss again," K'an said. She was a lean, long-limbed creature with tawny hair that best resembled a monkey, but there was also something wolfish about her long snout.

"I'll take a bite off your tail," Aj Kaab grumbled.

"Now, don't quarrel," Carlota said, shaking her head and touching Aj Kaab's arm. "Open wide, please."

Aj Kaab obeyed and showed her his maw. The teeth were razor-sharp and plentiful, but she did not hesitate, her fingers sliding against the jaw, then gently poking at a tender spot.

She found the tooth that had been bothering him. The difficulty was not in extracting it, but in diminishing the pain. For this, she must employ ether, which she dabbed on a handkerchief. Since she'd conducted this operation several times before, she was done quickly, and the long tooth was placed on a dish. Then she packed the empty tooth socket with iodoform-soaked gauze. It wouldn't take long for a new tooth to grow.

"How are you, K'an?" she asked. "Do you need anything?"

"My wrist is sore," K'an said.

"Bah! Bandage it tight and she'll be fine in a day," Aj Kaab said. "It's always the same thing, sprained wrist, sprained ankle. K'an is made of glass."

"And you're smelly and burly and not nice," K'an replied primly.

"I'm as big as I need to be," Aj Kaab said, proudly puffing his chest.

"I'll take a look," Carlota said.

The bones of some hybrids were brittle, and although Carlota suspected it was a sprained wrist, it might be a fracture, and the worst thing in that case would be to forego a splint. Her father said even a trained physician might mistake a Pouteau-Colles fracture for a sprain of the wrist, and the hybrids' peculiar anatomy and fur made it harder to make certain diagnoses, yet she had never failed to determine the proper course of treatment.

In the end, Carlota decided K'an had sprained her wrist after all, and a leather support would keep the wrist sufficiently at rest.

Once her tasks were concluded, Cachito poured water from the pitcher into the bowl, and Carlota washed her hands again.

From the corner of her eye she saw Montgomery walk by, who'd risen early and was also about his chores. She pretended she did not see him. He'd made fun of her the previous day, and she feared he'd tease her once more.

The green-eyed one, he'd said. And how had he known which of the gentlemen she favored? But he'd been right. She liked Eduardo's eyes.

Carlota gathered her medical instruments and headed back into the house. In the kitchen, her father's tray was ready. Some days, Carlota cut a flower and offered it to her father along with his toast and his jam. It was a pretty detail. But she'd been pressed for time, so on this occasion she simply took her smile with her.

She walked with quick, steady steps and knocked once before letting herself inside the room. Carefully she placed the tray on the bedside table and pulled the white curtains aside, opening the tall French doors to let a breeze in and also to offer a view of the greenery of the courtyard. At nights, one could stand in the courtyard and look up at a rectangle of night sky and survey the stars, but in the daytime the sun bathed the ivy growing on the walls and made the decorative tiles of the fountain glisten. Light, air, and water mixed together to produce a realm of enchantment.

"I've brought you your breakfast," she said. "And don't tell me you are not hungry."

"I am not," her father said, sitting up.

His mustache was white, and his dark hair had lost most of its color. When he moved now he was slower, though there was still determined strength in his body, which had always been as solid as a mahogany tree. He didn't like it when Carlota fussed too much around him, offended by her caring gestures. He liked to point out he was no invalid and to send her on her way when she grew too sticky-sweet.

"Have you had your medicine?"

"I have, which is why my stomach is upset and I don't feel hungry."

"I've made you tea to better settle your stomach," she said and carefully poured him a cup.

Her father smiled as he sipped the beverage. She took out the clothes he'd wear that day from the armoire and placed them on the back of a chair. The pretty blond woman in the oval painting smiled at Carlota. She wished she could cover it with a piece of cloth; it never ceased to unnerve her.

"You are good to me, Carlota," he said. He was in fine spirits that morning.

She smiled as she brushed her father's jacket, her hands careful against the fabric. She liked him to look poised and perfect.

"What did you think of the Lizalde boys?" he asked.

She grabbed a tiny white hair, stubbornly adhering to the lapels of the jacket, and pulled it away. "I don't have an opinion of them."

"It would be nice if they stayed for a few days. You're so alone here."

"I'm not. I have my work in the laboratory."

For a few years now Dr. Moreau had allowed Carlota to enter the antechamber and the laboratory more often, to assist him with his tasks. He had not forgotten that incident long before when they'd let a hybrid loose, but his attacks of gout were coming more often, and he needed her. Dr. Moreau tried all matter of remedies to ease his pain, cycling through lithium, colchicine, calomel, and morphine, but there was no easy cure for his malady.

The work her father gave Carlota was parceled carefully. She might tend to the hybrids, see to their aches and wounds, even mix certain compounds for him, clean flasks and receptacles, yet many things remained hidden. She didn't understand all the secrets of his scientific achievements. But then, neither did Montgomery, even if he also helped around the laboratory, fetching wood or animal specimens.

She hoped one day her father would allow her to do more, would let her pore over all his notes and books. She must be patient. Dr. Moreau did not rush himself.

"Work in the laboratory is not the same as being around people."

"I have you. I have Lupe."

"But to be able to spend time with gentlemen, it would be a welcome change."

"Montgomery is a gentleman."

"Mr. Laughton is many things, but not a gentleman. An outcast and a drunk, perhaps."

"Aren't you in a way an outcast?" Carlota asked, because even though she was still angry at Montgomery, her sense of fairness compelled Carlota to defend him, and she thought him gentle enough.

Her father raised his eyebrows at that. "What sort of rude chatter is this? Me? An outcast?"

"You said so once, papa. You were talking about your brother and you—"

"You misinterpreted me, surely," he said, although Carlota remembered him saying so—it had been during one of those episodes of his when he was terribly sad and wanted to see little of her, preferring to gaze at the oval portrait of his dead wife. "Outcast! Me! Besides, you couldn't possibly find Laughton's company more pleasant than that of the Lizalde boys."

His voice had hardened, and not wishing to displease him, she shook her head. "Of course not," she said quickly. "But I don't know them."

"That is easily remedied. You mustn't be shy. Be friendly and pleasant if they come to stay with us. We must please the Lizaldes at all times. You have nice dresses, it would be a good occasion to wear them, and your hair . . . perhaps you might do it in the style of the newer fashion plates."

Carlota's hair often fell in a single, thick braid down to her waist or else she wore it loose. But the magazines and newspapers Montgomery fetched for her from the city showed women with elaborate hairdos, strands twisted and looped and piled carefully with ornaments and hairpieces.

"You are a fine young woman, and these are fine young men. If we were in the city, you would have already been presented to society. But we are here and there's been no chance to properly show you to the world. A lady at your age might be courted, you know? You should practice your piano playing and we shall see what they think of you."

"Yes, papa," she said, although she wondered whether they'd find a fault in her demeanor or dress, no matter how many fashion plates she looked at.

"I don't want you to be anxious. When you are anxious it can trigger a relapse."

"No, papa. I'll be fine," she said, though her voice was small.

"What psalm shall we read today?" her father asked, motioning to the drawer where he kept his Bible, for weekday mornings he liked her to read to him from scientific texts, but on the mornings when they had a service he liked the Bible best. "*Dominus illuminatio mea.*"

"Though an army besiege me, my heart will not fear; though war break out against me, even then I will be confident," she said, and now her voice rose clear and sweet. The psalm was easy enough that she need not read it to recite it.

Her father smiled. He was pleased.

Once her father finished his tea and dressed himself, they walked together to the chapel. He held services each Saturday, reading from the leather-bound Bible with the red cover.

The chapel was modest and could hardly accommodate even this small congregation. It had been meant for the mayordomo of the ranch and the family that had lived there before them, and not for the workers who might have made their abode behind the stone walls. Thus they were packed together tightly and it was too warm, even in the morning before the sun set the land ablaze.

But Carlota liked the chapel, for all its smallness and simplicity. There was a pretty mural on one of the walls showing Eve in the Garden of Eden, which she gazed at with interest because Eve, rather than being rendered pale and golden-haired as in her father's Bible, rather than looking like the woman in the oval portrait, had instead been painted with a duskier hue that recalled Carlota's skin. The Christ on the cross, however, was pale as snow, and she didn't like the sight of him because his face was contorted in agony.

Her father's sermons often discussed the pain of the Christ, exhorting the hybrids to understand that God gifted the world with pain so that everything might be made perfect. Original sin must be erased, but this task could not be accomplished without suffering. God had entrusted her father with the labor of perfecting creation and delivering us all from sin, and thus the doctor had created the hybrids. Dr. Moreau was therefore a prophet, a holy man.

But Carlota knew the hybrids were confused by this notion. She'd heard them say that Dr. Moreau was the owner of the deep salt sea, the lord of stars in the sky and of the lightning bolt. And her father didn't always correct them.

She worried this was blasphemy. She worried about the tapestry of the world he wove for them and the purpose of Yaxaktun. Without her father's experiments and medical research she would have died, this was true. And he had told her often how many other wonders might be found by piercing the veil of nature. Cures that could provide hope to those who had none.

And yet . . . the hybrids were born with strange and odd ailments that could claim them in painful ways.

The hybrids suffered for the sake of humanity. Yet pain was a gift, that was her father's refrain. Pain must be endured, for without it there'd be no sweetness.

That morning her father told them that they should be obedient and meek, another common topic in the chapel.

"To speak evil of no one, to avoid quarreling, to be gentle, and to show perfect courtesy toward all people," he said.

In the back of the chapel she spotted Montgomery leaning by the doorway, looking dour. She doubted he was listening. She couldn't find Lupe among the congregation. When her father started in prayer, she bowed her head and whispered the words.

Behold the Lamb of God, behold him who takes away the sins of the world. Blessed are those called to the supper of the Lamb.

After the sermon finished and Montgomery and Cachito led the hybrids back to their homes and chores, she went looking for Lupe. She found her in the old building with the donkey's skull, gazing up at it. Carlota sat next to Lupe on a bench, and they both stared at the remains of the animal. She did not understand why Lupe sought this spot instead of the comfort of the chapel, but she knew by now that many of Lupe's preferences could hardly be understood. She did not explain herself to Carlota, and her inquiries were often rebuked.

"You weren't at the chapel again. My father will be upset."

"Maybe he will," Lupe said.

"You don't care."

"Cachito will repeat what he said all day today, as if he were a parrot."

"It doesn't matter. He'd prefer you to be there," she insisted. She didn't want Lupe to find herself in trouble, didn't want conflict to arise in their perfect household. But Lupe was distant now, her eyes turned from her.

She wishes to take flight, she thought. *If she had wings she'd have reached the horizon.*

"He says the same thing each time."

"He does not."

"You are deaf, Loti."

She did not reply, not wishing to start another row. Lupe stood up, and she followed her outside. Rather than walking back into the house they settled in the courtyard, by a wall painted oxblood red and crawling with ivy. Carlota rested her head against the other girl's shoulder and they looked at the fountain.

The silence was like a balm to soothe any wound. The birds sang in their cages, and the fountain bubbled. They forgot any ill feeling they'd held toward each other.

It was Carlota who broke that perfect bubble of comfort, watching the white curtains from her father's room flutter in the wind.

"I think my father wants the Lizaldes to notice me," she said.

"Notice you how?"

"He said I was of an age to be courted."

"Would you like that?"

In her pirate novels the women were kidnapped or met their lovers in exciting ways. To be courted implied a mundane process akin to the cooking of beans or the washing of linen. Yet it was also something alien, which she had yet to experience, and that itself might make it worthy of excitement even if other women were routinely courted.

"They are good-looking. I would have a handsome husband."

Lupe laughed, and she ran a thin nail down Carlota's braid, as they'd done when small. Lupe liked to braid her hair. Like a doll. Carlota was a doll to everyone.

"That's a silly reason to want a husband. Ask Ramona, she'll tell you. Her husband was pretty enough, and then he broke her nose with his fist. You can't tell what anything is by looking at it."

"Ramona didn't say that."

"She did. You—"

"Yes, I know. I'm deaf," Carlota muttered tiredly.

She supposed there was no reason why beauty and virtue must go hand in hand, but she also didn't want to resign herself to the idea of marrying an ugly stranger with rancid breath. If she could have a handsome husband and a gentleman, wouldn't that be nice? Not that she'd given marriage much thought. She'd assumed she'd always live at Yaxaktun, tend to her father, drift in and out of the laboratory, stroll down to the water hole for a swim. If she married, must she leave her home? Maybe if it was one of the Lizaldes she wouldn't have to go far. They could live at Vista Hermosa and visit often.

She didn't want things to change.

And yet.

The eyes of Eduardo Lizalde had been beautifully green, the color of the leaves of the ja'abin before the coming of the rains. She recalled them and blushed.

CHAPTER 10

Montgomery

IT TOOK EDUARDO Lizalde less than a week to send word that he'd be staying with them for a few days after all. Montgomery hadn't doubted he'd come back, but he was amused by his haste.

The arrival of the two young men necessitated a myriad of preparations. The house was carefully dusted, the porcelain locked in its cabinet was taken out and washed, the cutlery polished. Even Montgomery was compelled to pull his blue lounging jacket and the single-breasted waistcoat from the back of the armoire. Cachito laughed when he saw him standing in front of the mirror, adjusting his wide, primrose-yellow cravat. Fanny had liked yellow roses, and the cravat had been for her benefit.

"That bad?" he muttered.

"Not bad," Cachito said cheerfully. "Different."

Montgomery carefully grabbed a silver stick pin with the head of a fox and surveyed himself. He supposed he did look funny, different from what he thought of as his uniform—the white shirt and white trousers he wore every day.

Montgomery did not delude himself. His face was plain and prosy, always had been. When he'd courted Fanny he'd made an effort with his hair and clothing. He'd pursued her with zeal, and with the young woman at his side, he'd sometimes felt himself transformed into a prince. But those days were long past.

Yet he couldn't appear before the Lizaldes with dirt under his nails and his hair tangled. His coat wasn't of the newest style, but he supposed it would look fine, and grooming never did a man wrong, did it? Simply because he didn't tend to himself lately didn't mean he had to walk around looking like a bumpkin.

"Perhaps I should shave," he told Cachito, rubbing a hand against his cheek. The Lizaldes had tidy little mustaches. Montgomery had let his beard grow. "What do you think, should I get rid of these side whiskers?"

"You're ugly without the hair," Cachito said.

It was Montgomery's turn to laugh. "I suppose I'm no boy, but I might as well trim the damn thing before tomorrow," he said, and he pulled at the cravat.

"I wish I could see the visitors."

"You know you can't. You are to stay out of sight."

"Yes, yes. But I'm curious. These are men who want to kill Juan Cumux. They must be fearless to hunt him down."

"They're cowards and fools, the lot of them. If they really thought they would meet Cumux they'd turn around and flee."

Cachito cocked his head at him. "It doesn't matter. They'd never find him. Juan Cumux knows each tree in the jungle, and he has sixty men with him at all times. I read it in one of the papers that you brought from the city."

"You mustn't believe all the stories in there," he said and wondered what else Cachito had read in the papers.

"But he *is* fearless, and he fights for his kindred. Unlike the Lizaldes. I think they fight for themselves."

"You're still worried about the nohoch cuenta? You shouldn't be."

"But you don't like them."

"No I don't, but it's not my place to like them," Montgomery said simply.

The next morning he was up bright and early, not the slightest whiff of aguardiente on his lips. He did shave the beard, left it at a mustache, and then, feeling irritated, not wanting the boys to think he'd imitated them, he shaved all his facial hair off. Like that he looked gaunt, careworn, but he preferred it to attempting a stylishness he didn't possess.

Again he thought of Fanny, of the way she'd looked at him, of his days of courtship and yellow roses. He'd chipped a tooth since then, gained scars on his arm and lines under his eyes. He was thirty-five years old and couldn't remember who he'd wanted to be at twenty. He'd lost himself long ago.

He attended to his expected duties, then planted himself at the entrance of the house at the appointed time, awaiting the men. They were not punctual, and an hour after they'd said they'd arrive, they finally rode up to him, and he guided them and their horses to the stable. He needed to take the saddlebags off the animals and their belongings to their rooms, so he directed the gentlemen to please make their way to the sitting room.

Once he managed that, he asked Ramona to unpack the men's things and stopped by his room to change into the outfit he'd picked, quickly pinning the cravat in place. When he walked into the sitting room he saw Dr. Moreau was already there, chatting amicably with the gentlemen. Eduardo let his finger fall idly upon a piano key, banging out the same note three times.

They hardly noticed Montgomery as he stood stiffly to the side. Not that he expected to truly be included in these interactions. He was there merely because he must show his face. Dr. Moreau would consider it rude if he were to brick himself in his room with a bottle, which was what he looked forward to.

He forgot the bottle when Carlota Moreau walked into the room, forgot almost to breathe.

She wore a green dress strewn with a pattern of dainty white leaves that closely fitted her figure from neck to hip, then gave way to a wide skirt. Her hair was piled atop her head, soft tendrils falling charmingly around her face. In her right hand she carried a fan, and she moved with that wonderful ease of hers.

How lovely she was, the picture of youthful beauty, and how

quickly he looked away, fearing someone might notice the sudden, keen smile that had threatened to spread across his face, the pure joy at watching her, the embarrassing eagerness lighting his eyes.

Eduardo tugged at his jacket before stepping forward and throwing the girl a dazzling smile, capturing her hand and depositing a kiss on it. "Miss Moreau, we were wondering where you've been hiding," he said.

"Yes, indeed," Isidro said. "Eduardo has been threatening to play the piano. You mustn't let him."

"Would you play and sing for us?"

"If you wish," Carlota said, now allowing Isidro to kiss her hand, though her eyes remained on Eduardo, scarcely alighting on Isidro for a couple of seconds.

She didn't spare Montgomery, in his blue jacket and yellow cravat, which he thought fine enough, even a cursory glance.

She sat down at the piano and picked a simple melody. Her voice was clear and pleasant, despite the fact that she'd never been much of a musician. The gentlemen clapped politely, and after a couple of sweet, forgettable tunes Isidro volunteered to play.

Eduardo asked the girl to dance with him. Rather than reply with a touch of coquetry she looked frightened.

"I'm afraid I haven't learned," she admitted.

"It's simple. For someone as pretty as you, simpler still," Eduardo told her. "Don't you think, Mr. Laughton, that a girl as pretty as Miss Moreau will always find her footing?"

"I wouldn't know."

"You wouldn't know if she is pretty?"

Montgomery realized Eduardo had noticed the quick look he had thrown Carlota. Was Montgomery *that* transparent, or was Eduardo more perceptive than he'd thought? Maybe the young man simply wished to humiliate him in return for their confrontation the other day. It might be both things.

"Miss Moreau would no doubt appreciate compliments coming from your mouth rather than mine," he said.

The girl did glance at Montgomery now, curious and confused.

"Come, come, Mr. Laughton. You wouldn't be shy, would you? A lady always appreciates a compliment no matter who it comes from, and you must be an *old* acquaintance of hers. How long have you worked for her father, sir? Is it six or seven years? She must think of you as a kind uncle and no compliment would be taken poorly."

Montgomery did not reply. Eduardo took this as a triumph for himself. He turned to Carlota. "Let me show you a couple of simple steps," he said.

Carlota looked grateful for the change of topic and nodded bashfully. Despite her inexperience and uncertainty, the girl was graceful, swaying with him. She might never have danced before, but her body knew music and dexterity. She was lithe, supple, and he could imagine what glory it was like to hold her in one's arms.

When she looked up at Eduardo, her face expressed all the banality of youth and feeling.

Montgomery stood there with his hands in his pockets, watching the couple and remembering the last time he'd danced with a girl. It had been Fanny; they'd gone to a party. He didn't like parties, but she did, and he'd attended for her sake. The most popular quadrilles had French names: *le tiroir, les lignes, le molinet, les lanciers*. But the Viennese waltz was what Fanny danced best.

He remembered holding Fanny tight, his hand at her waist. He remembered her scintillant laugh, the garnet-colored dress she wore—satin and tulle, as soft as a butterfly's wing—and most of all the delicate, volatile notes of Otto of Roses perfuming her neck. He wondered if Carlota had dabbed perfume on her wrists and the hollow of her throat, or whether hers was the scent of salt on skin.

Montgomery muttered an excuse and stepped out of the room. The others did not take notice of his departure.

It was Saturday the next day, and since Dr. Moreau's usual religious service was canceled on account of their visitors, Montgomery took early to bed and let himself sleep in so he could avoid having to breakfast with the visitors. By the time he walked into the kitchen it was almost noon and Carlota was arguing with Ramona.

"There you are," Ramona said, turning to him. "Mr. Laughton, I've been trying to talk sense into this mulish girl but she won't listen. She wants to take those two men to the cenote by herself, and she shouldn't."

"They wish to go for a swim," Carlota said.

She was dressed in a simpler dress than the one from the previous evening. It was white with a floral print and trimmed with green ribbon. It appeared light and cool and becoming.

"In my town a woman wouldn't even be able to talk to a man before she married him, and here you are asking me to pack you food and let you go off with two of them."

"You are being silly, Ramona. It's a picnic."

"Don't worry, Ramona. I'll escort the three of them."

"I don't need an escort," Carlota replied quickly.

"You're not leaving without one," he said.

The girl looked peeved, but his tone had clearly indicated there would be no negotiation, and she was wise or proud enough to muffle any further complaints. "Forget the picnic, then. We will take them there without refreshments," she said, her voice cool.

"Fine with me."

She walked quick, almost running, until they reached the interior courtyard where the young men were chatting, then she slowed her steps and composed herself. As soon as the men saw Montgomery their merriment subsided.

"Good day, gentlemen. Miss Moreau told me you'd like to go for a swim," he said, lifting his straw hat in greeting.

"Yes. She said there's a pleasant cenote nearby and it's dreadfully hot. We thought we'd cool down." Eduardo smiled at him. "I don't think we'll need you to fetch the horses, from what she gave us to understand, we can walk it."

"Walking would be fine, indeed. Let's go, then," Montgomery

said cheerfully and began to walk without looking behind, though he could imagine the disappointment on their faces. It was not that he wished to play chaperone as much as he wished to irritate the men.

The conversation was patchy as they walked together, so he surmised he'd managed to sour their excursion as he'd planned. But he wasn't done yet.

When they arrived at the cenote he pointed at it. "There you have it, gentlemen. This is the cenote Báalam."

"Very nice," Eduardo said and didn't mean a word of it, that was clear enough. Both gentlemen stood a good distance from the water hole, as if they were afraid they might tumble in.

"Will you swim immediately?"

"Swim with you here, sir?"

"Why not?" Montgomery asked. "You wouldn't be shy, would you? The lady will turn her head away, as I'm sure that was the original plan."

Eduardo tipped his chin up but didn't say anything. Montgomery shrugged. "Well, if you won't, then I'll take a dip," he said and took off his hat, then his shirt. He was back to wearing the simple cotton shirt without a collar he always had on. No sense in trying to look like a damn dandy; no silk cravats, no silliness.

He removed his boots and saw Carlota turn her face away from him, blushing. He kept the white trousers on and walked down the stones, to the water, jumping in with gusto. The cenote was exquisitely cool, and normally he would have kept on swimming for a while, head thrown back and eyes closed, but after a few minutes Montgomery walked back up to the spot where his companions remained, his trousers sodden. He put on his boots again and slung the shirt over his back.

"Gentlemen, you really should take a dip," he proclaimed.

"We would if we were alone," Eduardo replied. His hand was pressed against the trunk of a tree, and his eyes were sharp. "Seeing as we have company, it would be rude to subject Miss Moreau to such a spectacle, as you have."

"But Miss Moreau and I are old acquaintances!"

"Are you," Eduardo said flatly.

"I can see you are indeed shy. Do not worry, Miss Moreau and I will let you be. I'm sure you can find your way to the house with ease, seeing as the path leads right back to Yaxaktun," Montgomery said, and he made a motion with his fingers, indicating the way. He pressed a hand against the small of Carlota's back and pushed her away from the gentlemen.

She moved quietly, without protest, but once they were at a good distance from the cenote, once they had passed the statue of the jaguar and only the birds in the trees could hear them speak, she planted herself in front of him, her hands balled into fists.

"How dare you, Montgomery!" she said

"What have I done? I walked the men to the cenote as we agreed, and now I'm walking you back home," he said innocently.

"No, you didn't. You humiliated them! What if they should be angry? What if they should tell my father? What if—"

"What if Eduardo Lizalde doesn't feel like marrying you? I suppose your father will have to sell you to another man. Don't worry, I think he'll find a customer."

She gritted her teeth and slapped him, which he had expected. Then her eyes filled with tears, which he hadn't planned for, and she hurried away.

"Carlota!" he yelled and tried to follow, but the girl picked up her skirts and ran like the devil. He might have caught up with her, no matter her speedy flight, but then he thought better of it and stopped suddenly.

He'd let his shirt fall somewhere behind him, and he cursed as he turned around and walked back. He found it, dirt-smeared, in the middle of the path, and he put it on again.

The girl was nowhere in sight when he walked into the house, and he didn't seek her out. Best he leave her alone, forever, if at all possible.

Chapter 11

Carlota

CARLOTA LOVED EVERYTHING about Yaxaktun, but most of all she loved her father. He was like the sun in the sky, lighting her days.

Yes, he could be stern and demanding at times. Nevertheless, she recalled all the evenings, many years before, when she had been small and he hadn't yet developed a treatment for her. She remembered how he smoothed her sweaty hair from her face, offered water, placed another pillow beneath her head. Lost in a haze of pain, there had been her father at her side, every night, promising he would make it better.

And he had. He'd kept his promise. As much as she had despised that feeling of helplessness, of being weak and left at the mercy of others, she had been grateful for his affection.

Carlota loved her father, loved to please him.

When she walked into the sitting room, Eduardo went toward her and deposited a kiss on her knuckles, and she grew flustered. When he suggested they dance together she could hardly reply.

She feared she'd take a wrong step, that they'd find her silly, and her first thought was to refuse him. But her father wanted her to socialize with the gentlemen, and Carlota forced her lips into a smile.

Eduardo gently held her hand and showed her the correct steps. "You're graceful," he said. "I wouldn't have guessed you've never danced before."

"It's kind of you to say so. I'm afraid I'll step on your toes," she replied, her voice so low she had to repeat herself and he had to lean down close to hear her.

"No danger of that. Why didn't your father send you to study in the city?"

"I was sick when I was a girl. I spent many hours in bed each day. I didn't mind being in my room, though. It gave me a chance to read."

Her voice was still a whisper. Her smile did not move; it was painted on.

"What's your favorite book?"

She enjoyed books about pirates and her father's science textbooks alike, but she wondered if he'd think her silly if she admitted to enjoying tales of great romance. "I like Sir Walter Scott and fell in love with Brian de Bois-Guilbert," she said at last.

"Don't tell me . . . he's from that book . . . oh, what is that?"

"*Ivanhoe.*"

"Of course! But isn't he a villain? Or am I misremembering?"

"Oh, no." Carlota shook her head, her voice now louder and more certain. "He's more complicated than that. He loves Rebecca, and she doesn't love him. He's vowed to never love again, and he's filled with conflicting emotions."

"I thought he was the villain, but thank you for correcting my flawed notion. You fancy *Ivanhoe* and what else?"

"Other books. I liked *Clemencia*. It's romantic. Have you read it?"

"I wasn't studious and skimmed my assigned readings," Eduardo said, sounding proud of himself.

"What did you learn in the city, then?"

"I did learn a little, even if I'm no scholar. My father wants me to pay attention to our properties now, so I suppose I should brush up on my math. The particulars of the hacienda are for the administrator and the mayordomo to handle, of course, but it doesn't hurt to take a look at the ledgers once in a while. My father hardly ever visits the estates, nobody really does, but he thought I should look at them, at least once. Vista Hermosa used to have cattle, but now it's a sugar-producing hacienda. That's all I knew about it until a few weeks ago."

"I can't understand how you wouldn't intimately know the places you own," Carlota said, frowning. "How can you tell all the different types of earth if you've never held them in your hands?"

"What different types of earth could there be?"

"All kinds! Tsek'el, which is bad for growing, and k'an kaab k'aat, which is thin and red. Boox lu'um is black and rich, and k'an kaab is yellow. If you don't know the soil, then you can't understand how to grow new things or how to burn it for the new crops. Learned men must know these things."

"I am a failure then," he said cheekily and gave her a big smile. "Will you be my teacher?"

"I don't presume to be so wise. Besides, *you* are teaching me how to dance."

"Bah. Dancing is not hard. Certainly simpler than Latin. I'm not very good at Latin."

"I'm good at languages."

"Perhaps in the end you surpass me at everything."

"Perhaps you are modest, sir."

"I'm not. But I can show you another step, would you like that?"

She felt more comfortable with him now that they were dancing. The newness of him was more exciting than frightful. Accustomed as she was to her father's stern, demanding exterior and Montgomery's somber musings, she much appreciated Eduardo's good humor. She smiled back at him and nodded, relishing the way his eyes fixed on her, full of infectious delight.

It followed her through the house, this delight, even after the dance had finished and they'd said their goodbyes. It almost itched; it was a strange, restless eagerness, and she wondered if he felt the same.

That evening, when Carlota brought her father his cup of tea, he congratulated her.

"You did well today," he said, as she placed the tray on the side table. "Eduardo seems impressed with you. Marriage would do you good, and it would give us options."

"What do you mean?" she asked softly.

"When I left Paris, it was without my family's support. You could say they disowned my studies, my work. I've had to build a new life for myself without them, without anyone. My brother owes me a share of the family fortune, but would he relinquish it? No. And would I get on my knees and beg for it? Never. Let him rot. I've survived without him."

Her father seldom talked about that part of his life. She knew he'd done revolutionary work related to blood transfusions, but why he'd abandoned France, how he'd made his way to Mexico, that he didn't like to talk about. It surprised her to hear him speak candidly, so rather than interjecting, she simply listened, nodding her head.

"I want to give us options, Carlota. The Lizalde name opens doors. Their fortune is immense. I've had to offer myself in the employment of others, to make do and follow the path set down by moneyed imbeciles. If you were to marry into such a family you'd have a chance to make your own choices."

"Then you think . . . you think you'd like one of them as a husband for me? Because they are wealthy?"

"Wealth is power. You can't go through this world without two pesos to rub together and when I pass away there will be little left. This house is not mine, Carlota. Neither is the furniture nor the equipment in the lab. This is all borrowed, girl."

"But then you speak as though I have no choice, papa, and you spoke of choice just now," she whispered as she stood by her father's bed.

He clasped her hand firmly. "Carlota, a girl must be sensible, and I need to count on you to be sensible. The Lizalde boys might be our best . . . no, our *sole* chance. Child, these might be the most important days of your young life."

She wasn't sure why he'd press this point. Didn't he have time to find a groom for her? Was it impossible for Carlota to meet a proper suitor in the capital or another city? Yet it was a daughter's duty to please her father. She nodded feebly.

"And you like Eduardo, don't you?" he asked.

"I like him fine, papa," she said, and she did. At least, she liked what she'd seen of him. The way he danced, the polite way he kissed her hand, his voice, and his beautiful eyes. She didn't like how he'd spoken to Montgomery; she couldn't understand the splinter of animosity between them, but she thought perhaps it was like that with men. They were like roosters, eager to peck at each other.

What did she know of men, after all, that she hadn't learned from the papers or from books or from hearsay? Nothing at all. But she liked the feeling Eduardo made bloom inside her chest and that odd eagerness that made her skin tingle.

The next morning, after a simple breakfast, her father asked Carlota to give their guests a tour of the property. She put on one of her newer summer dresses and bid them follow her. First she took them to their chapel and proudly showed them the mural that had caught her attention many times before.

Both men looked at it with care, but Isidro seemed put off.

"It doesn't please you?" she asked.

"The strokes of the brush themselves are fine, and yet there's something wrong about it," the young man said.

"Wrong?"

She looked at the black-haired Eve standing by a flowering tree and the vividly rendered birds on the branches. By her feet there was a deer and in the background one could spy lions, horses, a fox, a peacock. A stream flowed next to her, filled with fish.

"If this is Eve at the moment of her fall, then why isn't the snake on the ground? Nor is that an apple tree. Therefore this must be Eden before humanity sinned and yet Adam is nowhere to be found. It is Eve alone. Why, it reminds me of something *pagan*."

Eve held a crimson flower in her hand and had crimson flowers in her hair, and her skin was bronzed, and she stood below a round, round sun. Carlota could not understand why it would be pagan. She looked at Isidro in confusion, wondering if, like the steps to a dance, this was something she should have been taught but which her father neglected to instruct her on. But she'd read from their Bible and listened to her father speak about many of the passages contained within it.

"You must forgive my cousin; he was a seminarist and had his heart set on becoming a priest before the family thought better of it," Eduardo said. "He reckons almost everything is pagan."

"I do not," Isidro protested. "Besides, you can't deny these days the way the people twist the teachings of the priest, especially around this part of the country—"

"Don't start with that," Eduardo said dismissively.

Isidro frowned, but was silent. They exited the chapel, and she pointed to the wall and the main entrance that led to the hybrids' dwellings. That door was tightly closed, as it should be.

"My father's patients reside there, in the old workers' huts. My father doesn't want you to head there. There are many sickly people and they mustn't be disturbed," she said.

"We wouldn't dream of bothering them," Eduardo said. "They're charity cases, the lot of them, correct?"

"My father tends to them."

"It must be a pretty penny my uncle spends on Yaxaktun and all for charity," Isidro mused.

"Whoever sows sparingly will also reap sparingly, and whoever sows generously will also reap generously," she said.

She thought Isidro would be pleased to see she knew her Bible verses. But the young man merely stared at her and did not look amused. Carlota lowered her eyes and kept on walking, pointing to the stables, then taking them through the house.

To Carlota, Yaxaktun was more wonderful than the greatest museum in the world, but quickly she noticed that her guests were bored. By the time they reached the courtyard she half-expected them to begin yawning.

She stood there, listening to the birds chirp in their cages, not knowing what else to show them. They'd seen the lustrous hand-painted tiles, the stencils on the walls, the bougainvillea. She realized

Vista Hermosa must be grander than Yaxaktun, that their house in Mérida might also be magnificent. And as her father had said, they owned all this. Each glass and cup and even the bougainvillea blooming in the courtyard.

"It's going to be a blazingly hot day," Eduardo said. "I can't get used to it yet. It never gets this warm in Mexico City."

"We might go to the cenote. You could take a dip there," Carlota said. "The water is of the most wonderful shade of blue-green, and it's cool and lovely."

"That sounds like an excellent idea."

"We could have a picnic," Isidro added. "In the English style."

"I've heard about picnics at night. That might be better," Eduardo said.

"Perhaps, but I'm hungry now."

"I'll be a minute. I'll arrange it," she said and hurried to the kitchen.

Ramona was deveining chiles when Carlota rushed in. "Ramona, could you put together an English-style picnic for us?" she asked.

"What is that?"

"I don't know. Pieces of bread and cheese, I suppose."

"You'll have to explain."

"I'm not sure. Whatever would impress our guests. It must be done quick. We are going to eat it by the cenote."

"Why don't you ask Mr. Laughton to help you make it? He's English. He'd know how to."

"It's just us heading for a swim, Montgomery is not coming."

Ramona shook her head and wiped her hands on a kitchen rag. "Then you can't go."

"What do you mean?"

"You're going to swim with two men and no chaperone?"

"I don't see why not."

"It's bad, that's why not. There's no arrangement between you and those men, no mujul. You need to ask for a bride seven times before she'll marry you. Have these men asked even once?"

"It's not like that. They're not macehuales."

"The dzules need to court properly, too. It's not proper. I'm no fool, Loti."

"I am going," Carlota said, her gentle disposition giving way to mulish stubbornness.

But as Carlota spoke, she heard footsteps behind her. It was Montgomery. Of course, he took Ramona's side. Carlota thought he did it to exasperate her. She didn't understand why else he'd care where they went. It's not as if he'd ever made an effort to be sociable. She felt cheated as they walked toward the cenote, but she attempted to convince herself that the situation could be salvaged.

When they reached the cenote she was, for a moment, happy. The water was beautiful, and the birds sang in the trees, and there was all the magic and the glory that she was accustomed to. She thought they'd feel it, too, and this place would soothe them all.

Then Montgomery decided to act like a clown. With each word he spoke she felt the desire to press a hand against his mouth and bid him be quiet. He was breaking the spell that held the land and the water together, that knit the fish in the depths with the sun in the sky.

It was as if he was casting a hex.

When she thought it couldn't be worse, he tossed his hat aside, took off his shirt, and nonchalantly prepared to go for a swim.

She knew the names of muscles and bones from her father's medical textbooks, but she hadn't seen an unclothed man. Or half-clothed, in this case, since he had the decency of at least keeping his trousers in place. Though the trousers, white in color and of a thin material, turned almost transparent once wet, rendering modesty obsolete.

Montgomery was lean. Scars ran down his arm, and despite his gauntness, his body displayed the strength of coarse, constant work. She wondered whether beneath their magnificent clothes the Lizaldes looked different, whether they lacked Montgomery's sturdy efficiency. After all, they had bodies that had been tempered in front of pianos and desks, bodies that knew the motions of carriages and the sounds of a city.

Montgomery was like a chipped piece of pottery. She couldn't imagine he'd ever been whole, and his eyes, when they glanced at her, were watery gray. Not green and lush and full of promise like Eduardo's, but the gray of storms.

She turned her face away, blushing, and clasped her hands together.

Nobody said a thing.

She wished to tell the men that she didn't understand what was happening, that normally Montgomery didn't behave like this, that she hoped they weren't offended, but she could not think what to say or how to begin saying it.

He'd cast a hex, all right.

He'd ruined it all.

When Montgomery emerged from the water and pulled her away, still she couldn't speak, but each step filled her with anger, and at last she moved in front of him.

"How dare you, Montgomery!" she exclaimed.

Rather than looking contrite, he was indifferent. More than that: he was smug.

She slapped him, hand colliding with his smooth cheek. But all that did was make it worse, and she rushed away, tears in her eyes. The birds in the trees called out, their shrill cries an echo of his mockery.

When she reached her room she curled on the bed and wept. Many of the markers of Carlota's childhood still remained around her. The chest with toys was at the foot of the bed, and on the shelves sat her dolls. She stared into their smiling faces, hoping to find them comforting, but they looked old and ugly.

She remembered how Montgomery had seemed so confident in front of her, practically laughing. Unable to stand it, she raked her nails across the bedsheets, as if wishing she could slash his face.

How dare he! And yet he did, he dared, he cared for nothing, he made a fool of her. She was drunk on an intoxicating cocktail of emotions. Anxiety, anger, excitement, and shame mingled together, plunging her body into chaos.

Her nails snagged in the cloth, the fine linen was blemished, and she tossed around, pushing the top sheet off the bed. She hugged the pillow.

Later, when the evening's shadows began dancing through her window, Lupe knocked on the door and walked in. She was wearing the black dress, gloves, and veil she used whenever there were any outsiders at Yaxaktun, so that she might be concealed. The girl stayed out of the way, but this was an extra precaution.

Lupe had with her a tray, which she set down on a table.

"The gentlemen guests are going to have supper in their room, and Mr. Laughton says he's indisposed, so Ramona told me to bring you a plate rather than have her set the table."

Carlota felt the tears brimming in her eyes once more, eyes that were already red and raw from crying.

Lupe lifted her veil. She was frowning. "What happened? Why are you weeping?"

"We went to the cenote and Montgomery was completely awful to them. I'm sure they're offended and they find me dull. They probably want to leave come morning."

"What if they do want to leave?"

She pressed her hot cheek against the mahogany headboard. "You don't understand. My father will be furious. All he's done is tell me how wonderful it would be if I would marry, and then he said if he died we wouldn't have two pesos. I want to please my father and I want Eduardo to like me."

"I'm sure he does. Everybody likes you."

"You don't, not anymore," Carlota whispered. "You look toward the road all the time and talk only of what might be found in other places."

"I do like you, silly," Lupe muttered, and she sat on the bed and hugged Carlota. "You're odd. This is nothing. Who cares about those silly boys?"

When they'd been little they'd curled up together and looked through the stereoscope, watching distant vistas bloom before their eyes. They'd scared each other repeating Ramona's tales of spirits who drowned children in the water holes. But they hadn't been close like this in some time.

"You should come sit around the bonfire tonight," Lupe said.

"You're lighting the bonfire? But we have guests."

Lupe shrugged. "What will they care? They'll be in their rooms, and if what you say is true they'll be counting the hours until they leave. Why would they want to look behind the wall? Besides, Montgomery said it's fine."

"Of course he would. He wants to drink."

"I think he's been drinking all afternoon already. I think he'll be absolutely inebriated by the time he gets there. When he's like that, he doesn't care about anyone."

"I don't want to be near him," Carlota whispered, remembering the silly smirk on his face and, even worse, the tanned naked chest and shoulders. And his hair, normally untidy and falling before his eyes, slicked back when he stepped out of the water.

It was indecent of Montgomery to parade himself like that. It made her wonder, if they'd painted Adam on the mural, if he would have looked like Montgomery rather than Eduardo. She smothered the thought, furious at herself for even having it in the first place.

"What do you care if he's there? Toss the glass of aguardiente he's drinking in his face if he gives you trouble."

"You make everything sound easy," Carlota muttered.

"Then stay moping in here," Lupe said. "Maybe I'll toss the glass in his face for you if you won't. Would that help?"

Carlota smiled a little smile, and Lupe chuckled. "I should go. I'll leave the door open for you, in case you change your mind," Lupe said.

That night, when it was late, despite having told herself that she would not venture by the bonfire, Carlota ended up quickly changing into a white wrapper with an embroidered collar and put on a pair of slippers. She stepped outside quietly. She didn't need a candle.

The moon was up high, and she could see well. The darkness never frightened her, not even when she'd been small.

When she reached the door in the wall it opened easily, and she immediately spotted the bonfire and the circle of hybrids around it. They sat on rickety chairs and a few on the ground, the whole contingent, which numbered twenty-nine. A couple of them had fallen asleep, others were conversing happily, and some were eating and drinking.

Estrella and K'an played dice while Aj Kaab poked at his teeth with a stick, lazily closing his eyes. Cachito and Lupe sat together, laughing. Montgomery was half in shadow and sat next to Peek', who had the long snout of the tapir and deformed hands with only three digits tipped with long fingernails. The hands, despite their limitations, had once been nimble, but arthritis now afflicted the hybrid in his old age, and Montgomery helped him by holding up a bowl so that he could drink.

Carlota hesitated for a moment, thinking of stepping away. Peek' finished drinking and he stood up, then motioned to Parda and engaged her in conversation. Montgomery set the bowl aside and leaned forward, his long legs stretched out, popping a cigarette in his mouth. He raised an eyebrow when he saw her, and she walked close to the bonfire, her eyes fixed on him. He returned the look, observing her with a zeal she took to mean a challenge.

"You've come, Loti!" Cachito yelled, scrambling to his feet and holding up a bottle in his hands. "We weren't sure if you would. Do you want a drink?"

"Perhaps a half glass," she said. She wasn't used to drinking with them. She didn't like that her father allowed this type of merriment, but she felt bolder that night. Maybe it was the way Montgomery was looking at her that inspired Carlota. She wanted him to realize she didn't care about him or anything he did.

"I don't know if we have a spare glass. But here," Cachito said and handed her the bottle. "Go on."

It was a fiery drink, unlike the sips of anise or brandy they had after dinner, or the wine that might grace the table. She almost felt like spitting, but drank it down. She wiped her mouth.

Cachito patted her back and laughed when he noticed her grimace.

Montgomery walked over to where they stood. "What do you think you're doing?" he asked, his voice low.

"Having a drink. I assume you've had many yourself," she replied.

He tossed his cigarette on the ground and stepped on the smoldering stub. "You shouldn't be here. It's late and your father will not like it."

"I'm allowed to be here," she said, impertinent, wanting to push him and see where it got her. It was childish, she thought, to behave like this, and yet he'd been childish, too; he'd been a cretin that morning.

"Let's get you back to the house," he said, taking the bottle away from her and handing it to Cachito.

"You want me to walk with you?" Cachito asked. "We need more aguardiente, I can fetch it."

"I'll bring it."

"Montgomery, I can go. I don't mind."

"Don't bother," he said, without looking at Cachito.

He grabbed her by the arm and began marching her out the door, down the dirt path that led to the house. Tall grasses tickled her ankles. The humming of insects and the distant hooting of an owl punctuated the night.

The owl was a bad omen, and she ought to have been afraid of it and rushed quietly home, but instead she raised her voice.

"Lupe invited me! Let go!" she demanded.

"I don't care if the pope himself invited you. Your father doesn't want you drinking with the hybrids," he said dryly.

"Why can *you* do it, then?"

"Because you and I are not the same."

"How are we different?"

"Miss Moreau, you are my employer's daughter."

"Mr. Laughton, you don't seem to care about that when it's convenient for you," she said, her words fast, practically speaking over him.

"What has gotten into you?"

His grip was good, but she freed herself of it and peered up triumphantly at Montgomery. "I should have tossed the aguardiente in your face, like Lupe said. No matter. You were rude to me today and I don't see why I should obey you or make it easy or—"

"So you'll be a nuisance to me now?"

"Maybe! Perhaps next time you won't decide to ruin my life."

In that instant she honestly did think he'd ruined it all, that nothing would ever amount to much again. The food would lose its taste, the sun wouldn't rise in the morning. Her father would hate her, and no man would ever love her.

"For God's sake, you are giving me a headache," he said with a sigh and grabbed her arm again.

"You have a headache because you are drunk, you slob," she whispered.

He looked as if she'd really tossed the aguardiente in his face. No, worse. He looked somber, and he was standing close to her and smelled of the drink he'd been imbibing and the cigarettes he'd smoked.

She wondered what he'd do now, whether he'd insist on accompanying her or he'd turn back. Or he might be angry and they might bicker more. But something in his face made Carlota recall once or twice before, when she'd caught him looking at her and he'd quickly raised his eyes and fixed them on a point far beyond her. This time he didn't do that and kept looking at her.

"Sir! Let go of the lady!" Eduardo ordered.

They both turned their heads to discover the Lizaldes a few paces from them. Montgomery sighed. "Gentlemen, what are you doing sneaking around Yaxaktun at night?"

"I could ask the same question," Eduardo replied. "The lady looks distressed."

"I'm escorting Miss Moreau back to her room. Now, if you'll excuse us—"

Eduardo stepped forward, blocking Montgomery's path. "I want to know what you are up to," he said.

She opened her mouth to explain. Not the truth, of course. She meant to weave a pretty lie. But Montgomery spoke faster. "It's none of your business," he said, his voice a challenge.

Inevitably Eduardo responded to this challenge, straightening his coat.

"My father owns this place," Eduardo replied. "It is *mine*."

Montgomery had let go of her, and his fingers were curling into a fist. His face hardened, and she thought, *No, he wouldn't dare*. But then he *had* been drinking all evening, and he didn't look somber now. He looked furious. Before she had a chance to say anything he was stepping forward and throwing a punch.

He hit Eduardo in the face, and Eduardo yelped and stumbled back two paces looking so shocked you would have thought no man had ever dared to punch him before. Maybe no one had. Gentlemen fought duels.

But Montgomery was no gentleman, her father said.

Montgomery quickly went at Eduardo again, and this time Eduardo reacted, blocking him and hitting back. Isidro, not content to watch from the sidelines, jumped into the fray and also attacked. Montgomery, faced with two furious opponents, did not seem rattled.

"Gentlemen, no! Montgomery, don't!" she yelled. "Stop!"

Carlota thought Montgomery might obey her, because his eyes fell on her and he lowered his hands, looking almost mollified. Then Eduardo came from the side and hit Montgomery on the head with such vicious abandon she knew he had definitely been in fights.

Montgomery seemed stunned: he staggered, a hand pressed against his ear, and he winced, bending down as if he was about to retch. Isidro took the opportunity to kick Montgomery, and the blow threw him off balance. He fell, one hand still cupping his ear.

All of a sudden Cachito was roaring and leaping from the shadows. She clapped a hand against her mouth in shock. Carlota could not even tell where he came from or how long he'd been following them. Suddenly he was there, and he shoved Isidro against the ground with such force that the young man was unable to utter a scream. Cachito roared again before clamping his teeth on Isidro's outstretched hand.

Isidro tried to wrestle the hybrid off him, and Eduardo kicked Cachito. Isidro let out a hoarse scream at last, and she grabbed Cachito by the shoulders, pulling him back.

"Stop!" she pleaded. "Let go, stop!"

Cachito released Isidro. The man lay on the ground moaning in pain, and Cachito was crouching down, blood dribbling down his mouth and his ears pressed back against his skull. As Montgomery stood up she noticed there was also blood on his left temple, where one of Eduardo's rings must have cut him.

"What in God's name is that?" Eduardo whispered.

Cachito let out a low hiss, and Carlota crouched next to him, pressing a hand against his arm, her fingers digging into his fur.

"My father's patient," she whispered.

Eduardo did not reply. Isidro was moaning and attempting to scramble back up to his feet. Montgomery stretched out a hand and helped him up. The young man stared at the older one, but Montgomery was expressionless.

"Cachito, clean yourself and go to sleep. We'll get the doctor to look at your hand, Mr. Lizalde. Come on. Let's head back to the damn house," Montgomery said, then he spat on the ground.

The owl was still hooting in the distance, promising misery, as they began walking together. Montgomery had indeed cast a hex.

Chapter 12

Montgomery

THEY WENT INTO the laboratory, and the doctor had Carlota assist him, fetching gauze, rubbing alcohol, and other materials, while Isidro sat in a chair and the doctor examined him. Montgomery held up a lantern, and Eduardo lit two others, the shadows quickly receding and allowing a clear view of the patient.

"It's not as bad as I first thought," the doctor said, his voice calm. "Cachito is not a rabid animal. There will be no need to cauterize or rub the stick of lunar caustic into the wound. Cleaning and bandaging the hand will be enough."

Both of the young men looked relieved. Montgomery lowered the lantern and set it on a table. There was a great deal of blood smeared on Isidro's shirt, but the doctor was correct. The wound wasn't terribly deep. In the end, Cachito had held back.

"The treatment is sound enough, but will you tell us what the hell was that creature outside?" Eduardo asked. "Your daughter claimed it was a patient, but it was not human."

"Indeed not. It's an animal hybrid, part of the experiments I run at Yaxaktun for your father. Normally Cachito is docile."

"Docile! It almost ripped off my hand!" Isidro exclaimed.

"We were fighting. He must have been spooked by that," Montgomery said. "He probably sought to defend me. The hybrids trust me. Seeing me in trouble—"

"Hybrids, plural? There are several?" Eduardo asked.

"Yes. We are seeking many important answers here at Yaxaktun, answers to medical mysteries, and the hybrids may assist us in finding them. I assume your father never hinted at the nature of my work."

"No. Although that explains why he didn't want us coming alone here," Eduardo said. "I wrote to my father, telling him we'd be spending a few days with you, and he wrote back saying we shouldn't go without him. That he'd be coming down from Mérida and would visit Yaxaktun with us, as he wanted to discuss an important matter with you. I found it odd that he'd insist we couldn't proceed on our own. He hates leaving Mérida."

And you couldn't wait a few days for him, Montgomery thought. *You simply had to rush back and take another look at the girl.*

He had no doubts that had been the reason Eduardo had so eagerly grabbed a horse and set off to Yaxaktun. What other explanation was there? Montgomery looked at Carlota, who was deftly winding the bandage around Isidro's hand, her motions careful and gentle. Despite the commotion she'd composed herself quickly.

"My father has said you are a genius and that your medical research is important, but I couldn't have imagined it amounted to whatever that creature is."

"A thing belonging to the devil," Isidro said.

"Not the devil, a thing of science. I was going to show you the hybrids, but I thought it prudent to ease their introduction. We didn't aim to keep this a secret from you eternally," the doctor said. "I'd been planning a dinner to present them to you and to explain my methods."

"So much for that! How do you intend to punish that hellish animal?" Isidro asked, flexing his fingers and testing the bandage. "It deserves a good lashing. Let me whip it a few times and it won't have teeth to bite anyone ever again."

Carlota gasped in surprise. Montgomery kept his face blank. There wasn't anything he could say, and he was certain any intervention on his part would do more harm than good.

"We are all sorry. Please don't whip him," Carlota said with such breathless vehemence that a man would have to be made of stone not to be moved by her words.

All the same, Isidro didn't seem impressed by that answer, and he immediately opened his mouth, but Eduardo clasped his cousin's shoulder. "There must be an alternative," Eduardo said.

Carlota's magic seemed to have worked on him. She was pretty, her eyes were large and sweet, and either Eduardo was honestly touched by her or else he'd assessed the situation and wagered he'd best be served by playing the gallant man.

The doctor tapped his cane against the floor, as if in thought. "I'll punish him physically tomorrow morning. You may watch, but the whip would be excessive. I wouldn't wish to resort to it. Besides, he was intoxicated and had been drinking with Mr. Laughton and some of the other hybrids. The aguardiente must have muddled his thoughts."

"And what about Laughton? Will he go unpunished?" Isidro asked.

"Mr. Laughton will have his wages garnished for a couple of months. It'll teach him to mind his manners."

"That would be a feat."

"Tomorrow, after I administer the punishment, I will show you the hybrids and explain any lingering questions. I assure you: this has been a horrid accident. But it is a rare one. Please, gentlemen, I beg of you, let us speak in the morning."

"Very well. We shall talk tomorrow," Eduardo said.

Isidro stood up, grumbling a curse, and both of the men retired for the night. Once the three of them were alone, Carlota stepped closer to her father, her fingers hovering upon his arm.

"You won't really hit Cachito, will you?" she asked.

He made a sharp motion, almost like a horse rearing up, and brushed the girl's hand away. "Of course I will! Can't you see how close you've been in engineering my destruction? I should have said yes to the whip, so do not even think to demand another concession!"

Carlota looked at her father with wide, anxious eyes. Montgomery thought she'd say nothing else, but the girl surprised him by speaking up again. "But it wasn't Cachito's fault. It was us . . . it was *me*."

"Listen carefully, silly girl, since you don't seem to understand what we are faced with. If Hernando Lizalde is headed here to discuss important matters with me, it means he is about to yank the financial support he provides for my research. He's threatened as much already and now, no doubt, this incident with Isidro will serve as the perfect excuse. So I will not do anything to displease his relatives any further and I will punish that stupid animal. He best be grateful I don't skin him tomorrow morning! What would we do without the Lizaldes, girl? What?!"

Moreau's voice had been steadily rising, and his daughter had slowly retreated with each word until she bumped against a table. The instruments on it clattered.

"And you," the doctor muttered, turning around and pointing at Montgomery. "I thought you smarter than this. I thought you understood. Brawling, like you're at a cheap tavern! If we lose the Lizaldes then how will I be able to care for the hybrids? How will I engineer the medicine to sustain my daughter?"

"I'll get you a hundred jaguars if you need them," Montgomery said. "She won't suffer because of me."

"Jaguars! And the other ingredients? And the lab materials? And the lab space? Will you also get me that?" Moreau demanded. "Without the money from the Lizaldes my daughter would be doomed! You are a cretin and my child is a constant failure! My life's work . . . you threaten my life's work. Everything . . . life, the creation of life, life perfected . . ."

Montgomery knew that when Moreau got himself into a state like this he could roar for a good hour. Yet this time he winced and gripped his cane tight, and a strange expression fell upon his face. He'd gone pale.

"Father?" Carlota asked, moving close to him.

There were beads of sweat on the doctor's forehead. He shoved the girl aside, walking quickly out of the room. "Enough of you. Of all of you," he muttered.

Carlota gripped her hands together and stood in the middle of the lab, her lips quivering. "Let him go," Montgomery said tiredly. "You'll make it worse if you follow him now."

"What would you know?" she whispered.

"I know Dr. Moreau."

Carlota stood half in shadow and looked up at him. Her eyes almost seemed to glow, catlike. He'd idly wondered before what Moreau's treatment amounted to and how it might affect the mechanism of the girl's body. Was it merely her blood that it strengthened? The doctor had not said. He hunted jaguars for him, brought him the great cats' corpses every few months, and Moreau wove his strange alchemy. Gemmules from the jaguar, to keep her alive.

And without them, without this laboratory with its pipettes and measuring flasks, she'd wither as quickly as a cut flower. And the Lizaldes, they owned her safety and her future. She was an orchid, to be kept under glass.

"I'm sorry about today," he said.

"I'm sorry, too," she whispered and quickly stepped out of the laboratory.

He didn't sleep much after that. He was ready in the morning, dressed and shaved, when the doctor came knocking and curtly told Montgomery that he wanted him to fetch Cachito and take him to the donkey's hut.

Cachito was sitting outside, next to the spot where the bonfire had burned merrily the night before. Lupe sat next to him, wrapped in a rebozo. When they saw him they both stood up.

"The doctor says you are to go to the donkey's hut."

"Into the House of Pain," Lupe said.

Montgomery had never heard it called that. He didn't go in there for there was nothing inside he might want, and the old donkey's skull made him quiver with a certain superstitious fear. He felt as if a wicked feeling lingered in that spot. The hybrids felt the same, except perhaps for Lupe, whom he'd spotted in that old shack all by herself.

Moreau used that fear to his advantage. When he wished to scold or punish a hybrid, he had them taken to the donkey's hut. The alcohol kept them pliant, the medicine kept them loyal, the sermons burned the rules into their minds, and the hut ensured misdeeds were quickly corrected.

"Come on," Montgomery said.

They followed him without further comment, and the three of them waited outside the hut. Soon Moreau appeared. With him came the Lizaldes, and to his surprise there was also Carlota. Montgomery took off his straw hat as he crossed the threshold.

The building was in a bad state of disrepair. Montgomery did the minimal upkeep on this place. Spiders had woven their nests in all the corners and there was dust upon every surface. Light filtered through holes in the wooden boards and hit the donkey's skull nailed to the wall at such an angle that it made it gleam. It almost looked like it was grinning.

The gentlemen looked more curious than afraid of the old hut and the bones hanging from the wall.

"Cachito, you have bitten the hand of Mr. Lizalde and for that you will be punished," Moreau said as he took off his jacket and handed it to Carlota. "Do not withhold discipline from a child; if you strike him with a rod, he will not die. If you strike him with the rod, you will save his soul from Sheol. Say it."

"If you strike him with the rod, you will save his soul from Sheol."

"Punishment is sharp and sure and you will feel it now. Kneel and pray."

Cachito did as he was told, kneeling like he did in the chapel during one of the doctor's services. When Moreau preached, Montgomery paid little attention. He looked away and yawned and did not listen. When Moreau punished one of the hybrids, Montgomery was not present. But now there was no choice but to watch.

First, the doctor did nothing. Cachito kept praying and the man let him. Then the doctor raised his arm and brought it down, hammering against Cachito's head with his great fist. Even in his old age the doctor was tall, strong, a creature of Herculean proportions. Cachito was scrawny and small.

The boy yelped, and the doctor hit him again. And again. Montgomery was suddenly reminded of his father and the way his fingers had closed around the collar of his shirt, pulling him close, his breath smelling sour, and then the fierce sting of his knuckles against his flesh.

Montgomery hadn't cried when his father beat him, he hadn't protested. He'd known well enough that a single tear or a panicked scream would have resulted in harsher blows. He had simply breathed.

Cachito seemed to be doing the same. He quivered, but aside from that first, startled yelp, he had not said anything else. He accepted the blows and the blows came again, harsher.

All fathers are tyrants, he thought.

Until that moment Moreau had limited himself to hitting Cachito with his hands, but now he snatched his cane from Carlota's grasp and raised it. Its silver tip shone bright.

Montgomery crushed the hat between his hands, bits of straw falling on the ground. But it wasn't he who spoke up.

"Papa, please!" the girl cried out.

Her voice was like a clap of thunder. It startled them all. Moreau wavered, the cane still held up, but his face was contorted with doubt. Eduardo cleared his throat and spoke up. "I think the point has been made."

"Yes," Moreau muttered. His face was flushed. "Yes, it's been made."

Moreau lowered the cane and took his jacket from Carlota. The men walked out together. Montgomery's fingers relaxed and he felt like chuckling. *I'm a damn coward*, he told himself.

Lupe was helping Cachito stand up. She heard Carlota say something about cleaning Cachito's wounds, and he followed the three of them into the house. Why he followed them, he had no idea. They did not need him. He could do nothing for them. He couldn't even raise his voice against Moreau. When it mattered, he was useless.

Carlota brought rubbing alcohol, cotton balls, and other small supplies into her room.

Cachito sat on the girl's bed, while Lupe hovered next to him. Montgomery stood by the doorway. He wanted to open another bottle of aguardiente, quick, and he almost felt like laughing and had to press a hand against his mouth.

God. He was a worthless shit.

"How are you feeling, Cachito?" Montgomery asked, his voice hoarse.

"How do you think he's feeling?" Lupe asked, practically hissing at him.

"It's fine," Cachito said. "I'm fine."

"I'm sorry," Carlota said, kneeling next to Cachito and touching his hands. "I'm so sorry."

"I know where Juan Cumux can be found," Lupe told Cachito. "We should head there, away from this place. They wouldn't dare look for us there."

Carlota let go of Cachito's hands and looked at Lupe. "What are you talking about? You can't head anywhere. You'd die out there. You're always making up silly stories——"

"You're the one with stories in her brain. All the junk you read in books."

"Stop, please," Montgomery said, shaking his head. "Both of you, don't start bickering now. The last thing we want is the doctor or those boys coming here."

They quieted down. Montgomery walked into the room, closer to the trio, and spoke in a low voice. "Moreau is cash strapped. He wants these men to continue financing Yaxaktun, but I don't trust them. We need to stand together, not tear each other apart."

"What if we do tear each other apart? We cannot keep living like this. Dr. Moreau holds us by our throats. Without his secret formula, without a way to medicate ourselves, we cannot go anywhere."

"Do you really wish to leave?" Carlota asked Lupe.

"Yes. How many ways must I say it?"

"I could ask my father for the formula. Perhaps he might give it to me. But that would mean . . ." the girl said, her voice faltering.

"He'd never do that," Lupe muttered bitterly.

"He might," Montgomery said. "Perhaps Carlota could convince him. But you won't get anywhere talking about Juan Cumux in their company."

Lupe frowned. Eventually she nodded. "We'll keep quiet. But you need to help us." Lupe looked at Montgomery, then at Carlota. "Both of you. Come on, Cachito, you should rest."

Cachito stood up, and he leaned on Lupe, walking slowly. Carlota began stuffing her supplies back into the black medical bag.

"I shouldn't have said that. I shouldn't be putting ideas in their head," she whispered.

"Sweetheart, they already have those ideas in their head and they've had them for a while. This cannot go on forever, and your damn father himself has indicated—"

"Do not insult him. My father is trying to save us," she said vehemently as she snapped the medical bag closed.

"Your father is trying to follow a desperate plan that will never work. He's trying to save himself."

She drew a harsh breath, and her hands rested atop the bag. "I suppose you want to leave us, too."

"I should have decamped long ago. Maybe I could lead Lupe and Cachito and the others somewhere safe."

"You think yourself Moses?"

Your father thinks himself God, he thought. But he didn't want to antagonize her further. Unthinkingly he had walked in close to Carlota and now stood but a couple of paces before her and she was looking up at him, her wide eyes filled with what were not tears but which might well be in a minute or two.

She stretched out a hand to touch his own, her thumb brushing the scar that began below his wrist, where the jaguar had mauled him, and a shiver ran straight down his spine.

"I don't want anything to change," she said.

"It's inevitable."

She lifted her hand and placed it atop the bag, her nails digging into the leather and her lips pressed tight. How he wished to coax that hand back upon his skin. Nothing more than that single touch; her fingers laced tight with his own would be bliss.

His left arm lay useless against his side, his hand gripping his hat. He grasped the hat with both hands and stepped back from her. *Damn coward*, he thought. *In every way possible you're a coward.*

Chapter 13

Carlota

HER FATHER SPENT the day with the Lizaldes, explaining his experiments or simply trying to soothe their fears or both, she did not know. But he did send word through Ramona that they were to have a grand dinner and the hybrids would wait on them. He wanted it to be a demonstration, to show his creations were trustworthy.

The preparations for such an event would normally have thrilled Carlota, but she was subdued. She went to the kitchen, thinking to assist with a few chores. Despite needing the work, she was distracted, and Ramona chided her.

"Carlota, you're adding the sugar too quickly. The meringue won't fluff," the woman said. Her father loved meringues, even though they made them differently in France. She'd thought to whip up a treat and was failing.

"Sorry," Carlota muttered.

"Girl, what's wrong?" Ramona asked, tilting Carlota's chin up.

Carlota did not know what to say. *Everything* seemed wrong. Her stomach was aching and she wanted to speak to her father, but he was busy. And though perhaps it might have helped if she talked to Ramona and Lupe, laying clear her murky worries, she could not think what to say.

"Her mind's on that young mister," Lupe said.

"It's not," Carlota replied quickly.

"What else would you think about except yourself and your suitors? Not about us, you wouldn't. You haven't asked how Cachito is doing today. He spent the night in pain, you know? We could all hear him."

"I didn't hit him."

"No, your father did. For the sake of those clowns you are trying to impress."

Lupe stared at her, and Carlota looked away. There was the taste of bile in her mouth. She winced.

Ramona shook her head. "Carlota, you should ready yourself. Your father wants you to look nice."

Carlota nodded. She went to her room and splashed water on her face. Then she ran her hands over the dresses hanging in the great armoire. There was one that she'd seldom worn and which her father had bought her the previous year. All her dresses were made by a seamstress in Mérida who had been provided with her measurements. Montgomery hauled the garments back to Yaxaktun along with supplies and items they needed for the household.

This gown in particular was something of a folly, the most ostentatious thing she owned. It was an evening dress, suitable for a party, but she did not attend parties. She'd seen something like it in a lady's magazine and begged her father for it. It had a white skirt with pleated flounces of gauze and was trimmed all around with lace and swathed with an overskirt of blue satin. The décolleté bodice bared her shoulders daringly.

She worked slowly on her hair. When she looked in the mirror she felt as though there was an invisible crack in it, perhaps in her. That crack was slowly growing day after day, threatening to obliterate Carlota.

Twice she dropped the pins she was holding in one hand and had to take deep breaths before proceeding with the careful coiffing of her hair.

Eventually she marched into the dining room in the deep blue dress with its lovely accents of yellow. The tablecloth had been set, and upon it the silver candelabra glittered and the candles burned softly. Ramona or someone else had taken the trouble of cutting flowers and dropping them into a large crystal bowl filled with water. They would all fade by morning in the jungle's heat, but for now they retained their lush colors.

"My dear, you look lovely," her father said as she walked in, and then he leaned in closer to her, his voice low. "Be on your best behavior, we must charm them."

Carlota nodded and smiled at the guests. The dinner party consisted of her father, Eduardo and Isidro, and, surprisingly, Montgomery. She supposed her father was trying to make a point by having him sit with them after the brawl. As for the food, it was not the dishes that caught the attention of their guests, but the appearance of those serving them. Lupe, Aj Kaab, Parda, and La Pinta took turns bringing in plates laden with meat or filling glasses with Burgundy wine. Lupe acted as if Carlota were not there, her head held high, and again Carlota had that feeling that something in her was broken and jagged.

"It's remarkable the variety of shapes and looks that your hybrids take," Eduardo said. "I cannot tell at times what specific animal they derive from. One looks like a type of cat, another like an odd wolf."

La Pinta brushed crumbs off the corner of the table as Eduardo spoke, and Parda carefully set down a plate before her. Carlota thanked her in a whisper.

"As Mr. Darwin would point out, we are presented with endless forms most beautiful," her father said. "Though I must admit mammals are the most adequate for my work. My experiments with reptiles were disappointing.

"But what I want you to do, gentlemen, is to consider the other possibilities I mentioned to you earlier. There are many medical miracles we could accomplish. My daughter, for example, would not be sitting with us today if it were not for the treatment I have developed for her. She'd be an invalid, confined to her rooms. But it is not about Carlota, that is not the sole possibility, no sir. A cure for blindness or the ability to give speech to those who are mute may be within our grasp one day."

She watched a stray moth, which had managed to infiltrate the house, fly across the room and settle on the wall, like a small, quivering brown stain. When a dragonfly entered the home, it meant a visitor would be arriving soon. When a moth came in it could be a good or bad omen. If it was black it meant death. But the brown moth meant nothing.

"That is all well and good, but I don't think my uncle is looking for a cure for blindness, is he?" Isidro asked. "He is paying you to give him workers. Yet the ones you have here must be terribly expensive. How much money has he thrown into this venture?"

"Research always has a price," her father said dryly.

"I can see that. You don't exactly live a life without luxuries," Isidro replied, and he threw Carlota such a look that she imagined he must be trying to determine how many yards of satin had gone into the making of her dress. "The Indians in the eastern lands are spoiled. They must be punished, prudently, of course, or else they march around like heedless children. But can you guarantee your hybrids are any better? After all, I can attest to their temper."

With those words Isidro held up his bandaged hand as proudly as a man might display a trophy.

"Cachito was scared," Carlota said; her eyes were lowered and her voice was soft. So far she had maintained herself out of their discussion, mindful of her father and afraid she might make a mistake. "If someone you loved was in danger, you'd defend them."

"But then, you think that creature *loves* Mr. Laughton?" Isidro asked, incredulous.

"Cachito is sweet. If you knew him better, you'd see—"

"I see you have a tender heart. People take advantage of those with tender hearts. At our haciendas, if we let them, the Indians would work one day and rest for five. You don't have to take it from me, either, ask the local priest and he'll tell you."

"Yes. The priests claim their tariff, too," Montgomery said. "And I wouldn't trust them in these matters. I've seen them demand money to baptize a child that would soon die, and the parents selling anything they had to ensure their child would go to heaven. Does that sound right to you?"

"Are you an atheist, sir?"

"We are pious in this house," her father said. "Mr. Laughton attends our services each week. My daughter knows the Bible by heart."

"That is good. You are distant from civilization and close to those pagan wretches infecting the peninsula. I'd hate to think you'd absorbed their superstitions and turned your face away from God. Faith, Miss Moreau. One must have faith. That is what the Indians here lack. That is their flaw," Isidro said with a satisfied smile and a tone of finality.

Carlota smoothed a lock of hair, brushing it behind her ear. "We must have love for one another, sir."

Her voice was as muted as the colors of the moth on the wall, but nevertheless it reached Isidro's ear, for they were seated next to each other. "What?" he asked, looking surprised.

"And now these three remain: faith, hope, and love. But the greatest of these is love," she said, louder, more forceful.

"I don't see how love has any bearing in this discussion."

"Christ instructed us to love one another. If the macehuales lack faith, perhaps you lack love."

Isidro scoffed. She thought to explain herself better, but her father threw Carlota a look that clearly indicated she should mind her mouth. Montgomery, sitting across from her, was smirking, and Eduardo seemed surprised. Had she said something awful? She didn't think so. Yet Isidro's voice had turned icy.

"You simply cannot understand our situation. It might be best for us to get those Chinese workers people keep talking about. I've thought it an extravagant expense, but if my uncle is going to throw money to the wind at least they won't be biting me. Or else we can stick with the Indians. Love or not," Isidro concluded mordantly.

"I think a few of *them* would like to take a bite out of us," Eduardo said. "Some of the stories my father tells about the uprising of '47 would make any man's blood run cold."

The moth burst into flight and collided with one of the candles. It lay singed upon the tablecloth, by her hand. Carlota stretched her finger to touch its wing, but La Pinta came silently from behind her and brushed the insect away, then circled the table and refilled her father's glass.

"It was the execution of Manuel Antonio Ay which started the revolt," Montgomery pointed out, wiping his mouth and tossing his napkin carelessly by his plate.

"Yes? And?" Eduardo replied tersely. "Are you implying that somehow that made it fair for them to murder all those women and children in Tepich?"

"War is seldom fair for any party involved."

"You forget Mr. Laughton is English," Isidro said. "What is fair is what is best for the crown."

"Good point. I am curious, Mr. Laughton, being a citizen of the British crown as you are, do you favor the creation of an independent Mayan state? Of course 'independent' is not quite the right word, since I'm sure the British would oversee it in one way or another."

"Surely we are not going to launch into a needless dialogue on politics," her father said. As if in response, Montgomery reached into his jacket's pocket and took out a cigarette and a tiny matchbox.

It was the custom that when a man smoked he must offer his cigarettes to the others around him, but Montgomery made no such gesture even though it might give offense. Yet the others did not notice this, or perhaps they ignored him.

"You think politics is needless?" Isidro asked.

"I am a scientist. The study of Nature compels me. I proceed not heeding anything but the question I am pursuing. The research is the important part," her father said proudly. "The actual medical research. The cures—"

"Oh, yes. For blindness," Isidro said dismissively.

Though Carlota did not really like Isidro, she derived a little pleasure in seeing how neatly he cut off her father. No one ever spoke back to him at Yaxaktun. He was godlike. Yet in the company of other men he now didn't seem as great and massive as he always did. His treatment of Cachito dismayed her. It was cruel of the doctor to force them into this performance, to demand that they be merry even though Cachito must be writhing in pain.

He's a bad father, she told herself.

Almost immediately she felt guilty for having such an uncharitable thought. Again she sensed there was a crack inside her flesh, steadily growing, and she recalled how Montgomery had told her all things must change. She looked in his direction wondering what he was thinking, but his face was a sardonic mask.

Montgomery had lit a match and was pressing it against the tip of his cigarette, his eyes flickering up to look at her as he blew the match out.

Her hands fluttered against the smooth satin of her dress, sliding down her stomach until she caught them in her lap.

"Well, I think Dr. Moreau's research is interesting, even if the applications might not be practical yet," Eduardo said. "After all, as he's explained, if it were not for his work in the biological sciences his daughter wouldn't be whole and healthy and dining here with us. I think that would be a shame. You are a vision of loveliness, Miss Moreau."

She smiled at that, glad that someone seemed to be pleased with her presence at the table. Isidro certainly didn't look too thrilled to converse with her. Across from her, Montgomery leaned back on his chair and smirked for the quickest of seconds.

"Thank you," she said, blushing.

"Really, we shouldn't be talking about workers and their issues," Eduardo said. "It's a bore, and Miss Moreau shouldn't think us boring."

"Just like that he'll have us talking about horses for the rest of the evening," Isidro said with a roll of his eyes.

The conversation went on, the phrases spoken were airy and easy, and nothing of substance was touched upon. After dinner Isidro declared he was tired and would retire to his room. Carlota's father sat on a bench in the courtyard, and Montgomery stood leaning against the wall, arms crossed. Eduardo and Carlota walked together around the courtyard.

She felt odd, being watched by two pairs of eyes, and odder still to be walking with Eduardo. She thought it was as if the men were observing the courtship ritual of a colorful bird. She was there to provide a spectacle.

"You've been quiet today," Eduardo said. "I am worried I've displeased you."

"Here I was thinking the same."

"But how could you when you are enchanting?"

"Your cousin does not seem to like me," she whispered.

"He's upset. His hand aches."

"I am truly sorry. But you must believe me when I said Cachito is a kind boy. We've grown up together."

"You've grown up with those fearsome creatures?" Eduardo asked.

How strange to hear Eduardo referring to them as "fearsome creatures" when she thought of them as her friends. Aj Kaab had lifted her in the air, making her squeal with delight when she was a little girl; she had played hide-and-seek with Cachito and Lupe, and she'd taught the others the rhymes she read in books. Their prognathous jaws, strangely placed eyes, and malformed hands inspired in her no surprise.

However, she supposed it was not unexpected that Eduardo would regard the hybrids as fearsome. Montgomery himself had been flabbergasted by their appearance in the beginning, and yet now he joked and merrily worked with them. "You don't know them, but if you did, you'd see they are not to be feared," she said.

"That wolf thing has teeth that could tear through a man's neck in seconds. That doesn't bother you?"

Parda did have big teeth, they protruded from her snout, and her eyes were small and sharp, but she gnawed at her fur when it itched; she did not bite anyone else.

Carlota shook her head. "No. What's more, I couldn't ever imagine being parted from them."

"At some point they'll be sent to Vista Hermosa or another hacienda."

"Why?"

"They are to be workers, are they not?"

She knew that her father made the hybrids to please Hernando Lizalde and that ultimately he'd want them in his haciendas, yet she never thought they'd abandon the confines of Yaxaktun. Her father's research was not where it needed to be to allow that, and besides, she had lulled herself into a sense of safety.

"And you will also have to abandon Yaxaktun," Eduardo added.

"Why would I?" she asked, alarmed.

"What about the great cities of the world? Do you not wish to see them and explore distant shores? I could not wait to leave Mérida."

"You wanted to leave your father?"

"If you knew my father, you wouldn't want to be near him," Eduardo said sourly.

"Does he treat you poorly?"

"He's . . . Everything must be done his way. He dictates the steps of the dance and we must all follow. Surely you do not always wish to do what your father says."

"A daughter must be obedient," she answered quickly. But it was the force of habit that made her string the words together and she frowned, chafing at the thought of the blind deference that ordinarily came easily to her. "But I must admit, I'd also like to have my say sometimes."

"In what ways?"

"I want to care for my father, for the hybrids, for this place. I love my home, but it is . . . Sometimes my father dictates too many steps, like yours," she explained, looking up at him.

His fingers brushed her knuckles. "You are wasted here."

"How so?"

"If you were in Mérida, you'd be invited to a multitude of parties."

She knew of Mérida, of course. She knew about its great houses with their colonnaded porticos, the curving iron gates, the calesas drawn by beautiful horses, the alameda shaded by rows of trees where one might promenade when the day's heat gave way to the cool of the evening. But what of it? The cool of the evening also soothed her in Yaxaktun, in the inner courtyard with the potted plants.

"Mexico City is grander, of course. I enjoyed studying there. We have a house in the capital, obviously, and though I have not managed to visit Paris I expect to do so within a year or two. Surely you must want to see Paris? Your father is, after all, a Frenchman."

"I like it when my father talks about Paris, because I want to learn about it. I also like it when Mr. Laughton tells me of England or the islands he's seen. But I don't think there'd be anything I'd love in Paris," she said as she sat down at the edge of the fountain and dipped her fingers in the water.

"I must admit I'm puzzled. Every young woman I've ever met would want to be seen and admired by the greatest number of people possible."

Carlota shook her head demurely. "I feel as if Yaxaktun is a beautiful dream and I wish to dream it forever."

"But in the tale of the Sleeping Beauty the prince kisses the princess awake," Eduardo said, sitting close to her, his hand falling upon her own.

How easily he could raise a blush on her cheeks. Through the corner of her eye she could see her father had departed, but Montgomery remained rooted to his spot, his cigarette shining like a firefly in the dusk. "Mr. Laughton is watching us," she whispered.

Eduardo nodded. "He's a hawk. I'm tired of fathers and chaperones. Come."

He stood up, and she followed him. The bougainvillea trees that grew in the courtyard were bursting with color, extending upon walls and offering clusters of splendid magenta blossoms to the sky. Eduardo maneuvered her toward one of those patches of wild blooms, quickly tucking her in the shadow of the flowers. She realized that, wrapped in this perfumed darkness, they could not be seen from the angle where Montgomery stood.

Before she could elicit a question from Eduardo, he pressed her against the wall and pressed his lips over her own. Her mouth opened to him, and she felt his arms twine around her waist, the boldness of his embrace making her resent her unskilled response, for she didn't want to be thought an utter fool who knew nothing. But she didn't really know anything, shyness warring with the desire to press back, to kiss him hard on the mouth.

Ladies should be meek, she thought, yet she raised one hand to grasp the lapel of his coat, and she placed the other around his neck, to pull him as close as close could be so that they would not be seen.

She thought her heart might burst at the feel of him, and when he rested his chin against the top of her head she was certain everyone at Yaxaktun must have heard it, beating like a drum. But she still tipped her head up and initiated another kiss, which elicited a laugh from him.

"Aren't you bold?"

"I'm not," she whispered. She really wasn't, and she knew if Ramona or Montgomery saw them, they'd chide her, and this fear made her want to run away from him. But he was lovely, and she liked the way his body molded against her own, so she remained still.

"What might I give you that would please you?" he asked.

"Please me?"

"A gift, a trinket," he said, his voice low, laced with a delicious ferocity that made her shiver. "Ask for anything."

She thought the proper response might be to ask for flowers or bonbons, but she required neither. Her fingers brushed against the brass buttons of his jacket, and all she could say was the truth, the one thing she desired.

"Would you . . . if it was yours to give . . . would you ever give me Yaxaktun?"

"You are indeed bold," he said.

He didn't sound displeased, but she blushed. He kissed her quickly on the mouth before pulling away. Back again in the open they slowly walked around the courtyard, her hand resting on his arm. Montgomery was still standing where he'd been, smoking his cigarette, and on the ground there were the discarded ends of matches and a smoldering cigarette stub. When they walked by him he stomped on the stub and raised his eyes at them with such mockery that she was sure he'd seen them kissing after all and he'd scold them for it. But all he did was nod.

She hurried past him and back to her room. A little while later, Ramona came to help her out of her dress. The rustle of satin was loud against her sensitive ears, and she winced.

"Are you unwell?" Ramona asked.

"I'm tired," Carlota said, sitting down. "And my nerves . . . I'm dreadfully nervous."

Ramona took the pins from her hair. "Nervous about these menfolk? They're only men, Loti."

But they aren't, she thought and peered into the glass, watching as Ramona placed the pins in a cup.

"Montgomery doesn't like them," she said.

"Mr. Laughton doesn't like anyone. He's sick, needs a healer who can listen to his blood."

"He's not sick."

"Of course he is. Your papa can cure various sickness, but he doesn't know about all illnesses. Mr. Laughton lost his soul. It flew away and it's trapped somewhere. I told him once, go see a healer, wash away that sickness." Ramona shrugged. "It doesn't matter what Mr. Laughton thinks of anyone."

"It matters what my father thinks," Carlota muttered and turned her head. "Did a matchmaker arrange your marriage?"

Ramona nodded. "They consulted the stars and I had a fine necklace for my mujul. But it was not a good match."

"I have no mujul," she whispered, remembering what her father had said. That nothing in this house truly belonged to them. Not that Eduardo would have asked for a bride price, but she remembered the extent of her circumstances. "And how can you know whether the match will be good or bad?"

"You can't," Ramona said. "It is what it is. We all have a path to travel and a fate written in the book of days."

But what, Carlota wondered, was her path?

CHAPTER 14

Montgomery

THEY VENTURED BY the edge of the water, to the place where the mangrove trees knotted themselves together like slick snakes. They were supposedly there to check on the skiff that was at the landing. It was their fastest method of transportation and their key to the outside world when they required supplies. They had to check on it periodically and also tend to the path that allowed access to the landing in the first place.

But it wasn't necessary for them to sit down and dip their feet in the water, nor did they need to dawdle. Yet they did, because Montgomery was trying to keep Cachito out of sight and away from their guests. Cachito's right eye was swollen from the beating Moreau had given him. Montgomery didn't want them taking offense against him a second time.

"How's that feeling?" he asked, pointing at the eye.

"It's better, I guess. How's the cut on your forehead?"

"It won't spoil my looks."

Montgomery retrieved his battered cigarette case from his pocket and offered one to Cachito, who declined with a twist of his head. Not far from them, two snowy ibises stood by the shore, contrasting with the green of the trees behind them. Slowly, very slowly, one of them turned an inch and looked in their direction.

"He never hit me before. Melquíades hit me, and one time I bit him and he hit me even more, but the doctor never did. I always thought he was *better*. He talks about obedience and he talks about meekness and he says he loves us and then he . . . then he—"

"Then he's a hypocrite?" Montgomery replied. "I was in a village once where the priest preached fire and brimstone. He asked the young women to help him clean up the church after mass. And wouldn't you know it, for all his preaching those girls ended with bastards in their bellies who looked a lot like that priest."

He'd heard worse, too. He'd heard and seen a veritable litany of horrors. That was the world. Satan made it, he had thought when he was younger and on his way to becoming a budding heretic. Now he simply thought that it was the work of a cruel and wicked god.

"In the newspaper, sometimes, I've read ads from hacendados. They write that a worker has run away and they are giving a reward for whoever brings him back," Cachito said. "But they're not able to find all of them. Some hide away and they become bandits, or they slip away somewhere safe. If they can, who is to say we couldn't get away?"

Montgomery nodded, but he didn't want to offer a full answer. What could he say? If Cachito ran off he'd be dead within a few days without his medication, and if he made it longer perhaps Hernando Lizalde might send a bounty hunter after him. That's what they did with the laborers who dared to abandon their haciendas. Then the fee incurred on the bounty hunter was added to the debts the laborer owed the hacendado. This was also why Montgomery remained at his post. He owed money, and Lizalde might collect with blood if he dared to run off.

"Was it the same in Cuba?"

"People running away? They have indentured laborers there, too. They've been shipping Chinese people to work on the plantations for decades. They call it the yellow trade. Eight years, that's what Chinese people sign up for. Now they're sending rebel Maya Indians to the island. Instead of being dragged to jail you get put on a ship and dragged to Cuba. It's all the same," he said, waving his cigarette in the air. "Everyone is damned, and if they ban the trade of Indians, they'll find a way to circumvent it. The slave trade supposedly ceased sixty years ago, but they found ways around the laws."

"The rebels fight back. I always thought you were brave for fighting a jaguar, Montgomery. But I don't think you're so brave after all. You don't fight for anything. You just want to die," Cachito said gravely.

Montgomery shook his head and took a long drag from his cigarette. He didn't bother denying it. Yes, he was dead and dying, a fish flopping around and gasping for air, and for some damn reason the universe hadn't seen fit to completely cut off his supply of oxygen. That cruel, unflinching god enjoyed his suffering. Perhaps it feasted on it. That might be the ultimate face of god: the face of implacable horror.

The white ibises were flying away, and Cachito spoke again.

"Lupe said she saw Juan Cumux one time. It was near the cenote."

"How did she know it was him?"

"She knew. He didn't have his men, it was him alone. She says he's old, but not like Moreau. Moreau is old like he's made of stone, but Cumux is old like the mangrove. He stands against the storm."

He placed a hand on the boy's shoulder. "You'll be fine. Don't be afraid, Cachito."

"I'm not afraid," the boy said sharply.

Montgomery thought to tell him that there was nothing wrong with being afraid, that he'd been afraid many times in his life. That when his father beat him he closed his eyes and prayed he might fly away. But it was no use because he knew by the hardness of his stare such words would offend Cachito even more. So he let it be, and Cachito stretched out his hand and Montgomery gave him the cigarette.

He felt terribly old as they walked back together, and by the time he stopped in front of the doorway to the library he was exhausted. Then he saw Carlota, curled on the only couch in the room. She held a book in one hand and a fan with the other. She was biting her lower lip, deep in thought. It must be one of those books she liked about a pirate or a filibuster, soaked with heady adventure and romance.

"Where is Eduardo?" he asked.

The day before she'd been around and around the courtyard with him. Montgomery had expected the young man to stick by her side, like a barnacle. It was a rare pleasure to find her like this, alone, and for a moment he wished he hadn't spoken up and simply admired her from afar. She'd looked peaceful.

Carlota marked the page of her book with a ribbon before looking up at him. Behind her were tall bookcases crammed with many volumes, but the library was threadbare compared to the sitting room, with an old desk in a corner to serve as ornament.

"He's taking a nap. Where were you? My father was looking for you."

"Out for a walk with Cachito. Was it anything important?"

"I'm sure he'll find you if it's urgent."

"Well, fine. I wanted to talk to you, anyway."

"About?"

She sat up properly, indicating the couch with a movement of her fan and making space for him, should he wish to sit next to her. He did.

"I suppose you haven't talked to your father about the hybrids."

"You mean if I've asked him about the formula."

"That's right."

"I haven't had the chance."

"No, of course you wouldn't," he muttered. "Not with the young master around to distract you."

"What is that supposed to mean?" she asked sharply. "What do you want from me?"

"Nothing. I was thinking about you and Eduardo, but it's not for me to meddle with."

"That isn't 'nothing.' Speak up, sir."

"I said it's nothing."

"You will answer me," she said and slapped him on the arm with the fan.

When she was with Eduardo, she brandished the painted fan like the weapon of a coquette; it quivered in her hands in salutation, its movement punctuated her laughter. But with Montgomery, the fan was used to administer a punishment. And she had such a petulant look on her face, her chin up and airy, that he could not contain himself even though he knew, by the blush on her cheeks, that she was embarrassed and that was why she had reacted in such a way.

"Rather than doing something useful you're wasting your time with that Eduardo. No wonder you don't talk to your father, all your words are spent on someone else, that's what I think," he said bitterly and when she stared at him, wide-eyed, he pressed on, wanting to provoke her into further anger. "Or are you scared of the doctor? Is that why you won't talk to him?"

"*You* could talk to my father, Montgomery, if you wish it," she said.

"But I wasn't the one who said I would. You promised Cachito and Lupe you'd assist them. Fine, then. If you'll be a coward, then I'll stick my neck out."

"You have no right to call me a coward. You're as cruel as Lupe!"

Incensed, she threatened to slap him again with the closed fan, but he caught it and her hand. When he felt that hand beneath his and the quivering pulse under his fingertips he also felt the bitterness bleeding out.

"Carlota, I don't know what Lupe has told you, but I didn't say it to be cruel. It's just that Eduardo is no good for you," he explained, softening his tone.

"Have you any other suitors you'd present to me?"

"No. But there will come someone worthier. Another boy."

"My father would have me . . . What's wrong with him?" she asked, and she'd softened, too, and had not drawn her hand away. Instead she looked at him curiously.

"I know his type. It's the type of man who only takes. I don't think he'd love you properly, and you, Carlota . . . well, I know you. You share my same malady."

"A malady?" she asked, now more curious than irritated.

"Yes, of the heart. You are in love with love, Carlota," he said, gripping her hand tighter. "With the mere idea of it, I see it on your face. You yearn for *everything* and you are about to tumble into an abyss. Some people, they give a fraction of themselves, but there are others who give themselves completely. And you will. You'll give yourself utterly. I've been where you've been. I've been young and I chose badly and it broke me."

He thought of pretty Fanny Owen and the brief moments of his happiness that were obliterated by pain and sorrow. It was something that was impossible to explain. Most people would find it ridiculous that one could be so harmed by a single person. But he'd always been a romantic, and maybe he'd also been lonesome and scarred and he'd wanted to be saved, even back then. And Fanny had been the scent of a green forest and spring and hope, until it all wilted into nothing.

"I don't want the same to happen to you," he said, and he slid his hand away.

It was all true, too. He knew well she'd find a young boy to care about one day, and he'd never begrudge her that. But to end up in the arms of Eduardo Lizalde struck him as almost obscene. Why not another man? Any man. He'd happily dance at her wedding as long as the groom was not that tiresome toad.

Carlota frowned, as if thinking it through carefully. "But he might give me Yaxaktun," she said. "Otherwise what would we do for money?"

"A woman shouldn't marry solely for money," he said, and now he thought of his poor sister and her terrible, early death. He understood what a bad marriage did to a woman.

If he could go back! But he'd lost Elizabeth. He'd lost everything. Now he felt as though Carlota might face a similar, terrible end, and he could not allow that to happen, no matter how much Moreau salivated after the Lizalde fortune. He must speak up. But she didn't seem to be listening.

"Easy enough for you to say," she told him, shaking her head. "If Mr. Lizalde takes away this place from us you can work somewhere else. You can return to British Honduras, to Cuba or even England. But what would we do? What would *I* do?"

Then come with me, he thought suddenly. She might not have romantic notions about him, but he could whisk her away if she wished it, and if she liked him, even a little, then that would be enough for him. It was a foolish idea, and yet he thought to utter it. But then she spoke, quick, nervous.

"This house . . . this life . . . the trees and the hybrids and oh, even things like this book and my fan," she said, almost pleadingly. "What would I do without them?"

"Yes, I suppose it would be difficult to purchase fans with ivory handles if Mr. Lizalde stopped paying your bills," he replied, angrily. He was about to idiotically bare himself to her, and she was thinking about her fan.

"You are horrid."

"I am. And I should probably leave," he said, making a motion as if to stand.

But she caught his arm and pulled him down. "You judge me unkindly, but you give me no options. I don't understand what I've ever done to deserve this treatment."

"Let go, Loti," he said tiredly.

She did. He stood up, took a few leisurely steps, and she stood up, too, clutching her book between her hands. "I hate you! You're awful!" she yelled and tossed the book in his direction. It hit the wall.

Montgomery turned around. She stood in the middle of the library and was pressing a hand against her stomach, looking down.

"You might want to control yourself. If you destroy that book, I have no doubt it'll be discounted from my wages, which I already lack, seeing as I'm being punished," he said, and he expected her to throw her fan at him next.

But she was standing there, not looking at him. Her hands trembled.

"Carlota?" he asked, moving closer to her.

She didn't look well. Suddenly, she stumbled into his arms and held on to him, trying to regain her balance. "I can't breathe," she said. Her eyes, they seemed to gleam, they looked so yellow. Not amber, but gold.

The doctor had told him that when Carlota was younger she often had terrible fits and she spent most of her days in bed, sick and weak. But although Montgomery knew Carlota sometimes had to rest and that when she became agitated she might feel light-headed, she'd never had an attack he could remember. That was what her medication was for. It kept her safe.

"Montgomery," she whispered. Her voice was at the edge of breaking, and she was digging her nails into his arm with such force it made him wince.

"Give me a minute, sweetheart," he said, taking her in his arms like one might swoop up a bride at the threshold because she was about to collapse. "We'll get your father. It'll be a minute. For God's sake, only a minute."

CHAPTER 15

Carlota

AT FIRST SHE heard nothing. It was only the pressure of Montgomery's arms around her, lifting Carlota, holding her. She could perceive his heart beating and the blood drifting through his veins. She didn't hear the heart thumping, it was a vibration; a noiseless drum. Her chin was pressed against his shoulder blade and she could smell him. There was the soap he used to wash his face each morning, the laundered shirt that had been hung to dry the previous day, the scent of his sweat, and his body beneath all that.

He muttered something; she did not know what it was. Her head was a flash of red and yellow.

Then came her father's voice, loud and clear, the tinkle of metal and glass, and the pillow beneath her head. Montgomery had stepped away. She couldn't feel his pulse anymore. But he was still there, somewhere in the room. She could hear his heart. She almost wanted to ask him why it was so loud.

"Pass me that flask."

The syringe bit into her arm, and there was the pressure of her father's hand against her own. Distantly she heard the cry of a bird. She wondered if she might catch it if she was quick.

She turned her head. On the shelf sat her old dolls, staring back at her with glass eyes. She felt as if she were going back in time, to a childhood that was a cloud of sickness and pain, now half forgotten.

Then there came the cold compress against her forehead, and she breathed in. The minutes passed. When she opened her eyes, her father was still sitting by the bed.

"Papa," she said.

"There you are," her father said, and he squeezed her hand. "Have a sip of water."

He grabbed a pitcher and filled a glass. Carlota sat up and obediently drank the water. Her hands trembled, but she spilled only a couple of drops. She handed him back the glass.

"Daughter, you gave me a bit of a fright."

"I'm sorry, papa. I don't know what happened."

"We've talked about this. I've told you to be calm and avoid excitement. It's simply the medication. It needs to be adjusted."

"I lost my temper. I threw a book," she muttered.

"Why? What agitated you?"

"I was arguing with Montgomery. But I haven't had a relapse in years, papa. I don't even remember what it was like being sick," she said, and she really didn't. That cloud of pain was terribly distant, and her clearest memories were of her father at her side, comforting her, lifting her from her suffering.

But her body seemed to remember. Her body resonated with an ancient ache, as if there were scars beneath her skin, unseen, which now rose, like mushrooms after the rain.

"Perhaps you'll learn your lesson and quarrel less with him. You are no longer a child to be throwing tantrums."

"I know," she whispered, and she recalled her fight and all the things Montgomery had said. He was awful! But he was right about one thing: she had not asked her father about the hybrids, even though she'd promised them she would.

"What do you think would have happened if our guests had witnessed this episode? Or if they had seen you throwing books at Laughton and fighting like a madwoman? Their opinion of you would be greatly diminished."

"It was the two of us in the library."

"Carlota, you know better. It's not becoming."

"I understand."

"Fortunately for you Laughton got you to me quick. You'll recover soon enough. Nevertheless, you need to sleep. The medication must do its work, and it can't if you're running around the house," her father said, standing up, looking weary and perhaps eager to leave her side.

Carlota wished to close her eyes and sleep without another word. But it still rankled her, what Montgomery had said. Yes, that damnable man was right: she was a coward and she'd given her word. "Papa, I'd like to know the formula for my medication," she said quickly, before her father had a chance to make his escape, before her courage deserted her.

Her father frowned. "Why are you asking for that?"

"Because . . . I suppose it would make me feel safer. And I'd like the formula for the medication the hybrids take, too."

"Don't you feel safe with me?"

"I do, but we are all dependent on you, and you've said yourself that I'm no longer a child. If I am to marry and leave Yaxaktun, how can I manage my affairs if I cannot even ensure my health? Will you come visit me every time I should have an attack?"

Her father's mouth twitched ever so slightly. "You should not have an attack if you follow the rules I've set down. To go to bed at the same time each night and sleep soundly, to pray and read your Bible for comfort, to be gentle and serene and avoid exerting yourself physically."

"But one cannot be gentle perpetually," she said, her voice wavering.

"These are complicated medical matters."

"You've said yourself I'm smart. And I've been helping you in the laboratory for these past few years. I could learn, I'm sure of it."

"Not that smart," her father said. He hadn't raised his voice, but he was angry, his words were frost. "You and Laughton may be able to assist me with a small task here and there, but it is not the same as being a trained physician."

"Papa—"

"No more of this. I need you to rest. Will you be a good girl?"

She lowered her eyes and nodded. Her voice was mild, delicate as the lace of her dress. "Yes, papa."

"Blessed are the meek: for they shall inherit the earth. Say it."

"Blessed are the meek."

"Take a nap and you'll soon feel better," he said and kissed her forehead before departing.

But she couldn't rest because the paradox remained in her mind: that she must be a child to her father and also a grown woman. He wouldn't let her grow, and yet he expected her to behave like a sophisticated, mature person.

Moreau's daughter was forever supposed to remain a girl, like the dolls that watched her intently. But she was restless; she felt as if she'd overgrown her skin and must molt.

She lay in bed and closed her eyes but did not sleep.

Later, Lupe stopped by bearing a tray, a pot of tea and a cup, and a slice of bread with honey. The sun was setting, and the day's burdensome heat had given way to the cooler comfort of the evening. The hour made her want to stretch languidly and stare at the stars.

"Montgomery thought tea might do you good. I think a cup of chocolate is better. But you know him, he can't stand chocolate," Lupe said, making a face. "British men. Tea, tea, tea."

"That's thoughtful of him, I suppose."

"He's feeling remorseful, I can tell. The two of you quarreled?"

Carlota nodded. The tea was chamomile. She poured herself a cup and grabbed the silver tongs, picking a sugar cube. Lupe lit two candles and placed them on the large table on the other side of the room. Above it rested her mirror, her hairbrush, and the wooden boxes containing necklaces, bracelets, and a rosary.

"What did you fight about this time?"

Carlota couldn't tell her that Montgomery had called her a coward. She certainly didn't want to repeat Montgomery's talk about yearning. It almost made her head spin when she remembered the way he'd spoken. *In love with love.* Did he think her that foolish? And was he right? From what she knew, he'd loved but once. That wife of his who'd abandoned him long ago. If so, what wisdom could he offer her? Perhaps little, perhaps nothing.

Wasn't Eduardo pretty? And pretty wasn't everything, but it had been nice when he kissed her, and he was a great gentleman. Her father said so.

In love with love.

"We talked about this and that," Carlota said, stirring the tea.

"Someone's being evasive."

"I'm not. It was several things, and I'm not sure he'd like me repeating our whole conversation."

Lupe did not seem convinced. She went around the room, with the pretense of arranging a few things. She picked up a white shawl Carlota had left on a chair, placed a book back on its shelf. Carlota sipped her tea. It was too hot and scalded her tongue. She set the cup down.

"I asked my father about the formula. He wouldn't share it with me," she said as she resumed stirring her cup.

"I'd be surprised if he had given it to you."

"I can still obtain it."

"How?"

Carlota took a deep breath. It scared her to say it, but she did. "From his notebooks in the lab."

"Would you be able to do anything with that?"

"I don't know. My understanding of his work is rudimentary. But I should try, should I not?" she asked, disliking how shrill her voice sounded, how much it resembled pleading.

Lupe was still fluttering around the room. Finally, she returned to Carlota's bedside and took the chair her father had been occupying earlier.

"I'll tell you something, but you must keep it a secret. Will you?" Lupe asked, in the same tone she used when they were little and there was talk of some small mischief they might commit, like gorging on sweets.

"Yes, of course."

"There is a path nearby that goes straight to Juan Cumux's camp. It is well hidden, no one can tell it's there. But if you know the signs you can find it."

"He lives there? Juan Cumux?"

"If not him, one of his trusted men. Carlota, if Cachito and I and the others were to head there, they wouldn't be able to catch us. We could go far after that. We could go southeast, to the lands that are controlled by the rebels. We'd be safe there."

"But would they be friendly to you?"

"I think so. You could come. Why, Montgomery could come if he wants to. He might be able to help us get around. We could head into British Honduras. There're precipices and creeks and places to hide. I've read so, in the newspapers, and Montgomery has said as much, too."

Lupe looked so happy it made Carlota's heart hurt. She wondered if she could do what she had promised. Not only to discover the formula, but to then be able to reproduce it. Furthermore, to somehow assist the hybrids in their flight. It would be a betrayal of her father. Carlota might bicker with Montgomery or flounce off when Lupe irritated her, but she did not talk back to the doctor. She did his will. They all did.

"What if you could remain safely in Yaxaktun?" Carlota asked.

"How? The Lizaldes don't care about us. You heard them at that dinner. Talking about money, about how expensive Yaxaktun is and how little profit they can see coming from it. If they close this place down, what do you imagine they'll do to us?"

She thought of Eduardo's green eyes and how he'd told her to ask him for anything, and she'd told him she wanted Yaxaktun. He'd called her bold, but then he'd also kissed her. He liked her, and what was Yaxaktun to him? It was one farm, not much when one considered his vast fortune. It could be the same as giving her a hair comb.

"It might not come to that. Take the tray and sit here, sit with me and hold my hand," Carlota said.

She clutched Lupe's furry hand, felt the claws hidden in their sheaths.

"Are you feeling unwell again?"

"It's a bit of a fever, like when I was small. My father said to rest."

"Then I should go and let you rest. Unless you want me to call the doctor?"

"No, don't bother him," Carlota said. "I'll sleep and I'll feel better by the morning."

"Very well."

They sat together for a while. After Lupe left, Carlota tossed the covers away and stood in front of the mirror. The light of the candles made her reflection appear strange. She had that curious sensation, once again, that there was a crack, a seam, inside of her. She ran her hands down her neck, looking for a flaw she could not see. Her fingers, in the mirror, looked very long, the nails almost too sharp and the eyes . . .

She leaned forward and saw her eyes, bright, almost glowing. But it was the light of the candle, and when she angled her face differently the effect vanished.

She could hear, outside, the fluttering of a moth, and inside someone was walking down the hallway, and when she closed her eyes she could almost smell . . . was that Montgomery walking around? But it was her imagination. She couldn't smell anything from inside her room.

She went to the door and pressed a hand against it, listening intently. The steps had stopped. She waited for a knock to come, but there was nothing, no sound. Then the steps began once again. He was walking away.

She thought to open the door and ask him what he wanted.

But instead she went to the table, blew out the candles, and slipped back into bed.

CHAPTER 16

Montgomery

"SHE'S ALWAYS BEEN like this, though the past few years have been good to her," Moreau said, waving Montgomery's anxiety away as they spoke in the sitting room, white curtains fluttering with the breeze. "It's nothing more than a matter of changing the dose of her medication."

"But the way she looked, doctor. I've seen her fatigued before, but this was entirely different. I've never seen her like that."

Moreau was standing before the parrot's cage, and the parrot stared at him, cocking his head. The doctor glanced at Montgomery, sounding almost bored. "Fatigue, swelling of the joints, low fevers, headaches, hands feeling numb. It's a constellation of symptoms that may come and go. I've told you so."

Moreau was acting as though Carlota had simply stubbed a toe rather than collapsed into Montgomery's arms. It perplexed him, and even though he could tell Moreau didn't want to keep speaking about the incident, he pressed on.

"I thought she might die. I was frightened. I realize Carlota has an illness—"

"An illness of the blood. My wife had it . . . She died. I couldn't stop her bleeding. And the child . . ." Moreau trailed off, and his eyes fixed on a distant point. "For all my knowledge, it was impossible to stop the bleeding."

"I didn't realize you were married to Carlota's mother," Montgomery said. It had always been his understanding that Carlota was the doctor's natural daughter. As such, she could not enjoy all the rights of legitimate children. The doctor might not have a great deal of money, but there might be some pesos in his bank account back in Mérida. If Carlota was not an illegitimate child but his rightful heir, then upon his passing Carlota would surely be the recipient of this account. It gave the girl more leverage and social standing than he'd thought she had.

The doctor blinked, as if waking from a dream. He stepped away from the parrot's cage. "Carlota? No, I didn't marry her mother. I suppose I feel it was a situation similar to a marriage. You'll forgive me, I don't like to talk about her."

"I understand," he said assuming that in Moreau's aging mind both his first wife and his subsequent lover had merged and become one.

"Carlota said you were fighting when the attack came upon her."

"We had a difference of opinion."

"She's not supposed to make herself anxious."

"But is that all it was? She felt anxious and that generated such a violent reaction?"

He couldn't believe it. Carlota, for all her charm, was likely to argue with him about a number of topics. To argue with Lupe, too. She didn't go into a paroxysm over that.

"She's grown up. She's changed and changing." The doctor's voice had a dull edge, not quite irritation, closer perhaps to doubt. "I had a perfect handle on her when she was a child. I knew exactly the dose of her medication and how to keep her illness in check. But a living organism isn't stable. It's not carved in stone. I am using all my scientific knowledge of the laws of growth. But it's not enough."

"Then this is serious. She must be very ill, and it can't be an arbitrary episode as you've said."

"I can control it," Moreau insisted, banishing whatever doubt had strained his voice seconds earlier, like a magician performing an effortless trick. "Carlota has always been a work in progress. A project. That is what a child is, Laughton: one great project."

As usual, Moreau was grandiloquent, and Montgomery expected him to launch into a never-ending speech, but instead the man shot him a suspicious glance.

"I want you to be careful around Carlota. Please don't trouble her."

"Sir, I wouldn't. I don't."

Moreau did not seem terribly convinced. He leaned a hand on his cane and frowned. Eduardo and Isidro walked into the sitting room, both looking so healthy and in good spirits that Montgomery immediately felt irritated by their smiling faces and their loud voices.

"Gentlemen, where has Miss Moreau gone? We've been looking for her," Eduardo said.

"My cousin wants to invite the lady to go riding. Of course, with your permission, sir," Isidro added.

"I'm afraid that will have to wait until tomorrow. Carlota is feeling tired," Moreau said, but he had a cordial smile on his face for the sake of the young men.

"Is everything well?" Eduardo asked. He sounded solicitous, but his mere voice was grating. There were leeches and vampire bats Montgomery would have liked better.

"Perfectly fine. It's that minor malady that sometimes affects my daughter. But she's had her medication. There's nothing else she needs."

"Doctor, perhaps we should send tea to her room," Montgomery suggested, wishing to make a retreat into the kitchen, away from these men. "I can ask Ramona to prepare it."

"A good idea. And I would be happy to sit with her, too," Eduardo said. "It's rather depressing to have tea alone, after all."

"Sit in a lady's room, sir? It doesn't sound proper to me."

"I'm surprised you're so concerned with what is proper, Mr. Laughton. You strike me as a bit . . . unconventional," Eduardo said with a smile.

You strike me as an idiot, Montgomery thought.

"Why don't we find another way to entertain you," Moreau said, rising from his seat. "Perhaps you'd play a game of chess with me?"

"Gladly."

The men walked out of the room, to his great relief. Unfortunately, Isidro remained. He ran a hand by the mantelpiece, humming to himself, before heading to the piano and tapping a couple of keys.

"You don't play chess?" Montgomery asked, wishing the man would disappear.

"I can't say it's my favorite pastime. And you?"

"Cards," he said simply.

"That must mean you're a betting man."

"Sometimes."

"And someone who balances the odds."

"Do you have a point, sir?"

Isidro moved away from the piano to sit directly in front of Montgomery, leaning back in a chair with a practiced indolence. "I know my cousin, and if I were a betting man I'd say Carlota's odds are very good."

"At what?"

"At roping him in. Let's not be coy. She's trying to get her claws into the man."

"You don't like her."

"She's pretty enough. But there's something about her . . . something *wanton*," Isidro said, looking uncomfortable. "She hasn't been reared properly. No one would be, growing up in such a distant estate. And what does she have to offer him barring that pretty face?"

"Perhaps that is enough for the young master."

"Eduardo's emotions are like a fuse, they burn quickly. He has no patience and when he wants something, he won't desist. What's the girl's lineage, anyway? Dr. Moreau may be a physician, but he doesn't belong to any of the good families of Yucatán. God knows who her mother was. She's a bastard girl, I know that. And she's dark. Pretty, but dark."

What a toad you are, he thought, though the comment was not surprising. In Mexico, as in many other parts of the world, the tree of life was firmly structured. Color and lineage determined your spot upon a branch. The Spaniards had abandoned the country, but their customs remained. The castas were real, and so were ancient prejudices. Montgomery, as a foreigner with no money, occupied a nebulous space in this intricate web of people, and he could bypass classifications. Carlota's role, however, had been drawn with a firmer hand.

"She's a sweet young woman. Young Lizalde is lucky to have her attention," Montgomery said.

Isidro rearranged himself, now throwing an arm over the back of his chair. "I suppose you think he'll marry her. But what if he takes her as his mistress? What then?"

Montgomery's mouth twitched. "That would be unfortunate."

"Then we begin to understand each other. I know you don't like me, Mr. Laughton, and I don't like you one bit. But neither of us wants Eduardo and Carlota falling into each other's arms and causing mayhem. He'll ruin her and then we'll have to mop up this mess, somehow."

"What is it that you want of me?" Montgomery asked gruffly.

"I have written a letter to my uncle urging him to come to Yaxaktun and set his son straight," Isidro said, reaching into his jacket's pocket and taking out a folded piece of paper. "I would have you take it to Vista Hermosa. The mayordomo there will be able to send it to the city, quick."

"Why should I take it?"

"I can't leave. Eduardo would know immediately that I sent the letter. I can't have that."

"So you'd have me serve as your courier, in secret?"

"I'm sure you can saddle a horse and make it there and back safely."

"And ruin Carlota's future in the process."

"When we lived in Mexico City, Eduardo became enamored of a seamstress. He courted her for a season, loved her for another, and at the third he made a hasty retreat. How many months, do you think, would it take for him to tire of Carlota? I'm not a man who condones immorality. I don't want to see the lady's honor besmirched. My cousin is both foolish and impulsive."

He thought of his sister and her monster of a husband. He had not saved Elizabeth, he had not lifted a finger to impede her marriage. Could he let Carlota be lost to a cad? Suppose he did marry her and then flung before her a string of mistresses. Or, as Isidro said, suppose he should take her as a lover for a season or two? The laws of Mexico said if a man seduced and deflowered a woman he'd have to marry her or pay restitution. And yet despite estupro being clearly defined, and the penalties it might carry, he supposed this would not soothe the girl's wounds if she should be callously used and shunned afterward.

"Bring the matter up with her father."

"Moreau? We both know he won't help me and will do everything to hinder me."

"I could hinder you, too. Let me have the letter, I'll give it to the doctor."

"I don't think you will. I can tell you esteem her," Isidro said, and he held the letter up with two fingers.

"Precisely."

"Then do something."

"Break her heart, you mean."

"Better this way than the other, don't you think?"

Montgomery stood up and snatched the letter from his hand. "I won't promise you I'll deliver it."

Isidro nodded. "Fine. Think about it. I'm going to see how the game of chess is proceeding," he announced.

Montgomery, for his part, asked Ramona to make sure Carlota had tea sent to her room later in the evening, thinking it might do her good, while he went to consult with a bottle. After a few glasses he began composing a letter of his own in his head.

Dear Fanny,

Have you ever had the chance to do evil in order to produce some good? Carlota is a sweet girl. Too sweet to know heartache and misery. I find myself in a position to prevent said misery, and vacillate between my options. I realize what you might think: that I am merely attempting to rid myself of a rival. Yet that is preposterous, for to imagine Eduardo is my rival would imply that I have a chance to woo the girl or that I even wish to woo her. And yet I don't, I won't.

Fanny, when we were young, what did you ever see in me? What could a woman see in me now that the best parts of me are gone?

A few glasses later, the night shrouded his room. He lit a candle and turned Isidro's letter between his hands, examining the envelope. It would take a small movement of his hand to burn it and toss the ashes out the window.

Instead, he stuffed the letter in his pocket and stumbled out of his room. The house was quiet and he moved like a somnambulist, before stopping in front of Carlota's door. He ran a hand through his hair and tried to straighten himself up. His clothes were rumpled, and he knew he reeked of aguardiente. Again.

He raised a hand to knock. He wanted to show her Isidro's letter and to explain what the man had said. But as he rested a palm against the door he realized he couldn't do it. She wouldn't believe him, and even if she did, he was afraid he'd babble inanities.

He was drunk and stupid and if she opened the door he'd take her face between his hands and kiss her. First on the mouth, then on that long neck that was laid tantalizingly bare when her hair was plaited. He'd beg her not to marry that boy, beg her and be lost.

And she'd say no, he was sure of it.

She'd say no, slam the door on his face, and everything would be ruined. Moreau would rid himself of Montgomery, and Carlota would be disgusted.

Moreau had said not to trouble his daughter.

He wouldn't.

Montgomery turned around and stumbled back to his room instead.

CHAPTER 17

Carlota

THE MORNING AFTER her episode in the library, Carlota went to the laboratory.

Her father had been correct. She was fine. Her illness had been brief and lifted with the dawn. Nevertheless, she felt strange. That jagged, broken edge she feared grew under her flesh remained. She did not know what it meant, this baffling sensation that something was amiss, something was different, but she did not like it.

After a quick cup of coffee, she'd washed her face, changed into a blue tea gown, and left her room. Carlota looked around the antechamber, flipping through the many books and journals stacked on the shelves. Her father's sketches of wild animals were plentiful. There was a drawing showing the head of a dead rabbit from above. The skull had been removed and the position of the nerves neatly indicated. A drawing of a dog revealed its spinal cord.

Jaguars appeared in her father's sketches often. Sometimes they did not seem like scientific studies, but more artistic pursuits. She admired the animal's fangs and remembered that a jaguar had almost torn Montgomery's arm to shreds, leaving behind a net of rugged scars.

But her father's papers did not have any information on his medical formulas, despite all the drawings.

Carlota went from the antechamber into the lab space and eyed one cabinet that her father kept locked. Behind the glass doors she spied more leather-bound journals. She wondered if that was where he kept his notes on chemical matters. She didn't have a key to it, though.

She had spent the whole of the morning in the laboratory and uncovered nothing useful. However, there was much to go through. Her cursory explorations were clearly insufficient, and she was now afraid that, even if she should find the notes she needed, she'd be unable to interpret the information. Yes, she understood certain basics of her father's laboratory, she knew to distill sulfuric acid and alcohol to create ether, could name the bones in the human body and could insert a hypodermic needle with remarkable ease, but all this, she realized, amounted to little.

When she left the laboratory Carlota was crestfallen, though she had a thought that perhaps Montgomery could tell her if the notes she wanted were indeed in that glass cabinet or whether she should focus on a different section of the laboratory. Montgomery, however, was not in his room.

She searched for him throughout the rest of the house. As she ventured into the sitting room she spotted Eduardo, who was idly turning the pages of a book. When he saw her, he immediately stood up and smiled at Carlota.

"Miss Moreau. It's such a pleasure to see you up and about. Are you feeling better?" he asked and pressed a kiss upon her hand. "Your father said you were taken ill."

"I'm well. It was nothing. How are you?"

"A tad restless, to be honest with you," he said. "Look, I've found your old friend: Sir Walter Scott."

"You're reading *Ivanhoe*! But I believed you didn't like it?"

" 'I will tear this folly from my heart, though every fibre bleed as I rend it away!' " he declaimed, which pleased her. Montgomery and her father thought little of her adventure novels, and she took Eduardo's knowledge of the book to be a good omen. If he should enjoy the same literature she relished, she thought it must be indicative of a kindred spirit, perhaps of a good match. "I've read him, yes. It's not bad, but the day is hot. It makes it hard to turn the pages when you're sweating," he concluded, tossing the book on the chair he'd been occupying. "I was thinking of going back to that cenote you showed us. Do you want to come with me?"

"Mr. Laughton is not around to accompany us."

"I'd rather not have him with us. If I can be perfectly honest, he makes a horrid chaperone."

The clock ticked upon the mantelpiece. A dozen ticks and a dozen beats of her heart.

"I suppose I could walk with you part of the way," she offered. She didn't really want Montgomery with them, and God knew where he was hiding. She feared he'd cause another scene. Montgomery and Eduardo didn't mix well.

The walk to the cenote was slow and pleasant. Once they were following that familiar path, the failure of her morning pursuits and the sensation that something was amiss faded. She took a step and thought to turn back, bidding Eduardo goodbye, for she'd said she'd walk him part of the way there, but then she took another step because the day was lovely.

They reached the cenote together and sat next to it, under the shadow of the trees. They couldn't go swimming, for that would mean undressing in front of each other. Although she longed to feel the water against her skin, the light filtering through the branches and peaceful beauty of the oasis were enough for her.

The air was thick with the scent of red and white frangipani. She closed her eyes.

"What are you thinking?" Eduardo asked.

"I'm not thinking, I'm listening," she said. "I feel that if I close my eyes and pay attention I might hear the fish in the water."

The previous night her hearing had been terribly sharp. Ramona told her once that everything is alive, and everything speaks. Even stones have a language. She also said people who were sick with consumption were sharp of hearing. That might explain it, even if Carlota was not consumptive.

"You have such an imagination."

She opened her eyes and looked at him. "Is that bad?"

"Not at all. It's part of your charm."

"Montgomery says I daydream too often. And that my head is full from the plots of books."

And that I am in love with love, she thought.

They were sitting side by side but kept a modest distance. However, when he spoke, Eduardo extended a hand and touched her arm. It was a slight touch, as if he were trying to secure her attention.

"Mr. Laughton has a big mouth. I'll have him fired."

"You mustn't," she said quickly.

"Why not? He does nothing but act impertinently."

"He belongs at Yaxaktun."

"That fellow belongs back in the gutter where my father found him."

"Don't say that. It's cruel. Promise you won't be cruel to him. He's alone in the world."

Eduardo had snagged a lock of her hair, rolling it slowly around his finger. He frowned. "I'll grow jealous if you mention him again."

"Don't be silly."

"He looks at you."

"What's wrong with that?"

"Well, he does it without any decorum whatsoever. It worries me."

Carlota had indeed caught Montgomery looking at her with that steady, cool gaze of his a few times, but she hadn't realized this constituted impudence. Montgomery seemed always a little lost. She wouldn't imagine him capable of any harm to her, despite their verbal sparring.

"I've known Montgomery for ages," she protested.

Eduardo drew his hand away, frowning. "Perhaps you prefer him."

"Prefer him? How?"

"Come now," he said, lowering his voice, the implication obvious.

"Please don't mistake my affection for an old friend for something . . . oh, something . . ."

Something lewd, she thought. She couldn't say it. It was wrong to weave such fiction when Montgomery never spoke to her with any amorous affection, when he never touched her. Although, now that she thought about it, perhaps he wasn't indifferent to her after all. He'd seemed, for the span of a few minutes in the library, possessed of an eagerness that struck her as something close to passion. The thought made her want to hide her face.

"Montgomery is our mayordomo," she said, bunching her hands on the muslin of her skirt. "He is my father's confidant."

"Your confidant, too?"

He is *jealous,* she thought and looked at him in surprise.

"I said he is a friend. What else do you wish me to tell you?"

"Simply say that you prefer me," Eduardo told her, like a challenge, his tone petulant. "That if you had your choice, you'd share your bed with me."

She let go of her skirt and wondered how she was supposed to answer him. Montgomery said all she understood were the adventures on the printed page and that everything could not be learned from books. Maybe he was correct, and she did want to know everything, after all, curious to understand the many facts that escaped her. Yet it seemed improper to reply to Eduardo with an affirmative, but if she didn't reply he might think her foolish, a simpleton who couldn't match him in wit.

A painful silence stretched between them.

"What? You won't say it?"

He looked annoyed. She feared she was supposed to tease him, to reply with a pun. Her head was blank.

"There are so many things I want to tell you. I simply don't know how," she replied gently. "When I'm with you the world doesn't make sense. I am too nervous."

His face softened. "Are you?"

Eduardo drifted closer to Carlota, his fingers dancing over her wrists before he lifted her hand and planted a kiss on it. She drew her breath in. She wanted to lean into his touch, to press her face against his chest. She turned her head and pulled her hand away.

"You shouldn't," she whispered.

He seemed to consider something and grew serious. "What if I ask for your hand in marriage?"

She blinked and managed to mumble her reply. "You'd marry me?"

"I swear it."

"Your family . . . your father, he would like me? He'd give us his blessing?"

"I'm tired of asking for permission for everything," Eduardo said with a huff. "My father thinks me a boy, but I'm a man. If I say I'll marry you, I will. Do you doubt me?"

"No."

"Then? Perhaps you do not like me, after all."

Her heart quivered, and she stared at him as his hand cupped her cheek. "Do not start with that again," she said.

"Forgive me for sounding spiteful, for being mistrustful. But you're beautiful and I'm sure others would covet you. It sounds silly, I know, and you'll think me an impetuous fool, proposing like this, and yet I can do nothing else. I'll die without you."

"You speak like a character out of a book," she said in wonder, thrilled by the fierceness of his words and the dread of refusal lurking in his eyes.

"I thought you liked books. Volumes with romance and adventure."

"I do." Her fingertips brushed his lips. "And you like to speak of fairy tales."

"Scheherazade's one thousand and one nights. Snow White and Rose Red marrying princes at the end. Sleeping Beauty's kiss. All those."

Her hand now caressed his jaw and dipped down, stopping at the collar of his shirt. "Yes." The syllable was an exhale of breath, barely a word. She felt drowsy with desire.

He dragged her closer to him, his fingers trailed the path of her spine under the muslin tea gown before angling his mouth against her own for a sweet kiss. The kiss lingered, became more desperate until she felt his tongue in her mouth and he was sliding a hand up her thigh. "You'll give me Yaxaktun as a wedding gift? Like I asked before?" she said, although her throat was on fire and she could hardly speak.

"And more. Pearls around your neck and a carriage to take us to the Great National Theater and a thousand dresses. I want to spoil you. What's your favorite stone?"

"I don't know."

"Rubies? Emeralds, maybe?"

His eyes were a lovely shade of green. Brighter than any gemstone. "Emeralds."

"I knew I loved you the moment I met you and perhaps before that. Love me back," he pleaded.

She had no time to think of a proper answer because he was kissing her again, muffling any words she might have attempted to cobble together. Besides, she felt as though he was pulling at a seam and she was about to come undone. Her pulse drummed madly, and she seized his head between her hands, kissing him back until breathless she drew away and stared into his eyes.

"Take off your dress. I want to see you," he said.

She blushed and didn't move a muscle, too confused to comply. He was reaching for his own clothes and undressing, removing his jacket, the vest, finally the shirt. Despite her bewilderment, Carlota's hands crept over his chest. She was curious to feel his skin and the muscles beneath. Up close, he smelled of cinnamon and oranges. It was the scent of his cologne, fresh and bright, like him. Montgomery had a map of pain tattooed on his arm, large scars like rivers in an atlas, and fine lines fanned his eyes. Eduardo's body was not marked with scars, the world had had no chance to wound him.

"You're pretty," she told him. He laughed. The combination of his blatant joy and feverish yearning made him even more attractive.

He began helping her out of her dress, though he kept barraging her with so many kisses it became slow work. She did not mind. It was torture and also delicious. His body was a wonder, a mystery. She'd not seen anything like him before, and her own body felt also wildly new. She touched hard muscle and flesh and the coarseness of his pubic hair.

She felt his lips against her ear. His mouth was soft, and he was sweaty and warm; she tasted salt on his skin. He pressed his face down her neck, between her breasts and then drew her even closer still, upon his lap, until she was running her nails down his back and he was making promises she couldn't even make out.

Something about love.

She did love him, then, when he slid into her, when he pushed her back against the thin black earth, and they rocked against each other. His fingers clenched down hard against her wrists. A bird let out a few sharp notes, and she laughed softly when he cursed and his voice almost seemed to splinter with the effort. She thought she'd break, too. But no. They simply lay together, and she buried her face against his chest until the bird who'd been serenading them grew tired and flew away. Then they went down into the cenote to wash themselves. Her thighs were sticky with his seed and she could smell the coppery and sharp scent of her blood.

She jumped into the water, glad to feel its embrace. He went after her, caught her in his arms and kissed her, and it was different because he was less frenzied and his lips were cool.

"Are you pleased?" she asked.

"I've not had a virgin before. I half expected that you . . . well, never mind," he said, shaking his head.

"You've been with many girls?"

"You're not supposed to ask that," he said, looking embarrassed.

"I don't care. As long as you're mine now," she said, brushing a lock of hair away from his eyes. "Are you?"

"I said I'd marry you."

That's not what she'd asked, but she also wasn't sure how to explain what she meant. Hers was the water and the black soil and the trees and those birds in flight not because she owned them but because they had each other. But he looked desperately in love in that moment, when he smiled at her, and it was like a second sun warming her.

They perched themselves atop the rocks until they were dry and could slip back into their clothes. She buttoned his shirt and knotted his cravat, thinking from now on she could do this for him each morning and he could tie the laces of her corset. They could do a million wonderful things for each other and there'd be no one to say no to them. They could ensure Yaxaktun was a beautiful, quiet paradise.

The part of her that felt broken and torn that morning seemed to have healed. There were no jagged edges.

She knew she'd be happy forever.

On the walk back, they held hands.

CHAPTER 18

Montgomery

HE RODE FAST, and he hoped for a misfortune to strike. Perhaps his horse should lose its shoe and he might be thrown off the mount. But no troubles assailed him, and he reached the gates of Vista Hermosa with nary a scratch.

He wanted fate to intervene so that he might not deliver the missive in his pocket, yet he also felt compelled to complete the task at hand.

The mayordomo made him wait, and Montgomery tapped his foot impatiently. Finally, after what seemed hours, the man stepped into the patio, scratching his head.

"I have a letter that must be delivered to Mr. Hernando Lizalde. You are to send a man immediately," Montgomery said.

"Well, of course I can send someone tomorrow—"

"Immediately, I said. It's from the young master."

He handed the man the letter, and the mayordomo shrugged. "Very well."

Montgomery took his horse to the stone trough so that it might drink and also filled his flask with water rather than asking the mayordomo for a glass of aguardiente. His return home was considerably slower. He paused more than once under the shade of a tree and contemplated the land around him.

He'd done it. He'd intervened in Carlota's affairs, perhaps even precipitated a catastrophe, and he did not wish to reckon with the consequences. Should Moreau ever learn of this betrayal, he'd be yelled out of Yaxaktun.

He told himself he did it for her and still felt like a swine.

When he walked into the sitting room it was late in the afternoon. They were all gathered there, looking merry, glasses in hand.

"Mr. Laughton! You've made yourself scarce today," Moreau said.

"Yes, for a minute there we didn't think you'd be able to join the celebration," Eduardo said.

"What are we celebrating?"

"I've asked for Miss Moreau's hand in marriage, and she has accepted."

Eduardo's smile was a mile wide. At his side, Carlota smiled, too.

"Join us in a toast," Moreau said, quickly pouring him a glass of wine before Montgomery had a chance to properly react. "To my daughter, a more blessed child was never had. And to her fiancé, may he make her happy."

They all raised their glasses, although Isidro, sitting on the settee, did it without enthusiasm. He threw Montgomery a questioning look, as if trying to ascertain that he had completed his delivery. Montgomery looked away from the man and held his glass with two fingers, far and away from his mouth.

"I am the happiest of mortals, simply the happiest," Eduardo said. "I want to have the wedding by summer's end."

"That should constitute a short engagement," Isidro said.

"There is no need to wait. Where should we honeymoon? Mexico City is the logical choice, but I'd rather go farther away."

"As long as it's away from this spot, it ought to be fine. The creatures here make me shiver," Isidro said. As he spoke he spilled a couple of drops of wine on his pristine shirt.

"They are rather dreadful, aren't they?" Eduardo replied. "But it won't be our concern once we are living in Mérida."

"You wish to live in Mérida?" Carlota asked, turning to her future husband.

"Why not? We can't live here."

"But Yaxaktun is beautiful."

"Darling, Yaxaktun is an estate not suitable for the wife of a Lizalde," Eduardo said playfully, tipping her chin up. "Besides, I'll want you to meet my friends and accompany me to many functions."

"I'd like to stay closer to home, to my family."

"I want you to have the best."

No, you want to show her off, Montgomery thought. Like a man who has bought himself a valuable painting or a ring. A man at a shop, pointing to a trinket he'd like to buy and asking that it be wrapped for him. He stood next to Carlota with all the assurance of an owner.

"I think Yaxaktun is a nice estate."

"Carlota, you've seen nothing yet."

"Perhaps. But I'd rather have a say in these matters. After all, we must make a home, together, that is to both our liking," she said without losing her sweetness, her hand lightly touching her fiancé's arm. But her voice was firm.

Eduardo arched an eyebrow.

"We must toast again, for although I do not agree with Baudelaire's assertion that one should always be drunk, it is imperative we be drunk at my only daughter's engagement party. *Pour n'être pas les esclaves martyrisés du Temps, enivrez-vous sans cesse,*" Moreau said, grabbing the bottle and pouring more wine.

Ah, you smart devil, he thought. Trying to prevent any friction between the couple, quickly distracting them with the wine and a witty comment.

Montgomery had not taken a single sip, and there was no need to top his glass. He remained rooted to his spot, uncomfortable and wishing he might disappear without being conspicuous. As if sensing his thoughts, Eduardo approached him, bringing Carlota with him.

"Sir, I am trying to pick a stone for my bride-to-be. She says emeralds, but I almost feel inclined to choose a more unusual gemstone. Perhaps a yellow sapphire, which they say is the most valuable stone in Burmah. It might come close to matching her eyes, which are the most beautiful eyes in the world."

"I know little about weddings and jewels," Montgomery said, remembering Fanny and the magnificent earrings he'd once bought her. But he would not discuss her with this man.

"I forget a bachelor such as yourself wouldn't have the opportunity to think about gifts for a lady."

"Please don't tease Mr. Laughton," Carlota said, fingers sliding upon Eduardo's jacket sleeve.

"I won't. I'm very bad, sometimes, Mr. Laughton, and my jests don't make everyone laugh."

"Congratulations on your engagement," Montgomery said, his voice without inflection, his eyes fixed on the girl's face. Eduardo smiled at Carlota, and she bent her head slightly, shy as a deer.

They turned around, drifting away from Montgomery. Eduardo's hand rested on the small of Carlota's back. The way they looked at each other had the easy intimacy of lovers. He could picture them kissing and touching each other. In Eduardo's sharp smile he read the triumphant announcement of a conqueror. The fool couldn't see the silk threads of desire the girl had woven around him. Yet, in the end, even if he'd danced to her tune, or whether it had been the other way around, he held her tight in the palm of his hand. The hacendado, with a magnificent house, extravagant furniture, and a beautiful wife who was as shapely as a statue of Venus.

Girl, you've sold yourself, but did you calculate the price correctly? he wondered. The boy had a stinger. Maybe she didn't mind. Some people kept scorpions for pets, after all.

Montgomery reclined on a chair until the clock struck the hour and he made an excuse and his exit. Alone in his room he stretched out his legs and smoked a cigarette, throwing his head back and staring at the ceiling.

Once darkness blanketed the house, he took an oil lantern and walked into the courtyard, breathing in the scents of the night. The house felt small to him, for all its windows and rooms.

"You can't sleep again?" Carlota asked.

He turned around. She was standing in shadows, no lantern in hand, her head tipped to the side, watching him. Her wrapper was of a burgundy color and blended well with the night, and her hair was in a braid flowing down her back. She ought to have been abed. Everyone was.

"What are you doing, miss?" he asked and thought of a midnight rendezvous with a lover. She might be looking for Eduardo.

"I heard you walking around last night. You stopped in front of my door," she said, not bothering to answer his question and stepping forward. Her eyes gleamed for a second, as if catching the light. She slipped in and out of the darkness with remarkable ease, and when she moved, as she did now, it was with a finesse that made him want to sigh.

He lowered his lantern, setting it down by his feet. The ground was covered with a smattering of petals from the fiddlewood tree guarding the fountain.

"I was drinking. I don't remember where I went," he replied.

"You didn't drink today and you did not smile."

"You are observant. And smart and quick. It was an expert move, what you did. Queen takes king."

"Life is not a game," she said, the swish of her wrapper as she moved was a subtle sort of music. They walked side by side, moving in circles, spinning around the light like two moths.

"I beg to differ. We are all chess pieces on your father's ivory and mahogany set. But you are his queen, to move freely around the board in all directions and do his bidding. Good job."

"Must you sour my day?" she asked, with a toss of her head. "It has been a good day. I have Eduardo and I have Yaxaktun."

"Yes, indeed. I warn you off the man and you rush to him faster than a hummingbird. But I mustn't chide you."

"No, you shouldn't."

She swiveled on her heels, and he thought she was going to walk away from him, but she simply stood still, staring in the direction of the house.

"I must know I can trust you, Montgomery. Yaxaktun will have need of you."

"How?"

"Someone must watch over it and the hybrids when I am not here. You heard Eduardo, he wishes for us to live in Mérida, and even if we should make our home in Vista Hermosa, it must mean leaving Yaxaktun."

"Your father is here."

"We both know he is old and ill. Besides, I may decide to run things differently now that this is all to be mine. He's giving it to me, as a wedding gift. The whole of this," she said, spreading her arms.

"What are you thinking?"

"My father needs to offer the secrets of his formula to the hybrids. This is to be a sanctuary, not my father's playground."

"What a strange thing for you to say, since you are the obedient child who loves him so well."

"I love Lupe and Cachito, too. And they are unhappy. I want to make sure they will never be mistreated. My father wishes me to be a woman grown, then I must be one. But such a position conveys responsibilities I cannot shirk."

"You have spoken to your father, then?"

"I asked him for the formula. I'm not as big a coward as you assume."

"I apologize for saying you were."

She seemed surprised at that and nodded. Her back was very straight. She clasped her hands together. "When I asked my father to give me the formula, he said he would not and that I was too foolish to understand his science. I looked through my father's notes, trying to discern the answer. I've not found the information I need. But I will keep my promise."

"You are angry at him, then."

"I am not. Anger is not what drives me to this. It is, as I said, my love of Lupe and Cachito and the others."

"And there is also all your love for Eduardo. A mighty amount of love you have," he said, unable to control his tongue.

"I am happy and wish for others to be happy, too. Is that such a terrible thing?" she asked. "Do you not wish others joy?"

"What should I know?" he muttered, remembering that he had taken that blasted letter to Vista Hermosa hours before. Her happiness was bound to be short-lived if Hernando Lizalde caught wind of this situation. Perhaps that was why Eduardo wanted a quick wedding, hoping he might seal the bargain before his family could intervene. Or else it was the pull of the blood, the want for the girl to begin warming his bed as soon as possible.

"If we should all be safe, then I would be happy."

"Is that all, then? Are you sacrificing yourself for the well-being of others?" he asked.

"I love Eduardo."

Love at that age was a fire that sparked quickly, so it shouldn't have surprised him when she spoke earnestly, but it still stung to hear her voice her affection with such ease. She'd known the boy for a second and a half, and already her lips curled with honeyed sweetness when she spoke his name. Give her a month and she'd be ready to press an asp to her breast if the spoiled brat ever left her.

"How would you know love? From thumbing through a thesaurus or an encyclopedia? From the pen of Altamirano or another writer you fancy? Love! He is rich and that is good," Montgomery said, even though he didn't want to be spiteful.

"Why should you define love for me?" she asked, eyes narrowing with indignation.

"Love is easy when you can dangle exotic jewels in front of a lady. If he were a cobbler, for all his prettiness, you wouldn't have accepted him."

He thought she might respond with a passionate tirade, but instead Carlota's eyes grew sad.

"Monty, I do not like you when you are cruel."

"I am always cruel," he said, more for the sake of contradicting her than to make a real point. He was about to accede to anything she wished and now simply delayed his surrender.

"No, you are not," she said, shaking her head. "You like to tell yourself you are and to hide from the world. But you are a decent man and I believe I can trust you to take care of this place. I know you love Yaxaktun. My father resides here, but he doesn't love it."

"Carlota, I promise I will assist you if you ask it of me," he said. He didn't want to say he'd care for Yaxaktun, because he could hardly promise such a thing knowing that Hernando Lizalde might not sanction his son's engagement with the girl.

That letter! Why had he sent the damn letter? How could he look the girl in the eye with such a sword dangling over their heads? And after she'd said she loved Eduardo, that fool.

She scrutinized his face, perhaps trying to find a lie, and he looked down.

"Thank you," she said.

"Don't thank me, Carlota. I've done you no favors today," he muttered.

But she couldn't possibly understand what he meant and merely shrugged, moving away, out of his reach, her feet light, her wrapper fluttering behind her as a breeze blew through the courtyard, sending flower petals splashing against the lantern.

CHAPTER 19

Carlota

AFTER EDUARDO ASKED for her hand in marriage, he announced that he would remain at Yaxaktun until their wedding. His cousin did not seem pleased by this, but Eduardo was besotted and he told Carlota he would not part from her side. She suspected that he also hoped to find an occasion that they might sneak away to the cenote again, but that was not to be had. Isidro had appointed himself their chaperone, and if he wasn't around, then Montgomery emerged, walking a few paces behind the couple as they went around the courtyard.

Carlota dearly wished to have more than a fleeting kiss on the cheek from her betrothed, but she reminded herself patience is a virtue and instead distracted herself going through more of her father's papers. It was a fruitless pursuit, and although she'd asked Montgomery, he'd said he did not have the key to the glass cabinet that had drawn Carlota's attention. Patience, again, must be had.

It was after one of these incursions into the laboratory that her father walked in and found her dusting a shelf. She had already put away the notebooks she'd been reading so there was no guilty clue he could discern.

"I've been tidying a little," she explained when she saw the question in his eyes. "There's plenty of dust to go around."

"Yes. No wonder. It's not as if I can do anything here, so why should I bother with it?" her father grumbled. "Hernando Lizalde has reduced my funding to a trickle these past three years. You can't accomplish much when you must economize like this. I shall be happy when I can have better equipment and my funding back. Carlota, my dear, you must ensure this takes place as quickly as possible, the same way as you managed to propel this marriage forward. I must be able to conduct my experiments. New experiments."

"Fresh funding would permit you to conduct new experiments, yet I've heard you complain that the hybrids always fall below your expectations."

"They do. The human shape I can achieve, almost with ease, but there is trouble with the hands and the claws, and there are painful gaps . . . but that must not concern you. There are secrets to be had, the treasures of nature to be pried open. The hybrids are not the treasure I seek, they're merely a piece in a puzzle, one more key that shall unlock one more lock."

Behind him the glass and metal gleamed, and she saw the elaborate instruments of his trade. For the first time ever she truly wondered what the meaning of all of this was. His father said it was for the benefit of humanity, that it might be healed and elevated, but she did not believe it when he spoke to her now.

"Could you cure Lupe and Cachito? So that they don't require your treatments?"

"They cannot be mended," her father said firmly.

"Then can the treatment be improved? So that it is less onerous and they administer it themselves?"

"There you come again with that same idea! Didn't I tell you I did not want to discuss it? You waste your time with those hybrids. You and Montgomery, schooling them and petting them and making them soft. I know you want to fix them, but they are broken."

When she'd been a girl Carlota had showed Lupe and Cachito how to read, and she'd also seen Montgomery pointing at a word in a newspaper and saying it out loud for them. Did her father truly mean what he'd said? Were her conversations with Lupe and Cachito something that softened them? And why was softness wrong when her father asked meekness of them all?

"The hybrids are not important anymore, Carlota. They were

meant for Hernando Lizalde. I prostituted my intelligence for him, to obtain the money I required. I have not pursued other avenues of research that are more compelling, but now I will have the chance. Your husband will be my patron and I will have free rein."

"If you refuse to help the hybrids then I shall not tell my husband to give you rein of anything, if—"

"If what?" her father asked, his voice as sharp as a scalpel. "Are you to threaten me, now?"

Her father was tall and had the strength of an ox. Age was nibbling at his body, but it had not brought him to ruin yet, and to look at him when he stood up straight and imposing, to see those great hands of his and his piercing eyes and his lips pressed together, was to fear him.

Carlota swallowed. "I want to have my say, too."

If Eduardo was tired of asking for permission for everything, then so was she.

Her father stared at her. "Ingrate child. You were not raised to speak to me like that."

"I've said nothing rude or foolish. I ask for mere decency."

"My experiments will allow for enormous scientific leaps. And remember, without my knowledge you would not be here Carlota."

His voice was now glacial, but there was a fierceness beneath each syllable which made Carlota wish to clasp a hand against her mouth and be quiet. She spoke up again.

"I am grateful for the medical treatment I have received, but the price of it is high."

"The study of Nature makes a man at last as remorseless as Nature. Knowledge is not freely granted."

"Then perhaps if you were to use that knowledge to improve the life of the hybrids and grant them better care—"

"Children, obey your parents in everything, for this pleases the Lord. Have you forgotten your lessons?"

"I can quote scripture, too. Fathers, do not provoke your children to anger."

"How dare you," her father said, his gaze leaden.

The bitter rebuke was caught in her throat, jagged, and Carlota pressed a trembling hand against her forehead. She felt faint, short of breath.

"Sit down, Carlota. I will not have you overexciting yourself again," her father muttered. "Sit, sit. I'll get the smelling salts."

She sat down and heard him rummaging in a cabinet, but when he approached her with the flask in his hand she waved him away.

"I'm fine. It was nothing," she said and stood up, holding on to the chair.

"Carlota, I must adjust your medication, but I need to be careful. In the meantime, I don't want you exerting yourself. We had this conversation before."

He put the flask down on the table and gently clasped her hand. That same hand that had wiped the sweat from her forehead when she was ill and turned the pages of storybooks when he was teaching Carlota her letters. That hand she loved and respected.

"Everything I do, I do it for you, Carlota," her father said.

"I know."

Yet for the rest of the day Carlota felt doubt gnaw at her gut again. She had managed to convince herself the path forward was clear and good, but now she worried again about what she might truly accomplish. Her father was intractable, and worse than that, she doubted him.

He who was so flawless had, in recent days, seemed to her wholly diminished. Worst of all, she could find no comfort in others, for Lupe was sure to be cross at her and Montgomery was distant. She thought to speak to Ramona, but then Carlota realized it would be impossible to explain how she felt.

All she had was that dreadful, anxious knot in her stomach.

Her spirits were buoyed by Eduardo at dinner, who seemed determined to be particularly charming that evening and made her laugh.

She was not surprised when, upon rising from the table, he whispered in her ear. "I'll come to your room later."

She did not blush, merely glancing down at her plate, a discreet smile on her lips. The dread was replaced by eagerness.

That night, she changed into a simple nightgown and carefully brushed her hair, watching her reflection between the candles on her table.

Eduardo arrived at midnight, his knock soft, and she opened the door, letting him in and planting a quick kiss on his lips. He tried to kiss her with more ardor, and she took a step back.

"You should go to sleep," she whispered, but she was smiling. She loved his impetuous spirit and the intensity of his affection.

He turned the key that normally lay undisturbed in the lock, shutting them in.

"I'll be quiet, not a single sound," he swore and clasped her hand, drawing her to the bed, where he pulled the nightgown up her thighs, exposing her legs to him.

"How can we? Without—"

"I promised, not a single sound," he said, divesting himself of his clothes with nimble fingers.

She took his vow of silence as a challenge, and then he said they might make love another way this time, which was a second, most interesting challenge.

His body looked different in the candlelight, every detail smoothed, but he was still handsome and cocky as he guided her atop him, hands sliding down her breasts and belly. At first, she had no idea what he was about, and it didn't feel right because he kept staring at her and she wanted to hide her face. Then it changed, they found a rhythm. His hips bucked up, and she shushed him even though she wanted to giggle.

Stretched out beneath her, he had to press a hand against his mouth to keep from crying out. It was then, when he had betrayed himself, that she pressed her breasts against his chest, her lips finding their way to the side of his throat, nipping ever so slightly at the delicate skin.

She didn't move away, resting atop him, even though he'd already spent himself. He lazily traced circles down the small of her back.

"It's silly of you to be here, you know," she told him.

"Maybe bold, but not silly. We don't have a single moment alone. What am I supposed to do?"

"Wait for the wedding day?"

"That might be asking too much. It does remind me I must make a few inquiries. There was a handsome house I once visited in Mérida, with palm trees in the courtyard. I must see if I can obtain something like that for us. And I must write to my mother so that she can tell my father I've decided to marry."

"Why can't you write to him?"

"My mother has a softer touch when it comes to him," Eduardo said, but she sensed a hesitant wariness to his words. She guessed Hernando Lizalde must be like her own father: a formidable force that sometimes frightened his children.

"I should also see about the papers for Yaxaktun. I want it to be yours before the ceremony, otherwise it wouldn't be a wedding gift. Do you think you'll need money for alterations? I don't want to have it fall to pieces."

She remembered what her father had said about money, how he wanted Eduardo to be his patron. She realized that Eduardo was a creature who focused on the concrete and who was moved quickly and passionately. If she should whisper that she needed the funds, he'd be sure to grant them. She also suspected that the bed was the right place to ask Eduardo for favors, to trap him when he was pliant.

And though it would have been simple to do her father's bidding, she found herself tracing a line down Eduardo's stomach instead and shrugging. "I don't think I need a great deal of money for the upkeep. But it would be nice to visit Yaxaktun when we can."

"Carlota, Mérida is better than this place."

"Perhaps. But you've told me you have many friends there and that we must go to all those soirees—it sounds exhausting. Besides, in Mérida we'll have to do what your family wants. What your *father* says."

He frowned. The other thing she had realized about Eduardo was that the excitement of a wedding for him was tied around the notion of independence. It would mark a milestone. He'd be a man, with his own household and his wife, no longer the child. Carlota understood this feeling because she had similar reasoning. The last thing one wanted, in this case, was a father telling them what to do and when to do it.

"But your father will be in Yaxaktun," Eduardo said. "It would be the same."

"Then perhaps we ought to settle in Valladolid. Yaxaktun can be our getaway. My father won't bother us. He respects you too much to give you orders. And we could walk to the cenote every day, spend the morning indolent in bed, and go riding when we feel like it. Didn't you say you'd spoil me?"

She was still straddling him, and his member was growing hard again as she raked a nail across his breastbone and raised an eyebrow at him questioningly. He laughed.

"Fine, fine, do as you wish. By god, you are a stubborn girl."

I didn't use to be one, she thought. She did everything she was told. But now she was beginning to understand there was such a thing as choice and that there were ways to nudge her fiancé in the direction she wanted, like one guides a horse. Her father might think she'd parrot his words in Eduardo's ear and Montgomery believe her naïve, but Carlota was a quick learner.

He frowned, but only for a minute. Then he became interested in the motion of her nails and sighed. "You know, you look like a girl in a book I read as a child."

"Truly?" she said, skeptical.

"It was *The One Thousand and One Nights*. Scheherazade sat together with the king and her hair was violet-black, the color of grapes, and her shoulders were bare."

"When I was a child I had a book that made me afraid of being devoured by salmon."

"Goodness! My book was better, then."

"Why? Did you hope Scheherazade would tell you stories all night long?" she asked, leaning down, close to him, her long hair falling like a velvet curtain around his face.

"No. I don't expect you to tell me stories."

"We'll be quiet, then."

"Very quiet," he whispered, brushing his fingertips against her lips.

CHAPTER 20

Montgomery

THE DAY WAS terribly hot, and even under the shade of his straw hat Montgomery felt the sun baking his skull. Montgomery and Cachito fed the pigs and the chickens; afterward he went back into the house, soaked a rag in a bowl of water, and dragged it across his sweaty brow.

When he'd accomplished this task Montgomery found his way to the courtyard for a smoke, sitting by a window. The gentlemen were playing the piano; he could hear the tinkling of the keys under Isidro's hands and the sound of laughter. He could picture Carlota fanning herself. Their merriment was like a splinter under his skin, and he grimaced.

He took out the box of matches and turned it between his fingers while he rubbed his free hand on the back of his neck.

Before he had a chance to light his cigarette he heard a banging at the doors of the hacienda. He stood up and walked to the portón, his hand brushing the pistol at his hip.

"Moreau! Open up, Moreau!" someone yelled.

The racket continued, and Montgomery unbolted the decorative iron gate and then the postigo. The smaller door would allow people to enter on foot. He was not about to throw the double doors open.

"Finally!" Hernando Lizalde exclaimed, looking frazzled and dusty from the road.

Montgomery was not surprised to see him. He'd been expecting him each morning that week. But he still felt a sour taste in his mouth at the realization the letter had had its intended effect. Lizalde had come to fetch his brat of a son, and for once Montgomery was not glad to rid himself of Eduardo because he'd had a chance to witness Carlota's happy smiles and the way she clung to the boy's arm.

"Mr. Lizalde," Montgomery said, stepping aside and allowing him in. Behind him came two men, and he spotted two more sitting atop their horses. "How can I assist you?"

"I'm looking for my son. Where is that rascal?" Hernando asked, briskly walking into the courtyard, his riding crop under his arm. His leather boots were like slaps upon the stone floor.

"I believe he is in the sitting room."

"Take me to him. You two, wait here," the man said, pointing to his companions.

Montgomery quickly catalogued the men, taking note of the two guns they carried. Hernando was also armed, the ivory handle of his pistol stark white against his dark clothes. Pistols for a man of this caliber were purely ornamental, but Montgomery was wary of the detail. "This way, sir," he said without inflection.

When they walked into the sitting room, the first one to spot Hernando was his son. Eduardo stood up quickly and swallowed. Then it was Moreau who turned his head and looked in their direction.

"Mr. Lizalde," Moreau said, leaning on his cane and standing, too. "What a surprise. I didn't receive any letter saying you'd be by."

"I didn't send one," Hernando said. His eyes were fixed on Carlota, who had been fanning herself on the settee and now sat still, her fan on her lap. Isidro had stopped his playing and leaned against the piano. A smile danced on his lips.

"You seem to be having a merry time."

"Dr. Moreau is a good host, father," Eduardo said, his voice straining to sound cheerful. "I'm happy to see you. Won't you take a seat?"

The man did not. Atop the mantelpiece the French clock ticked and ticked.

"I didn't say you could come here. I explicitly told you we'd visit Yaxaktun together, yet here you are."

"I didn't think it would matter."

"It does."

"Is something wrong?" the doctor asked. He looked surprisingly calm while everyone else seemed to be stricken with terror.

"I was going to be more measured about this matter, Moreau, but seeing as you have a complete lack of respect for me I might as well be direct and quick about it: your research is at an end. You are to surrender all those hybrids to me and get on your way," Hernando said, and as he spoke he held his riding crop tight, swatting the arm of the settee where Carlota sat. The girl scooted closer to the other end, where Eduardo was standing.

Moreau stared at Hernando with cold eyes. "May I ask what has happened? Or am I supposed to be dismissed without an explanation?"

"You can try to explain, but I doubt you can. For years you've provided me with nothing except bills and excuses. I asked for workers, you give me nothing. I told you I could not continue to so generously sponsor you."

"I know. You have been rather frugal when it comes to my research these past few years."

"Because there is nothing to be had, Moreau! Nothing but overblown speeches and sickly animals. Yet I would not have minded if talk hadn't come that someone at Yaxaktun had been providing Juan Cumux with assistance."

"That is ridiculous," Moreau said flatly.

"I thought so, too, until I did more research. An escaped Indian was captured recently, a rascal who had worked once at Vista Hermosa, and upon interrogating him the man confessed that he had been living near Yaxaktun and that the people there were friendly with Cumux."

"You believe an escaped laborer? He is inventing it all."

"I believe it when he's been under the lash more than a dozen times," Hernando declared, and he swished his crop again, cracking it against the arm of the settee. Carlota jumped up in her seat.

Montgomery saw her extending her hand up and Eduardo clutching it tight.

"Your son spoke similar words when he first came here," Montgomery said, "but as I told him that day, we know nothing of that. You can't trust gossip."

Hernando now looked at Montgomery, a contemptuous smirk on his lips. "Gossip has a source in fact, Mr. Laughton. And when you consider all the facts, it seems to me I've spent a fortune for nothing, and perhaps all I'm doing is feeding Cumux's men and providing them with weapons so they can ransack my properties. I have a thought to go look for that Indian bastard with a few of those useless animals of yours, doctor, and kill the pig. What else might they be good for if not that?"

"Hernando, you cannot possibly think you can take the hybrids and what . . . put knives in their hands and ask them to search for a phantom?" Moreau asked.

"Why would they need knives? They have claws, don't they? They bit my nephew, didn't they?" Hernando said, pointing at Isidro. "If they can bite him, they can feast on other flesh. As I said, your research has been fruitless. Someone else can continue the work for a fraction of your price."

"No one can do what I do," Moreau said fiercely. "Try and bring a silly hack in here, he won't find a way to ever approximate my genius."

It is too bloody hot to be quarreling, Montgomery thought. On days like this he'd entered into senseless brawls, driven by idiotic rage. That was what was happening now. Hernando looked no better than a buffoon in a cheap drinking den, wailing about being cheated at cards, and Montgomery feared the worst. Days like this never ended well. They were soaked in blood.

"Gentlemen, father, please, let us sit down and discuss this over drinks," Eduardo said, his voice laced with panic. The boy, despite all his stupidity, seemed to smell the blood in the air, too. "We cannot quarrel. The doctor is the father of my bride-to-be."

He surely could not have said a worse thing. Hernando's face immediately grew flushed with anger.

"Bride-to-be?" Hernando asked. He looked at Isidro. "When did this happen? The letter did not mention anything about a marriage."

"He asked for her hand in marriage a few days ago," Isidro said.

"And you did not think to stop him?"

"Uncle, I wrote to you before the fact and could do nothing else."

"You are not going to marry her," Hernando said. "I'll be dead before you do such a thing."

Eduardo shook his head. "Sir, I have given my word and my heart—"

"Your heart be damned! Are you blind! Can you not see?!" Hernando roared, pointing the riding crop in the direction of the girl. When he spoke, spittle flew from his mouth. He resembled a rabid dog.

In a few quick strides, he was before the young woman, tilting her chin up with the riding crop, making her gasp. He looked down at Carlota, scorching hatred in his eyes. He'd seen drunkards knife another man with that same look plastered on their face. Montgomery restlessly circled closer to them, his left hand forming a fist.

"What are you doing, Mr. Lizalde?" Montgomery asked, his voice low.

"Admiring the doctor's handiwork," Hernando muttered and stepped back, releasing her. "She is like them, one of the doctor's creations."

The girl grasped Eduardo's arm, and her fiancé laughed. "Father, you must be joking. She is a woman and nothing like the hybrids."

"She is one of them, I tell you. When I met Moreau, he had no daughter. Still, it wasn't my business if he had a hidden bastard and brought her to live with him. But when Isidro wrote and said you were interested in the girl, I had to give the matter more care.

"Do you remember your old assistant, Moreau? I met with him a few months ago, trying to discuss the possibility of his return to Yaxaktun. I contacted him again and asked the man if he knew anything about your daughter. I thought he'd tell me the doctor had availed himself of a servant and that I'd have to inform you, Eduardo, that you were infatuated with a maid's bastard spawn, a girl with no prospects. I did not expect him to tell me the doctor's daughter was the literal child of a *wildcat*."

"Melquíades was trying to steal my research," the doctor said. "He has reason to be my enemy and speak his poison."

"Prove to me this is not a monster, an unholy cross between a jaguar and a human," Hernando demanded, pointing at the girl again, who was now clinging to Eduardo and had buried her face in his chest. She was shaking, perhaps weeping. She seemed to want to make herself smaller, to hide between the folds of her betrothed's jacket. "Prove it to me if you can."

"I can haul your son before a magistrate for estupro, Lizalde, so don't start demanding that I prove anything, or I'll prove more than you want and he'll have to marry her anyway," Moreau warned.

Hernando looked at his son, his face going slack. "For God's sake, say that isn't true. You did not let yourself be seduced by the whore?"

"She is no whore. Father, when I bedded her she was untouched," the boy said earnestly.

Hernando blanched and no wonder. If his son had indeed deflowered Carlota, Moreau had a case, and it would be a humiliation for Eduardo. Carlota would have to be examined by physicians, but the boy might also be examined to determine if he was capable of deflowering a virgin. Imagine that, a Lizalde with his trousers down and a doctor looking at his penis as if he were a dirty, common lout. And then there would be the nastiness of standing in front of a judge, the threat of arrest, names splashed in the papers.

The girl's body was racked by great sobs, and when she turned her head and looked at Hernando her eyes were shining with tears. Montgomery wanted to yell at Lizalde, tell him that enough was enough.

"My lord, promised in marriage to an abomination," Hernando said, and he turned to Moreau, the crop ready. "You did this, you madman!"

Hernando launched himself at the man, and he was so quick he managed to hit the doctor in the face, the leather slapping him with such viciousness Moreau dropped his cane and let out a loud groan. He stepped back and almost lost his footing.

Carlota rushed to his side, helping steady the doctor before he could be toppled. "Get away from my father!" she yelled.

"Stand aside or I'll whip you bloody," Hernando warned her, raising his crop again.

Montgomery had had enough, and he made a motion, intending to drag Hernando Lizalde to the other side of the room, since distance seemed the most prudent course. But he didn't have a chance because as the man held the crop tight, the girl launched forward.

She moved swiftly, and at first Montgomery did not understand what had happened. All he heard was Hernando's terrified cry. Then he saw the red lines on the man's cheek. She'd scratched him.

The girl lifted her head, and Montgomery had a perfect view of her wide, angry eyes. They gleamed now, saturated with color. Carlota's eyes were a beautiful shade of honey, but this was a different hue. The eyes seemed to glow, and the pupils were all wrong; pinpricks of blackness against a citrine background.

These were not a woman's eyes, and when she turned around, chest heaving, Isidro almost toppled a vase as he stepped back. Montgomery, for his part, did not move a muscle.

He'd seen eyes like that, once, close against his face. Those were the eyes of a jaguar. The girl's stance, the way she held her head up, the neck stretched out, and her body tense, that was the furious stance of a cat.

Dazedly he thought of all the times he'd been near her, of how he had admired the way she moved, like an acrobat, terribly graceful. How her eyes sometimes seemed to gleam in the dark for the briefest of moments. She could see so well in the dark, walked without a candle in the middle of the night, and her feet were quiet, a whisper. You couldn't tell she was approaching you if she didn't wish to announce herself. The shadows cradled her: she slipped in and out of them in the darkness of the courtyard, in the greenery of the jungle. Fluid, like water, like a ghost, like the jaguar when it hunts.

And he knew it was true. The lot of it. She was a hybrid. And the others knew, too.

"How dare you!" Hernando said and pulled out his pistol with one hand while he pressed the other hand against his wounded cheek.

Montgomery reached for his own gun, pointing it at the man's head. "Let go of that," he said, his voice low.

At first Hernando did not seem to understand. He stared at Montgomery with more shock than rage. Then he snorted. "Mr. Laughton, do not dare to threaten me. My men are right outside this house and will shoot you down."

Although Montgomery had spoken defiantly to Eduardo the first time they had met, this was a different situation. This was Hernando Lizalde, the man who ultimately held his debt and who paid his wages. He was dooming himself by speaking against him, yet he swallowed any misgivings and held the gun with a steady grip. It was time he summoned his courage.

"Not before I put a bullet in your skull," Montgomery said. "Need I remind you I'm an excellent shot?"

"Think about what you are saying and who are you siding with."

"Toss that on the floor. I want you out of here. I've had enough of the lot of you."

The hacendado sneered, but placed the pistol on the floor and straightened himself up. Montgomery kept the gun pointed at him and picked up the ivory-handled pistol.

"Get out of here, all three of you," he ordered.

"If we are made to leave, we will come back, Moreau," Hernando said, now looking at the doctor. "And when I come back it will be with a dozen men, and we will grab those hybrids of yours, use them to kill the Indians that have been bothering us, and then punish you thoroughly. It is best if you surrender to me now. If you obey, then I will be merciful. Do not force my hand because I will harm you."

Moreau clasped his daughter's arm so he could stand up straight and stared back at Hernando. "You need to leave."

"You heard the doctor," Montgomery said, motioning with one of the pistols to Eduardo. "Get the hell out of this house."

Eduardo and Isidro slowly walked to the door, behind Hernando.

"Eduardo," Carlota said. The name was a plea, and she extended a hand in his direction. That single gesture would have broken any man's heart.

But the boy flinched, his eyes skittered across Carlota's face, filled with dread, before he crossed the threshold. Montgomery followed behind the three men, the guns pointed at their backs.

When they reached the patio, Hernando's two men immediately looked at him in alarm and reached for their pistols.

"We are leaving; don't draw your guns," Hernando said, wisely surmising that there was a revolver aimed at his spine.

The men were shocked, but they did as their boss said and walked toward the doors of the hacienda. Once they were all outside Montgomery barred the door and moved quickly back toward the house.

PART

THREE

(1877)

CHAPTER 21

Carlota

"COME, SIT HERE," her father said. "Montgomery, fetch me a syringe. There, yes, there."

She was trembling all over. She felt as if she might vomit, and her hands ached terribly. They looked wrong, the fingers were unnaturally long, somewhat crooked, and her nails were too sharp, slightly hooked. She caught sight of her reflection in the surface of a glass cabinet. Her eyes were also altered. They shined, as if they were polished stones.

She pressed her arm across her midsection and bent down, weeping, not wanting to see herself.

"Let me have your arm," her father said.

"No!" she yelled, swatting his hand away. "Don't touch me! Don't get close to me, neither one of you!"

Montgomery stared at her, and her father raised his hands in the air. His face was calm. "Carlota, you need your injection. My lamb, remember: blessed—"

"I need an explanation. You will explain this to me! What is happening to me!" she demanded and stood up, toppling the chair upon which she had been sitting and pushing aside a tray with medical instruments that had been placed on the table next to her. They clattered and fell on the ground.

The antechamber to the laboratory, which she knew so well, was alien to her. The animals in their jars and on the shelves, the books, the charts showing the bones and muscles of the body, they were wrong. She felt as if she'd never seen them before, and through her body there coursed a terrible, awful pain.

"He said I'm a hybrid! Look at my hands!" she exclaimed, raising them in the air and spreading her fingers. "Why do my hands look like this? I have claws!"

She did. Like a cat, nails long and curved and sharp, and she couldn't understand how this was her body and these were her hands.

"You must calm down. You simply must. I don't want to restrain you but I will."

"Tell me why!"

"Carlota, little one, stop it."

She hissed at him. The sound sprung from her lips involuntarily as she stretched her neck forward. She whirled away, placing the table between herself and the men. She began walking quickly, from one side of the room to the other. Her heart was beating fast, and she closed her hands into fists, pressing them against her temples.

"Carlota, you are like this because there is a part of you that is not human and which I have controlled and kept at bay for years. But your body has changed in ways that have baffled me in recent months and the treatment that suppressed those traits is not working."

"How can there be a part of me that is not human? Am I not your child? Ramona said a woman came to see you. A pretty woman from the city," she said, clutching at that strand of gossip. "That was your mistress. That was my mother."

"The woman *knew* your mother." Her father shook his head.

Her muscles ached as if she'd been running for a long time, and she breathed in quickly, her nostrils flaring. She could smell the one hundred scents of the laboratory, the chemicals and solutions and also the sweat pooling on her father's brow and Montgomery's scent. They were sharp and clear, all layered against one another.

"I was married once to a lovely woman. My Madeleine," her father said, and he smiled a little. "You've seen her portrait in my room. But my wife suffered from a congenital ailment. She died while she was in the final trimester of her pregnancy. It should not have been so. But there was nothing I could do. The flaw lay in Madeleine's body. The priests tell us God made us perfect, in his image, but they lie. Look at all the defects! All the mistakes nature wreaks upon our flesh. The deformed and the infirm and the ones who go to their grave early. I sought to rectify that. To perfect God's creation. To eliminate the ills of man."

Her father's face had appeared calm up until this moment. Now it turned sour, and he frowned. "My experiments were too esoteric and wild to be understood in Paris. I was forced to leave the country of my birth and sought refuge in Mexico. But I needed money. Lizalde had money aplenty. Some of my research tickled his fancy. I had, at that point, managed to create rudimentary hybrids, and I'd had a thought that this line of investigation would be appreciated by someone like him. He offered Yaxaktun to me and his patronage, and my work was able to proceed at a more assured pace. You must understand, the hybrids were not what I wished to study, it was what I was forced to study. Workers! What would I possibly have wanted with field hands? That was Hernando's concern.

"I bred the hybrids in the bellies of pigs, then transferred the viable fetuses to my tanks. But there were mistakes, details that went . . . well, I thought perhaps the problem was the materials I was utilizing. I was employing the gemmules of criminals and vagabonds. I decided my own gemmules would be more fitting. And I also decided a woman would bear the child, not a hog. I found Teodora in a whorehouse. That was . . . that was the woman who birthed you."

Carlota stopped in her pacing. She stared at him. "Then I did have a mother, and Hernando Lizalde is wrong. I'm not a jaguar's child."

Her father's lips were pressed into a grim, thin line. He let out a sigh.

"I took Teodora out of that whorehouse, and she agreed to birth me a child in exchange for money, and the child did grow in her womb. It had some of her traits, yes, and some of mine. But it also had the gemmules of a jaguar. Carlota, you are not the child of two parents. I made you, like I made the other hybrids. You are an impossibility, practically a creature from myth. A sphynx, my love."

She did not know what to say and remained still, standing behind the table, as her father slowly rounded it, leaning on his cane. Her eyes darted toward Montgomery, who was rubbing a hand against his jaw.

"Like the other hybrids," she whispered slowly.

"When you were born you didn't look like them. My other creations had been wretched and flawed in some way, but you looked exceedingly human! There was work to be done, yes, but I had never seen anything like you. I had to correct certain traits and express others more fully, and there was an amount of pain in the beginning—"

"I remember nothing but pain when I was a child," she said sharply, recalling the black cloud of suffering of her youth and her father's cool hand upon her brow. "Was that your doing?"

"You've seen what happens with the hybrids. I needed to tweak certain components. But you cannot deny the genius of my work. Your face is perfectly balanced, your features are most pleasing."

"So you made and remade me?"

"Yes. Because you were close to perfection. Unlike the others. That lot of miscreants have too much of the animal inside, they're riddled with mistakes. Not you. There has never been another who has approximated you in form and thought. You are a gentle child and obedient and . . . ah, Carlota, don't you see? You are a work in progress, a—"

"A project," Montgomery said, with a sneer on his lips. He had been leaning against the wall and now pushed himself forward. "Isn't that what you said to me, doctor? One great project. Well, you were not lying about that, I suppose."

"Yes, and what is wrong with it?" her father asked, turning around in exasperation and looking at Montgomery. "Every child is a project! Mine happened to be better than the dirty, low projects of common men who simply wish to have children so they might help farm their meager plots of land."

"It's not the same."

"But it is. And I have been a good father. I have clothed, fed, and educated my child. She did not have to endure the beatings of a violent man, as you did, Montgomery. Nor was she unfortunate enough to inherit the traits of a vicious alcoholic which would have doomed her to the exact same life of inebriation. She has grown whole and healthy, and if I should choose to exhibit her this instant, before learned men, no one would be able to deny I've created a chimera to surpass any ordinary woman."

"My father was a lowlife, yes, but so are you," Montgomery said, pointing an accusing finger at the doctor. "I always knew you were a little mad, but to treat your own child like a *thing* you would wish to exhibit at a fair?"

Moreau slapped his chest, his voice rising. "I never said I would exhibit her. I said I could. There is a difference there."

"No wonder you've been trying to sell her like one sells a horse!"

"Spare me your idiotic rantings, Laughton. All men marry their daughters off. I simply wanted her married to the best. There is nothing wrong in ambition."

"Where is my mother?" Carlota asked, staring at the ground. She felt exhausted, and at some point her hands had stopped aching, as if a spell was breaking, as if slowly something inside herself was drawing back and reassembling itself. The nails looked smaller and rounded. "Where is Teodora?"

Both men turned their heads to look at her.

Her father licked his lips and raised a hand in conciliatory fashion. "It was a difficult birth. She died not long after it. That is why I never pursued the option of growing another hybrid in a human womb. It seemed too risky. But that might be the trick. Nothing else has ever approximated you. Or perhaps it was a quirk, a miraculous alchemy I cannot hope to recapture."

"She had no family? No siblings?"

"None that I knew of. She was a foundling who'd been whoring herself since the age of fifteen. The lady who visited me was the woman who owned the brothel where she worked. She wrote a few times, asking for money; she even came in person on one occasion. She probably believed I'd done the girl in. Well, I didn't kill her. She slipped away. Like my wife. My poor wife . . ." he said, trailing off.

"Where is my mother buried? Is she here?"

"No. The corpse is in the lagoon. I weighed it down. It will never be found. Oh, don't look at me like that, Carlota. I did not intend to harm her, never. I even liked to pretend, sometimes, that she had been my paramour and you had been no experiment. It was a pretty fiction."

Her whole life had been a pretty fiction, a story the doctor spun. She took a deep breath and closed her eyes. She felt the tears thick against her eyelids, and her voice wavered. "The treatments you give me each week, you say they no longer work. What shall happen to me?"

"Without them you seem to express certain animal traits. It happens when you are agitated, which is why I've sought to provide a soothing environment for you."

"Then I'll always change. As I did now."

"No, no, my girl," her father said, and he placed his cane aside, resting it against the table, and caught her hands with his own, pressing them against his lips. "I'll perfect the dose. It's a tiny detail."

She wanted her father to embrace her and tell her everything would be fine, but she also wanted to run out of the room and far from him.

"What about the others? I need to know the formula for their medication," she murmured.

"They are not important."

"How can they not be important?" she asked, stepping back and pulling her hands away. "You hold them in thrall. They can go nowhere without their treatment."

"Where would they go? To the circus? To show themselves in a freak show?"

"A freak show? That is what you think of us?"

"You are not like them," her father said. "You've never been like them. That's the whole point. They are *beasts*."

She felt such rage then that for a moment she was unable to see. The world went crimson. She had been scared and angry in the sitting room. But this was pure fury, and while before she had been trying to control herself, to calm down as her father demanded, she now let this fury flow and opened her mouth wide to a roar. She stretched out a hand, and her fingers dug into her father's neck. With one quick motion she was slamming him against a glass cabinet.

He was tall and big and powerful, but she pinned him against the furniture, and the glass shattered against his back. She felt her teeth large in her mouth and sharp like knives.

"I want that formula!" she yelled.

"I . . . there isn't . . . ." her father muttered.

"I want it!"

"Carlota, let go of him," Montgomery said, and he was trying to pull her away, holding her arm, then grabbing her by the back of the neck. Somehow he managed to drag her from her father.

She tried to bite him, but her teeth snapped in the air rather than sinking into flesh. He turned her around, grabbed her by the shoulders and stared into her eyes until she hissed at him. But as unlikely as it seemed, he did not appear to be frightened. She remembered he was a hunter, used to dealing with wild animals, and it made her wish to throw her head back and laugh.

"You need to take a deep breath," he said, his voice low. "Can you take a deep breath for me?"

She had no idea if this was possible. She felt as though she had forgotten how to breathe, but somehow she nodded and opened her mouth. Her lungs were burning. She took a shaky breath, and a wave of exhaustion and terror hit her. What was she doing?

"Good girl," Montgomery whispered.

"Carlota," her father muttered.

They both turned their heads. Moreau was lifting himself up, clasping his arm. She had held him so hard there would be bruises on his pale throat.

"There is no formula, Carlota," he mumbled, wincing and wiping the sweat dripping down his brow. "I made it up. It's the same lithium or morphine I use to treat my gout. It's been employed in cases of acute mania, and it seems to keep them soothed. It helped you, too . . . when you were younger."

She did laugh then: she pressed her fingers against her lips and erupted in laughter. No formula! And she was one of his creations, something inhuman, something that could fling a grown man across the room.

"I always . . . I always wanted a daughter. And you were mine." Her father straightened himself up, and then he stumbled back, glass crunching under his feet. "My heart," he said, clutching at his chest.

Then he collapsed, and the giant that was Dr. Moreau was sprawled upon the floor of his laboratory.

Chapter 22

Montgomery

THEY'D BEEN SITTING by the doctor's bed for hours now. Dr. Moreau slept and they waited. Ramona brought tea and handed Montgomery a cup. He thanked her, and she nodded, going around the room and handing the others their coffee and their tea, depending on their choice. When she was done, Ramona left her tray on a table.

He'd seldom been in this room and felt uncomfortable sitting there, among Moreau's things, with the oval portrait of his dead wife guarding the wall and his clothes hanging in the armoire, with the doctor on the great mahogany bed and the curtains around it open. It reminded him of his mother's final days, when he and Elizabeth had to remain still, quiet, while the fire burned.

Carlota clutched a handkerchief between her hands. She was by the head of the bed. At turns, she wept. Cachito and Lupe did not cry. Their faces were masks of frightful calmness and their voices were whispers when they spoke, sitting side by side. Montgomery shifted from one spot to another. He didn't want to sit, afraid he'd fall asleep in a chair and wake up in the morning with his back a mess.

He wondered what would happen if the doctor died during the night, and then he wondered what would happen if he lived. He'd seen men who'd been afflicted with apoplexy and could hardly move their body or speak. What would Carlota do, left to fend for herself and perhaps also for her father?

It was late, and the candles burned low.

"Lizalde will return with his men in tow, and we have choices to make before that," he said, because somebody had to say it, and he was tired. He wanted to lay his head down, and he couldn't if they were sitting there, crammed into the doctor's room, following a vow of silence.

"What choices?" Carlota muttered.

"Hernando Lizalde said he's coming to take the hybrids and also to wage war on Cumux's men."

She shook her head. "Cumux's men are not real. It's a lie. No one at Yaxaktun ever helped insurgents."

"Lizalde was not wrong about that," Lupe said. "There is a trail nearby, I told you. It'll take you to one of their camps. And Lizalde is going to find it, and he is going to follow it."

"Those are stories you tell yourself," Carlota said, twisting her handkerchief.

"It's not a story," Ramona said. They all turned to look at her. She stood firm and straight. "There's a path the macehuales follow to get here when they come for supplies, and now that these dzules know of it they'll be looking for it, and they'll find them."

Carlota dropped the handkerchief. "It was you then? You've been helping Cumux's men? And Lupe, you've known all this time?"

"I told you it wasn't my imagination," Lupe said.

"But how could you! You never told me so!" Carlota yelled, turning to Lupe.

"I've told you that you are blind! Besides, he knew, too," Lupe said, pointing at Montgomery.

Carlota's eyes narrowed, and she stared at him. "Did you?"

"How couldn't he? He's the mayordomo. Food goes missing, supplies go missing . . . you think he can't tell? Yell at *him*," Lupe said.

"I didn't know for sure," Montgomery said.

"But you must have suspected."

"A sack of flour, some beans and rice. Do you think it would have been worth much to Lizalde?" Montgomery asked. "It's nothing to him. I didn't know exactly who was dipping into our supplies and even how much they were taking, but why would I have been miserly?"

"You mean why would you have cared? You got us into this situation."

"It's not his doing, that," Lupe said. "That's your precious Lizalde. Why couldn't you have married him and left immediately?"

"I was going to," Carlota muttered, and she stood up and turned her back to them.

He thought of the stupid letter, the confrontation. Perhaps Hernando's interference could have been avoided or handled more elegantly, but Montgomery couldn't turn back time. He'd have the space to berate himself for it later, in the privacy of his room. Right now, there were other matters to be handled.

"What's done is done. It won't get us out of this mess. Cumux's men are in danger, as are we," Montgomery said.

"They'll come with rifles and shoot us," Cachito declared glumly.

"Then we'll close the doors and shut ourselves inside," Lupe told him. "They can't walk through walls."

"They can break doors down."

"Then we'll run," Lupe said firmly. "Carlota said we don't need the doctor's drugs anymore. We'll run away. They won't find us. We can head south to British Honduras, to English territory. We'll be fast."

"Not all the hybrids are fast," Montgomery said, thinking of old Aj Kaab and Peek' and the others with the quirks in their bodies.

"And what about the macehuales? What of Cumux and his men?" Cachito asked. "They are also in danger."

"They can fend for themselves," Lupe said.

"They can't fend much if they don't know what's coming their way."

"It's not our problem. We need to run."

"Running won't do any good. We'll fight them," Montgomery said firmly.

Carlota turned around. Her eyes looked red from all her crying, and tendrils were escaping from her braid. Her lips were trembling. "You want to kill them."

"If it comes to that, yes," he said.

"If you hurt them, then they'll come again. You kill ten men, they'll come back with thirty."

"We are isolated. If we kill ten, people wouldn't know of it for days, and by then we all could be gone. It's better to have a week's head start than none. And it's difficult to put together men for this sort of chase," Montgomery said. "When there are large Indian raids, the hacendados have to either fetch the peninsular authorities, which is a quest in itself, or beg their neighbors to send men. If they think there's been a raid, the other estates will either take their time, or even panic and flee to the safety of a city. They won't come back here. More than a week. We'd have more than that if we kill the first wave of attackers."

Carlota shook her head. "This is not an Indian raid."

"All I know is Hernando Lizalde intends to return. We should receive him with pistols and rifles," Montgomery said.

"Yes," Cachito said excitedly. "We tear them apart."

"Are you listening to yourselves?" Carlota asked. "You are planning the murder of people!"

"What do you think they've been planning for us, Carlota? Do you think they planned to have us for tea?" Lupe asked and brushed the silver tray with the teapot and cups aside. The sugar tongs clattered and fell on the floor.

"No. I can talk to them. I can negotiate something."

"What something?"

"An agreement, I don't know. You are not going to do this."

"It's not for you to decide for us."

"Is it for you to decide?" Carlota asked. "You don't speak for anyone."

"Then let's ask the others," Lupe exclaimed. "But don't stand here, thinking you are our mistress."

"We'll put it up for a vote in the morning," Montgomery said, touching the bridge of his nose and wincing. "I must rest."

He stepped out of the room. He couldn't take it anymore. He'd never been good when someone was ill. He remembered the hours crouching by his mother's bed when she'd convalesced, the need to speak in a low voice. When his mother had been alive things had been better with his father, but not much. But at least back then he'd had his sister, he'd had Elizabeth. He realized Carlota might be all alone without Moreau.

In his room he removed his jacket and washed his face, then lit a cigarette and shook his head.

He'd liked this place. It had been good to him. It had offered him safety, and now its safety was vanishing with astonishing speed. He let the ashes fall into a cup while he took out his gun and placed it on the desk. He placed Hernando Lizalde's ivory-handled pistol next to his own. His favorite rifle rested on the wall, by the desk.

He'd killed a jaguar, hunted animals, knew his way with weapons, but he was no cold-blooded murderer. He wasn't one of those men who goes around with quick threats, despite the rough-and-tumble places he'd ventured into. When he was drunk, sometimes there was trouble. But even in his inebriation he knew a measure of restraint.

When the knock came, he wasn't surprised, but he was dismayed. He really did wish to sleep, not to bicker, and Carlota's face when he opened the door was that of a general going to war.

"You always have a bottle of aguardiente in your room so I thought I'd ask you for a glass," she said.

"You don't drink aguardiente. Certainly not the cheap kind I keep."

"I don't toss my father against a cabinet either, and yet I did a few hours ago," she said, elbowing him aside and walking in with the breezy air of a conqueror. Her hair now fell loose along her back. She'd undone the modest braid.

He went to the desk, opened a drawer, pulled out the bottle and two glasses. He poured her a couple of fingers' worth of the drink. "It's stronger than the stuff you sipped by the bonfire, it's a cheap and awful swill," he warned her. "A few sips and you'll be tipsy."

"Let me taste it."

She downed it with a quick twist of her wrist and wiped her mouth with the back of her hand. She had a beautiful mouth, generous lips. The lamp on his desk made her hair look like it was sketched with charcoal pressed hard against the paper.

"How do you like it?" he asked.

"It's not as bad as I thought it would be. Cachito says your preferred drinks are vile," she replied and grabbed the bottle, filling the glass to the top.

"It grows on you if you let it. Did you want me to lecture you on different kinds of spirits? Somehow I don't think so. What is so important you've come to see me in the middle of the night?"

"It'll be dawn soon."

"My point precisely."

She sat on the chair he'd been occupying; he took the bed. Her nightgown was properly hidden by a crimson robe, and she demurely crossed her ankles, but the look she hurled him above the rim of her glass was bold.

"I can't have you killing those men," she said.

"You mean you don't want Eduardo killed."

"I don't want anyone killed. Are you prepared to see the others hurt? To see Cachito and Lupe bleeding? I want to attempt a peaceful negotiation."

"Wave a white flag and all that? I suppose you'd be conducting the treaty, hmm?"

"Why not?"

"They may not like you now. Not anymore."

She smirked and drank. He had to give it to her. She did not grimace as the aguardiente went down her throat. She stretched her hand and dangled the glass above the pistols while with one finger she traced their handles, following the whorls in the ivory.

"I still want to try. You need to push for a peaceful solution."

"I said we'd take a vote in the morning."

"Cachito will listen to you. And so will most of the hybrids. They respect you almost as much as my father. You and I could sway them."

"You've come to plot and to manipulate, then."

"I've come to beg you to think this over. I do not want to see anyone harmed. Before we consider bullets, let us consider words. Montgomery, we must try this. You think I want to protect Eduardo, but I'm trying to protect *us*. I'm trying to save our home."

He gave an exasperated sigh. "Carlota, I am king of no realm. I said my piece, others will say theirs. You'll say yours, too."

She grabbed the glass again and poured and drank more. She would be sick in the morning, but it wasn't his concern.

She wanted peace, yes? But as he watched her, as he examined the softness of her profile, he remembered how she had dug her fingers into Moreau's throat, and instead he pictured the girl committing violence. The macehuales told tales of warlocks who slipped into a second skin, who turned into dogs and cats and wreaked evil across the land. He didn't believe those stories, yet his hands trembled. His cigarette was burning down quickly. He tossed the butt into the teacup and set it on the night table.

Carlota's head was angled sharply to the left, and she was looking down.

"I can smell your fear, you know?" she muttered.

"What?"

"My senses are sharper. I can smell you. If you should snuff out all the lights in this house, I'd be able to find you in pitch darkness," she said. He couldn't see her eyes with her head tipped down; couldn't see whether they gleamed strange and terrible, or they looked human. "Don't worry. Eduardo was afraid, too. Did you see his face when he looked at me? He was afraid. He was also disgusted. My father was not disgusted. Only terrified. Are you disgusted right now, Mr. Laughton? On top of the fear, I mean."

"I'm not afraid."

She strode over toward him, cradling the glass of aguardiente against her chest. "Did you ever know? Did Dr. Moreau tell you what I am?"

"No."

"But you keep secrets. You knew Ramona was taking our supplies."

"As I said, I simply chose not to investigate the matter."

"If you knew and you didn't tell me, I'll hate you forever."

"I didn't know."

He hadn't even guessed. Maybe that made him stupid, but it would have been too wild a thought. She'd never appeared to him anything other than entirely human.

She was standing in front of him, looking pensive. The folds of her robe brushed his knees, and she nodded, a hand going up to her lips as she nibbled at a nail. Human hands and human nails. For now.

"He said I'm a sphynx, but sphynxes aren't real," she whispered, and she was still glancing down, evading his gaze. "I don't know if I even exist anymore."

"Have you exhausted the self-pity? Can I get that glass back from you?" he asked angrily, because he'd had a sufficient measure of her theatrics, and he was truly tired. He couldn't take more of her.

"You are trembling in fear! Tell me you're afraid of me!" she yelled, tossing the glass away. It shattered against the wall and sent shards flying everywhere across the floor.

Her eyes, when she stared at him, were like marigolds, a burst of yellow, but still human. If they hadn't been, it would not have changed things. He pulled her down and kissed her on the mouth, felt her nails against his skin as she clutched him tight. It made him shiver.

He drew her under him. He thought maybe she'd kill him for the impertinence. But Carlota sighed, and there she was, willing and eager, with her hair spread across his pillow. Carlota Moreau, who was inhuman, a hybrid dreamed by the old doctor. If she'd been a siren luring him to the bottom of the sea, he would have followed. If she'd been a gorgon he'd have let himself be turned into stone.

Let him be mangled and devoured. It didn't matter. That was what she'd come for, and he wouldn't dance around it a second longer; he wanted her too badly. Let her be rough with him, let her bruise him if that was what would bring her to the edge.

But her hands were careful, and she kissed him slow and gentle, in a way he hadn't been kissed for years and years. He knew it would be easy to lose himself in her, and he could make it pleasant for Carlota; he could trace her body with his fingers, take his time. Her boy was pretty but he was young. Age at least gives hands a certain skill, and Montgomery had learned a thing or two through the years.

The robe she wore was velvet with a green lining and gold trim. It had grown shabby, like everything else in the house. Perhaps it had belonged once to the doctor's wife, who must have been a fine lady. Carlota was fine, too; finer than anything he'd ever gazed at. Fanny Owen, she'd been pretty, and she'd peppered his face with kisses the day they wed, but she hadn't pressed her forehead against his own the way Carlota did. Nor had he slid the robe off Fanny the way he did with Carlota, because back then he had been both shy and too keen.

He wanted to please her, make her happy. She was sweet and tender and the world was bitter. He didn't want her to know sorrows.

But her eyes were closed. He wasn't so stupid as to think it a sign of passion. He'd done things like this in the past, sought the anonymous embrace of women in drinking dens and whorehouses. Closed his eyes tight. He knew what she was after, and it wasn't him. If he took her now, he wagered she would whisper the wrong name in his ear. All that yearning, all the featherlight touches, they were for another man.

He sighed. "Look at me."

She did. There were tears there, unshed yet but bright. Her hands were on his chest.

"You don't love me," he said. It was a statement of fact. He wasn't going to bother with a question.

"So?" she replied, her voice defiant. Her breath was perfumed with the aguardiente. "You don't love me, either."

"You are in love with Eduardo Lizalde," he said, and she looked away, her jaw tight.

He was dizzy from the alcohol, exhaustion, and desire, but he sat up and scooted closer to the foot of the bed while she rose and pressed a hand against the headboard, hair askew and looking prettier than she'd ever seemed to him. She must have been a sight after Eduardo made love to her, content and smiling. He'd always envy the boy that.

He ran a hand through his hair. "I know the way it is. You are hurt and you are lonely. When my wife left me I sought solace, but you are not going to find it between the sheets and definitely not at the bottom of a bottle."

"That's wise of you, and yet you drink yourself to death."

"Maybe I don't want you to be like me."

"I'll never be like you. I wasn't *made* like you."

"Copulating with me won't make you any more human. It'll make you sadder, when you open your eyes and see my face instead of his. Copulating with me won't make up for what happened in the lab, it won't wipe away the things your father confessed, and it won't heal him."

She looked offended, perhaps by his choice of words or his acrid tone. The tie of her nightgown was undone and offered him a perfect view of her neck as she swallowed and tipped her chin up.

"Maybe it's not about any of that."

"It's about all of that, and even if it wasn't I'll tell you something else: I'm afraid."

"I knew it," she muttered.

"Not of *you*. But of loving you."

"I don't understand."

For a minute he had a notion to keep quiet, and he even had the selfish craving to take back his previous words, to instead kiss her and damn the world. But he wanted to be honest, not play a card game with her despite his predilection for gambling.

"I once loved a woman who didn't love me back and it broke me. I don't want that again," he said, his voice smooth and low.

Maybe it was not the only thing that had broken him. The brunt of cruelty, of the world, had taken its toll and marked him. But she'd been his solace and his hope, the balm from ugliness and wrongdoings. Then she'd left him and admitted that she'd never really loved him. It had been solely her misguided thought that he might have some money that led her to the altar; it had been his uncle's business that had led her to him. When there were no coins to collect, she'd abandoned him. She'd written it all in a wonderfully brutal letter after he was mangled by the jaguar, and he'd written back, but in his dreams.

And afterward there had been no beauty in the world, nothing good or compassionate, so he'd wandered, aimless, and hoped maybe God might smite him, because Montgomery was too much of a coward to take a knife to his neck.

"You'll share yourself with me for the span of an hour and then what? I'm two paces from loving you, two paces from having my heart destroyed," he said and smirked. "Because you are not going to love me back, and when you leave me, like a ship run aground, you won't care. It's not because you'll be cruel, it's because it's the way of the world. So if you want me, you'll have to say you love me, and make a liar of yourself."

She did not speak a single word, curling up on the center of the bed, blinking through the tears, not letting herself cry, holding back, but still terribly sad. At least she was calmer now; the aguardiente was making her lids heavy.

"I need someone who won't leave me," she whispered at last.

"You'll have me for as long as you require my assistance."

He could give her that. She needed it more than she needed his body.

"You'll swear to it?"

"Yes."

He felt exhausted, but he watched her until she fell asleep, knowing he'd never have the pleasure of that sight again.

CHAPTER 23

Carlota

IT WAS EARLY when she awoke and stretched her body, her fingers touching the headboard. She turned her head on the pillow and saw Montgomery asleep in a chair next to his desk, his arms crossed against his chest. It did not look like a comfortable position, and she felt sorry for him sleeping like that.

Then she remembered that she'd kissed him the previous night and how he'd touched her before pushing her aside. The embarrassment should have killed her on the spot, but instead she felt better, even if she'd made a fool of herself.

She'd been heartbroken and raw. When Eduardo had looked at her it had been like a dagger to the heart. The way he flinched, the way his eyes fell on her before he walked out of the room . . . she wouldn't forget that look.

She'd wanted to pretend that everything was fine and that she was still loved, that someone cared about her, because her father was a liar and she was monstrous and she thought the well of affection had run dry. But Montgomery had seen through her despair.

She stood up, picked her discarded robe from the floor, and touched him on the arm. He grunted and looked up at her.

"Good morning, Montgomery," she said.

"Morning?" he muttered and rubbed his eyes. "Doesn't feel like it."

"The sun is up."

"Mmm . . . let me sleep longer and maybe lend me a pillow."

"I'm afraid that wouldn't be a good idea. We have plenty to discuss with the others, and the Lizaldes will be back soon enough."

"If they have any decency, they'll be back after I have my breakfast," he muttered.

She smiled, appreciating his attempt at humor. He hadn't shaved in a couple of days and was becoming scruffier, but he looked more like himself than when he attempted to shave his face clean.

"I have a great big headache and I'm up. You can get up, too."

"No surprises there, the way you guzzled my aguardiente. You'll feel better after you have a cup of coffee," he said, cracking his knuckles and shaking his head as if to rouse himself.

"I must apologize for that. I shouldn't have . . . It must have been bad for you," she said, not sure exactly how to put it.

He smiled. "Sweetheart, that was the most fun I've had in ages."

"You mustn't jest with me," she said, swatting him on the arm, but he laughed harder.

"I'm serious, you swine. It's not . . . I don't want you to think poorly of me or to have that be something . . . I don't want to break anything," she said, brushing the edge of the desk with her index finger.

He went quiet and looked at her solemnly. "Nothing's broken and I don't think less of you for it. There's nothing wrong with kissing a man if you want to and it feels right. But it didn't last night, and I don't need lies. Not from you. We are friends, Carlota. That won't change."

The relief she felt was great. She had feared rejection would sour him against her, but he truly didn't look upset. Maybe he was good at concealing his disappointments, unlike Carlota, who cried and ranted and burned, unable to mask anything at all. Not anymore.

"No lies, then," she said and extended her hand. "We shall maintain our friendship."

"I'd toast to it, but you drank my aguardiente," he said, shaking her hand.

"I know you have another bottle hidden in this desk," she said, tapping a drawer with her knuckles.

"Yes, but I'm not letting you drink it and get fresh with me again."

She blushed, and he laughed louder, but it was better now. This was themselves, as they normally were, less complicated. Her heart was already in knots, and she didn't want to twist it any further, didn't want to hurt him out of selfishness, either.

"I'm going to change. You might want to splash a few drops of water on yourself. You don't smell nice this morning," she said, wrinkling her nose, and he gave her another smile and a shake of the head.

Before going back to her room she went to see her father. Ramona was sitting next to him, drinking a cup of coffee, when she peeked her head inside the room. Carlota stood by the doorway, biting her lip, unsure whether she should step any closer. Never had she spoken back to her father. Never had she dreamed she'd hurt him. She thought she ought to pray for him but feared God would strike her dead.

Then again, Dr. Moreau had been the God of Yaxaktun, dispensing wisdom and punishment and love. If he were to perish, it would be like the sun being extinguished in the sky, and yet she could not stop herself from wishing him ill.

I am a bad daughter, she thought.

"He's still sleeping," Ramona said, catching sight of her. "You want coffee?"

"No change at all? He has not woken up?" she asked timidly, finally walking into the room.

"No. It takes time to heal."

Maybe, but Carlota didn't know if he'd heal from this, and it was not as if they could send for a physician. She bent down and touched his arm, pressing her palm against it. Her father was such a strong man, but strength had fled him, and she could now see the marks of age clearly on his body, the white hair and wrinkles that he strived to hide behind that commanding voice of his. Even when the gout struck him Dr. Moreau was no invalid.

"Why were you giving them supplies?" she asked Ramona, drawing her hand away.

"I didn't plan it. I went to the cenote of Báalam and stumbled on to a young man hiding there. He was a fugitive who'd ran off from a hacienda. He was looking for Cumux and his men. I knew nothing about that, but I fed him and sent him on his way. He came back later, thanking me for my help, and said he'd found what he was looking for. But he looked scrawny and I told him, take this food. Then he'd come back, and if not him, others."

"And Lupe knew."

"Lupe's always in the kitchen, helping me. She noticed, even followed me a couple of times when I went to leave supplies for them. You shouldn't be angry at her or at Mr. Laughton. It's a hard world out there, Loti. They lash the workers in the fields. I had to help the boy."

"I'm not angry," Carlota said tiredly. "But I do wish there was a way to make this whole thing go away."

She tugged at a corner of her father's bedsheet, smoothing it with her hand. "Ramona, were you aware I am a hybrid?"

"No, Loti. You were a girl when I came here. You were sick often, but the doctor explained it was a thing of your blood and you didn't look anything like the animal folk."

"Montgomery says he didn't know, either. I can't understand how I could have been so stupid and never guessed the truth, or how others wouldn't have known."

"Cachito and Lupe didn't know, either, so how could anyone understand what he'd done?"

Carlota looked at her father's face, trying to recall the features they shared. But he seemed to have transformed during the night, and she could see little of him in herself. She stood up. "Thanks for watching over my father. I'll come back in a bit and take your place."

Carlota changed quickly into a day dress and brushed her hair with firm strokes. Her father had always asked her to be meek and sweet. He hadn't prepared her to make difficult decisions or deal with strife. But she had many issues to consider now and could not back down. When she was ready, she fetched Montgomery, and together they walked to the area with the workers' huts, where Cachito and Lupe and the others were waiting for them.

They'd all gathered outside as they did when her father administered their medication. The old ones and the younger hybrids, the small, scrawny ones and the great lumbering creatures. Most of them were sitting, like they might have been around the bonfire, and all of them looked solemn and a few outright frightened under the blazing blue sky. Twenty-nine pairs of eyes fixed on Carlota.

When the hybrids gathered, it was the doctor who spoke. Carlota did not address the congregation. She felt shy standing before them, aware she did not possess her father's voice, which was a clap of thunder.

"I'm sure Lupe and Cachito have told you what happened last night and the ramifications of it," she began, because they were all looking at her. "Suffice to say my father has fallen ill, and what's worse the owner of Yaxaktun intends to take us from this land."

The hybrids whispered and stared at her.

She took a deep breath. "Several options have been proposed between us. The others will speak of that. For myself, I do not wish any violence, nor to flee, though we might, seeing as my father's treatments were a sham. I hope that we may reason with the Lizaldes. They might not be as intractable as we think."

She thought again of Eduardo's face and his look of disgust, but she didn't care if he helped her out of pity and did not turn with love to her ever again. Though such desertion would hurt, she'd gladly suffer the breaking of her heart if it meant the salvation of Yaxaktun.

She did not dare to consider that he cared for her still, though a small spark burned inside her mind, hoping and yearning. She wished to snuff it and couldn't bring herself to do it yet.

"Carlota thinks we may negotiate, but it's mighty difficult to speak when men carry rifles," Lupe said, wiping her palms against her skirt and standing up. "I've heard these gentlemen talking. They'll have no qualms in putting a bullet in our chest. Ramona knows a path through the jungle that can lead us away, to a place where Juan Cumux and his men live. We can hide there."

"And should they follow?" Carlota asked. "Should they hunt you down?"

"Better than to sit here and wait for them, don't you think?"

"Is this place far? Would we have to walk many days?" one of the hybrids asked. Her furry face and tusks resembled those of a boar. It was Paquita, one of the youngest ones, and she spoke in a voice as thin as a reed.

"Yes," Lupe said. "But all journeys end."

"Where would this one end exactly?" asked Estrella. "And what will the humans do, if they should see us on the road?"

"Roast us in a pit," piped La Pinta and yelped.

The faces of the hybrids were grim. Old Aj Kaab picked at his large fangs with a twig and smacked his lips. "What say you, Mr. Laughton? You are quiet this morning."

Montgomery was standing with his arms crossed, looking at the ground. She stared at him, fearing he'd talk again about taking up arms and slaughtering men.

"I had thought to propose that we ambush and kill them," he said, and she felt her breath hot against her fingertips as she pressed her hand against her mouth. "But it's not right to ask you to risk yourselves and engage in such violence. Lupe is correct, it might be best to escape while it's possible. We can gather supplies, grab whatever can be taken. With luck, Ramona might be able to ensure safe passage for everyone through macehual territory, since she knows Cumux's men. Should we vote on it?"

"I don't think there's much to vote on," Peek' said, scratching his long tapir's snout with a sharp nail. "Only a fool would stay here."

"Skinny coward," Aj Kaab said, his voice was almost a grumble. "I'll face them if the others won't."

"And be roasted in a pit," La Pinta said, repeating the grim picture and letting out another yelp.

"What do you say, K'an?" Lupe asked.

The hybrid shook her long yellow mane and slapped her long arms against her thighs. "I say Aj Kaab is too lazy to make a run for it, but I'm ready for a sprint."

Some of the hybrids chuckled. Lupe asked for a show of hands. The consensus was clear: they'd leave. Cachito began telling the others to gather their belongings. Lupe and Montgomery stood next to Carlota as they watched the hybrids shuffle into their huts, looking for sacks and clothes and whatever they could find.

"I have jewelry you must take, Lupe," Carlota said. "Most of what my father gave me was paste jewelry and colored glass, but there's my fan with the ivory handle, and maybe Aj Kaab can carry some of the silver. He's slow, but strong. You'll need money."

"You intend to remain at Yaxaktun?" Lupe asked.

"I can't leave my father here," Carlota said, and she began walking back toward the house. Lupe walked close to her. Montgomery frowned and followed a few paces behind them.

"Loti, you can't stay in the house alone. Besides, the doctor is a bad man. He lied to you. To all of us!"

"I can't leave him to rot alone in bed. Maybe you don't care, but I do."

"No, I don't care," Lupe said vehemently. "He made us knowing full well Lizalde would come to collect his due one day. He told us lies. Worst of all, he tattooed death in our flesh. Have you seen us? Have you seen the elders and the way their muscles and bones ache? And Cachito and I will be old before our time. He deserves his fate. Don't be stupid, Loti. Run away while you can."

"You must get ready," Carlota muttered, walking faster, not wanting to consider the idea. Lupe picked up the pace, too.

"Is it that you still want that man? Are you thinking Eduardo Lizalde is going to save you?" Lupe asked.

Carlota did not reply, her hands pressed against her skirts. Lupe stared at her incredulously and chuckled. "Are you really thinking of him?"

"No. I'm thinking of my father. But if I could talk to Eduardo, perhaps he would convince Hernando Lizalde not to pursue you."

"You are a great fool. Fine! Stay behind. I'm leaving," Lupe said, and she turned around and walked back toward the huts of the hybrids.

Carlota took a deep breath and closed her eyes. Her head throbbed, aching with the excess of the previous night. She didn't understand how Montgomery could make a habit out of drinking, nor how she could have thought liquor would fix her problems. Well, she knew now that neither flesh nor spirits provided the comfort she sought. As Montgomery had said, what she wanted was not to be found at the bottom of a bottle, but she had no idea where it might be.

She wished to be unafraid and for the world to be good. Neither thing seemed possible.

"Lupe's not wrong," Montgomery said. He had his hands in the pockets of his trousers, and despite his bleary appearance a little while ago he seemed alert now, gray eyes inviting her to debate, as he often did.

"You think I'm stupid, too?" she asked, unable to stop herself from sounding bitter and more disagreeable than she wanted to.

"I think you should leave."

"My father can't be moved, and I can't leave without him."

"Hernando Lizalde will not be nice. That man is out for blood, and I doubt Eduardo will protect you."

"I realize the risk I'm taking," she said, voice firm.

"I'm not sure you do," he muttered.

The grass grew tall by the white limestone path that led from the dividing wall back to the house. When she'd been a child, the grass had been taller than her and she'd crouched there, giggling; she'd played hide-and-seek with her father. Now she pulled a couple of blades, twisting them between her hands.

"You won't change my mind. To leave him alone would mean to leave him to die. I won't do that, never."

"We could take Dr. Moreau with us. Make a stretcher or a contraption of some sort," Montgomery suggested, but she shook her head.

"It would slow the others down and it might kill him. I'll stay."

"Then I'll stay with you," he said quickly.

"You don't—"

"I promised I would last night, didn't I?"

"It doesn't mean you knew then what you'd be promising."

"I keep my promises, Miss Moreau, whatever they may be."

"On this occasion you might wish to reconsider and break your vow."

"No, I won't."

"It's not as if you'd be any help if you did stay."

"You know, Carlota, there will be a day when you'll actually agree with me, but that day will be the day the world ends. Still, I look forward to it."

She could tell by the look in his eyes that he wasn't going anywhere, and she let out a sigh, but she felt terribly grateful.

"Thank you, Monty," she said and took his hand between her own.

He scratched his head and looked at her with no small amount of nervousness. She wondered what he was thinking and what made him anxious. "Look here, Carlota, I should tell you—"

"Montgomery!" Cachito waved at them from the door that led to the workers' living area. "What should we do about the horses and the donkeys? And Aj Kaab insists we should take a pig with us. He's a glutton. I don't think we should!"

Montgomery sighed and frowned, turning to look at Cachito with ill-concealed irritation.

Carlota smiled and released his hand. "Go ahead, sir. We'll talk later," she told him.

"Carlota, I take my leave for now," Montgomery said, very formally, tipping his straw hat at her before walking toward Cachito and yelling back at him. "What, then, doesn't he want a turkey to go with it? Let me talk to him!"

CHAPTER 24

Montgomery

HE'D NEVER BEEN skilled at goodbyes and would have preferred to simply wave away silently. Still, he talked to the boy.

"You be careful," Montgomery told Cachito. "Take care of each other and be smart."

"I'll try. But, Montgomery, I'm not sure we can get far," Cachito said. The hybrids were still finishing packing clothes and wrapping things with twine, moving in and out of the huts, while Montgomery and Cachito spoke. The excitement and nervousness were palpable, and Cachito looked half terrified. "I thought your idea to ambush them was good."

"And should you be wounded? Or die?"

"Some of us want to fight."

"*You* want to fight. Most of the others don't."

"Well, you want to fight, too," Cachito said defensively. "Maybe you even want to die heroically for Loti."

"Trust me, boy. I'd rather not die soon."

"You used to want to. And it's really stupid, Montgomery, to simply send us off like this."

"We took a vote, remember?"

Cachito grumbled, and Montgomery placed a hand on the boy's shoulder and smiled. He handed Cachito his old compass and a map.

"My uncle gave it to me as a gift. It's made of silver, engraved with my initials. See? Now it's yours. Maybe it'll help you find the way. At worst, it might be worth something."

"Montgomery, but it's your compass."

"It was. Don't lose it in a card game. If you do, steal it back. I know I have from time to time."

Cachito laughed at that. After that there were more preparations and a few matters to be sorted out, but soon enough came the time to walk to the portón and throw open the double doors.

Ramona wept and told Carlota to be a good girl, and Carlota wept, too. But there was no tearful, drawn-out goodbye between Lupe and the girl. Lupe seemed eager to depart and gave Carlota a quick hug before slipping aside.

The hybrids hoisted their belongings—food, clothes, the other supplies they'd scrounged—and they began to walk together. The ones with crippled limbs were at the rear, moving slower, and the younger ones, afflicted with less deformities, at the front. It was a tapestry of glossy and mangy furs, misshapen arms brushing against the dirt, crooked spines. Yet they moved with an odd grace despite the disproportion of their bodies as they went past the gates of Yaxaktun, past the Moorish arch and the two ceiba trees. Past the many enclosures that separated them from the outside, until the last of the hybrids was out of sight. The sun was ending its journey and the land would soon be swathed in darkness. It would hopefully conceal them. In this distant spot visitors and wanderers were few, yet the veil of night would be an extra precaution.

"Lupe hardly said a word to me," Carlota whispered.

"It's not always easy to say goodbye. I'm no good at it."

"Yes, but still . . . I wish she'd said more. I may never see her again, and she—"

The girl seemed to choke on her words and rushed back inside the house. He closed the doors, barred them, and walked into the house. He found Carlota back at her father's bedside, as she'd been most of the day, and quietly stepped away. He wasn't any good with tears, either.

He walked around the empty workers' huts and stopped to admire the herb garden Ramona and Carlota had carefully assembled. He wondered what would happen to it when no one could tend to it, and he glanced at the hogs and the chickens. He would have to open the gates for them, he'd have to let the horses and the donkeys run free, too, and to open the birdcages in the courtyard. He'd have to do that before Lizalde's men arrived.

He pictured the courtyard, which now grew lush and beautiful, and imagined it neglected, full of weeds and dead vegetation. He'd liked Yaxaktun. Not because of the doctor, who had his grandiose dreams. Montgomery had smaller dreams he'd casually planted in this soil; the dream of quiet and distance from the world.

Night was thick around them now. Montgomery lit a few lamps. He retreated to the sitting room and listened to the rococo clock ticking before seeking the dome of the starry sky. In the courtyard the fountain gurgled, and he dipped a hand in the water, then rubbed it against the back of his neck, relishing the coolness of the water.

Dear Fanny, he thought. But he could put none of his emotions or thoughts into sentences. For once in his life that familiar mechanism failed him. He was left alone, with nothing to anchor him.

"What are you doing?" Carlota asked.

She'd come up quietly to him, as she often did, and he was not startled. "Wasting time," he said. "Any change in the doctor's condition?"

"None. I don't know what to do," she whispered, her hands fluttering up, fingers grazing her lips for a second.

"Nothing but wait and hope."

"I thought of going to the chapel and praying for him. But then I thought God might strike me dead."

"God is not real."

"I'd be angrier at your blasphemy, but I'm too tired," she said.

"Do you want me to watch over the doctor for a bit?" he asked, thinking it couldn't be easy for her to be sitting by the old man's bed for hours and hours.

"I need a few minutes and a bit of fresh air," she paused, her voice low. "I feel like we must speak in whispers, though I don't understand why."

"One often does, when someone is ill," he said, thinking of his mother's final days. He didn't know what Elizabeth's final days had been like. Thoughts of suicide were, perhaps, as much an illness as the tumor that drained their mother's life.

"How old were you, when your parents died?"

"I was a child when my mother passed away, and older than you when my father finally perished."

"And did you mourn him? Even though he'd wronged you?"

"No. I didn't wear black, I didn't pray for him. I hoped he went to hell."

"But you don't believe in hell."

"And yet I'd like to believe in hell."

Her eyes were soft and dark and sad. She tilted her face up to the sky, and he thought of wrapping his arms around her, but he shoved his hands into his pockets and contemplated the patio stones.

"The house seems awfully large and lonely now, don't you think? It seems haunted, although I've grown up here and never seen a ghost," she whispered. "Ramona told us about a house in Villahermosa that is haunted. There's a ghost that smells like rotten meat that moves through the rooms. I wonder if they'll say this house is haunted one day."

"Come, Carlota, we should head inside and I'll watch over your father," he said. He didn't like it when she spoke like that.

"No, I'm fine. Don't mind me, I'm simply tired."

"The more reason to go to bed. Let me look after the doctor."

"You can't stay up all night. It would be worse, if they come in the morning and you're exhausted, then what will we do?"

"I can still shoot even if I've slept only a couple of hours."

"You must not mention that again," she said, shaking her head. "Please, don't receive them with weapons drawn."

"Perhaps I ought to greet them with a warm embrace."

"No, but let's attempt to speak first, then draw weapons second. Please. You are too quick to anger, sometimes."

"The same could be said about you."

"Yes, and I do not like myself for it. If I hadn't lost my temper when Eduardo's father was in the sitting room, if I hadn't leaped up like I did and scratched him . . . if I hadn't done that, then maybe we could have resolved this simply."

"You mean maybe he'd have let you marry?"

"If he hadn't been so ill-disposed toward me . . ." Carlota said, wringing her hands together. "I ruined it, I did."

"I must tell you something. They would not have allowed it. Isidro wrote to his uncle. I didn't read the letter, but I delivered it to the mayordomo at Vista Hermosa, to be sent to Mérida. I didn't read it, but I can imagine what it said because Isidro told me, before posting it, that he didn't like you. That you were an unsuitable bride. I regret sending it, but I suspect it would have always been the same. They would have hated you."

She gave him a deep, grave look, her large eyes fixed on his face. "You were the one who summoned him, then?"

"Isidro did, but I helped him," he said in a choking voice, though he didn't want to say it. But he must. He had wanted to tell her that morning when they stood together outside, before Cachito interrupted them. He didn't think it fair to keep such secrets.

"Why would you do that? Do you despise me?"

"Carlota, I did it because I thought you'd be hurt. Because I was sure he'd be bad for you and he'd use you and cast you away. It was before you announced your engagement, before—"

"And maybe you were jealous," she said sharply.

For a second he wished to swear that his intentions had been good and pure, that he had sought to protect Carlota, but looking at her it was impossible to deny the truth: he'd wanted to rid himself of the young man, and yes, he had been jealous and petty.

"I was," he said. "And I'm sorry for that, too."

" 'Sorry' is not enough. I should slap you," she muttered, but she did not raise a hand against him. She sounded exhausted with grief. Instead, her fingers rested on his arm.

The gentle quietude of the house induced in them a torpor. He wanted not to speak to her but to simply bask in Carlota's presence for a few minutes, and he felt that she, too, had little need for words at the moment. Maybe they'd fight later and she'd reproach him and that slap would land on his cheek.

There was knocking at the portón, and Montgomery immediately tensed, hand at his pistol.

"Montgomery, please," she whispered, squeezing his arm. "Don't shoot before we have a chance to speak."

"I won't shoot first," he muttered. "But I'll still need my rifle. Go, run fast for it."

She looked uncertain, but nodded and rushed away. While the knocking continued, he slowly approached the door and opened the iron gate, then stood by the postigo. Carlota ran back to him, swift and looking scared, and handed him the rifle. He supposed neither pistol nor rifle could ensure their safety, but he felt a tad better with something more solid in his hands.

He drew a slow, determined breath. "Who goes there?" Montgomery asked.

"It's Lupe," a voice said.

He opened the door, and indeed it was Lupe, her clothes dusty from the road.

CHAPTER 25

Carlota

CARLOTA MADE COFFEE and offered Lupe a cup. She also pulled out a loaf of bread Ramona had baked the day before, and they dipped pieces of crusty bread into their coffee while they sat at the kitchen table. Lupe unwound her rebozo from around her head and folded it, setting it next to her. Her closely set eyes observed Carlota carefully.

"I went with them and followed the trail. It's not far from here. But I turned back after a while," Lupe said. She had not said much since they'd walked into the house. Montgomery had told them he'd go see how the doctor was doing, therefore giving them a chance to converse.

"I thought you wanted to leave."

"I talked it over with Cachito while we walked. We both think you are foolish, and I decided you might need me here."

"I'm glad you came back," Carlota said and squeezed Lupe's furry hand. "You were angry at me, you hardly said a word when you left."

Lupe drew her hand away; she clacked her nails against her clay cup. Her lips twitched but no sound emerged.

"You are my sister," Carlota said softly, and Lupe stared at her.

"That is a lie."

"It is true. I don't care how we came to be. You're still my sister. Cachito is my brother. You're my family."

"An interesting family we are," Lupe muttered. "Dr. Moreau's twisted mistakes."

"My father said he created the hybrids for a great purpose, in order to solve humanity's ills. Even when he mentioned that Hernando Lizalde funded his research in order to secure new workers, he always emphasized that other point. I've wanted to believe that he was indeed searching for an important piece of knowledge and that he would never let any of the hybrids come to harm. But now, knowing the ease with which he lied, and thinking about all the things he said, I can't . . . Lupe, I am sorry."

Silence settled between them. Carlota clenched her hands together.

"You asked me a few times why I liked going to the hut with the donkey's skull rather than the chapel," Lupe said. "I think it was because I thought a more truthful God lived there than the God your father spoke about. Your father said God willed him to right the mistakes of nature by fashioning our flesh, and gifted us pain, but that must be a cruel God who could do such a thing. He held that Bible up and read from it, but I don't think he knew the words."

"My father has been irresponsible, utterly careless," Carlota whispered.

His investigations had birthed creatures bound to suffer, to die painfully, and he'd masked his aimless pursuits with talk of God and great purposes, then padded all this with careful lies she didn't fully understand yet.

"Yes. And for all of that you should leave him to die in his own piss and go away with me, but I know you won't and I won't ask you to do it. So here we are, to stand vigil by a dying man. I came back, because I didn't want you to face this without me."

"Lupe."

"Don't cry, Carlota. You cry far too easily."

Carlota smiled at that, and Lupe smiled back. When they'd been little, Lupe had braided Carlota's hair, and Carlota giggled and ran a brush across the soft fur of Lupe's back. They'd followed rows of ants back to their anthill and clapped their hands together, played games of hide-and-seek throughout the house. She'd liked Cachito, but she'd been closest to Lupe. Then, somewhere in the past few months, the divide between them had surfaced and grown very wide. But she felt that, for the first time, this chasm might be crossed.

"Your father is awake," Montgomery said, standing at the doorway. "He wishes to speak to you."

Carlota rose quickly. They walked back to her father's room. Montgomery had lit two lamps, so that the bed was bathed in a yellowish light. Dr. Moreau lay pale and frail under the bedsheets. He was indeed awake, and when Carlota sat next to the bed, he turned his face in her direction and raised a hand, his fingers reaching for her. Carlota grasped his hand, but weakly, where before she would have kissed it and laid her cheek against it.

"Carlota, there you are," he muttered.

She said nothing. She was ashamed of her fury, of having hurt him. She feared for his life. She also couldn't look him in the eye. She poured him a glass of water and held it up so he could drink. He did so slowly. When he was done, she put the glass back on the night table.

The roles were now reversed. In her earliest years her father had sat by her bed and she had clutched his hand for comfort, powerless and weak. Now the doctor lay there, his sturdy body looking as if it might dissolve under her fingertips, sinews and bones coming loose.

"Child, I do not blame you for what has happened," her father said, his voice low.

"I do blame you for it. For keeping secrets from me. For not telling me who I am," she said in turn, calmly, and saw him wince as if she'd struck him again.

"I could not speak freely, Carlota."

"You told me I was your daughter and that I was ill and needed a special treatment. You said the hybrids needed to have their medication, too, but that wasn't true, either. You were trying to maintain us docile and quiet."

"I had to tell you that you needed constant medicating. I couldn't have you leaving Yaxaktun. It was also necessary to maintain the fiction because of Hernando Lizalde. This way, he couldn't take the hybrids from me."

"Was it also necessary to give us painful, truncated lives?" Lupe asked. She stood on the other side of the bed, eyes fixed on the doctor.

Her father sighed. "I admit I blundered. But sometimes I struck gold, and could claim a near-perfect victory. Carlota, for example . . . Carlota, you provided me with such valuable information!" he said, his voice filled with excitement. "The younger hybrids are much improved. No more monstrosities like Aj Kaab with his ever-growing teeth or the tumors previous hybrids developed. And it was thanks to you that I was able to create stronger hybrids with less defects and extended life spans."

"Extended how?" Carlota asked. "Thirty years, that's the life span of a hybrid. That is what you told Mr. Lizalde."

"I crossed that limit but never revealed it for fear he'd think the project was at an end, for fear he'd snatch you from my arms. You, Lupe, Cachito, the younger ones, you should all live the life span of a common adult. I improved my work."

He stretched out a trembling hand, as if to touch her face. "Can't you see how difficult a feat you are? You are better than human. Almost flawless."

She turned her head so that he might not reach her. "What of the other hybrids? Didn't you hear what Lupe said? Their bodies pain them. Their joints ache. Their sight grows poor quickly or they have growths over their skin. You've always dismissed their complaints and even if they are stronger than previous creations, they are far from healthy."

Lupe had turned her back to the doctor and moved close to the window, grasping the curtains and looking outside.

"I had to create the hybrids for Lizalde, Carlota. I did. Without them, I'd have had no funding, nothing. The intermingling of human and animal traits had unexpected side effects. Birth defects, illness. It's as if by ripping out the front page of a book you also ripped three from the back of it. I've attempted to correct the course, but it is hard, and the funding dwindled with each year. Hernando Lizalde grew deaf to my pleas. I did what I could for you, my daughter."

But not for the others, she thought. Had there been treatments that he could have developed for them instead of spinning an elaborate fiction? Could there have been relief for them?

"You had Montgomery bring jaguars periodically," Carlota said, frowning. "You said they were used for my treatment, but since that was a lie, what did you use them for?"

"At first, to try and replicate my success with you. I thought the jaguar had been the key ingredient, but as the years went by I suspected it was your mother who in some mysterious way made the difference. But I did not dare have another woman carry a child and limited myself to using the hogs and my incubating chamber rather than a human womb. Still, I held hope the jaguar might be an important clue. Later, it became a necessary pretense. If you should ever manifest any animal traits, I thought I could convince you it was the injections I had given you. I could tell my assistant the same story."

"But Melquíades knew the truth. It couldn't have been much of a pretense."

"Melquíades suspected, but toward the end. It was why I had him thrown out and hired Montgomery. He was also trying to steal my research, which didn't help matters. He was putting his nose where it didn't belong, going through my journals." Her father's face had grown agitated, regaining a fraction of his furious vitality. "And it worked, it did work. Montgomery didn't know, Hernando didn't, either. Melquíades guessed. He guessed. But I could have fixed it. If you hadn't attacked Hernando . . . but, ah, I might still fix it.

"Yes, think about your youth! You've been whole and healthy for many years now. Gone are the migraines, the pain. Even now, this transformation that overtook you is but a brief episode. Your limbs are strong and straight, your eyes are clear. I took care of you, and I will continue to do so. Tweaks . . . everything can be tweaked."

She thought he might try to reach for her again, and this made her want to weep. But instead she raised her head high. "For you everything is still a work in progress. Something that must be tweaked.

But sometimes you break something, father, and you can't put it back together again."

Her father muttered a couple of words and then he groaned, seemingly running out of breath, his burst of energy quickly spent. He compressed his lips and then turned his eyes to a corner of the room, where Montgomery stood silently.

"Mr. Laughton, can you grab pen and paper and take dictation?"

"I can."

"Then do so now, please."

She heard Montgomery fiddling with drawers and pulling a chair, sitting at the table where her father scribbled notes. Then her father spoke again.

"Are you ready?"

"Yes."

"Date the document, please. I, Gustave Moreau, being of sound mind and body, hereby bequeath all my possessions and the monies in my bank account to my natural daughter, Carlota Moreau. I designate as my executor Francisco Ritter of Mérida and to him I also assign the task of contacting my brother, Émile, that he may know of the existence of his niece. I have asked for nothing for myself, but do request of you, Émile, that my daughter be granted the fortune I was denied, that she be provided as would befit a Moreau. This, I beg of my brother, as my dying wish. Now you must sign as my witness, Montgomery, and I will sign my name, too."

"What are you doing?" she asked.

"Leaving behind what I have. And ensuring someone will look after you. My family banished me, but it's been many years since then, and my brother will feel obligated to his kin, even if it's a girl he's never met."

"A girl who is not human."

"A girl who is my daughter. You will always be the better part of me," he said with a terrible tenderness and a sadness that made his voice tremble.

Carlota watched quietly as her father signed his name, then handed her the piece of paper. She looked at it as if she'd never seen such an item before, inspecting Montgomery's compact handwriting and her father's signature, then carefully folding it.

"This is the one other thing I can give you," her father said tiredly, pulling at a silver chain which encircled his neck and holding up a small key. "There is a glass cabinet in my laboratory. It is always closed. That is where I store my journals and all the notes on my research. I've kept secrets from you but will not any longer. I need to rest now. I'll feel better afterward."

She clutched both the key and the letter between her hands and watched as her father closed his eyes. His breathing was shallow.

She stood up, dizzy with an awful mixture of emotions. Lupe had turned to look in her direction again and threw her a questioning glance. She remembered what she'd said, that Carlota cried too easily, and she brushed the back of her hand against her eyes.

"Carlota, I'll keep watch over him. You and Lupe go to sleep. I'll wake you in a few hours," Montgomery offered.

Her first instinct was to say no. She feared her father might die during the night and she would not be there when it happened. But she also feared she would be next to him when his demise took place. Despite the fact that she had stayed in the house for his sake, she now wished to run away so that she did not witness the terrible event.

"Yes, I think, I'll retire," Carlota said.

Lupe accompanied her out of the room. They walked side by side, and Carlota leaned on Lupe as they stepped into the hallway; she could hardly see where she was going. "Lupe, what will I do if he dies?"

"Loti, I'm sorry," Lupe said, her fingers running through Carlota's hair. "I know you love him."

"I do. I can't help it. And he's sick and . . . God, I'm afraid," Carlota admitted. "I want to cry and cry and nothing helps. I tried to drink and I tried . . . Lupe, I'm scared."

Each hour of the day was laced with anxiety. The dread pressed against her lungs, making it hard to breathe, and she was terrified of so many things, even of herself.

"Don't be scared and don't cry. I came back, right? You're a milk-sop, Loti, and you'd die of fright without me. It's fine, you silly cow-ard."

Carlota's lips trembled, but when she looked at Lupe she managed a smile. "You're not making it any better by insulting me."

"You're a crying, annoying baby."

"Oh, you're bad," Carlota said, giving Lupe a little shove, and Lupe shoved her back. This was how they played. Lupe pulled her closer, wrapping an arm around Carlota's waist. They stood still.

Carlota took a deep breath. "I think I'll go to the laboratory tomorrow," she whispered, opening her hand and looking at the key.

CHAPTER 26

Montgomery

HE THOUGHT ABOUT drinking the whole day. From the moment Carlota relieved him and took his place at the doctor's side to the morning, when he washed his face and had his breakfast, to the hour when the sun was highest in the sky and he opened the pens so the chickens and the pigs could roam free. He thought about it as he dabbed at the sweat on his forehead and before he lay down for a nap, with his arm pressed across his eyes.

Granted, it hadn't been that long since he'd had a drink, but he wanted another and another. He wanted to be stinking drunk because he was nervous and he was upset, and alcohol had always been his trusty friend.

He thought about Cachito and wondered where he was and felt his gut churning. Then he pictured Lizalde's men banging at the doors, and he selfishly wished Dr. Moreau would perish within the next five minutes so the three of them could run off. He hadn't lied when he told Cachito he wasn't especially interested in dying. Not from a bullet or a knife. If that had been the case, he would have gotten himself into a fight years ago and would have been happy to end his days in a pool of blood.

No, stupid masochist that he was, he had intended to die slowly and quietly.

He wanted to drink because whenever the world was bitter the alcohol muffled the pain, and he wanted to slip away for a bit. But he couldn't now, not with the way things were. He felt damn low that day, and he really would have liked to polish off a bottle all alone in his room. Instead he sent it flying out the window, to crash against the ground.

Dear Fanny, it's not the best time to be sober, he thought. His long letters to his former wife were now turning into telegrams.

It was nearly dusk when he found Carlota in the laboratory, leaning over one of the long tables, books and papers spread all around her. He carefully brushed a book aside and placed the bowl of rice and beans on the table and the mug filled with coffee next to it. Rather than looking for more aguardiente, he'd made himself useful and ventured into the kitchen. He had never been a good cook and appreciated Ramona's abilities to render tasty treats for all of them.

The dish he'd conjured was probably deficient despite its simplicity, yet it was what he could manage, and Lupe had at least appreciated the coffee that he'd brewed.

"I thought you and Lupe would want supper," he said.

The young woman raised her head and stared at him but did not reply.

"You can't be here in the dark, you'll strain your eyes. Let me light the lamp."

"I can see in the dark," she said, her voice flat.

"Carlota?" he asked cautiously. "Are you well?"

She nodded; the line of her lips told him nothing. He lit the lamp and placed it on the table. He stood across from her, glancing at the papers she had taken out of the glass case. She did not touch the food nor the coffee.

"Come now, sweetheart, talk to me," he said.

She sighed deeply but provided no response at all. They seemed at an impasse. Then she began drawing invisible figures with her fingertip, brushing the page of an open notebook. He spied on it the drawing of a jaguar.

"I've been reading my father's journals. There are a few of them. I went looking for information on my mother. She was twenty years of age when she had me. She died of sepsis. He weighed her, measured her, noted her coloration, kept notes on her pregnancy and my delivery. Yet he said almost nothing about who she was. And when he wrote about me it was the same. I know my reflexes were abnormally fast, but I do not know if he celebrated my first birthday. My life and that of everyone at Yaxaktun is recorded in these papers, yet he says nothing about us, not truly. And in his monstrous selfishness he wonders, constantly, how we are to be of use to him."

She tucked her hands in her lap, looking down. "I have blindly loved my father, and in doing so I have ignored the atrocities he bequeathed us. I have followed him without question and for that God will punish me."

"I've told you, there is no God."

"Maybe not for you, sir," she said angrily. "But I do believe in God. Maybe not the God whose face my father showed me, but a God. In doing what we've done here, in the needless cruelty of my father's experiments and the creation of the hybrids, we have sinned. I thought Yaxaktun a paradise, but it is not so. He shaped pain into flesh.

"He made me and he wrote . . . do you know what he wrote? That I was 'the most humanlike of his cursed lot.' *Hi non sunt homines; sunt animalia.* We are *animals.* And being animals our only purpose was to serve him," she said and held up a journal, reading from it. " 'Similar research has been undertaken by breeders of horses and dogs, by all kinds of untrained clumsy-handed men working for their own immediate ends. The difference is that I operate with more finesse.' That is what my father said. And you know how he ends this entry? He wonders out loud about the great reception he'll have in Europe once he demonstrates his scientific accomplishments, he imagines the glory heaped upon his shoulders. And he says 'when Carlota understands the full extent of my achievements and experiments, she might resent me. But then all children come to hold grudges against their progenitors, and her discomfort is no great consideration when weighed against my intellectual passions. Although I have made monsters, I have also performed miracles.' "

She let the journal fall upon the table and stared at it.

"There is no perfect place on Earth. Everywhere I've gone, I've seen the cruelties and excesses of men. It is why I came to Yaxaktun and remained here, because at least it offered a semblance of happiness. I never saw monsters," he said.

Her face had taken on a severe, sharp appearance, and she was breathing faster. "It doesn't matter what you saw. It was wrong. And what shall become of the hybrids now? I should have gone with them, this is my responsibility. I am the doctor's daughter, after all. I should have, but I could not."

"Hush now," he said and walked around the table, holding the girl, for she looked feverish, and he feared she'd collapse as she'd once done before him.

"You don't care," she muttered, and he felt her hands pressed against his chest.

"I do. I wonder if Cachito is afraid almost every hour of the day and whether trackers would be able to hunt them down."

"Trackers! Hernando Lizalde wouldn't be able to get trackers that quickly, would he?"

"I suspect not. But even if he does in a month, in two, the danger will still be there."

He felt a pinprick of pain above his heart and let out a gruff complaint. The girl yelped in shock, pushing him away with a coiled strength that surprised him. He moved two paces back, softly stumbled against a cabinet, making specimens behind glass tremble.

"I'm sorry, I didn't realize I was—"

Her fingers were tapered into long, sharp nails, like a cat that shows its claws, and like a cat she retracted the nails. The spot where she'd nicked him was blooming into a tiny red flower, staining his shirt.

"I've hurt you." She raised a hand to cover her face. "I can't control it. My father said to be good and calm. But I don't know what to do. I don't know how to make it stop."

Her free hand rested on an open book, and her fingers curled together, drawing a slash across the page. The jaguar was thus mangled, the perfect lines of its body broken.

"It's fine. Sit, Carlota. Give me a minute to tend to myself," he said, his voice shaky. He had no idea what to do, either.

He looked among the shelves and found a piece of gauze. Then he proceeded to unbutton his shirt and dab at the wound. It was shallow, like a paper cut. She'd applied little force, and he was reminded once again of a cat, this time kneading upon a human's lap. What an odd thought! And she was strong, despite her slimness. He'd witnessed that already when she'd hoisted Moreau up.

When he buttoned up, she had her back turned toward him and had sat down again.

He thought Carlota might have herself a good cry, but instead the girl reached for the bowl and the spoon and began eating. She sipped her coffee but wrinkled her nose at it. When she was done he asked her if she wanted him to boil her a cup of tea in case she preferred something else to drink. She nodded her head and pushed the mug aside.

"Carlota, look at me," he said, and she raised her eyes to him. "I've met monsters. They weren't hybrids and they weren't you."

"I could kill a man," she said and held her hands up, examining them carefully. But her fingers were once again the long, elegant fingers of a lady.

"So could I, if he meant me harm." He placed a hand over her own, brushing her knuckles with his fingertips. "I don't know how to help you, but you can't start by hating yourself."

"You don't like yourself, Montgomery," she said accusingly.

He smiled, a lopsided grin. He thought of Elizabeth, dead and gone long ago, and her specter knotted around his heart. He thought of the mistakes he'd made, the crimes of omission he committed, his numerous weaknesses, and the vices he'd nurtured.

"No, I don't like myself," he said, shaking his head. "I've spent a long time loathing myself and trying to accelerate my demise. But you shouldn't be like me. Take it from someone who knows."

"I don't know who I should be. I'm Dr. Moreau's obedient daughter, and that's not enough anymore."

"Fortunately you don't have to determine everything this instant."

"I don't think there's much time left," she said. "The Lizaldes said they'd return."

True enough, but he didn't feel like exploring that line of thought at this time, so he raised the mug to his lips and sipped the coffee.

"Look," he said, when he was done and he had wiped his mouth with the back of his hand for wont of a handkerchief, "we can help the others by staying alive and then we'll see how we fare. If the Lizaldes stay away for a couple more days, perhaps we could try to move the doctor and take the boat."

"He remains rather frail."

"But he's drinking and eating a little, isn't he?"

"Only soup."

"That's one good sign, and he has woken up. The doctor is strong. I don't think this malady is going to kill him."

"You really think we'd be able to take him away?"

Montgomery wasn't really sure of anything, but Moreau was damn stubborn. Besides, he wanted the girl to calm down. She was all nerves and haunted eyes, and he himself wasn't faring well that day. He wondered if they could make their way to Yalajau. It had once been a den of criminals and filibusters, but that was in the past, elements left to fabricate romantic novels. It was now simply a port. From there one could try to gain passage to Corozal. Once in British territory, they'd be safe.

Of course, this plan required a chain of events that were hardly set in stone.

"I think we'd better pray to that God of yours that we may fare well," Montgomery said. "And save another prayer for the hybrids."

"I'll pray with you, sir, but afterward we should build a stretcher," Carlota said. "We'll need it if we are to transport my father."

"Perhaps you ought to rest," he said, wary that if they moved

Moreau that instant they'd end up dragging a corpse across the jungle.

"You were the one who suggested it."

True. But it was supposed to be an imaginary palliative. He hadn't imagined she'd spring into action, though he supposed it might be a good distraction.

"Do you not know how to make one?" Carlota asked.

"Do you?"

"Yes, I've read it in a book," she said, tipping her chin up proudly.

He smiled. "Open it to the right page, then," he said and thought perhaps this might work after all. He couldn't ferry all the hybrids across a lagoon, but he might be able to move a single man.

CHAPTER 27

Carlota

ON THE THIRD day after her father was seized with apoplexy they tried to move him and failed.

Their improvised stretcher was made of flour and bean sacks looped around two pieces of wood with rope, with crosspieces nailed to the poles. It was sturdy, and Montgomery and Lupe were strong enough to carry it and the doctor.

But when the time came to move her father, he seemed to have taken a turn for the worse. His face was flushed and his forehead hot to the touch. Carlota administered aconite to lower his blood pressure and sat next to his bed.

Montgomery had joked she should pray, and now she did, bowing her head and lacing her hands together. Lupe and Montgomery watched her with worry. After a few hours her father's condition improved, and he slept soundly.

It was nighttime. Carlota went back to her room, and Lupe relieved her. When she walked down the hallway she heard Montgomery speaking in his room. *Dear Fanny*, he said. The door was closed, and he was speaking in a low voice. She shouldn't have been able to hear him, but she did.

It was strange how her senses seemed to be growing sharper. Perhaps it was the fact that her father was no longer plying her with lithium and whatever other substances he thought might soothe her. Perhaps it was that a process that had started long ago only now fully came to bloom. But that strange dividing line inside her body, the crack that seemed to nestle at the center of her being, now felt deep and solid. A fault line, filled with dread and anger. Weighed with bone-combusting fury, her mouth was ready to open in a snarl.

She had to clench her fists tight and close her eyes.

It scared her, this capacity for strength, for violence. It also awed her.

Once inside her room Carlota divested herself of her clothes and stood before the mirror, naked—like Eve, like the painting in the chapel—and examined her body with the kind of care she had never examined it with before. She felt the muscles under her fingertips and the pulse beating at her wrists; she observed her eyes, glowing, in the semidarkness.

Her father had taught her to be meek. But her hands could pluck flowers or hurt a man.

Did she wish to hurt? No. Not Montgomery, not her father, not even Hernando Lizalde. Yet she might. And how strange it was to think of this possibility.

There were stories Ramona told of wizards who could change their skins and fly through the night. But Carlota was not like one of them. She couldn't shed her skin at will; it was an uncontrollable transformation that rippled through her body.

It terrified her. She terrified herself. She changed into her night-gown and slid beneath the bedsheets, hiding like a child might hide from ghosts or chaneques.

On the fourth day after her father was seized with apoplexy, Lizalde and his men came. They made such a racket that even without her finely tuned ear, Carlota would have been able to hear them.

She was with Montgomery in the kitchen when they arrived, and he quickly walked out in search of his rifle. She followed him, clasping her left wrist with her right hand and pressing it against her chest, and for a minute or two she didn't know what to say. Then she let her hands fall by her sides and breathed in.

"We don't want them thinking we mean them any harm," she said, practicing the calm she wished him to also convey. "Please, bring them to the sitting room. I asked you not to shoot before we have a chance to speak. Remember that."

"Very well," he said.

Lupe, who had also heard the noise, the banging and hollering, came into the sitting room and stood next to Carlota.

"Lupe, you should go to my father's room. He might need you, and in case the men prove intractable you'd have a chance to run away," Carlota said.

"I came back to be with you, Loti."

"Don't be stubborn."

But Lupe wouldn't move, and soon Montgomery returned, and with him came the Lizaldes and four of their men. Montgomery did not look uneasy, despite being outnumbered and the fact that they had apparently taken his rifle.

She saw Eduardo and her hands shook, but she clasped them together. Hernando Lizalde had a bandage on his cheek and glared at her. Isidro was not too pleased to see her, either.

"Fetch Moreau," Hernando Lizalde ordered her. "We'll need him here."

"My father has taken ill. He is in bed and cannot rise."

"How convenient."

"If you wish me to take you to him, I will. But I do not lie," she said, her voice still calm.

"Then let him lie in his sickbed, if that's what he wants. I don't care if he wishes to hide under the covers. We've come for my hybrids. Round them up."

"They've left."

"What do you mean they've left? How could they?"

"I opened the doors for them."

"You better point me in their direction, then," the irate man said. This time he had brought no riding crop with him, but his voice was a whip. "That is my valuable property you've released into the wild."

"My father has a little money, which I can tender to you if you'll leave us all at peace."

Hernando Lizalde let out an irritated grunt. "Whatever pathetic sum Moreau has in his bank account cannot compare with the investment I've made. This is my house, these are my furnishings, and those hybrids remain my property."

She glanced down, her lips pinched tight. "I cannot help you," she said.

"I'll beat the answer out of you."

She said nothing to that and remained motionless, her hands knit together as if in prayer. This seemed to incense the man further, and he began swearing at her.

"Whore," he said. "Filthy beast."

"Damn your tongue, you pig!" Montgomery yelled and surged forward, fist in the air.

But Lizalde's men leaped after him, and one of them swung Montgomery's rifle against his back with such brutal force she thought the weapon might break. Montgomery let out a strangled cry and fell down.

"Don't!" she said, but they ignored her. Two men had grabbed Montgomery and hauled him to his feet while a third one punched him in the stomach. Isidro seemed amused. She looked to Eduardo, who was observing the scene, impassive.

"Sir, please!"

He stared at her, green eyes sharp. "This is not necessary. Perhaps I might speak to her in private and find out more about the situation?" Eduardo asked, raising his voice against the tumultuous struggle.

The men stopped their beating and turned in Hernando Lizalde's direction as if awaiting a cue. Montgomery glared at Eduardo, muttering a curse under his breath, and then he spat.

"Fine. Come on, out, all of you. Out," Hernando Lizalde said, waving a hand.

"Should I stay?" Lupe whispered in her ear.

"No, it's fine. Be careful," she whispered back, squeezing her hand.

Lupe nodded and went with Montgomery and the rest of them. The doors closed. They were sealed in the room, the clock ticking on the mantelpiece. She stood straight, her whole body rigid, and her hands warm, like she was running a fever. Her heart was beating fast.

"I'm sorry about that," Eduardo said. "The men were promised a fight and they're eager to taste blood."

"Are you eager for blood, too? Is that why you've come?"

"I wanted to see you again."

She thought she had learned each and every one of his looks in the short time she had known him. Yet the way he walked toward her and the manner in which his eyes raked over her were different. Curious and alien.

"Your body is a perfect mimicry," he said. "Like the chameleon that changes colors. I cannot pinpoint the animal part of you."

"I am not a puzzle that is made of different pieces," she said.

"Do my words offend you?"

"They do not please me."

He was quiet, with that same inquisitive gaze, still trying to make sense of how she fit together.

"Where are the hybrids, Carlota?"

"Gone, forever."

"They couldn't have all vanished into thin air."

She took a deep breath. "I know that at this point I cannot expect you to keep your promise to me. I will not demand marriage, nor Yaxaktun as a gift, nor the slightest show of affection. But I would hope that we might part amicably, despite what transpired the last time we met," she said. "I do not know where the hybrids are. This is the truth. I have not lied to your father. I would ask, as a kindness to me, that you speak to him and convince him not to seek them out, wherever they may have gone."

"There is every reason for us to go after them. Aside from the fact that they are our property, they pose a danger to us."

"They do not pose a danger. I had hoped that we would all continue to live together at Yaxaktun. I know now that is impossible. We will vacate the house, I will tender the money I promised. But I beg of you, call off whatever hunt you have in mind. My father is terribly ill. I might soon be an orphan with no home and no one to turn to."

He slid closer to her, so close she couldn't help the nervous flit of her gaze. She turned her head away, her heart stuttering.

"Please, do not burden me with further misery. Please help me."

"Carlota, you look near tears. Only a sadist would wish to see you weep. You're too pretty for that. You must know that when I gazed at you the first time, I was lost."

The last time they'd seen each other he'd looked at her with loathing and fear. But now his face reflected neither. It was as if he recalled their meeting by the cenote or the stolen hours of that night they'd spent together. His hands found her waist with certainty and tilted her face up to him. And her body in turn remembered the burning caresses he'd shared with her, and the memory of that delight made her open her mouth, kiss him back with the simple, frank sweetness she'd always bestowed upon him.

"What are you doing?" she whispered.

"Isn't it obvious?" he replied.

"I thought you didn't want me anymore."

"Don't be silly. Of course I do," he said with the same ferocity that had drawn her to him in the first place, which had the effect of only baffling Carlota further.

"You seemed so upset when you left. I thought—"

"I was upset. The doctor and you tried to deceive me."

"But I didn't!" she said vehemently. "My father kept many secrets from me. And I didn't lie when I said I cared for you. I didn't manufacture my love."

"No, I don't believe you did. I've thought about you and what we might do about this mess. Then I decided, why should it be complicated?"

"There's nothing to be done. What other option do I have but to abandon Yaxaktun?"

"What would you do out there? The world is dangerous for a young woman such as yourself."

She looked at him, mute with confusion.

"Carlota, my dear," he said in a caressing tone. "I cannot let you go."

Could he mean . . . did he mean his love was steadfast? Perhaps he wished to run away with her. Perhaps he'd conjured a clever solution to all their problems.

He held her tight, his lips gliding over her neck. She pictured not lonesome misery in her future, but a warm island of safety. She thought of the haven they might still build together, perhaps not at Yaxaktun, but somewhere else. She thought of all the hybrids left unharmed, of all of them happy. She allowed herself to dream of this. She inhaled, her lips parting.

"You'll be my mistress at Vista Hermosa. It will be pleasant. My father has agreed to it. He was reluctant at first, but I talked him into it. A mistress is cleaner and safer than the whores in brothels, and the hybrids cannot bear children, meaning I'll have no bastards."

Eduardo had buried a hand in her dark hair. Now his grip tightened as she tilted her head and looked at him. "You cannot . . . I wouldn't agree to that."

"You said it yourself. You can't expect me to marry you. It's no perfect fairy tale, but we'll make the most of it."

"Neither would I expect such an arrangement."

"Carlota, you will be safe and content in the countryside. I won't mind spoiling you, and you in turn will be generous to me. It's not unusual for a man to take a mistress, and it is definitely more than you would be able to hope for under the circumstances."

Her fingers found purchase on his shoulder. "What would you do with the hybrids? If you had me, would you let them go?"

"Goodness, no," he said with a smirk. "They're ours to keep. Your father's former assistant will take over the operations here. You'll be more comfortable at Vista Hermosa, with me. Yes, I'll be in Mérida for a few weeks at a time, but—"

She wrenched his hand away from her and took two steps back.

"I do not wish to be your mistress, nor am I willing to live at Vista Hermosa. If you think this offer a kindness, then you are mistaken."

"You'd refuse me."

She felt as though there were a knot in her throat, and she swallowed. "I might agree to it, but only if you let the others be."

"You think you can give *me* terms?" he asked, his voice turning rough. "You don't have a choice."

She closed her eyes, scalding tears threatening to drown her. But when she opened her eyes again she spoke without a hitch. "Then I'll refuse you."

With a violent movement he bent down and pressed her to him again, throwing her head back and savaging her lips. It startled her, and she froze in fury, feeling his tongue in her mouth, before regaining her wits and shoving him away. Eduardo stumbled back, bumping against the mantelpiece and accidentally knocking down the delicate clock that rested there. It fell with a resounding crash that made her yelp.

She stared at the ground and let out a soft *oh*. That clock had presided over each of her waking hours; its bells marked the rhythm of her days. The beautiful courting scene it showed had entranced her young eyes. The gentleman kissed the hand of the beautiful lady and above them the cherubs smiled their blessing at the couple.

But now it was shards on the ground, the mechanism of the clock lying naked and exposed.

"What have you done?" she asked in a murmur.

"I am trying to be good to you!" Eduardo yelled.

The doors to the sitting room flung open, and the men walked in again, weapons at the ready, throwing her hard looks. She noticed that Lupe's and Montgomery's wrists had been bound.

"What is this racket?" Hernando Lizalde demanded.

Eduardo ran a hand through his hair, then rubbed his wrist. "Nothing."

"Has she told you anything useful?"

"No," Eduardo muttered.

"Well, then, you better start talking, girl."

"I do not know where they are. I've said so already," she said, her eyes fixed on the broken clock.

"You're a stubborn cat. Let's see exactly how stubborn. Bring Laughton next to me," Lizalde said, and two men shoved Montgomery forward.

Without further preamble Hernando Lizalde pressed the barrel of his gun against Montgomery's cheek and stared at Carlota. She crushed a hand against her chest.

"It's hard to miss at this distance."

"Montgomery doesn't know anything, either," she said quickly. "We aren't trying to lie to you."

"No, you are trying to trick us."

"I'm not. Truly, I'm not."

"I don't think you want your friend's brains decorating these walls, do you? Where are the damn hybrids?!" he roared.

She couldn't breathe again. Her warm hands were now burning, and she felt the tears searing a trail down her cheeks as she grabbed on to the settee and knelt on the ground with a sob.

She thought another fainting fit was coming upon her. Carlota opened her mouth and pressed a hand against her throat.

"I know where they went. I can take you," Lupe said, surprising Carlota when she spoke, sounding resolute. "It's not far."

"At least someone has common sense around here," Hernando Lizalde rumbled.

She hardly heard the rest of what they said. Her breath was shallow, and she clung to the settee, shivering.

"Eduardo, you'll come with us. As will you, Laughton. I don't trust you to leave you behind. Isidro, you'll stay with Moreau's daughter. I don't want her running off. Well, what's the matter with this bitch? Is she ill?"

"It's her nerves," Lupe replied, staring at her. "It will be fine, Loti."

Carlota swallowed, the taste of bile in her mouth. Eduardo's fingers closed around her arm as he helped her to her feet. She swayed, unsteady, and tried feebly to push him away, but her strength had drained from her body.

"Where is my gun with the ivory handle?" Hernando Lizalde asked. "I'll want that."

"I didn't mean to yell at you. But don't talk to me the way you did again," Eduardo whispered, guiding her toward the doorway, where Isidro was standing. "I do love you, silly girl. Don't you understand? We belong together."

He tipped her head up and looked into her eyes, a confident smile on his lips.

She felt, as she stood there and looked into his beautiful, youthful face, another wave of nausea and recoiled from him in disgust when his hand brushed down her face. Carlota thought the fracture in her body might finally cleave her in two, but she did not tumble to the ground, instead stumbling forward as Eduardo pulled her with him.

CHAPTER 28

Montgomery

THEY'D TIED HIS wrists together so tightly they ached, and he had no way of undoing the knot. Even if he had found a means to untie himself, he would be left in the company of more than two dozen armed men. Not exactly an enticing prospect.

Montgomery had hoped the trail would be narrow and overgrown, making it difficult to proceed on horse and therefore slowing them down, but it proved to be in decent shape. They could ride without need of hacking their way through the jungle and would cover ground quickly enough like this, even when moving in single file.

Lupe rode at the front of the group, while Montgomery was toward the middle of the pack, followed closely by Eduardo. Her hands were also tied. Neither of them had a chance at escape.

Montgomery lamented his current predicament and cursed his situation, wishing he'd done things differently. Not just his damn encounter with these men, but the whole of it. He'd spent six years in the service of Dr. Moreau, watching over Yaxaktun, and always telling himself his position was not immoral. He neither created the hybrids nor did he wish to profit from them. He was merely a man doing a job.

He'd loved the distance and peace of Yaxaktun, he'd cared for everyone there, regarding the hybrids as the only friends he could ever hope to have. Yet what good had his sympathy done in the end? The hybrids were in thrall to Moreau and to Lizalde, and now they were hunting them down.

And what about Carlota, left behind with her father? What should become of her? Moreau could not protect her; the man couldn't even rise from his bed. Although, Montgomery supposed right that second he should be more concerned about what might happen to Lupe and him. If they'd wanted him dead they would have killed him already, and Lupe was somewhat valuable if only because Lizalde considered her his property. But that did not mean there wasn't a bullet with his name on it awaiting Montgomery at the end of this trail.

The narrow path snaked to the left. Montgomery's horse had not rounded the bend when a shot rang through the air. Three more shots followed. The man right ahead of him fell from his horse. Montgomery, knowing he was an easy target simply sitting there, threw himself to the ground and rolled to the side of the road. The white dust of the path clung to his clothes as he gritted his teeth, pressing as low as he could.

Lizalde's men grabbed their rifles and began shooting back, but with the trees and the foliage it was hard to see exactly where the shots came from. The man who'd fallen from his horse had not gotten up, and Montgomery stood and rushed forward, pulling him to the side and turning him over. The fellow was dead. Montgomery crouched by the road, holding his breath, hoping he wasn't the next one to get shot.

Their attackers had ceased their brisk fire. Hernando Lizalde was yelling ahead of them, and he saw Eduardo, atop his horse, reins in hand, looking nervous.

"What's happening?" the young man asked.

Welcome to a real fight, Montgomery thought, and he walked ahead, past the bend of the road, to get a better look at what was going on there. Eduardo cautiously followed.

A couple of Lizalde's men had been injured. Lupe was still toward the front of the column and looked fine. Everyone was alert, waiting for another volley of fire and the chance to pinpoint the location of the shooter. There were two or three people shooting at them, he wagered. Had there been more, there would have been considerably more damage. Still, two or three men with decent rifles could create a pretty big amount of trouble.

"Get back on your mount," Eduardo said.

"Hush," Montgomery muttered. He heard a rustling, the breaking of twigs.

"You don't give *me* orders."

"Shut the hell up."

"Grab him," Eduardo ordered to one of the men. "Grab this bastard."

Something moved quickly between the trees, and one of Lizalde's men pointed in its direction. He was probably expecting another volley of fire, but instead a lithe creature sprang from the shadows and leaped atop the man, tossing him to the ground. Then a second and a third emerged.

He recognized K'an, her long yellow hair a whirl and her mouth a snarl, as she grabbed on to the legs of a rider and pulled him down as he screamed. There, too, were the wolfish Pinta and Áayin, his caiman's tale swishing back and forth. They slid forward, jumping on top of the men. Their fists pounded upon their heads and backs.

It was a frightening sight. Yet the brute that Eduardo had ordered to grab Montgomery either did not see the three hybrids jumping around or he did not care. His single focus was Montgomery. Hands tied, Montgomery could do little more than dodge his blows. One struck him in the stomach, while the other met his chin. Montgomery stumbled back and fell.

The brute stepped forward, slamming his foot against Montgomery's right leg. God damn it! He groaned and narrowly avoided a swift kick by rolling over on his belly, which didn't improve the situation. The man kicked him again, robbing him of breath. He scrambled in the dirt, trying to get away. Montgomery was kneeling, trying to steady himself, when he felt the barrel of a pistol pressed against his skull.

"Stand up slowly," the brute said.

"You don't need to point that at me," Montgomery muttered.

The man grinned. He didn't help Montgomery stand up, but at least he stepped back, though the pistol was still aimed at his head. Montgomery pulled himself to his feet.

"Might as well let me go now," Montgomery said. Through the corner of his eye he'd glimpsed a familiar gray shape.

"No chance of that."

"You sure? It'd be better if you did."

"Shut up."

And then Aj Kaab, slow and big, came from the left and showed his rows of vicious teeth to the brute, who immediately lost his courage and pointed his pistol in the hybrid's direction and attempted to shoot, only to find the weapon wrenched from his hands. The pistol fell to the ground. Aj Kaab's teeth closed around the man's hand, and he screamed.

Montgomery winced, hearing the unmistakable crunching of bone, as Aj Kaab roared and bit and chewed loudly.

Montgomery quickly picked up the weapon on the ground, maintaining a difficult grip on it with his hands still bound together, but at least he had a pistol now.

"What is this!" Eduardo yelled. The young mister had deigned to finally get his hands dirty and jumped off his horse.

Montgomery looked at the young man, and Eduardo stared at him. He slammed the butt of his gun against Eduardo's head, pushing him away. Then he ran toward the spot where he'd last seen Lupe. She wasn't atop her horse anymore.

It was chaos. Their mounts were spooked by the hybrids. They bucked up, snorted, and they kicked. Montgomery narrowly avoided being trampled by one of the riders by swooping low and slamming into a tree.

"Lupe!" he yelled.

He couldn't see her anywhere. Had she been hurt? Bullets were raining around him as some of the men tried shooting liberally in any direction. Others, perhaps more cautious, had dismounted and held their pistols or knives close, eyes darting back and forth.

He ducked again. A man screamed as one of the hybrids tackled him. It was a shrill, brief sound. Montgomery counted two more hybrids besides Pinta, Áayin, K'an, and Aj Kaab, a total of six furious, snarling creatures, slim and small, or lumbering and strong, whirling, darting, roaring. Spooking the horses, making the men launch into a prayer.

Lizalde yelled, ordered his men to kill the animals, but the hybrids were quick and they slipped away and slipped back into view, and the men were growing more and more desperate. It was like the strangest of dances, men suddenly paired with animal and twirling for a few moments, their steps tracing patterns etched in blood.

"Get them!" Lizalde kept saying.

Instead of finding Lupe, Montgomery bumped into Aj Kaab, who was slowly stumbling down the path. His tongue was poking out of his mouth as he huffed and sat down in the middle of the path, his great head falling forward.

"Aj Kaab! Old chap," he said, kneeling in front of him. "Come on, get up."

"Laughton," the hybrid said, showing him his big teeth and making a fist, pressing it against his chest. "I told you, I'm old but strong. I need a rest."

"Rest later, Aj Kaab," he said and gripped the hybrid's shoulder. But the hybrid wasn't moving, and Montgomery saw the handle of the knife protruding from his furry belly. Montgomery held his breath.

Aj Kaab was dead.

"Laughton!" Lupe yelled.

He blinked, and she rushed to him, jumping over a corpse. Her hands were untied. She grabbed the rope holding him prisoner and gnawed at it until he was able to brush the bindings away. Men were screaming and dropping to the ground.

Their fear worked in the hybrids' favor, but they were severely outnumbered and Hernando Lizalde was still shouting commands, saying they were merely animals. There were men scrambling, trying to reload their guns, and there were those who had decided to flee and were rushing off on foot or on the back of a terrified mount. Horses trampled upon the bodies of the ones who had fallen while the hybrids darted back and forth, spitting blood and chunks of flesh.

"Are you hurt?" Montgomery asked Lupe, as they quickly went along the trail.

"No. I'm fine."

A gray-haired man with a red kerchief stepped next to them, a rifle in his wrinkled hands. With him was Cachito, who smiled at Montgomery.

"Montgomery!"

"What is happening here?" Montgomery asked.

"Can't you guess? This is one of Cumux's lieutenants."

"Sir," Montgomery said, reaching for the brim of his straw hat, but he'd lost it at some point and he ended simply brushing the hair away from his face.

"We're fighting," Cachito said excitedly.

"Down! Get down!" Lupe yelled.

Behind Cachito's shoulder Montgomery saw Hernando Lizalde, his son standing next to him. The older man was aiming his beloved pistol with the ivory handle in their direction. Montgomery shoved the boy away and extended his arm, pulling the trigger of his own gun. When he hunted, he did it with finesse. Right then and there, there was no elegance to it. He clumsily pulled the trigger.

The bullet hit Hernando, and he saw the man stumble.

He wasn't sure how badly he'd hurt Hernando Lizalde, but he did not have time to find out, because two riders flew toward them and Montgomery turned his gun in their direction, hitting one of the horses. Then he was out of bullets, and there was the loud blast of the rifle as someone shot the other rider. A fountain of blood sprouted from the horse's neck, spraying Montgomery across the cheek even as he turned away and tried to distance himself from the poor creature, lest he be trampled.

In his hurry he tripped and fell, hitting his head as he landed at an awkward angle. The horse collapsed right in front of Montgomery's feet with a wet thud, and he lay staring into its eye.

The blow to his head stung, and everything went muffled and dark. He heard himself groaning. He could not feel his own body. Something was dragging him through the jungle, and he remembered the time when the jaguar had pounced on him and its claws sunk into his flesh.

Dear Fanny, he wrote. *I may indeed be dying.*

Jaguar. He ought to have died that day, when it gnawed at his arm. But he hadn't and he'd lived and lived still. Well . . . maybe not for long. He thought of Carlota, wondered if he might die with the memory of her face and the whisper of her voice in his ears.

He blinked. Montgomery lay on the ground of a small hut. There were two hammocks to his left and a couple of chairs. Bare bones, even when the houses of macehuales were often simple affairs.

Sweat rolled down Montgomery's sore back. It still ached with the memory of the rifle they had beaten him with, and his mouth was dry.

"He opened his eyes! Hey, Montgomery, you're safe," Cachito said.

He wiped his mouth with the back of his hand and turned his head, looking at the boy. The scent of viscera and death from the road still lingered in his memory, though he'd obviously been moved somewhere else.

"Where are we?"

"The camp! Ramona was right. There's a camp that Cumux's men use."

Montgomery frowned. The sleeve of Cachito's shirt was stained with blood. "Are you hurt?"

"It's a flesh wound. Stings if I move," Cachito said, looking down at his arm. "They got me here, too."

He lifted his shirt and showed him his ribs, where someone had wrapped him in a thick bandage. When he moved his arms, the boy winced.

"Next time don't be getting in fights. What the hell were you doing there?"

"We figured you were being stubborn, Montgomery, when you said not to fight, and we hatched a plan. A few of us waited for you to come this way. Lupe said you would, and if you didn't come in five days' time then we should continue on our way. She also said she wouldn't tell you any of this because you'd probably say no and ruin it."

Montgomery frowned. "She did, did she?"

"You would have thought to stop us."

"Probably," Montgomery admitted, remembering poor Aj Kaab, his corpse left in the middle of the road. "Where are your new friends?"

"Outside. We have three of Cumux's men and the hybrids who would fight. Not everyone was willing to wait or fight. It's the best I could do."

"Englishman, you live," the old man in the red kerchief said, rifle over his shoulder, standing at the doorway of the hut. At his side there was a younger fellow, also carrying a rifle, and Lupe. "Good. We need to go."

"One second, go where?" Montgomery asked, rubbing his head. It still ached like the devil. He wondered how long he'd been knocked out and how far Cumux's camp was from the place where the confrontation had taken place.

"Somewhere else. We killed some of the folk who were holding you prisoners, scared others off, but it doesn't mean we should stay. We are not safe."

"The other hybrids have gone ahead," Cachito said. "Cumux's men have also moved. We're supposed to catch up with the others."

"I must return to Yaxaktun," Montgomery said, rubbing his forehead. "Carlota and Moreau are there."

"Yaxaktun has thick walls," the man in the red kerchief told him. He had a stern, serious face that did not invite rebukes. "It can't be breached. And there will be more of those men there. You've been lucky today. I owed Ramona a favor, which is why we came with your companions and waited for you. We will do no more."

Carlota. He'd said she could have him for as long as she required him. It seemed to him if she ever needed him, it was now.

"I won't ask you to come with me."

"But you want to go back alone?" Cachito asked.

"I have to," Montgomery said, and he pushed himself up on his feet, a little wobbly still. If there had been a thousand men between him and Carlota, and as many spears as stars in the heavens, still he'd have gone back for her.

"You can't even walk," Lupe said accusingly.

"I don't need to walk. I need to ride. If you can spare a bit of aguardiente, that'll make it better, and if not I'll manage without it."

They didn't offer him a bottle, so he supposed there wasn't any to be had or they had not taken him seriously. Well, he could do this sober, although he wouldn't have minded a couple of fortifying sips for luck.

Montgomery stepped out of the hut. Outside waited four of the hybrids—Pinta, K'an, and two more—looking tattered and tired, their nails caked with blood. Aj Kaab was dead, and he didn't see Áayin, so he assumed he must also have perished.

They gave Montgomery a grim nod. He saw three other palm-thatched dwellings like the one he'd been in and a black-haired man who was tending to three horses. There were no other animals, nor any more structures. This camp was small. Cumux had probably employed it as a waypoint to move supplies and weapons.

"We can give you weapons and a horse, Englishman, but I caution you that this is not wise. You're better off going with your companions," the old man said. "They worry about you."

Montgomery looked at the hybrids, bloodied and tired, and then back at the old man, who was slowly rolling a cigarette.

"The little one thinks you are both brave and foolish," the man said. His eyes were fixed on Cachito. "But he's brave and foolish, too. He said he'd bite me if I didn't help you."

"He didn't."

"Of course he did, and he convinced the others to help him and stay back."

"And you went along with him."

"He reminds me of myself."

"You're not afraid of them," Montgomery said, which struck him as odd.

"I'd seen one of them before, at the water's edge," the man replied. "We all have an animal double, Englishman."

He remembered what Cachito had said, that Lupe had once seen Juan Cumux near the cenote. That he was old, but not like Moreau.

"You're not one of his lieutenants," Montgomery said, frowning. "You are Juan Cumux."

The man did not reply, but he didn't need to. Montgomery spoke again. "You took a great risk helping us."

"Those men were coming for us. It was a good thing we knew they were coming, this time. And now maybe they'll think twice about heading in this direction."

"You're hoping people will be frightened away?"

"Maybe. It would be good if they said this area is dangerous."

"I suppose so."

"I also owed a favor. And maybe now you owe me one, too, Englishman."

"The name's Laughton," he said. "And that's fine. I pay my debts."

"I can't take more risks, Laughton. My men can't hide your friends. They'll have to fend for themselves. We can take them farther east, but we must also return to our people."

But you are Juan Cumux, he thought. Lupe and Cachito's hero. Yet he supposed the truth of it was that Moreau had not been a god and Cumux could not be divine, either.

"If you'd be able to reunite my friends with the others who have already gone ahead, I'd be eternally grateful. And I would beg you that they might remain hidden somewhere. I cannot have them come to any further harm."

"We can take them farther east, but I told you, I cannot shelter them."

"A cave, a camp you don't use anymore," Montgomery pleaded. "Anything will do. Please, sir."

Cumux had finished rolling his cigarette and shook his head. He lit it and took a puff. "You owe me twice now."

"In that case, lend me a horse and a rifle and make it thrice."

"Things are better done in threes, so yes."

They shook hands and walked toward the horses. Lupe and Cachito came after them quickly. "Don't you think about it," he told Cachito before he could attempt a word. The boy looked at Montgomery with large, startled eyes. "You're wounded."

"A flesh wound!"

"Wounded," Montgomery repeated.

"Maybe he is, but I'm not," Lupe said, grabbing hold of the bridle of a horse.

"Lupe," Montgomery told her tiredly.

"You can't leave me, Laughton. I stayed behind because I didn't want to see Carlota or you dead, and I'm going to make sure neither one of you is stupid," she replied stubbornly. "If it weren't for Cachito and me, those men would have killed you. You should let me go with you for both your sakes."

"Fine. But at the first sign of trouble I want you to turn back."

Montgomery and Lupe were handed a rifle, which they carried on the saddlebow, as well as a couple of jicaras filled with water. Cachito didn't want to let them go, insisting that he wasn't that badly hurt, but Montgomery could tell by the way he spoke and how he winced that there was no way he'd be in any shape to put up a fight.

"Listen to me," Montgomery said, pulling the boy aside, "the others have need of you."

"Not of me, Montgomery. What do I know?"

"Cumux likes you and you are smart. Keep everyone together and keep them safe. You'll have a chance if you stick together. We'll find you. Go southeast, get far away. You understand?"

"Please don't leave us alone again. God knows if you'll make it back this time," the boy said, and he had tears in his eyes.

"I have to go back for Carlota, you know that. Cachito, you saved me and Lupe today, but now we have to fetch her. Juan Cumux can't keep the hybrids safe, but I know *you* can."

"Montgomery, no."

"You have my compass and my map."

"That's not enough. That's why we decided to fetch you, so you'd help us. I can't do this."

He embraced the boy. Cachito finally quieted and nodded when Montgomery stepped away.

They bid the others goodbye, and Montgomery shook Cumux's hand before they started off. When they reached the portion of the road where the confrontation had occurred, Montgomery jumped off his saddle and looked around, surveying the dead horses and dead men. In the heat of these latitudes, the bodies would soon reek.

He found Aj Kaab's corpse in the middle of the path with the knife sticking out of his belly. He pulled the weapon out and wiped it against his trousers. He began dragging the corpse to the side of the road. Lupe, seeing what he was doing, also dismounted and helped him. They left the corpse at enough of a distance from the path that it wouldn't be spotted easily if anyone went by. They repeated the procedure when they stumbled upon Áayin, who was facedown by a dead horse. Later they'd have to give them a proper burial, but they had no tools now.

Montgomery shook his head and looked among the corpses of the men, grabbing a couple of pouches that contained bullets. He also found a holster and a pistol. While he searched he looked for Eduardo and Hernando among the fallen, but could not find them.

Lupe watched him, impassive. When he was done, they guided their horse across the white road, which had been painted red with blood.

"There's still time to turn around, Lupe," he said. "There's nothing but more death ahead."

"It doesn't frighten me."

"Frightens me plenty."

"She's my kin, Montgomery."

"Does she know that?"

Lupe looked at him in the eye, her face serious. "We are sisters and I love her. It doesn't mean I have to say it every morning and every night."

"It might be good if you said it once in a while."

"It might be good if you minded your own business. I don't tell you what to say to her. Besides, if anyone has an obligation to Carlota, it's me, not you. You are no proper nothing of hers," Lupe declared.

"Well, then I guess we'll have to fetch her together," he muttered.

Montgomery drank from the gourd at his saddle. His wrists were raw and red, his back ached, and they were going back for Dr. Moreau's daughter.

CHAPTER 29

Carlota

SHE'D SPENT THE day at her father's bedside, under the watchful eye of either Isidro or one of his men. Late in the evening Dr. Moreau awoke, and she gave him a little food and water. He looked at Isidro curiously.

"They came back today," Carlota explained.

"Where is Hernando? I must have a word with him," her father said.

"He's not here."

"He's chasing after the hybrids your daughter let loose," Isidro interjected.

"Is that true? You've set them free? They are my life's work."

"It had to be done."

"Carlota, these experiments are my great accomplishment, my legacy. I didn't mean for you to rid yourself of them." Her father's voice was growing rough and pained. "This is sacred knowledge that must be preserved."

Your legacy is misery and pain, she thought and turned her head. "I have your notes, but I could not have kept the hybrids here. To do so would have been cruel."

Isidro smirked. "Yes, well, since it's not *your* money. Let us toss a fortune to the wind."

"You have no compassion, do you, sir," she said flatly.

"Compassion? For a pack of animals? The reason for their existence, their function, is to serve us, and yet you thought you might meddle with that. What do you imagine you will achieve? How will they feed themselves or brave the jungle?"

"At least they have a chance."

"Do you think if they come in contact with people they will survive? They'll be shot and skinned."

"I'll have my tea now, if I may," Moreau said, raising his voice above theirs.

Isidro blinked and looked at the doctor. "I can get it," Carlota said.

"No," Isidro muttered. "Stay here. I'll have it brought over."

He opened the door and yelled for someone. Isidro truly was not taking any chances, never letting her out of his sight. Not that she would have gone far. Carlota had counted four other men in the house who could make quick work of finding her, should she step out of the room.

"Are they all truly gone?" her father asked, his voice low.

"Yes."

"Where is Laughton?"

"Hernando Lizalde took Lupe and Montgomery with him while they search for the others."

"Then you are alone. In that drawer, Carlota, by the bed, there is my Bible and next to it the box with the pistol. Fetch it and go."

"Father—"

"Fetch it and go," he demanded, his hands grasping the covers tight. "Go out through the courtyard."

She pulled open the drawer and saw the Bible and the wooden box inside. She breathed in, her eyes wide, considering the implications of such a choice, and stared at the French doors that led to the courtyard with their white curtains .

Slowly she stepped toward the doors. She thought of running out, fleeing into the night. She thought of running until she was out of breath, until the stars burned out. Then she looked at her father on the bed, frail and broken. And she couldn't leave him, despite everything, even though the price might be high.

Shadows moved in the courtyard, behind the curtains, and she heard voices. She moved back quickly and sat back in her chair.

"I can't," she whispered and pressed her hands against her face, a sob lodging in her throat.

"It's fine," her father said. "Don't worry, child."

The voices were now coming from the hallway and getting louder. Eduardo walked in, his hair wild and his shirt stained with blood. Isidro and another man followed him.

"Doctor, you must get up," he said. "My father was shot and requires medical care."

"Hernando?"

"Yes, who else? Come, doctor. Where is your cane?" Eduardo asked, looking around the room.

"Are you mad? He cannot get up," Carlota said, rising instead.

"My father needs to have someone look at his wounds, what else—"

"We'll take your father to the laboratory and I'll see to him."

"But you!" Eduardo exclaimed in surprise.

"I can take care of this."

"Carlota is correct," her father said. "She knows enough."

The men looked at her dubiously, but Eduardo muttered something to Isidro and then he nodded at her. Carlota moved briskly. When they reached the laboratory, the doors were still open, as she'd left them before the men's arrival, and her father's papers were strewn around the anteroom. She asked Eduardo and the man accompanying him to light the lamps.

Carlota looked among the shelves and grabbed her father's medical bag. She had no experience dealing with bullet wounds. But she'd read about injuries sustained in the battlefield from one of the doctor's volumes. She pulled that book and paged through it. After a few minutes, Isidro walked in with his uncle. The older man grimaced as he clutched his arm.

"Where is Moreau?" he asked.

"It's only me. My father is still abed."

"That won't do. Get that man up."

"He is in no condition to assist you. Please sit down."

"And you are supposed to be a physician now? You'd put me in her hands?" Hernando asked, turning to his son.

"I've learned from my father, and I'll do you no harm. I have no desire to assist you, but I am compelled to do so. Where are you wounded?"

"My shoulder."

The man looked weary, but he sat, apparently concluding he was fighting a losing battle. Or perhaps it was simply the pain that softened him. She asked him to remove his jacket and his shirt while she boiled water. When she was ready, she wiped his shoulder clean. Now she was able to see the ugly puncture of the bullet. It had entered near the shoulder and exited neatly. Neither the bone nor joint had been injured. Hernando had been lucky, torn, ugly flesh and all.

Carlota's main concern must be ensuring her instruments were clean and making sure no foreign substance was introduced, infection being the greatest risk. She dusted iodoform liberally on the skin. Then she applied a dressing and bandaged the injured arm, taking care to also place a good amount of gauze under the armpit.

The man complained loudly and grunted as she worked, as though he'd been blasted by a cannonball, sucking in a deep breath, then clenching his teeth.

When she was done she brushed her hand across her forehead and took a step back.

"Where are the others?"

Hernando Lizalde winced and looked at the bandage. "Those damn animals of yours attacked us."

"The hybrids?" she asked in surprise.

"Yes, your hybrids. And someone else. There were three Indians with them! But we are going to fetch the army, we are going to fetch soldiers right away—"

"It's dark," Isidro said warily. "They could be hiding in ambush outside, in the dark. We ought to wait until daybreak."

"What if they should come here?" the older man asked.

"The doors are thick," Eduardo mused. "It's not as if they could knock them down. Isidro is right, we'd be exposed out there in the dark. There're seven of us, but outside that might not be enough, and to make things worse the lot of our rifles are now lost, left in the middle of the jungle."

"But the men here have bullets and pistols. And there must be other weapons around the house."

"I haven't done an inventory, but it might well be that Laughton has rifles stashed around," Isidro said. "He hunts, after all."

"That still leaves us with the problem of moving around in the dark," Eduardo said. "And, father, I frankly feel exhausted. I am guessing you feel the same."

"I admit this has been a long, difficult day," the older man said, flexing his fingers. "We should proceed at first light. I need a strong drink and I need to lie down. Come on, show me to a room."

"There's a room that would be perfect for you, uncle."

"And my drink?"

"You can fetch it from the kitchen," Carlota said dryly.

"This way," Isidro said as they went out into the hallway.

Carlota began following them, but Eduardo stopped her, grabbing her by the arm. "I have cuts and bruises that need looking after," he said, as he took off his jacket, as if to allow her an easy inspection of said lesions.

"I must to return to my father's side. You can have his medical bag and tend to those yourself."

"No, I don't think so."

"But someone has to watch over him."

"Isidro, will you keep an eye on Dr. Moreau after you've helped my father into his bed?" Eduardo called out.

His cousin turned to look at Eduardo. "You are not coming?"

"I'll keep an eye on her."

"Keep an eye, of course," Isidro muttered, his tone spiteful. But he didn't say anything else.

Eduardo's man was still by the doorway, looking at them. He seemed amused.

Carlota asked the man to move the lamps, then she fetched the bag and opened it again, pushing the journals aside. She placed the bag atop the table in the anteroom. From what she could see, Eduardo had but a few cuts on his knuckles, which she cleaned. There was blood on his right temple, and she wiped that clean, too.

"You'd make a decent nurse," he said. "You're very careful."

"As I've said, my father taught me."

"I thought you'd be less kind after our last conversation."

"It's not kindness."

It was the restraint her father had tutored her in as well as her own sense of decency. She was not a monster. She didn't wish to hate and she didn't wish to hurt.

"What happened out there?" she asked.

"The hybrids came out of nowhere and began attacking us. There were also men with rifles. Indians, as my father said. I spotted three of them. They caused mayhem. Men were killed, others ran off."

"What about Lupe? And Montgomery?"

"Your friend Montgomery shot my father and hit me here," Eduardo said, pointing to his temple. "When we meet again I intend to return the favor."

Carlota turned her head and bit her lip to keep herself from smiling. "Then they're alive."

"Maybe."

But they must be; Hernando and Eduardo lived, after all. Yet she worried that they might be injured and that no one would be there to assist them, as she'd assisted these men. She began placing the items back inside the medical bag.

"I'm tired. Let's lie down," Eduardo said.

"You know where the rooms are," she replied, her hands stilling.

"I meant we should go to your room."

"I don't want you with me."

"You did last time. Come now, I wager you're also tired. How much sleep did you have last night?"

He took her by the arm; in his free hand he carried a lamp. He did not hold her roughly, simply directing her steps. She thought to protest, but she saw the man at the doorway, looking at them, a hand casually resting on his gun. She ought to have taken the pistol by her father's bedside. She felt like such a coward.

Once they reached her room Eduardo turned around and dismissed the man, who had been walking behind them in silence. The key to her room was in the lock, and after they walked in, he turned it, locking them in. Carlota stepped away from Eduardo, her eyes fixed on him, taking stock of the holster at his waist and the revolver there.

He looked at her curiously. "Why are you making that face?" he asked. "You aren't afraid of me, are you?"

She didn't reply, rubbing her arms instead and taking another step back, putting the bed between them. On the bookcases were all her novels of dashing pirates and her old dolls, and in a chest at the foot of the bed sat the toy soldiers of her childhood.

He set the lamp down and took off the holster, placing it on a table.

"I'm not going to hurt you. Come, sit down," he said and sat on the bed, extending a hand.

She shook her head. "I don't want you with me."

"The safest place is at my side. Those men outside are hired brutes. And although you've done my father a service, he doesn't like you. But he'll let me keep you, don't worry."

"How kind of him."

Eduardo brushed a hand against his face and pinched the bridge of his nose, sighing deeply. "Carlota, you are taking all of this the wrong way. You must be reasonable. Sit with me," he said, patting the covers.

She stared at him. "Let me go, please."

"Look, I've done everything I can for you and more."

"What have you done? Aside from chasing the hybrids and harming my friends."

"What about the part where they tried to massacre us?" Eduardo asked. "What about that? As for the rest, I told you: I'm keeping you safe. I fought for you with my father. I am ensuring no harm comes to you and that you remain mine."

"Yours," she said. "As if you bought me at a market."

"Damn it, I don't mean it like that!" he yelled.

She shrank back, wanting to make herself tiny, but the gesture seemed to upset him even more, and he stomped toward her, reaching for her waist. Her palm rose quickly against his chest, pushing him back, rebuffing him. She was reminded of when she'd stood with Montgomery and accidentally scratched him. And yet now, when she might wish to inflict true pain on a man, she had no claws to attack. There was that awful feeling of weakness, of being near fainting. She didn't want him thinking she was acquiescing to him, but Eduardo was pulling her toward the bed, and she almost tripped over his feet.

"You feel feverish," he said, sliding a hand across her cheek.

"I'm unwell. You should let me be."

"I am tired. We'll rest together."

"I don't want you," she whispered.

He laid her down and stretched out next to her. It was a parody of the night they'd spent together. They'd lain like that, slept until it was almost morning and he'd sneaked out of her room. But she'd loved him, then, and now she dreaded him. Now he caged her with his arms and forced her to look at him.

"You'll want me again, one day."

"I will not. You ruined it all. I'll run away."

"And leave your poor father behind? What about your friends? We are going to find them, you know."

She hit his temple, where Montgomery had injured him, with the palm of her hand. He hissed in pain and squeezed her chin with one hand.

"Don't disrespect me," he said, his voice low. "I can make life difficult for you. Or it can be simple and good."

When Carlota said nothing he simply repositioned her so that her back was to him. He wrapped an arm around her waist. It felt like a chain of iron holding her tight. "Don't you want to go to Vista Hermosa with me?" he asked, whispering in her ear, iron turning to silk, and yet there remained that undertone of sweet savagery to his words. "Don't you want to ride a calesa and wear emeralds and pearls around your neck? I told you, I fell in love with you the moment I saw you. I won't let you go. I won't hurt you."

He was running a hand through her hair, and she heard him breathing in slowly. After a while, she thought he'd fallen asleep, the whole of the day hitting him hard. But his grip didn't slacken on her. He clutched her tight, like a greedy child that holds on to a favorite toy.

She supposed that's what she was to him: merely a doll to be carried around. Life with him would be, as he said, simple and good as long as she agreed with everything he said. And then, if she didn't, his fingers would dig too tightly into her skin, his words would scrape low and dangerous against her ear.

She had the furious desire to pull his fingers into her mouth and bite them off. Her skin was like a burning coal.

A loud scream made both of them jump up.

"What was that?" she asked.

Eduardo pushed himself out of the bed and rushed to the door, pausing to snatch his revolver up. He fetched the key.

"Wait," she said, running behind him, but before she could reach him he was closing the door behind him and locking it from the outside. She slammed her palms against it.

CHAPTER 30

Montgomery

BY THE TIME they reached Yaxaktun and tied their horse to the trees by the Moorish arches, night had fallen and the house was a collage of shadows. He stared at the stout front door. He had no experience with picking locks, and the portón would not yield to brute force. Montgomery was still considering their quandary when he realized Lupe had tied her rifle to her back with her rebozo and had begun to scale the doors of the house.

He watched in awe as she moved as quick as a lizard, her nails digging into the wood, and disappeared over the door. Two minutes later she was opening the portón to let him in.

"I didn't realize you could do that," he said.

"It's not hard," she replied with a shrug.

Montgomery walked at the ready with his rifle. The light from the doctor's room spilled dimly into the courtyard. The rest of the house was dark. He had counted the number of men who had stayed behind with Isidro. There were four of them in addition to Eduardo's cousin. Hernando and Eduardo Lizalde had not been among the fallen, so he had to assume they might have returned to Yaxaktun. That meant there were at least seven men inside the house.

The windows at Yaxaktun had decorative iron grilles, and the auxiliary patio doors tended to be of the same sturdy black wood as the one used at the front of the hacienda, but Moreau's room and the sitting room had French doors with glass, so he moved toward the sitting room and smashed one of the panes with the butt of his rifle, then reached in through the broken window and flung the door open.

There were many rooms in the house, and he couldn't be sure where the men or Carlota would be holing up. If they had half a brain they would be at the ready, weapons within easy reach.

"You see if she's in her bedroom and I'll check on the doctor. I'll grab him and haul him out," Montgomery told Lupe in a whisper. "We'll meet you by the horses. Be careful, rifle against the shoulder, as I told you. Otherwise it'll kick."

"It's just pulling a trigger," Lupe whispered back, scuttling quickly away.

Montgomery headed down the hallway leading to the doctor's room with steady steps. When he reached the door he held his breath for a moment and stepped in quickly. Moreau lay on the bed, and next to him there was a man in a chair.

The man turned toward Montgomery and immediately clasped his pistol. Montgomery shot first, killing the man where he sat. Then he turned to Moreau, who was sitting up, hands trembling and staring at him with wide eyes. Montgomery looked around the room, but Carlota was nowhere to be found.

"Where is she?"

The doctor swallowed, reaching for his night table. "I don't know, they— Laughton! Behind you!"

He heard the French doors swing open, and before he could react there came a bang and he felt the pain of a bullet hitting his arm. He turned around, threw himself to the ground, onto his stomach. A shadow drifted by the window.

There was another shot.

He assumed he was about to be riddled with bullets. But the second bullet didn't hit him and neither did a third. Then he blinked and realized that it was Isidro who had shot him, but he now lay slumped by the French doors. The doctor was cradling a pistol against his chest and had shot the man, then been shot in turn.

Montgomery got up, wincing, and walked to the spot where Isidro lay. He checked for a pulse, but the man was dead. By his body there lay the beautiful, ivory handled pistol Lizalde had fancied. Montgomery spun around and went back to the doctor.

"All right, Moreau, let me see."

"Nothing to see," the doctor said, pushing his hand away.

"Moreau, I—"

Moreau's eyes were filled with death, and his chest was a splatter of crimson. Montgomery clutched his hand, seeing as that was the only thing he could do for him.

"My daughter, watch over my daughter."

"She'll be fine, doctor."

"Tell her I loved her. Carlota . . ."

That was the last thing the doctor said, the girl's name spilling from his lips. The doctor's Bible had toppled and fallen onto the floor. Montgomery did not believe in God, so he said no prayer for the man, simply closed his eyes and placed the Bible next to his body. Then he cursed under his breath and looked at his arm.

He discarded the rifle. He couldn't use his right arm now, so he would have to do with the pistol and his left hand. He also had the knife he'd tucked at his belt. He rushed toward Moreau's armoire and pulled out a shirt, ripping it and tying it around the wound. It was the best he could manage considering the circumstances. That and pray he didn't bleed to death that night.

Five, he thought. *With luck that means there're five men left.* He didn't like those odds but they were not going to improve with him standing there, so he held his pistol up and walked out into the hallway.

He decided his best bet was to simply follow Lupe's path to Carlota's room and hope the three of them could run away before the other men came at them. But the racket they'd made had clearly been heard, and a door slammed open. A fellow pointed a pistol at him and shot. He was a bad shot and missed, the bullet hitting the wall behind Montgomery. He returned the favor with two quick bullets to the man's chest.

Montgomery stood at the doorway and looked into the room, pistol at the ready. Hernando Lizalde stood by a bed and stared back at Montgomery in wild-eyed terror. He saw the bandage around the man's arm and shoulder. There was a rifle on a table, by a window, but Hernando wasn't anywhere close to it.

"Laughton," he said, his voice raspy. "You live."

"As do you."

"I'm unarmed."

"Where's Carlota?"

"I wouldn't know."

"Get on your knees," Montgomery said, still at the doorway.

"God, Laughton. Don't shoot an unarmed man."

"I intend to tie you down, you pig. Kneel!"

Hernando obeyed. "Now, Laughton, think carefully. Why should you be going against me? I have money. I can pay you. Moreau doesn't have anything. You should be with me."

"All I want is to take Carlota away from here," he said and stepped into the room. Just as he did, he noticed Hernando's eyes shifting to the right of him. On the floor a shadow moved.

Quick as he could, Montgomery tried to slam the door against the wall, attempting to fend off whoever was hiding behind it, but he felt the sharp sting of a knife driving into his injured arm. The man tried to pull the knife out, and Montgomery shot with his left hand, hitting his attacker in the groin. The man let out a terrible scream and collapsed.

When he looked up he saw Hernando Lizalde had rushed toward the table with the rifle and was holding it up, attempting to shoot Montgomery in the belly. Montgomery slammed himself back against the door and took a shot. The bullet struck Hernando's face and knocked him to the floor.

Montgomery breathed in deeply and stuffed his gun back in the holster, looking at the mess that was his arm with the knife still sticking out of it. He pulled it out with a loud grunt. He stood there with the damn knife at his feet and his arm throbbing. Then he heard footsteps and whirled around to find Eduardo Lizalde looking in confusion at him.

The confusion lasted for a second. Then Lizalde was raising his gun. Montgomery shoved the young man against the door and twisted his hand, the motion knocking the weapon from his fingers.

He should have been able to subdue him, but Eduardo smashed a fist against Montgomery's head in frustrated fury, and then he went for the injured arm. Pain roared through Montgomery's body, and he stumbled back, wincing. Eduardo's fists connected with his jaw, then his stomach. Montgomery, reeling from the agony of his injuries, could not block the blows. Blood was dripping down his forehead, down his face, staining one eye and making it hard to see, and there again came another blow and he had fallen on the floor, belly up.

Eduardo was kicking him now, going for the ribs, and Montgomery felt a fresh sting of pain there. A rib. He'd broken a rib. As he lay on the ground he remembered the time he had faced off against a jaguar and the way the beast had sunk its fangs into his flesh. It was the memory of that terrible confrontation that made him snap out of this swamp of distress into which he was sinking.

When he had met the jaguar he had known, during one crystal-clear instant, that he needed to fight back now or he'd be killed. And he had fought, rousing all his strength, all his feverish need to survive, into one single blow when he sunk the knife into the head of the creature.

Bloodied, on the floor, with pain racking his body, Montgomery pushed his way out of the agony. He'd done it once. He could do it again.

Eduardo raised a leg, intending to stomp down on Montgomery's face, and Montgomery raised both hands, caught the man's foot and twisted his ankle with a satisfying crunch. Eduardo screamed and threw himself away from Montgomery. Montgomery reached for the knife and sat up.

He spat and showed Eduardo his teeth, looking wilder than any of the hybrids. The taste of blood in his mouth spurred him forward, because he was not going to die that night. Not like this, not by the hand of fucking Eduardo Lizalde, so he clutched the knife and he grunted through the burning pain and he knew his face must be that of a madman right that instant.

The young man's eyes narrowed, but he had no gun, and he stepped back, limping. His courage had deserted him. Montgomery heard the man moving, away and down the hallway, in the direction of the doctor's room.

Montgomery wanted to simply collapse on the floor. Every breath he took hurt and his head was throbbing. But he couldn't remain there. Eduardo would return with a weapon. Carlota and Lupe might still be somewhere in the house.

He clutched his midsection, pulling himself up a bit, then fell back again. He breathed in, straightened his shoulders, and forced himself up with a grunt. Montgomery tottered forward like a poorly wound-up toy and bit his lip.

CHAPTER 31

Carlota

SHE SLAMMED HER hands against the door to no avail, and the more Carlota screamed, the more her strength seemed to desert her. The fever she was running now seemed to reach the point of boiling, and she slid down against the door feeling as though she'd spent the whole day racing through the paths near Yaxaktun. Carlota clutched her hands and pressed her knuckles against her lips, praying.

"Carlota!"

"Lupe?" she muttered, at first thinking she was imagining the voice, then pressing her cheek against the door. She scrabbled against it, pushing herself up. "Lupe, I'm locked in here."

"Move away from the door."

Carlota stepped back. She heard a loud thumping as Lupe banged something heavy against the door until splinters flew through the air and she had made a hole, and the entire doorknob came tumbling down with a resounding clang. Lupe opened the door and rushed toward her.

"Lupe, you came back!"

"Yes, for the last time, I hope," Lupe said, but she was smiling. "God, you do get yourself in trouble! Come on, we better run to the horses and hope Montgomery and the doctor find us quick."

"He's here?"

"He's with your father. He'll get the doctor, don't worry."

"My father can't walk."

"The stretcher is still in the room, isn't it?"

"Yes, but——"

"Come on! The others are waiting!"

Carlota was trembling. "The others? They're well?"

"They're fine. Come on, I'll tell you later."

Carlota wasn't sure Montgomery would be able to get her father anywhere, but Lupe looked scared, and they couldn't stay in the room. She took a few steps but stumbled as if she had been imbibing aguardiente for hours and hours.

"What's the matter?"

"I can't breathe right," Carlota muttered. Sweat beaded her forehead, and her body tingled. It was like before, like her other fits. This couldn't be happening at a worse time.

Lupe wrapped one of Carlota's arms around her shoulders and pulled her up, with her free hand she clutched the rifle. "I can't get you smelling salts so you'll have to help me here. Come on, take a step. There, yes."

She obeyed Lupe, even though she felt as though someone was sticking needles into her skin. They shuffled forward in the dark. When they were about to reach the courtyard a man with a rifle stepped in front of them and without preamble fired at Lupe, hitting her in the leg.

Lupe yelped and pushed Carlota away. Carlota hit the wall, feeling boneless. She let out a scream that made the man pause, startled.

Before the man could shoot again Lupe leaped forward and swung her rifle, hitting the man in the head with it. The man yelled and tried to raise his weapon, but she hit him again and he dropped his rifle. They struggled mightily; Lupe clenched her teeth as he tried to punch her and she swung at him, slamming the butt of the rifle into his stomach, which seemed to do the trick. Then she hit him again and again, going for the stomach first, then the head. His limbs flailed, reminding Carlota of the pigs when they butchered them.

Blood spattered across the floor, staining the tiles. The man had grown still, and Lupe let the rifle fall down with a loud clatter. She turned to Carlota.

Carlota lay with her back pressed against the wall and had slid down, sitting on the floor. The scent of blood assailed her nostrils, making her stomach churn in revulsion.

"Come on," Lupe said and extended her arms, trying to help her up, but when Carlota leaned on Lupe she winced.

"My leg," Lupe muttered, and she clutched the wall. "We'll have to go slow."

They began walking across the courtyard. Lupe limped, and Carlota tried not to lean her weight on her. But it was terribly hard to drag her feet. It was as if the anguish of the night had turned her legs into lead, and she was terrified that she might transform into a beast, as she had with her father. She had slammed him against the cabinet and harmed him, and then she had left claw marks on Montgomery's chest.

No, that must not happen.

No, she wouldn't.

Oh, and her father. Her father, her father. She wished she might run to his room and embrace him.

"I need to stop."

"You can't stop!"

"My . . . my lungs."

Her body had caught on fire; her heart was a blazing coal.

"Breathe in. Come on, Loti, as your father says, slow breath then let it out."

She closed her eyes and tried to calm down her desperate heart. She took a deep breath, then exhaled. God, it hurt! Her eyes were stinging. Finally, Carlota gathered her resolve and began walking. They had gone half the length of the courtyard when she heard the unmistakable sound of boots upon the tiles and Eduardo's voice, rough and loud.

"I am aiming at your dog's head," he said. "Turn around."

They turned. Carlota clutched Lupe's arm and stared at the young man. He had a gun pointed at Lupe and gripped the ivory handle fiercely. Carlota's mouth was dry as dust; she could hardly speak.

On the patio floor the two women had left a thin trail of blood that seemed to tether them to the house, making it easy to trace their steps.

"Eduardo, please," she whispered. "It's all over."

"Over? It's not over. You've ruined my life!" he yelled, taking a step and wincing, as if he was injured, though his grasp on the gun did not slacken. "The lot of you, mongrel monsters! But if you think you are ever going to leave me, you are sorely mistaken. You are mine!"

"Yes," she said, stepping forward, away from Lupe, holding her hands up to him. "Yes, I'm yours, but don't hurt her."

"I'm going to kill every last one of them and you . . . you get over here! I said you're mine!"

He looked feverish, too, as if he were racked by a terrible disease. His hair was wild and sweaty. But his illness was hate, plain and simple. She knew he would shoot if she didn't obey him, and she moved toward him even though Lupe tried to clutch her hand and hold her back, muttering a curse.

"I'll go wherever you want."

"Good," he said, nodding. "That's right, come here."

"But put the gun down," she begged him, because there was something terrible in his eyes, something wicked, and the way he clutched the pistol frightened her. It was still aimed squarely at Lupe's head. He shook his head and licked his lips.

"My father is gone. That bastard killed him."

"We had nothing to do with that."

"You have everything to do with that! Get here, I said!"

She could hardly draw a breath, but she shambled toward him until she was at his side, and he gripped her waist with one arm, pulling her close to his side while he held the weapon in the other.

"I'm here," she muttered, trying to soothe him.

His arm still held the weapon firmly in place, but for a second he wavered, his gaze skirting over Carlota with the slightest promise of sweetness. Then something foul clouded his eyes; she felt his muscles tensing around her, observed the telltale clenching of his lips, and she knew he would pull the trigger. She hit his arm, and the bullet flew through the air, missing its target. The pistol made a noise so deafening she felt the need to cover her ears.

He shoved her back, and she fell on her knees, her knuckles brushing stray weeds growing between the pretty, polished stones decorating the courtyard floor. Lupe had darted away, but he shot once more, and the girl yelped, wincing and stumbling.

Lupe was clutching her arm, and Eduardo was hurriedly cocking the hammer, pressing forward, intending to shoot a third time. He'd kill Lupe. She knew it. Now or tomorrow, but he'd kill her. His hunger had to be sated. She felt that same boiling pain she'd felt before, that rage in the pit of her stomach that she'd always tried to erase, that pressure in her chest that made it hard to breathe. Rather than attempting to fight it she let it explode, bright and scorching, like the fires that torched the fields in preparation of the new harvest, and she pounced forward with all her might, knocking him down.

The gun went flying through the air, landing with a splash in the fountain. Her hands were on his shoulders and she lay atop him, holding him down.

"You bitch," he said and made an attempt to shove her off, but she pressed down harder, strength suddenly coursing through her muscles.

"Stop! Stop it!" she ordered. But he fought back. He bucked, tried to hit her, landed a punch that made her gasp.

"You!" he said and nothing more, but the word was laced with a corrosive hatred, and she knew he'd kill Lupe and her both.

Carlota arched her back and felt her vertebrae popping, bones and tendons shifting with a series of loud cracks, like the wood when heat and moisture make it bend with the season.

She felt herself changing, weaving herself into something else. The something her father had always feared, always warned her away from. But it wasn't an ailment and it wasn't a defect, it was raw power that she'd seldom tasted. It was the mystery of her body. At that moment, it was her salvation, and she let the change take place, spurred it forward, not even knowing *how*, feeling the lacerating agony of bone and marrow reshaping themselves in the span of a breath.

His hands went to her neck, squeezing her throat, holding her tight. His long fingers were digging into her skin, and he roared in a fury.

She was afraid of him, for a moment. Afraid of his strength, his frenzied rage. Afraid, too, at what she was doing. There was the pain of his hands, squeezing her, and the burning agony of her body.

Her jaw unhinged, tendons straining. She growled, low and harsh, right before she bit into his face. Her teeth felt bigger, her mouth was full of blades, and he screamed as she took a chunk of him and spat it out, throwing her head back, then slashing at his face and throat with her claws.

She ceased to be Carlota and became fear, became anger, became death, became fur and fang and fury. She slashed and she bit and she tore apart.

His jugular vein was sliced neatly, and she heard him gasp and felt him shiver. But she didn't move away, she kept pressing him down, she kept thinking, *No, not my sister. You'll never hurt my sister.*

The sound of boots upon the tiles of the courtyard made her lift her head, and she stared at Montgomery, who had stumbled out of the house and stood heaving and bloodied, one arm slung against his chest, the other barely dangling a gun from trembling fingers.

"Carlota!" Lupe said, and she was next to her, pulling her up from Eduardo.

Carlota let herself be lifted; she felt Lupe's arms around her. She shook her head and was slowly moved aside. Montgomery looked down at Eduardo's body. She could hear a gurgling, not unlike the fountain, as Eduardo lay there, bleeding to death.

There was blood in her mouth and running down her chin. It felt as hot as burning tar and she spat it out, nostrils flaring, mouth pulling in a breath of air. She hadn't noticed it, but there were also tears in her eyes.

"He's not dead yet," Carlota muttered.

Montgomery pointed his gun to the man's head, pulled the trigger, and the charge exploded, burying itself in Eduardo's skull. The sound was like the clap of thunder.

Carlota and Montgomery stared at each other. His arm lay limply at his side, and she rubbed the back of her hand against her mouth, wiping away the blood that stained her lips. She didn't bother wiping the tears, lacing her fingers together with Lupe's instead.

The patio lay quiet, for they had let all the birds in the cages go and besides, night had fallen, painting the greenery and the flowers black, and her eyes glowed yellow in that darkness.

Carlota

SHE COULDN'T SLEEP, and thus she rose early and brushed her hair and dressed long before she ought to ready herself. Lupe came into her room with a cup of coffee, surprising her.

"He's up already, too," Lupe said, rolling her eyes. "I thought I'd make all of us something to drink, seeing as you insist on waking me up with your pacing."

"Thank you," Carlota said, and she stepped into the interior courtyard.

The house they were renting came furnished, and she appreciated it for its location and price, but it was bare-bones and the courtyard was ugly and did not have any cages with canaries, as they'd had in Yaxaktun. Nor did it have a fountain. She had loved the fountain.

After she finished her coffee, Carlota helped Lupe into her black dress, her gloves, and her thick veil. Lupe seldom went out in Mérida, which was one reason why they must move; it was impossible to be out in a city where she might be seen, but on this occasion her presence was necessary. As was Montgomery's. He'd spent a good many weeks in bed, healing, and although he swore he was fine by now, she didn't like to see him moving around, and he had therefore played the role of the good patient.

Once Lupe was correctly outfitted, Carlota took one final look in the mirror and they stepped into the courtyard. Montgomery had also donned black. He had a cheap black hat and a black necktie and that look in his gray eyes he sometimes still got, like he was going to

smuggle a bottle of aguardiente into his room. But at least his conva-
lescence had rid him of the drink. If this might last, she did not know.

"Ladies," he said, and they stepped out into the street. They
walked the length of the trip. Francisco Ritter's office was a few blocks
away, which was another reason they had picked this house.

They reached the lawyer's place of business at exactly the
appointed time, and he let them into the room that Carlota knew
well. She had been there a couple of times before, but on this occasion there was a new element: the man with a sandy mustache sitting
in one of the chairs, which had been arranged in a semicircle so that
the three of them would be facing the lawyers as they sat behind a
large desk.

"Mr. Maquet, may I present Miss Carlota Moreau? This is Lupe,
her attendant and companion. And this is Mr. Laughton, who was
Dr. Moreau's mayordomo at Yaxaktun."

"I'm pleased to meet you," Maquet said.

"Likewise," she replied and sat down, pressing her gloved hands
primly together.

The others also sat down.

"First of all, I must offer my condolences on your father's passing and the whole tragedy at Yaxaktun," Maquet said, and Carlota
nodded.

The "tragedy," as far as the lawyers knew, was that Hernando
Lizalde had marched into the jungle intent on killing a group of
Indians from the area, only to be killed by them instead. He had been
accompanied in this venture by Moreau and Laughton. Although
neither Moreau's corpse nor the corpses of the Lizaldes had been
found, they were presumed to be very much dead.

It had taken Lupe and Carlota a great deal of effort to bury Aj
Kaab and Áayin and also to drag the men who had perished inside
the house to a pyre where they watched the bodies go up in flames.
Whatever remained after that, they had sunk into the bottom of the
lagoon, where skulls and bits of bones might mix with ancient roots.

These tasks had been completed in haste and without the assistance of Montgomery, who was forced to lie in bed after Carlota attended to him. Fortunately, Lupe's constitution was strong, her wounds minor, and the women managed the task without aid. Not long after the corpses were disposed of, men from Vista Hermosa had come, intent on seeing about the whereabouts of the Lizaldes. One of the men who arrived was a physician who tended to the injured mayordomo, though he declared that Moreau's daughter had done a good job patching up Montgomery.

Carlota assured their visitors that there had been few patients staying with them because of previous rebel incursions in the vicinity of their home, which had scared most of the people away, and also due to their precarious funding situation. In fact, she told them that Hernando Lizalde had been thinking of closing down the farm for fear of the Indian rebels. Now, after Montgomery had ridden back home bloodied and severely injured, the patients had departed and only Carlota, Montgomery, and a servant remained.

If there were other questions, Carlota deflected them, and the men hesitated to upset a lady in mourning. Besides, they were more worried about the whereabouts of the Lizaldes than the gaps in a young woman's tale.

With everyone panicked and attempting to follow the trail of the missing Lizaldes, Carlota had been able to gather her father's notes and his most important possessions and arrange to have them shipped to Mérida. The three of them quickly departed—in the end, the stretcher had been used to move Montgomery—afterward alleging that they were too afraid to remain in the area. In Mérida they rented the house and sought Moreau's lawyer.

After a few weeks of Ritter pushing the authorities to make a declaration about the situation, they had finally obtained a death certificate for the doctor. But now that this business was achieved, there remained other matters to be sorted—mainly Moreau's testament and bank account. They had, for now, been subsisting on Ritter's generosity and the promise of future profit. She intended to repay the lawyer and settle this affair once and for all.

"Thank you for the sincere condolences, sir," Carlota said, her voice soft and low.

"My client, Émile Moreau, has been very much stricken by this matter," Maquet said. "He was not close to his brother, but it is a strange and sudden passing. Though, at the same time, he admits he half expected something like this, Dr. Moreau having chosen dangerous activities and distant locations for his work. What he did not expect, however, was this testament and the addition of a daughter."

"The addition, sir?"

"Your father never wrote to his brother telling him about you."

Carlota nodded. "But as you say, they were not close."

Ritter let out an irritated sigh. "Mr. Maquet, I thought we had established that although no baptismal record was ever drawn, Miss Moreau is the doctor's natural daughter. I met the girl when she was a child, and Mr. Laughton here has signed a notarized document stating that he, too, has known of Miss Moreau's existence, having worked for her family for the past six years."

"Be that as it may, you must understand how troublesome this is for my client. A daughter is one thing, but a natural daughter is another. Would he be expected to take her to France with him, to dwell with his family? He has never met her, never received a single letter even hinting at her existence."

"I cannot say why Dr. Moreau never chose to introduce Miss Moreau to her uncle. But she remains his niece."

"And yet a natural daughter. And yet dreadfully young. She is not yet twenty-one and the kind of support she is requesting . . . for a woman, it is a great fortune."

"Come now, sir, Miss Moreau is a lady. You can't expect her to live like a street urchin," Ritter said. "Her father certainly didn't expect her to go around the city begging for her supper."

"Who should oversee money matters for her when she possesses no male kin, nor a husband? You must understand how this might concern my client. A young lady might spend it all on frivolous pursuits; she might buy herself too many dresses and shoes."

Carlota did not flinch or react to his words; her hands were clasped lightly. "I wish to open a sanatorium for the poor. There are many people in need, and I might be of assistance."

"That is pious of you," Maquet said. "But once again, how might a girl manage such a thing?"

"My father's testament is valid, sir," Carlota said, turning her eyes toward the man and speaking calmly. "And though I may not have full control of my father's estate until I turn twenty-one, I have been assured that Mr. Ritter may help oversee my affairs until such a time comes, which should be a matter of a few months. If the Moreaus should seek to interfere with my father's wishes, I will have no choice but to take my fight to the proper authorities. In France, if need be."

"In France?" Maquet replied, frowning.

"I have no aversion to arranging a visit with my uncle, should he wish to discuss the matter in person."

"That wouldn't be necessary," Maquet said quickly, and she imagined by his tone that the last thing Émile Moreau wished to do was to meet his brother's bastard daughter, something that she had already gathered thanks to the letters and telegrams that had made their way into Ritter's hands.

"Then, sir? What does my uncle propose?"

Ritter and Maquet whispered to each other. It was obvious the Moreaus' lawyer had thought to shortchange her, but Carlota had not budged, and now a true offer must be made.

"My client will honor Dr. Moreau's commitments. He will not contest the testament, and he offers to grant you the annuity you've requested, to ensure that you are well taken care of. However, he makes one stipulation."

"What is that?"

"That you may not style yourself as Carlota Moreau. You cannot bear the doctor's surname, nor should you ever claim any relation to his family, nor seek friendship or contact of any sort with them. The Moreaus are a proud lot. They cannot affirm a link with a bastard child."

Carlota let out a crystalline laugh that seemed to startle the lawyers. "Mr. Maquet," she said, "the terms appear to me agreeable."

Afterward they signed the proper documents and shook hands. With the stroke of a pen Carlota was thus anointed with a small fortune and stricken of her surname.

"You do not mind?" Lupe asked her later, when they were back in the house and they sat in Carlota's room, as Carlota undid the tangles in her hair and readied for sleep.

"I don't. For I feel this way I may choose who I wish to be," Carlota said. "I've only ever been 'the doctor's daughter,' but I feel as if I may now be someone else and chart my path."

"But it's your family's name."

"He was my father. But that is not my family."

In the mirror she saw a grin spreading on Lupe's furry face, but still Lupe scoffed, as if making fun of her.

The next day, Carlota went to church. The prettiest spot in Mérida, to her eyes, was a small square with a marble fountain and flower beds and elegant iron seats. This plaza was located not far from the cathedral, which she didn't like because it was massive and she missed her small chapel with the painting of Eve. In this cathedral she felt adrift, just as she felt lost in the city.

Now that she had the means to put her plan in motion, she yearned to find a small plot of land, hidden from others, where all of them might live together. Not just the three of them, but all the hybrids. She did not know what had become of the others, but she hoped they were well and safe. So far, despite multiple discreet inquiries, no rumors had come from the eastern or southern portion of the peninsula of animals that moved like men. The men from Vista Hermosa who had fled the confrontation with the hybrids had either wisely kept their mouths shut, could not give credence to what they had seen, or the stories they had whispered had gone unheard.

Dr. Moreau had helped himself. Carlota wished to help others. In the eastern shores there'd be people who would need medical care. She might fund a clinic and also keep their house, where all the hybrids might live together safe and sound. It could be tucked away in a little town. It could work.

She lit a candle for her father and bent her head, saying a prayer for him. She asked God to guard his soul. For herself, she did not beg for clemency. The terrible deed she'd done, the death she'd claimed, she'd carry that inside and face her judgment one day. Perhaps God would understand.

On the way out, she dipped her fingers in the font with holy water. The sky was clear, and she sat in the small square with the marble fountain, watching the pigeons as they searched for crumbs, and she smiled.

When Carlota reached the house she noticed a calesa with a driver waiting outside, and when she walked in she saw Montgomery was standing in the courtyard with one hand in his pocket and a single piece of luggage by his side. The rest must have already been loaded onto the vehicle.

He was dressed in travel clothes, with a new straw hat on his head.

"You're leaving?" she asked, rather surprised.

"We agreed I would, if the money came in. You want me to find the others, do you not? And I know British Honduras well."

"Well, yes, but I didn't think you'd go so soon."

"I'm feeling better," he said, giving his ribs a pat. "Besides, I don't want the trail growing any colder."

"That's all good and well, but I suspect you do not intend to return," she said, looking at him with reproachful eyes.

He shook his head with something that was not quite a sigh. "I'll find the others and I will make sure they find you in turn."

"Now I almost wish I was going with you, if this is the case and you wish to so easily abandon us."

"I ought to travel alone. I know the territory, I can move quickly, and besides—"

"Besides, you wouldn't want me with you." He gave her no answer, which irritated her. "Why must you leave? Truly?"

"Because I am restless. I've done things that have not been right and ignored the correct path, and I need to think long and hard about that."

"You won't be absolved of your sins on a dusty road," she said, yet even as she spoke she knew that although absolution was not to be found so simply, God might be glimpsed there. She knew Montgomery did not believe in God and her father had preached a different God, but the God that lived in every stone and every flower and every beast of the jungle was real.

Perhaps he did require this. To go forth and find the true face of God. She had once glimpsed a God of joy in between the orchids and the vines of Yaxaktun. To this God she prayed.

"You said you'd stay with me if I needed you," she reproached him, nevertheless, because she was selfish.

"You don't need me now," he said cheerfully. "You've got yourself, and your strength, and you have Lupe."

"I know. Yet I do not like this parting, and besides, there's something you're not saying, and I hate it when people keep secrets."

He took off his hat, and his easy mirth was spoiled as he gave her a wry smile. "I think it's no secret," he said, but his voice was low. "I need a little distance from you. Those two paces I told you about? They're more like an inch now. Perhaps I'll gain a measure of perspective, perhaps not. I'd like to try."

As if to punctuate his words he took a couple of steps toward her, and she did not move away, but she did not come closer, either. There was no tremor of her lashes; she regarded him straightforwardly, as she always had. The silence between them had a weight to it.

"If I said I loved you, then you would stay, wouldn't you?" she muttered at last.

Again he smiled his wry smile. "Then I wouldn't love you, for you'd be dishonest and I'd know it."

"I never wished to drive you away."

"You aren't. Not truly. Don't apologize."

She felt sad, but she stood straight and dignified, extending her hand. "Whatever may happen, I will stay in touch with the lawyer and forward my address. Should you wish to find us, you can turn to him. Look for us at journey's end. Whether something changes or nothing at all, look for us. I'll make an offering for you, so that you may find your way back."

He shook her hand and smiled. Then he placed his hat back on his head and grabbed his small suitcase. "Good luck to you, Carlota, on your own journey," he said.

She closed the door behind him, not waiting for the calesa to take off, and walked back inside, contemplating the floor. Lupe came out into the courtyard and stood next to her.

"Montgomery's gone," Carlota said.

"I know. He was waiting to say goodbye to you. He didn't want to *look* like he was waiting, but he doesn't have a gambler's bone in his body. You can tell anything he's thinking by staring at his face," Lupe said with a shrug. "At poker he is terrible and probably not any good at any other game of chance. Cachito beat him more than once, you know? I'm not sure he can play chess, either."

"Yes, well, maybe he shouldn't play cards if that's the case."

"You will miss him."

"Yes," Carlota said simply.

Because he was dear to her, if not in the way he wished, then in other ways. But Carlota wouldn't lie and distort reality, she wouldn't cheapen her heart with half-truths. He wouldn't want it, either, he'd said so. She would speak no shallow promises.

"Don't cry, now, Carlota. You're a sentimental ninny, sometimes."

"Hush, I'm not going to!"

She held Lupe's hand, her sister's hand, and leaned her head against her shoulder, smiling.

"It'll be fine. We'll meet him again. When we find the others, when Cachito and everyone else is reunited with us. We'll meet then," Carlota said.

She pictured it, crystal clear, the house in a secluded spot, away from prying eyes and curious questions. In the southeast, near mountains, by the bend of a river or the ocean. She wasn't sure of the exact spot, but she could smell the flowers and the dew and the leaves in young trees. They'd be safe and the world would be good, and the house would be filled with the laughter of her family and the people she cherished most.

They were out there, the others, and they'd find their way back to her. The tide comes out, but then returns. They would be reunited.

She thought of the jokes Cachito would tell and how Lupe would roll her eyes at her when Carlota became sentimental and wept for joy. She heard the voices of all of them, engaged in animated conversation.

In the chapel where they prayed she had spotted an Eden without flaw and knew that there need be no bitterness in God's creation. The heaven they would build would be theirs and not built by a man.

The heaven they'd build would be true. For she had hope and she had faith, and as she clutched her sister's hand, she had, most of all, love.

She pictured the dusty road that led to the house. It would be perfectly visible from her window, from her room, which would be bathed golden and soft each day by the sun's rays.

Until one morning, when the weather was fair and the birds sang in the trees, there'd come a single rider down that road. He'd move without haste, and she would walk slowly to the gates of the house and wait there, patient, until he reined his horse and dismounted.

Then she'd smile and she'd say: welcome home.

Afterword

THE DAUGHTER OF DOCTOR MOREAU is loosely inspired by the novel *The Island of Doctor Moreau* by H. G. Wells. That book tells the story of a shipwrecked man who discovers an island inhabited by strange creatures that have been operated on as part of Dr. Moreau's vivisection experiments. Vivisection was a controversial practice in the late nineteenth century, and Moreau seeks to discover the "extreme limit of plasticity in a living shape" by literally changing animals into men.

The Daughter of Doctor Moreau takes place in Mexico, against the backdrop of a real conflict. Because of its location and the difficulty of maintaining contact with the rest of Mexico, Yucatán, although a peninsula, sometimes felt like an island. Some old Spanish maps indeed showed it as such. Hence the original spark for this novel.

The Caste War of Yucatán began in 1847 and lasted more than five decades. The native Maya people of the peninsula rose against the Mexican, European-descended, and mixed population.

The reasons for the conflict were complex and rooted in long-simmering animosities. Landowners expanded their haciendas, seeking to raise cattle or cultivate sugar. The Maya people were the principal source of labor, and landowners employed an abusive system of debt and punishment to keep them in check. Taxes were also a point of contention, as well as the violence and discrimination heaped on the Maya.

Conflicts and interactions in the Yucatán peninsula did not only involve Mexican and Maya communities. There were Black people in Mexico who tended to occupy a higher social position than the Maya and served what Matthew Restall calls an "interstitial position." There were also some Chinese and Korean laborers, especially toward the end of the nineteenth century, and it is true that hacendados even tried hiring Italians, who grew ill and died. There were mixed-race people in a dizzying array of combinations (pardos, mulattoes, mestizos were some of the terms used to describe them, borrowed from Spanish colonial racial classifications). And there were the British.

The British had established themselves in what is present-day Belize and formed what was then called British Honduras. The British traded with the Maya, and in 1850 they recognized a free Maya state (Chan Santa Cruz), as a move to undermine Mexico's claim in the region and also in order to benefit from the natural resources in the area.

Relations between the British and the Maya were complex because the Maya rebels did not necessarily represent a unified faction. In 1849, rebel leader José Venancio Pec murdered another important leader, Jacinto Pat, accusing him of using the armed struggled for his own enrichment. Another leader, Cecilio Chí, was killed by one of his followers. As the years advanced, Maya rebels clustered in the east, while hacendados in the western portion of the peninsula switched from sugar plantations to the cultivation of henequen, a type of fiber and a very profitable crop. A henequen boom began in 1880 and lasted until the beginning of the Mexican Revolution, around 1910. The treatment of the Maya did not improve during those years. The system of debt and peonage continued.

In 1893, the British government signed a new treaty with the Mexican government, recognizing its control of all of the Yucatán. They ceased in their support of Chan Santa Cruz and the Maya rebels.

The Island of Doctor Moreau was originally published in 1896. Five years later, the Mexican army had occupied Chan Santa Cruz.

Acknowledgments

A BIG THANK-YOU to the production team at Del Rey, led by editor Tricia Narwani, who trusted me to write this novel as well as other books. Also a big thank-you to my agency and my longtime agent, Eddie Schneider. Thanks as usual to my family and to my first reader, my husband.

FOR THIS NOVEL, I utilized modern Mayan Yucatec spelling rather than nineteenth-century Mayan spelling. Although the spelling is intended to be as accurate as possible, Ya'ax Áaktun (green grotto) is rendered as Yaxaktun, in an attempt to reflect a plausible colonial transliteration. Thanks to David Bowles who revised my Mayan vocabulary.

Read on for a sneak peek at

SILVER NITRATE

by

SILVIA MORENO-GARCIA

A dark thriller about a curse
that haunts a legendary lost film—
and awakens one woman's hidden powers.

Enjoy this special preview!

CHAPTER 1

AN ENGORGED, YELLOW moon painted the sky a sickly amber hue, illuminating a solitary figure. A woman, standing between two sycamore trees.

It had rained, and the earth was slippery as, breathing with difficulty, she ventured toward the cabin. The woods felt awake and dangerous, with the sounds of crickets and rolling thunder in the distance. There was a thin humming. Was that a bird? It was too high-pitched, that noise.

The woman pressed a hand against her lips and stared at the cabin, with its welcoming lights. But that oasis of warmth was distant. A twig snapped, and the woman looked behind her in terror. She began to run.

The noises of the night were now mixed with the patter of her feet. She flew forward, and her hands desperately pulled at the front door—there was a *thump*, so loud it sounded like a cannon—until she finally managed to burst into the cabin. She immediately shut the door, bolted it, and stepped back, waiting. Her eyes were wide.

The crash of an axe against the wood made the woman jump. Splinters flew. The woman screamed, pressing back farther into the room as a man hacked his way through the door. The scream was an annoying squeal that made the levels jump into the red. The man lingered at the threshold, clutching the axe. He began advancing; his breath was heavy, punctuated with an annoying pop.

"Demon possession again?" Montserrat asked. Her eyes were on the VU meter; on her knee she balanced a notepad.

"Ghosts," Paco said.

She scribbled in the notepad. "I thought you were into ninjas."

"We're still doing the ninjas. Just not now."

"A ninja moratorium."

The woman screamed again. Montserrat pressed a button. The image froze on the screen. She spun her chair around.

The padded room smelled faintly of the pine-scented air freshener that the other sound editors liked to spray around to cover up the fact that they were smoking inside. The whole place was a bit of a mess. The editors regularly left pizza boxes and empty bottles of Pepsi around the mixing room, along with the scent of cigarettes. "No food or smoking in the editing room" said a sign half hidden behind the random stickers the editors had pasted on it over the years. In theory, this admonition made sense, especially when you were dealing with film. You didn't want to smear a workprint with grease. In practice, though, all editors were supposed to eat in front of the monitors. You were constantly working your ass off in post-production, trying to make up for missed deadlines. Montserrat had never been in a facility that was perfectly neat and organized. Editing rooms all looked like war zones unless a client was poking their head around.

Still, she might have tidied up if Paco hadn't ambushed her. Unfortunately for him, this particular mixing room was small and, unlike the bigger rooms, didn't have a client area with a couch. Paco was sitting uncomfortably on a chair, by the door, next to a pile of tapes and vinyl records, and from the look of his position he was probably getting a cramp.

"So, what do you think?" Paco asked.

"I think this is the kind of shit you shouldn't have to be fixing in post-production. Did you shoot these scenes inside a washing machine? The sound is terrible. Those levels are way too hot."

"I know, I know. But what can you expect with these budgets?"

"It's going to take me a couple of weeks."

"I need it to be done in five days."

Montserrat shot him a skeptical look. "Not likely. Mario will tell you as much."

"Come on, I'm not asking Mario, I'm asking you."

"I don't want to be stuck here from the crack of dawn until midnight because you forgot to hire a person who can hold a boom mike in the right position."

"Don't do this to me. I've got hundreds of units due at Videocentro and can't run the duplicates if the master is a mess. Don't you get overtime for this stuff? Must be a hefty check."

"I wish," she said.

Though there was the yearly discretionary bonus. The full-timers got the aguinaldo mandated by the law, but freelancers like Montserrat couldn't count on that. They had to rely on the gratitude of their employers. At Antares, Mario gave his editors a turkey, a bottle of cheap whiskey, and a Christmas bonus. It was never a generous bonus—it shrank or expanded at whim—this despite the fact she was by far the best sound editor at Antares. She was also the only woman on the Antares team, aside from the receptionist, which was probably why she never became a full-timer, never had the right to an aguinaldo, and instead had to rely on Mario's mercurial temper: the editing business was a boys' club. There were a few women working at studios writing the scripts that were used for subtitling and dubbing. There were also female translators, though those were often freelancers who were contracted for single projects. But full-time female sound editors? Those were as rare as unicorns.

"Look, I have to meet someone for lunch," Montserrat said, grabbing her leather jacket from the hook by the door and slipping it on. "Why don't you talk to Mario and we'll see what he says? I'd love to help, but he was raging about an unpaid dubbing—"

"Come on, guys, I always pay even if I'm a few days late. As soon as I offload those videos I'll be golden, I swear."

Montserrat didn't know how true that was. Paco had scored a modest hit with an *Exorcist* ripoff a few years before. Mexican horror

movies were scarce these days. Paco had reaped the benefits of a
nascent home video market a few years back. But he wasn't doing well
anymore. Four years before, René Cardona III had tried the same
concept: shooting a low-budget horror copy of a hot American film
with *Vacaciones de Terror*. Although *Vacaciones* was a blatant attempt at
mixing *Child's Play* with *Amityville*, the film had one semi-famous star
in the form of Pedro Fernández, whose singing career had assured at
least a few butts in seats. *Vacaciones de Terror* and its obligatory sequel
had performed decently, but the market for local horror productions wasn't substantial enough to support two filmmakers intent on
churning out scary flicks, and Paco didn't have a singer to put on the
marquee.

Not that there was a market to produce anything with a semi-
decent budget at this point. The best that most people could hope
for were exploitation flicks like *Lola La Trailera*. Paco was, if anything,
a little better off than most Mexican filmmakers, since he'd managed to rope a few Spanish financiers into his moviemaking schemes
and so the bulk of his output was meant for the European market.
He'd dump a bunch of copies at Videocentro, then sell the rest to
Italy, Germany, or whoever had any dough to spare. Paco's work was
slightly more nutritious fare than what most of the other exploitation
hounds offered, but nothing to get excited about.

"Montserrat, come on, darling, you know I'm solid. How about we
do this: *I* pay you the overtime. I'll throw in . . . oh, how much would
you want?" he asked, reaching into his pocket and producing a wallet.

"God, Paco, you don't have to bribe me."

"Then you'll do it?"

Montserrat had been working at Antares for the past seven years.
She'd never made it into the two big film studios, but you had to
be the son of someone to edit at a place like that. Positions were
passed down through the STPC and STIC like knighthoods. Now
that Estudios América was being dismantled, the movie business
was even more of a mess than before, and competition for positions

was cutthroat. Antares had been, when you added all the pluses and minuses, not that bad.

Not that bad, that is, until the previous year, when the company had hired a new sound editor. Everyone loved young people and despised old ones. Help wanted ads always specified "35 and under," sometimes even "30 and under." Samuel, the newest member of the team, was definitely under thirty. Mario had funneled a bunch of assignments to Samuel, in part because his youth meant he was one of their lowest paid employees. Antares saved money with Samuel. And, as a result, Montserrat had been pulled from several projects. She'd gone from working five, sometimes six days a week, to three, and she was sure Mario was going to cut her down to two by December. Maybe they'd end up assigning *this* job to Samuel.

Crap, she needed to make more money. Her sister didn't ask her for anything, but Montserrat knew she was hurting a little. She had been working only part-time for half a year now; the cancer treatments were too exhausting for her to manage her usual workload at the accounting firm. Montserrat tried to chip in when she could.

"Follow me," she muttered, looking at her watch. She'd be late if she didn't step out now.

Paco and Montserrat walked down a long hallway decorated with wall-to-ceiling mirrors and back toward the reception area. The mirrors were supposed to be "wall art" and lend an air of class to the joint, but the results were more tacky than elegant. The reception area was the only part of the studio that looked semi-decent. Instead of shabby, patched-up furniture, the room boasted two black leather couches. Behind a big desk a big sign with silver letters said "ANTARES" all in caps.

Candy was behind the desk. She had bright yellow neon nails that week—she changed them often—and smiled at Montserrat happily. Candida, who liked to go by Candy, handled reception and all manner of assorted tasks. She was the person who kept track of who was using which editing bay at any given hour of the day. She wasn't supposed to schedule anything until Mario said so, but Montserrat sometimes skipped the queue.

"Candy, is Mario back from that business lunch yet?" she asked, hoping the answer was yes but the receptionist shook her head.

"Nope."

"Crap," Montserrat said. "Okay, this is what we'll do: Candy, can you slot me in for some night work tomorrow? Put me for the whole week, beginning at seven in my usual room. I need to work on Paco's latest picture."

"Oh, what's it called?" Candy asked, looking at Paco with interest.

"*Murder Weekend*," Paco said proudly.

"Sounds cool. But, Montserrat, I need to know the pricing, the green form—"

"Put it down before someone grabs the time slot," she said. "I'll show it to Mario later and fill in the green form."

Before Candy could ask another question, Montserrat waved them a curt goodbye and stepped outside.

She shook her head, thinking about the long nights that awaited her. Too many people thought they could skimp on the audio portion of a shoot. Then they ended up with ambient noise, cutoff tracks, or low sound quality. They often expected miracles, too, from their sound editors, and Montserrat had to deliver those miracles for a measly amount of cash. She wasn't even on staff, for God's sake. Mario didn't believe in hiring people full-time because it was cheaper and easier to keep them coming in by the hour. That way, when he didn't need someone, as he had with Montserrat lately, he could cut them off without sweating it.

The problem was that Montserrat *liked* editing at Antares. A full-time job for a TV show would be steady money, but it also meant she'd have to work with a lot more people. Two audio editors in the same room, and then maybe the lead editor and the director giving notes while they worked. She knew someone who had made the switch to working as a sound recordist because it at least meant less insane schedules, but she despised sets, with all their technicians and actors. Small productions, low-budget flicks, these appealed to her because she often worked alone, no need for a gigantic team of ADR experts, foley artists, and music supervisors to suffocate her. People. She didn't wish to deal with people, although sometimes she feared she'd end up with a vitamin deficiency from spending all daylight hours inside, and she'd start talking back to the characters on screen, like an editor she knew did.

Montserrat wondered if she shouldn't poke her head around the set of *Enigma*. Cornelia could introduce her to her contacts, or there might even be an opening with Cornelia's TV show. She hated the idea of a desk job, but maybe there was freelancing she could do on the side to augment her paycheck. Research. Administrative work. Something other than audio editing, because audio was uncertain: canceled gigs, clients changing their minds, or the composer scoring a film being late, which meant *hurry, hurry, hurry*.

No one cared about the audio, anyway. People noticed only when you fucked it up, not when you got it right. It was a thankless job that had her sometimes catching three hours of sleep on one of the couches around Antares so she could keep working through the night.

Montserrat made it into the restaurant on time and took a booth, ordered a coffee and a slice of pie. Tristán arrived twenty-five minutes later. His coat was a lush plum color with big buttons and a wide belt.

His hair looked a little ruffled, and he was wearing his sunglasses, which he took off with practiced theatrical panache as he sat down at the table. "Well! They were out of Benson and Hedges at my usual newspaper stand, so I had to walk around."

"I thought you were a snob who only bought imported cigarettes."

"I'm trying to save money this month. Dunhills are out of the question for a few weeks," he said, taking out his lighter and a cigarette. "You've been waiting long?"

"Yes," she said. "You shouldn't smoke."

"Keeps me thin, and I have to have at least one vice."

"Maybe, but we're sitting in the non-smoking section," she said, pointing to the sign behind him.

Tristán looked around and sighed. "Now why'd you seat us here?"

"Because it's full in the smoking area and they said there's no way we're getting in there."

"Maybe I can ask for us to be moved," he said and raised his hand, trying to attract the attention of a waitress.

"Please don't," she said, poking at the slice of pie she had almost finished eating. She'd assumed he'd be late and had been wise enough to order quickly.

"Miss?" he said.

A waitress turned around. He threw her his careless, sixty-watt smile that was all teeth. The smile had a success rate of 70 percent. The waitress approached him, notepad in hand.

"Are you ready to order?"

"I'd like a Diet Coke. Could you move us to the smoking section?"

"It's full."

"If there was a table that opened up, could we move there? What's your name? Mari. That's nice. Mari, would you be able to keep an eye out for a table for us?" he asked. "As a special favor for me, please."

He spoke with that deep, velvet-smooth voice he always used when he wanted to get something. The voice had a success rate of 90 percent. The waitress smiled at him. Montserrat could tell by her expression that she was wondering if she didn't know Tristán from somewhere. She had that curious look people got around him. Maybe she'd remember him later.

"Well, all right," the waitress said, blushing.

"Thank you, Mari," he said.

Tristán Abascal, born Tristán Said Abaid, was Montserrat's age. Thirty-eight. They'd grown up in the same building, and they both loved movies. But their similarities ended there. Tristán was tall and handsome. Even the years of drug use and the car accident hadn't completely marred his looks. He wasn't the same crazy-beautiful boy he'd been, but he still cut a striking figure. And although it had been about ten years since he'd acted in a soap opera, some people still recognized him.

Montserrat, on the other hand, was small and plain. When they were kids, the others mocked her limp. After three surgeries, her foot had improved quite a bit, though it pained her when it got cold. Now that there were bits of silver in her hair, her plain face was only growing plainer.

"So, the good news is I found a place. It's in Polanco and it's the right size," he said spinning his sunglasses with one hand and smirking. The doctors had done a good job with his left eye; there was but a faint scar under it, and the eye was still smaller than the right one, a little lopsided, that pupil permanently dilated just a tad more than the other. It gave his face a faintly mismatched air where once before it had possessed an elegant, near-perfect symmetry. Nothing terrible, but he was self-conscious about it, even after many years. He wore the sunglasses all year long, everywhere he went. In the first few months after the accident, he even wore them indoors.

"How much is it?"

He gave her a figure, and when she raised her eyebrow at him the smirk grew into a big smile. "It's a bit pricey, I know. That's why I'm laying off the Dunhills. I'll need all the voice work I can get. Work has slowed to a trickle."

"You too? We should buy a lottery ticket."

"Cash flow problems?"

"Not dire, yet. But I'd like to help Araceli with her expenses."

"How's she doing?"

"Good. I mean, as good as she can get. We're hoping it'll go into remission, but despite all the treatments and the limpias, nothing's changed."

"I should stop by and say hi to her some time."

"She'd love that."

The waitress came back with his Diet Coke and a glass filled with ice. Tristán smiled at her as she poured the soda. He ordered a Monte Cristo sandwich and fries. She knew he'd poke at his food and eat little.

"I need to be out by the thirtieth, and I have the movers booked

and everything, but I'll have the keys sooner than that. I was thinking
we could look at it before the move. How about Friday?"

"I'm probably going to be stuck doing a rush job all week."

"In that case could I borrow your car? I wanted to take a few small
things on my own."

Montserrat had three loves. One was horror movies. The other
was her car. The third was Tristán.

She'd always loved him, first when he'd been simply "El Norte-
ñito," that slightly confused boy from Matamoros with the funny
accent. She grew up in Tristán's kitchen and had even learned to cook
meatballs the way his Lebanese mother did. Montserrat's parents
were divorced, her mother was seldom home, and her sister Araceli
was a terrible cook, so she much preferred eating with him.

Theirs was the bountiful affection of children who sat close to the
TV set, mouth open, and watched monsters carrying maidens away.
After his braces were removed, Tristán morphed into a cute teen-
ager, the one all the girls had a crush on; she too had a crush on him.
Around that time, Tristán started taking acting and singing lessons.
He was no good with the singing, but he did get work modeling for
fotonovelas and as an extra in several forgettable flicks before landing
a steady gig at Televisa.

By 1977, when the twenty-two-year-old made his debut in a soap
opera, he had the chiseled good looks of a star, and Montserrat's love
became a roaring passion that was eventually dampened by his utter
indifference. She loved him still, but it was not with the desperate
romantic yearning of her younger years. She'd eventually admitted
that Tristán was a bit of a shit at times and more than a little fucked
up. He could be a horrible, selfish prick, and his numerous personal
problems took their toll on their friendship.

Yet she loved him.

However, despite this deep affection, she would not give him her
car. She immediately tensed and put her cup down.

"Is that all you wanted? To borrow my car?"

"Come on, no. It's been a while since I last saw you. I wanted to say hello."

"And conveniently borrow my car."

"It would only be a tiny trip."

"No. You're not going to lug around your mattress on top of my car to save yourself money with the movers."

He laughed. "I'm not tying the mattress to the roof of your car. Come on, Momo."

"No. That's it, no. Take a cab. Or have Yolanda drive you there."

Tristán's lips were pressed tight together, and he was staring at her. But she wasn't going to let him have the car. She'd wanted a car the Saint drove on the TV when they were kids, a Volvo P1800. Since she couldn't get one, she'd settled on a Volkswagen that ran like a dream. It was white, immaculate, and kept safe and sound in a reliable garage spot she rented a block from her home. It was not the car of a TV hero, but it was her precious four wheels, and she didn't need Tristán stinking it up with his cigarettes, imported or not.

The waitress came by and told them she could move them to the smoking section. Montserrat took her cup of coffee, and he grabbed his soft drink. When they sat down again Tristán again toyed with his box of cigarettes. Montserrat extended a hand and placed it over his. "I'd like it if you stopped smoking."

"I've told you, it keeps me thin."

"If not for your health, think about your teeth."

"That's why I have veneers."

"Tristán."

"We switched sections so I could smoke."

"We switched because you're a stubborn fucker," she said, almost hissing at him.

"Mmm," he replied as he lit his cigarette and took a drag. "Yolanda and I broke up, so she's not driving me anywhere."

This startled her. Usually, Tristán called Montserrat at the end of his relationships. He used her as a confessional booth.

"What? When?"

"Two weeks ago."

"You didn't say anything over the phone."

"I was trying to figure out if I could patch it over. I mean, seriously patch it over, not just flowers and a box of chocolates. Therapy, maybe. Couples counseling."

"That's a bit—"

"Mature of me?" he asked.

"Unusual," Montserrat said. "I thought you two were going to work on that movie."

"We're not on speaking terms. It's impossible to get funding, anyway. You have to beg for grants and kneel in front of Conaculta," he said.

"What did you do?"

"Why do you always assume *I* did something?"

"You didn't cheat on her, did you? She was nice."

"You didn't even like Yolanda," he muttered, irritated.

"Well, she was nice for *you*," Montserrat said. "She was a bit of a snob, but you enjoy that."

"Are you still seeing that vet with the bad hair?" Tristán asked. He sounded a little spiteful, but she didn't take the bait.

"That was a year and a half ago. And 'seeing' is a big word. If you go out with someone twice you are not seeing them," she said calmly. "Anyway, we're talking about you and Yolanda, not me."

"I didn't cheat on her," Tristán said, tapping his cigarette against the small, amber-colored ashtray. "If you must know, she wanted to get married and have a baby."

"Kiss of death, that," Montserrat muttered.

"Maybe I should get serious about someone, do the whole wedding and baby thing."

"Do you want to have a baby?"

"No! But I would like to be happy, and sometimes I think I'm too fucked up to make it work with anyone. I'm going to die alone, wrinkled and ugly, devoured by my cat."

"Don't be stupid. You don't even have a cat. Besides, you're lovely."

"My God, I like it when you lie to me like that," he said, grinning with unmitigated pleasure. He really was too vain.

"I guess now I understand why you said you needed a new apartment. And I thought it was because your old apartment had a roach problem."

"Roaches and silverfish. I'm hoping the good thing about this new place is I'll at least avoid an insect infestation."

"Silverfish love eating starches, you know?" Montserrat said. "They'll eat books and photos. They're ravenous little monsters."

"That's why I never had you over. It wasn't a nice apartment. It was cheap, though," Tristán said with a sigh.

She knew he had never had her over because he had been fully immersed in Yolanda, and he didn't need Montserrat when he was captivated by the fresh bloom of a new relationship. When he was single, though, he stuck to her like glue. It irritated her when she recalled Tristán's inconsiderate behavior, his patterns. In six months, he would meet someone new and forget Montserrat's phone number until a malady befell him or he started getting bored.

"I need to run," Montserrat said and checked her watch. She folded her napkin and placed it by the empty cup of coffee.

"Where are you going?"

"I told you I had less than an hour for lunch and you were late."

"You can't leave me eating by myself."

"I am," she said. She grabbed her jacket and put it on.

"What about marriage? Should I crawl back to Yolanda?"

She took out a couple of bills and placed them on the table. "Because you're afraid of growing old and being alone?" she asked, her voice coarse, even though she didn't want to sound angry.

"Yes. What? Don't stare at me, it's a good enough reason. Isn't it?"

"It's not," Montserrat said as she zipped up the jacket. He was irritating her with his little lost boy look, that wounded, wide-eyed expression. "Maybe you'll meet someone interesting in your new building."

"Sit down and eat with me, I'm not done chatting with you."

"Maybe you'll learn to be punctual," she said, which earned her a glare and a huff from him.

She slid her hands into her pockets and walked out of the restaurant. When she got back to Antares the reception area was empty and there was a sign that said "Ring the bell," which meant Candy had gone to fetch herself lunch. Montserrat meant to head to Mario's office to see if he was back, but he ambushed her in the tiny closet-like space that passed as their staff room, with a sad, half-dried fern in a corner and a toaster that had a broken lever so you had to keep pressing on it. There was a working coffeepot, which was the reason Montserrat had headed there. She placed her jacket on the back of a chair and poured herself a cup.

Before she had a chance to take a sip, Mario walked in. He had splashed soup on his cheap tie during lunch. "Who exactly do you think you are, booking time for Paco without my permission?" he asked.

"I told Candy we'd fill out the green form when you came back."

"You are not supposed to do that. If I'm not around, you're supposed to talk to Samuel and let him figure out the schedule."

"I didn't see Samuel."

"He was right in the office. If you'd checked with him, you might have seen Paco has an overdue bill—"

"Fine. I'll fill out the green form."

"You have to start paying attention. I can't run a business if you're goofing around. You're a decent sound editor, but you have a terrible attitude," Mario said, moving past her and almost making her spill her cup of coffee as he elbowed her on the way to the coffeepot.

"What? How do I have a terrible attitude?"

"You do. Everyone complains about it."

"Who?"

"Samuel, for one. He organized that team-building exercise last month, and you were the only one who didn't show up."

"You're kidding me, right? The 'team-building exercise' was drinking beer in very big glasses and pinching waitresses' behinds. I don't need to play sexist caveman games with the boys to do my job."

"Sexist," Mario said, crossing his arms. "I suppose now you're going to say that you're getting picked on because we're all being sexist here."

"I *am* getting picked on. You're giving Samuel the best jobs, you're pushing me to the sidelines," Montserrat said, knowing she shouldn't be getting this worked up or speaking this honestly about the situation, but it infuriated her when people tried to belittle her. "Come on, Mario, we both know you're fucking with me."

"See? That's what I'm talking about. No one can talk to you because you simply explode," Mario said, rolling his eyes. "It's as if you get your period twenty out of thirty days of the month."

"I'm not the asshole pitching a hissy fit over a green form."

"That's it. Out you go. You're not scheduled this week," Mario said, majestically pointing a finger at the door.

"What? No! I'm doing that job for Paco."

"You're not. You call next week to see if you have shifts. You're getting seven days off unless you apologize for being disrespectful."

"I haven't done anything!"

When Mario was in a bad mood, he became a petty tyrant. She knew from experience that the answer was to bow her head and blurt out a half-assed apology. That's what Samuel or the boys did when Mario was grumbling and stomping through the building. But if there was anything she hated, it was having to stomach a bully. Every single fiber of her body resisted the impulse to grovel, even when she could see by the look in Mario's eye that he expected her to. Maybe it had been the comment on sexism that had gotten him riled up. Whatever it was, Montserrat would be damned if she was going to take a reaming from this guy.

"Well? Are you going to apologize?"

Montserrat slammed her cup down on the rickety plastic table where they were supposed to have their meals. "I'll take the seven days off. Maybe when I come back you won't be such an ass," she said, gathering her jacket under her arm and storming out of the room.

As soon as she opened the front door, she knew she'd messed up. She shouldn't have gone off on him. Mario had been baiting her. He was probably itching for excuses to let her go, and she was giving them to him on a platter. Well, there was nothing to be done about it that day. Mario would probably change his mind in a few hours. He usually did. If he didn't call her in the morning . . . well, fuck.

Montserrat put on her jacket with a quick, fierce motion and hurried to her car. She desperately needed to find alternative sources of income, because this job wasn't cutting it anymore.

MARTIN DEE

SILVIA MORENO-GARCIA is the *New York Times* bestselling author of the critically acclaimed speculative novels *Mexican Gothic, Gods of Jade and Shadow, Signal to Noise, Certain Dark Things,* and *The Beautiful Ones;* and the crime novels *Untamed Shore* and *Velvet Was the Night,* and she has edited several anthologies, including the World Fantasy Award–winning *She Walks in Shadows* (aka *Cthulhu's Daughters*). She lives in Vancouver, British Columbia.

silviamoreno-garcia.com
Facebook.com/smorenogarcia
Instagram: @silviamg.author

ABOUT THE TYPE

This book was set in Baskerville, a typeface designed by John Baskerville (1706–75), an amateur printer and typefounder, and cut for him by John Handy in 1750. The type became popular again when the Lanston Monotype Corporation of London revived the classic roman face in 1923. The Mergenthaler Linotype Company in England and the United States cut a version of Baskerville in 1931, making it one of the most widely used typefaces today.

EXPLORE THE WORLDS OF DEL REY BOOKS

READ EXCERPTS from hot new titles.

STAY UP-TO-DATE on your favorite authors.

FIND OUT about exclusive giveaways and sweepstakes.

CONNECT WITH US ONLINE!

@DelReyBooks

RandomHouseBooks.com/DelReyNewsletter